NO TURNING BACK

"Would you fetch my soap from my saddlebag, English?" Three Wolves called from the river.

When he waded ashore, she gasped in embarrassment as her gaze dipped below his waist. "Why did you do that?"

"A man can't bathe without soap, can he? Why don't you join me?"

"Kindly turn your back," Jennifer said, and began to unbutton her shirt. Her hair drifted around her like a golden cloud.

"Give me your hand," he said, reaching out to her. "If you don't mind touching me . . ."

Gently, he drew her toward him, deep in the water. She allowed him to guide her body against his muscular contours. "Do you trust me, English?" he whispered.

"You know I do. The only reason I am alive now is because of you."

"Would you trust me with your body, if it was good for your soul?"

Jennifer tilted her face up to study his shadowy features. "I trust you," she murmured. "No one but you."

"Come," he said, as he turned toward shore. Moonlight spotlighted his nude body, glistening with water droplets. "Aren't you coming out of the water?"

"Aren't you going to turn your back?" she asked playfully. But there was no need. She trusted him—with her life, and now with her body. He was her salvation . . . the answer to her prayers. She longed for his exquisite touch, for every pleasurable sensation he could call forth, like a wizard whispering the incantations of a magic spell . . .

COMANCHE PROMISE

Carol Finch

Zebra Books
Kensington Publishing Corp.

http://www.zebrabooks.com

ZEBRA BOOKS are published by

Kensington Publishing Corp.
850 Third Avenue
New York, NY 10022

First Printing: July, 1998
10 9 8 7 6 5 4 3 2 1

Printed in the United States of America

This book is dedicated to my husband, Ed, and our children, Kurt, Jill, Christie, Jon, and Jeff, with much love. And to our granddaughter, Brooklynn, hugs and Kisses!

One

Dodge City, Kansas
April, 1882

"No credit?" Jennifer Reynolds Templeton stared in frustrated disbelief at the plump, balding clerk in Rath and Company Mercantile Store. "But I've already explained we were robbed on our way up from Mobeetie, Texas. If you doubt me, you can ask Sheriff Hartman. I reported the incident to him yesterday and he sent out his deputy to track down the thieves. Surely you can make allowances for unforeseen difficulties. I have promised to pay my bill when our cattle are driven up to Dodge next month."

The clerk chewed on his unlit cigar as he swiped a beefy hand over his shiny head. "Miss, you've got my sympathy, you truly do, but them's the company rules. No cash, no supplies. We've got folks hopping in and out of Dodge faster than migrating frogs, don't ya know. The company would be bankrupt if we extended credit to everybody who had a sad tale to tell."

Bloody hell! Jennifer swallowed the oath and glanced helplessly around the untidy piles of clothing, dry goods, and tools that lined the rough-hewn walls of the frontier store. Blast it, the past three months had held nothing but disappointment and heartache. Despite Jennifer's strong will and optimism, one stumbling block after another kept tripping her up. Her father's dream of making a new beginning in the United States was crumbling so fast it made her head spin.

At times, she considered throwing up her hands, selling the Texas ranch, and returning to her birthplace in England. But that would be admitting defeat, and *defeat* was not a word in the Templeton vocabulary!

"Now, Miss Jenny, don't you fret," Jawbone Drake consoled his employer. "Me and Sunset will find a way to pay for the supplies."

"You bet we will," Sunset Greer seconded. "There's ways of making quick money if we git downright desperate."

Jennifer was already downright desperate! That's why she had made a beeline to her lawyer's office the moment she reached Dodge City, hoping to take control of the trust fund bequeathed to her by her maternal grandfather, the Duke of Calverdon. The family attorney had smiled regretfully and told Jennifer that until she and her younger brother met the stipulations of their trusts, the funds would remain beyond her reach.

Drat it, now this! Jennifer fumed silently.

"I appreciate your concern," she told Sunset and Jawbone, "but the ranch is my responsibility and I shall find a way to resolve the problems."

"And we'll help," Jawbone repeated.

Jennifer stared at the bowlegged cowboy, a point rider for cattle drives and roughstring rider—not to mention her foreman, mentor, and friend. The same held true for Sunset Greer. The wrangler, whose crop of flaming red hair earned him the nickname, had also taken Jennifer under his wing to help her run the Texas ranch. But, with complications developing weekly, Jennifer needed more than moral support from two cowboys. She needed a knight in shining armor.

Unfortunately, this was the wild West, not Camelot, and

there was a scarcity of gallant knights who could rescue English ladies in distress.

"Holy jumping hell!"

Jawbone's shocked exclamation prompted Jennifer to glance over her shoulder. The crusty cowboy was staring toward the entrance of the crowded store. Conversation screeched to a halt. The clerk champed down on his cigar and stared at the new arrivals.

"Three Wolves . . ." Sunset wheezed.

Jennifer pivoted to determine what—or who—commanded such attention. She found herself staring at two full-grown, gray timber wolves. "Three wolves? But I only see two—" Her voice dried up when an ominous shadow fell across the planked floor.

There was no longer any question who the third wolf was.

Jennifer's rapt attention drifted from a pair of moccasins and fringed leather leggings to trim-fitting buckskin breeches. She took note of the crisscrossed holsters that held pearl-handled Colt .45s. A sheathed knife—that looked to be a foot long if it was an inch—was strapped to a thick, muscular thigh.

Stunned, Jennifer surveyed a broad male chest covered by a black shirt and bleached-bone breastplate. A lock of copper-red hair formed a decorative braid interwoven with silver conchos that dangled in the middle of the breastplate. The colorful beads, conchos, and bones "chinked" as the brawny giant of a man strode into the store.

The rattle of beads and bones, and the panting of wolves, were the only sounds penetrating the silence. Jennifer stared into the man's granite-like features framed with shoulder-length black hair. A dark braid, adorned with a gray feather, brushed the side of his bronzed face.

A jolt of electrifying awareness sizzled through Jennifer when she met piercing silver-gray eyes beneath jutting black brows. Although the other patrons cleared a path to let Three Wolves approach, Jennifer remained rooted to her spot. In all her twenty-two years, she had never found herself so captivated.

No man remotely compared to this six-foot-three-inch mass of brawn and muscle. Indeed, he rendered *all* other men invisible!

Destiny, fate ... Jennifer's lips twitched in a smile. She, who was desperate for assistance, had whimsically wished for a gallant knight. And poof! Here he was—the epitome of invincible strength and rugged savagery. No need for the customary suit of armor, Jennifer decided. This hulk of a man was a walking arsenal.

Spellbound, Jennifer watched Three Wolves' black brow rise when she smiled at him. His expression softened slightly, but in the blink of an eye, he shifted his attention to the bald-headed clerk who cleared his throat nervously and chewed on his unlit cigar.

"We don't allow animals in the store," the clerk bleated. "Company rules, you understand."

Three Wolves rattled off a command in an Indian dialect. The wolves rose from their haunches and disappeared.

While Three Wolves ordered his supplies, Jennifer stood there appraising his striking profile. A sense of peace flooded over her when a quiet voice whispered: *Here is the answer to your prayers, Jennifer. Help has arrived.*

Jennifer wasn't sure how she was supposed to link that comforting knowledge to a plan of action, but she sensed this imposing figure could resolve her problems. It was as simple as that.

When Three Wolves gathered his supplies, paid the clerk, and turned to leave, Jennifer scurried forward to block his path. Those eyes hypnotized her instantly, freezing her tongue to the roof of her mouth. She stood there like an idiot while Three Wolves veered around her and walked off, the soft "chink" marking the tempo of his long, lithe strides.

Jennifer was jolted to her senses when Jawbone and Sunset drew her protectively between them. Suddenly, conversation struck up around the store like a five-piece band.

"Damn, Miss Jenny, you should've backed off from that savage," Jawbone chirped. "Don't you realize who that is?"

"Well, of course she don't," Sunset broke in. "How could

she? She's only been in Dodge City four times her whole life. Three Wolves don't hang around civilization more than he has to . . . Where the devil are you going, Miss Jenny?"

Jennifer hurried through the door, determined to waylay Three Wolves. Unfortunately, he was already striding down Front Street to deal with the two drunken cowboys who staggered from the Old House Saloon and drew their six-shooters to take target practice on the wolves standing beside a coal-black stallion.

Jennifer had never seen a man move so quickly! Three Wolves didn't reach for his pistol or dagger. With a snarl, he leaped in the air, his right leg thrusting out to take the first cowboy's feet out from under him. A hatchet chop to the wrist sent the cowboy's pistol cartwheeling in the dirt.

The second cowboy caught a moccasined foot in the under-belly. When he doubled over reflexively, Three Wolves kicked the pistol and sent it skidding down the boardwalk. Fascinated, Jennifer hurried over to stare at the drunken cowboys sprawled in the dirt, squinting into the late afternoon sun.

A sharp command brought the wolves to the cowboys' throats. With fangs bared, they stood guard while Three Wolves plucked up the six-shooters. The crowd of onlookers hung back as Three Wolves hauled the cowboys to their feet and shepherded them toward the sheriff's office. Once again, Jennifer stood directly in this ominous giant's path.

"Sir, I daresay that was the most incredible display of hand-to-hand combat I have ever seen," she complimented. "I wonder if I might have a private chat with you. Perhaps we could share a cup of tea."

Jennifer's bold request elicited the kind of silence Boot Hill Cemetery was famous for. Nobody on the street moved when she broke the cardinal rule of Western etiquette: respectable folks did not associate with gunslingers—especially one of Three Wolves' caliber and reputation.

Three Wolves stared down at the bundle of refined beauty who blocked his path for the second time in fifteen minutes. He couldn't believe a proper lady would risk her reputation by speaking to him. He was considered an outcast. Decent women flung their noses in the air and refused to look at him. Most folks walked on the opposite side of the street to avoid him, so he usually saved them the trouble of snubbing him by walking in the street.

Three Wolves had overheard the rumors circulating about him enough times to know why people stayed out of his way. He was reported to be a devil who carried every curse of hell with him. So why was this lovely female, whose crisp British accent was so pleasing to his ears, trying to strike up a conversation and invite him to tea?

The woman's stylish clothes and regal carriage testified to superb breeding. Probably a royal pedigree, he speculated. One look at this lady indicated she was as out of place in this rowdy cowtown as he would have been in the English court.

Three Wolves found himself staring down into intriguing violet eyes surrounded by long, thick lashes. Wisps of blond hair curled around the edge of the purple bonnet, forming corkscrew ringlets around a face as smooth as cream and soft as silk. Each breath the woman inhaled caused her full breasts to rise against the scooped neckline of her trim-fitting gown. The scent of lilacs floated toward him, overriding the stench of blood and death that had become his constant companion. Damn, but this lady looked good enough to eat in her stylish, grape-colored gown, bonnet, and parasol.

Although he and this sophisticated female were separated by cultural gaps as wide as the seven seas, he did admire her courage. Because of his Comanche upbringing, he had learned to appreciate tenacity and bravery. Every pair of eyes on Front Street were riveted on them—a mismatched twosome if ever there was one. The woman didn't belong on the street, mingling with gamblers, drunken cowboys, and gunslingers whose reputations were known in every dusty cowtown from Kansas to Texas.

"What's your name, honey?" Three Wolves asked gruffly.

"Lady Jennifer Reynolds Templeton."

"Well, Lady Jennifer, you dammed well better hightail it

out of here. You're standing close enough to the devil to melt your English pedigree. If you don't believe it, you can ask anybody here."

Jennifer's brows rose. "Is that so? And whose decree makes you the devil, may I ask?"

"*My* decree."

"Begging your pardon, sir, but if you expect me to be terrified of you, I assure you I am not." She leaned closer to convey her confidential comment—and the crowd gasped in amazement. "I may be English, but I am no shrinking violet. Indeed, you might be shocked to know that I have even uttered a few salty curses in my time."

It was all Three Wolves could do not to burst out laughing, but he forced himself not to change expression. He had to get Jennifer out of his way—now.

"English," he growled, his eyes narrowing into silvery slits. "If you don't move your pretty fanny off the street right now, you're going to have hell to pay."

He expected the insulting remark to spark her indignation and send her storming away. Instead, she stared at him with a wounded expression. He had bruised her pride and hurt her feelings—the very last thing he wanted to do.

Three Wolves scowled. Was his conscience bothering him? He wasn't sure. He had stashed his emotions in cold storage so long ago that nothing got to him, yet this woman with luminous amethyst eyes and silky blond hair was definitely affecting him. That wasn't good. In his dangerous profession, he couldn't afford to feel a cursed thing. Sentiment got a man killed in a hurry in these parts.

"Curse it, woman, get off the street," he hissed. "If you don't, I'll carry you off. Now move it!"

When Jennifer backed away, Three Wolves marched his prisoners into Sheriff Hartman's office. L.C. Hartman stepped aside as Three Wolves trooped in to lock up the drunken cowboys.

"What was that conversation on the street about?" L.C. asked as Three Wolves stashed his captives in a cell.

"Nothing."

"Come on now, I'm not blind. God and everybody else saw you and the lady on the street together."

"Drop it, Hartman. Nothing happened," Three Wolves snapped.

L.C. plunked down at his desk to retrieve the telegram he had received that morning. "The marshal in Denver sent you a message. The three surviving members of the Yates Gang put a death wish on your head after you killed their leader. Word is that the gang has decided to track *you* down."

That was old news to Three Wolves. He had spotted the bloodthirsty cutthroats two days earlier, but he planned to confront his vengeful shadows on his own terms—at his designated time and place.

"Where did you bury the leader of the Yates Gang?" the sheriff inquired as he filled out the necessary paperwork so he could pay Three Wolves his due.

Three Wolves tossed the pouch of bank notes that had been stolen from the Denver bank on the desk. "I didn't bury the son of a bitch."

L.C. glanced up, then frowned. "You brought the stinking corpse with you?"

"Nope." A devilish grin pursed his lips as he pocketed the bounty money.

"Then what did you do with that murdering bastard?" the sheriff wanted to know.

Three Wolves stared pointedly at his well-fed wolves, then grinned.

"Damn it, there you go again," the sheriff grumbled. "There are enough rumors circulating without implying you turn your victims into wolf bait."

Three Wolves shrugged. "Why shouldn't I live up to the gossip? Most folks are hell-bent on believing the worst about me. They prefer wild rumors to dull truth."

"And what is the truth in this case?"

Three Wolves braced his hands on the desk and stared at

the lean, leather-faced sheriff. "Truth is that son of a bitch tried to shoot me in the back."

"And?" the sheriff prompted.

"And my sawed-off shotgun packed enough wallop to send Edgar Yates toppling over the edge of the cliff. After that, I was not in the mood to sidestep down the ravine to retrieve what was left of his worthless carcass."

"Then you should have said so in the first place," the sheriff grumbled as he slapped down three bench warrants. "These WANTED posters came up from Abilene, Texas. Murder, rape, and robbery. The deputy marshal was killed in a showdown with Frank Irving, Bernie Giles, and Yancy Wyatt. They're wanted dead or alive. If you ask the marshal, he prefers dead. He was mighty partial to that deputy—he was his nephew."

Three Wolves nodded as he tucked the warrants inside his breastplate. "Soon as I deal with the Yates Gang, I'll see what I can do about avenging the Abilene deputy."

"Now, about that pretty female on the street," the sheriff added. "She is off limits to you. If you're hankering for female companionship, do your looking on the south side of the railroad tracks."

"I intend to."

"Good. Another encounter like that one and the Women's Christian Temperance Union will be in here raising hell with me. All the old hens are trying to make Dodge respectable. I would appreciate it if you wouldn't give them anything else to complain about."

When Three Wolves turned on his heels and headed for the door, the sheriff called after him. "I don't want a showdown between you and the Yates Gang on Front Street."

"Don't worry, Hartman, I'll take care of the matter in an out of the way place."

"Thanks, me and the Women's Christian Temperance Union appreciate that."

* * *

"Miss Jenny, what in the name of heaven has gotten into you?" Jawbone muttered as he ushered her toward the hotel. "Don't ever go near that headhunting devil again."

Despite Jennifer's objections—and she had plenty of them— Jawbone and Sunset whisked her up the steps and locked the door of her hotel room behind them.

"What is the matter with you two?" Jennifer demanded as she tossed her parasol on the lumpy mattress. "I was only complimenting a man on his impressive combat skills. What was the harm in that?"

"Lord, Miss Jenny," Jawbone crowed. "That ain't a man. That's Three Wolves. He's a bounty hunter who'd just as soon shoot you as look at you. You just don't waltz up and pass the time of day with a ruthless half-breed like him. Sweet Jesus, yer poor daddy would roll over in his grave if he knew what you did."

"When you git within five feet of an hombre like Three Wolves, you're close enough to hell to smell smoke," Sunset chimed in.

Why was it, Jennifer wondered, that everyone—including Three Wolves himself—used his name and *hell* in the same sentence? That was preposterous!

True, Three Wolves possessed a formidable aura that set him apart from the common masses. Also true, he commanded grudging attention. But he was not evil. If he were, Jennifer would have sensed it the moment she stared into his silver-gray eyes. The fire she felt burning inside her had nothing to do with hell's inferno. It was a warm tingle of physical attraction and admiring respect—feelings stronger than any reaction she had ever had to a man. Besides, Three Wolves was her much-needed knight.

"Sit yerself down, Miss Jenny," Sunset requested as he pulled out a chair for her. "You've always been too optimistic and goodhearted. But not everybody deserves yer kindness and generosity. There are things you should know about Three Wolves. Tell her, Jaw."

Jawbone paced the floorboards, hands clasped behind his

back. "I realize yer old enough to pick and choose the company you keep, and all that, but I feel obliged to offer advice since yer daddy ain't here to do it.

"First off, it's said that Lucifer himself holds the mortgage on Three Wolves' soul. He's mad-dog mean. Rumor is he was raised by wolves and he feeds on rattlesnakes, scorpions, and cactus."

Jennifer tossed her well-meaning friends a withering glance. "That is the most absurd—"

Jawbone flung up a hand when Jennifer tried to interrupt. "When that two-legged hound from hell starts tracking you, it's said you better save yer last bullet for yerself. Three Wolves' brand of torture makes you welcome death."

"He's half Comanche," Sunset added, as if that was the worst curse ever heaped on a man.

Jennifer smiled wryly. "I see. Naturally it must follow that I should avoid Three Wolves, because he is as different as I am. Is that true?"

"Well, no, I s'pose not," Jawbone mumbled. "But being Comanche indicates the man's got a streak of hell in his heart." He stared grimly at Jennifer. "Do you know what kind of assignments Three Wolves pulls down at three hundred fifty dollars a month, plus the cash he collects as bounty?"

When Jennifer shook her head, Jawbone stared at her grimly. "Well, I'll tell ya, Miss Jenny. Law officers send for Three Wolves after their best agents fail to hunt down the worst vermin terrorizing the West."

Jennifer was mightily impressed. Apparently, Three Wolves was without equal when it came to resolving the worst problems imaginable. She definitely needed an efficient problem-solver—and she needed him *now*.

"When renegades and outlaws leave trails of blood and violence in their wakes, federal marshals call out the wolves— so to speak," Jawbone continued. "The Mexicans call him *El Lobo Diablo,* the Devil Wolf. Comanches call him Three Wolves because of some legend that began years ago. White folks refer to him as Hell's Fury."

Jawbone shook his head bleakly. "Don't let yerself be fooled, Miss Jenny. That headhunting gunslinger don't wear all that hardware and artillery for decoration or bluff."

"I saw Three Wolves in a gunfight in Tascosa five years back," Sunset said gravely. "I ain't never seen anybody that fast on the draw. The local tough in Tascosa called Three Wolves out to make a name for himself. But the man didn't get to breathe his last breath, because Three Wolves blew it clean out of him."

Although Jawbone and Sunset were trying to put the fear of God in Jennifer, they had defeated their purpose. They had assured her that Three Wolves was *exactly* the man she needed. She had seen him take on two-to-one odds when drunken cowboys tried to take potshots at his wolves. Three Wolves certainly hadn't hesitated to attack. It made her wonder what odds he *did* consider risky.

While Jawbone and Sunset continued to warn her away from Three Wolves, a plan was hatching in Jennifer's mind. Learning that the Comanche half-breed had a reputation that left men quaking in their boots added to his appeal. A living legend was the perfect solution to her problems!

"Me and Sunset are gonna look up a few old friends in the area to see if we can borrow some money," Jawbone announced as he wheeled toward the door.

"That won't be necessary," Jennifer insisted.

"Of course it's necessary," Sunset said as he followed in Jawbone's wake. "We'll git a loan to pay for yer supplies, so don't worry about a thing."

"And if that don't work out, we'll try our hands at the poker tables." Jawbone smiled encouragingly. "You just stay here where it's safe and we'll be back in a few hours."

Jennifer waited until the sound of footsteps receded down the hall before she scooped up her parasol. Radiating her customary optimism, Jennifer hiked off to resolve her financial and personal problems while her well-meaning friends weren't around to object.

* * *

"Bloody hell!" Jennifer muttered, wielding her parasol like a sword.

The besotted cowboy who had draped his arm over her shoulder staggered back when she whacked him over the head. Giving the big galoot one last thump for good measure, Jennifer scurried off to hail Three Wolves.

A few minutes earlier, she had seen the bounty hunter ambling across the sagebrush "plaza" that abutted the railroad tracks. When Three Wolves entered South Side—the disreputable part of town lined with gaming halls, saloons, and brothels—Jennifer hurried to catch up.

By the time Jennifer meted out punishment with her parasol and zigzagged through the rowdy crowd, she spotted the famed shootist trotting his stallion across the wooden bridge that spanned the Arkansas River. Three "Bloody Hell"'s later, Jennifer tramped down the dirt road, determined to have a private conference with Three Wolves. She should have realized the gunfighter would not be renting a room at a hotel. Traveling with wolves appeared to be a trifle inconvenient. From all indication, Three Wolves intended to pitch camp beside the river.

As darkness descended on the countryside, Jennifer crossed the bridge. She noticed the blazing campfire beneath a canopy of cottonwood trees. Three Wolves had not wasted any time setting up housekeeping, had he? Bright orange flames lit up the night sky. Of course, she reminded herself, a man with a legendary reputation need not fret about attracting trouble. Yet, she saw no need for a billowing bonfire, unless he planned to roast an entire buffalo for supper.

Jennifer hiked up her skirts and blazed a trail through the thick underbrush and prickly locust trees that lined the river. Every few steps she had to stop to free her cumbersome skirt from thorny briars. When she reached the clearing she paused to pluck thistles from the delicate lace of her sleeve.

Threatening growls erupted around her. Jennifer jerked

upright, seeing glowing eyes reflecting the firelight. She instinctively stepped back when she heard rustling underbrush beside her.

"Don't move . . ." The hollow voice came out of nowhere. Jennifer didn't move a muscle.

Three Wolves barked another command in Comanche, and the two menacing lobos—standing thirty inches high and weighing close to one hundred and twenty-five pounds apiece—sniffed her up and down. Willfully, she ignored the intimidating creatures and scanned the darkness to locate the man whose odd-sounding voice seemed to come from a different direction each time he spoke to the wolves.

And then she saw him—or at least she thought she did. For a befuddled moment, Jennifer swore the man had materialized from the thick black smoke that rolled off the campfire. His eyes were like twin pinpoints of starlight gleaming inside a swirling, shapeless fog—like the disembodied spirit of the newly damned, she caught herself thinking.

Impossible! Jennifer assured herself quickly, shaking off the unsettling sensations and eerie visions. Though her nerves were standing on end and her pulse raced, she was certain her eyes had played tricks on her . . . hadn't they?

Just because Jawbone and Sunset said that standing close to Three Wolves was like smelling the smoke of hell . . .

Rubbish. You're being ridiculous, Jen, she admonished herself. Three Wolves was not a terrifying demon. She had no fear of this extraordinary man. And furthermore, snarling wolves and smoky shadows were not about to deter her from her purpose. She needed assistance—the kind this legendary pistolero could provide—and she was not leaving until she spoke to him.

When Three Wolves emerged from the floating wreath of smoke, garbed in a breechcloth, moccasins, and leggings, Jennifer blushed profusely. She had never seen a man so scantily dressed. Hopelessly fascinated, she studied every magnificently-crafted inch of him. With each silent step he took toward her, brawn and muscle rippled down his sleek chest and washboarded belly. Corrugated muscle disappeared beneath the flap of buckskin that covered the most private parts of his anatomy. A thin leather strap was all that concealed his hips. Jennifer forced herself to raise her gaze to meet the unwelcoming frown stamped on Three Wolves' stony features.

"What the hell are you doing here, English?"

Jennifer's mouth opened and shut, but no words came out. Her attention was fixed on the man's symmetrical beauty. He was absolute perfection, except for a few battle scars on his right arm and left ribcage . . .

Her gaze drifted up to the gray feather tied to the braid dangling by the side of his face. "Is there some symbolic meaning for that feather?" she murmured, her fingertips brushing the quill.

Three Wolves pushed her hand away. "It's the breath feather of the war eagle. Comanches believe the eagle's tail feather allows a warrior to move as silently as air whispering from a man's body."

"And what about the copper braid on the breastplate you were wearing this afternoon?" she asked curiously.

"A lock of my white mother's hair," he said gruffly. "Now answer my question, English. Why are you here?"

Jennifer gave herself a mental pinch and adjusted the cock-eyed bonnet that had snagged on tree limbs. "Mister Three . . . um . . . Mister Wolf?" She frowned, puzzled. "I daresay, just what should I call you, sir?"

The faintest hint of a smile pursed Three Wolves' lips. This pert beauty, who had trounced through South Side on foot, braving the dangers of ruffians, with only her parasol for protection, thoroughly amused him. The woman had no regard for damaging gossip, either. He wondered if her lofty British upbringing had her thinking she was immune to danger and scandal. Probably. He had heard it said that the misplaced English aristocrats who had established vast ranches in West Texas were as arrogant as they were stuffy. Still, Three Wolves could not help but admire the lady's gumption . . . and appreciate her alluring beauty.

"Three Wolves is the name the Comanches gave me," he said belatedly. "My white mother's name was MacTavish. My friends call me Trey." What few he had, he added silently.

"And what do your enemies call you?"

He smiled in wry amusement. "I would rather not repeat the names, if you don't mind, English."

"I suppose that is none of my business," she murmured.

"No, it isn't. Just what *is* your business here?"

Jennifer graced him with her best smile. "I was hoping you and I might have a private chat."

One black brow jackknifed. "A *chat?* Well, isn't that just ducky, duchess," he smirked, imitating her English brogue. "I would offer you a spot of tea, but I am all bloody out of it at the moment. I am also expecting company and you are interrupting."

His rude comment brought her head up with a start, causing the corkscrew curls to spring around her oval face. "Sir, I have been taught that it requires no more effort to be polite than it does to be purposely rude. If I have come at a bad time, I apologize. I can call on you tomorrow morning if you prefer."

"No."

"But I have a proposition for you," Jennifer rushed on determinedly. "A profitable one, I daresay. It would be worth your while to—"

Jennifer's voice evaporated when the wolves growled simultaneously and pounced into the underbrush. Trey—or Three Wolves, or whatever he preferred to be called—sprang at her without warning. Jennifer didn't have time to scream. She landed flat on her back, the air gushing from her lungs. The scantily-dressed gunslinger sprawled on top of her, his arm sliding between her breasts to cup his hand over her gaping mouth.

Trey peered down into Jennifer's enchanting face, expecting to see those lavender eyes rounded with fear. What he saw instead surprised the hell out of him. Jennifer was staring up at him in blatant curiosity, but Trey didn't have time to explain. The trouble he had been expecting from Colorado had arrived.

His campfire had been an open invitation to the Yates Gang, who wanted his head in exchange for killing their bloodthirsty leader. Trey intended to deal with the bastards quickly and quietly. He didn't want this pretty English aristocrat caught in the crossfire when all hell broke loose.

"Stay where you are," he whispered against Jennifer's cheek.

Jennifer felt his hand slide across her hip to grab her right arm—which was pinned beneath his leg. Her eyes widened when she felt his fingers flex in her palm. When he removed his hand she was left holding the butt end of the dagger that had been stashed in his moccasin.

In a flash, Trey was up and gone, disappearing into the underbrush like an evaporating shadow. Jennifer heard the eerie bay of a wolf, followed by vicious snarls. Pained yelps erupted from the clump of trees to the west of camp. Another howl rose in the air, preceded by an agonized wail from the east side of camp. And then bullets started flying from every direction at once!

Astonished, Jennifer watched Three Wolves rise up in the smoke from the fire—like a shadow within a shadow. That eerie wolf howl rose again, and more shots barked in the night, pinpointing the location of the snipers.

Intrigued by the strange, otherworldly image she had seen twice in the same night, Jennifer disregarded Trey's command and propped upright to watch the smoky figure swirl into the bushes. The yapping of wolves mingled with the thrash of underbrush and terrified yelps.

Another shot rang out, and Jennifer glanced sideways to see a darkly-clad figure leaping at her. Her wide-eyed gaze bounced from the sneering desperado to the knife clasped in her fist. Before she could think to defend herself, the outlaw kicked the dagger from her hand and yanked her up by the nape of her gown.

"Come out here in the open, you Comanche bastard, or I'll blow her brains out. I swear I will!" Bob Yates bellowed.

Two

Jennifer was dreadfully sorry she had not remained flat on her back, concealed in the tall grass. She hoped she lived long enough to apologize for disobeying Trey's command.

"Well? Are you coming out or not?" the foul-smelling outlaw roared.

A bloodcurdling scream rose from the underbrush on the north side of camp. Jennifer felt her captor flinch, aware that one of his cohorts had been attacked. When the wolves bounded from the thicket to leap on Bob Yates, he slammed into Jennifer. Thrashing wildly, Bob tried to counter the vicious bites. When Jennifer and Bob toppled to the ground in a tangle of arms and legs, her nose was smashed into the grass, making it impossible for her to see what was going on.

As if Bob had sprouted wings, his oppressive weight was lifted from her. Jennifer peered over her shoulder to see Trey swooping down to retrieve the knife. He stalked toward Bob, who was whimpering from the bloody bites the wolves had left on his arms and neck.

In the blink of an eye, Trey pounced. He slashed the outlaw's breeches' leg—just above the back of his knee. Bob howled in pain and clutched at his left leg. He cursed the Comanche half-breed with the foulest oaths Jennifer had ever heard.

When Trey attacked a second time, Jennifer latched onto his forearm. "No! Please don't!"

Trey froze when Jennifer clung to his arm, preventing him from severing Bob's right hamstring. Whimpering, the desperado slithered off like the snake he was, and Trey was left staring into the bewitching face that represented all that was pure and wholesome and decent in this world. He felt himself withdrawing from the cold depths, coming back to himself, responding to Jennifer's insistent plea.

He had subjected this gentle-hearted blue blood to the kind of vicious savagery that kept him alive. She was too naive to understand that in the dark, sinister world of brutal killers, harsh punishment and ruthless battles were the only way to survive. But because of this lovely English aristocrat, Trey had not crippled both of Bob Yates' legs—though the murdering bastard deserved the punishment.

Trey was not happy with the decision he had made. He shouldn't care what Jennifer thought of him. He should have executed the desperadoes who put a death sentence on his head. That kind of generosity got men killed, and Trey could not afford to be charitable.

There were damned few allowances for mistakes in Trey's profession. He had learned years ago that succumbing to emotion during a life-and-death crisis cost a man his edge. Now, Trey's would-be assassins had the chance to lick their wounds and bide their time. They would be back, bearing a fierce grudge against him. Next time, Trey might not be as well prepared to deal with them.

Muttering, Trey listened to the thunder of retreating hooves as he jerked Jennifer to her feet.

"I am sorry I disobeyed you," Jennifer apologized hurriedly. "I was not expecting to be attacked. This sort of thing is not quite up my street, you see."

"Not up your street?" Trey snorted sardonically. "Damn, English, you've got a strange way of saying things, and a bad habit of ignoring orders that can mean the difference between life and death!''

"I was worried about you. The odds were three to one, if the flare from the pistols was anything to go by. I wanted to determine where you were, in case you needed my assistance.''

He stared at Jennifer. No one had ever worried about him before. *She* intended to lend *him* assistance? Was she kidding?

"Worried about me?'' Trey repeated, dumbfounded.

"Most certainly,'' she assured him as she fluffed her rumpled skirt. "I have taken a liking to you. I wanted to be prepared to come to your rescue, just as you came to mine.''

Trey scowled at her. "Lady, Bob Yates was about to blow your head off because you didn't stay down like I told you to do. If you had a lick of sense you would be scared stiff right now.''

Jennifer peered at him as if he had voiced the most ridiculous remark anybody had ever made. "I daresay, I had no reason whatsoever to be alarmed.''

Trey stared incredulously at her. "You didn't?''

"Certainly not.''

"Damn it, English, you could have been the deadest woman who ever lived!''

"With you here to protect me?'' she sniffed in contradiction. "Do not be absurd. You are more invincible than any knight ever to serve the British realm.''

While Jennifer scooped up her crushed purple bonnet and reshaped it, Trey stared at her in astonishment. His jaw was still scraping his chest when she drew herself up and marched toward the campfire. As bold as you please, she plunked down between the two wolves sprawled in the grass, their broad faces resting on their oversize paws.

"You are either amazingly brave or incredibly stupid,'' he muttered. "As for the two wolves you're ignoring, they still have the taste of blood on their lips. What makes you so damned sure they won't make a meal of you, English?''

"Because they dutifully obey you,'' she pointed out, an

injured expression on her face. "I trust you will not order them to devour me just because you think I am incredibly stupid."

Trey sank down Indian style—on the opposite side of the campfire. The blaze separating them prevented him from strangling her . . . or kissing the breath out of her. He couldn't decide which he wanted to do first.

"What do you want from me, English?" he demanded to know.

Jennifer stared through the dancing flames that flickered on his chiseled features, watching those glittering silver eyes bear down on her with fierce intensity. The vision reminded her of the strange sight she had witnessed earlier—a man materializing from smoke. No, she assured herself. Her eyes had played tricks on her. Whatever she thought she saw must have been an illusionary, flickering flames and rolling smoke. And when Trey yanked her to her feet after he had attacked Bob Yates, the iciness she thought she felt in his fingers was undoubtedly . . . Well, she was not quite sure what caused that, but it did not matter. The incident was over and done and she had business to tend to.

Jennifer marshaled her determination, met Trey's steely gaze, and said very simply, "I have come here to ask for your name, sir."

"I already gave you my names in both the white and Indian worlds."

Jennifer's soft laughter sent a forbidden throb pulsing through Trey's body. He tried exceptionally hard to ignore the beguiling woman who sat beyond the flames, but it was impossible. Never in all his miserable life had he been this close to pure, sweet innocence.

"You misunderstand. I wish to *share* your name, Mr. Mac-Tavish."

Trey didn't think he could be shocked, not after all he had seen and done in thirty years of hard living. He had witnessed atrocities too ghoulish to describe when his tribe was massacred by the Army. He had watched life's last breath ebb tortuously from men's bodies, and he had seen lives snuffed out with the speed of a hiccup. But he had *never* been propositioned by a woman, especially not a blue-blooded English aristocrat whose beauty and breeding allowed her to pick and choose suitors from two continents!

"You want me to marry you?" he croaked, frog-eyed.

"Blast and be damned," Jennifer said indignantly. "You do not have to look so ruddy appalled by the idea. The marriage will not restrict or inhibit you in any manner whatsoever. I would never think to do that, especially since you have made it glaringly apparent that you have such a strong aversion to my stupidity."

"Damn it, English, I didn't say you were stupid," he muttered.

"No? We both know I am not amazingly brave, else I would have used the dagger on Yates. So that makes me incredibly stupid, does it not, sir?"

"Quit calling me *sir,*" Trey snapped grouchily. "The name is Trey or Three Wolves, or Lobo, but it sure as hell isn't *sir!*"

Jennifer contemplated his thunderous glower. "Are you always this surly after doing battle?"

"What the hell do you think, English?" Trey bared his teeth and growled for effect.

Jennifer smiled, undaunted. "I think you are prone to believe those ridiculous rumors circulating about you. Indeed, I think you enjoy misleading gossipmongers, just to amuse yourself. But the truth is that you are a kind, caring, and very remarkable man who is deserving of respect and admiration. As for myself, I am greatly impressed by your capabilities and your amazing art of self-defense."

"Is that so?" Hard as he tried, Trey couldn't stifle his grin. This spirited female was a constant source of amusement— when she wasn't frustrating the hell out of him, that is. For sure, Trey didn't feel in control when Jennifer was underfoot. Her forthright honesty kept knocking him off balance.

"Yes, that is so," she said with great conviction. "As I said before, I have developed a fond attachment for you."

"And you think you're perfectly safe in camp with two

wolves and an uncivilized half-breed Comanche? Nobody else does, you know.''

"I have never felt safer, or more secure, in all my life," she declared grandly.

"Then you are a fool, English." Trey bounded up to circle the fire. He hauled her roughly to her feet and breathed down her neck. "I could take you right here, right now, and to hell with giving you my name. You are nowhere near as safe as you think. I could make a meal of you. By the time my wolves finished devouring the leftovers there would be no evidence that you had come or gone from my camp."

Jennifer peered up into his formidable frown, refusing to be intimidated or frightened. The expression in his eyes gave his game away. She had seen the merciless glint in his gaze when he attacked Bob Yates. There wasn't the slightest hint of savagery now, and she had no fear of him.

"You are not as wicked as you want me to think," she insisted. "You simply project that ferocious persona to give you the needed edge so you can intimidate your enemies. Furthermore, you are not a man who would mistreat a woman. It is your very nature to defend."

Trey scoffed derisively. "Guess again, English."

His mouth came down hard on hers. He encircled her in his arms, pressing her against his muscled torso. His hands clamped on her buttocks, guiding her into the cradle of his thighs, holding her to him as if they were sharing the same space, the same skin. Flicking his heel, he knocked her legs out from under her, taking Jennifer to her back. His body half-covered hers, holding her effortlessly in place.

Three faces appeared above Jennifer—three wolves, two of which were snarling. The third was grinning in wicked challenge. Unafraid, she traced the full, sensuous lips that had purposely bruised hers in a show of male domination. But Jennifer was not fooled, and fright was not the emotion flooding through her.

Disappointment was.

Jennifer longed to know what it would be like to have that

masculine mouth whispering tenderly over hers, to feel Trey's
hands caressing her with gentleness. He felt so right to her,
looked so utterly appealing. Why was he resisting what seemed
so natural and welcome to her? Didn't he understand that she
was inexorably attracted to him? She had told him so twice,
but he seemed reluctant to believe it.

When Trey nipped at her fingertips, trying to convince her
that he was not as easily tamed as she thought, Jennifer met
his challenge. Her lips drifted over his knuckles. And to assure
him that she could be just as ornery and playful as he, she bit
his fingertip.

Trey yelped in surprise.

The wolves threw back their heads and bayed at the moon.

When Trey spoke in Comanche the wolves slinked away,
leaving him alone with Jennifer. He studied her in a silence
broken only by the crackling embers of the fire. No one had
ever stared at him so trustingly. He was accustomed to being
regarded with wary trepidation and nervous apprehension. But
this well-bred English lady, who seemed so far out of her
element that it was laughable, was relaxed and at ease around
him. He wasn't sure how to respond.

Trey had been an outsider all his life, a nomad who belonged
nowhere. The Comanches had accepted him more readily than
anyone, and yet he had never been one of them.

White men refused to associate with him, though they tolerated him when they needed him to fight their most difficult
battles. He was an outcast, living on the fringe of civilization,
going about his deadly business for exorbitant fees. He had
acquired wealth he never had time to spend, and he had grown
more cynical and isolated with each dangerous mission he
accepted.

And then along came this lovely, vivacious female who had
proposed to him—of all things! To say that Lady Jennifer
Reynolds Templeton was a novel experience was the understatement of the decade! Truth be told, Trey couldn't find it in
what was left of his shriveled heart to send her away, not with
the memory of his rough handling fresh on her mind.

If this was as close to paradise as he would ever get, Trey wanted to savor the heady pleasure he sensed was awaiting him—for one fleeting moment out of time. Jennifer was his forbidden fantasy, he realized as his mind and body yielded to delicious temptation.

Reverently, Trey brushed his lips over Jennifer's petal-soft mouth. He felt her body melt beneath him, marveled at her innocent, generous response. His probing tongue glided into the soft recesses behind her lips to savor the honeyed sweetness.

Trey swore he would never forget the taste of her, the compelling fragrance of lilacs that filled his senses, the feel of her lush body molded familiarly—and willingly—to his.

After a long, pleasurable moment, Trey retreated, but he lost himself in the shimmering depths of her amethyst eyes. Damn, the woman had entrapped him in her potent spell, and he became mesmerized after one gentle kiss.

"Trey?" Jennifer whispered as she limned the curve of his lips, his high cheekbones.

"What, English?" His voice was nowhere near as steady as he had hoped. And worse, he felt all soft and mushy inside. What the hell had happened to him? Must've been some strange side effect from going in so deep when he dealt with the Yates Gang, he supposed.

"Could we move a tad farther from the fire? All these layers of clothes are making me a trifle hot."

Trey was a trifle hot himself, but he was experienced enough to know the heat Jennifer referred to came from within. "You could shed all those clothes," he said, grinning scampishly.

Jennifer chortled. "I daresay, I would not look as magnificent as you do if I did."

Trey disagreed. Jennifer was the most enticing female he had ever seen. The seven wonders of the world—collectively— could not compare to the prospect of seeing her dressed in nothing but her dazzling smile.

When Jennifer levered up on an elbow, Trey eased away, permitting her to sit upright.

"There, you see, it is just as I thought," she proclaimed.

Trey frowned, bemused. "What is just as you thought, English?"

"You are not a vicious, devouring beast at all. When I indicated I wanted to sit up, you did not restrain me in the least. Beneath that fierce veneer, necessary to your dangerous profession, there is a tremendous potential for tenderness. It seems to me that you simply have not cultivated the gentler side of your nature, but it is there. You have become accustomed to living down to those preposterous rumors that declare you wicked to the bone. Utter rubbish! There is nothing but goodness in your soul, and I have been drawn to it since the moment I saw you."

Trey gaped at her, then burst out laughing. Her precise British accent and her optimistic conclusions beat anything he'd ever heard.

"Hell's teeth," Jennifer muttered in offended dignity. "I am bloody serious. I have more faith in you than you have in yourself. And drat it, I refuse to let you sell yourself short!"

Trey swallowed his laughter, wondering if this goodhearted beauty always sought—and found—the best in everybody.

"I suppose you are curious to know why I have asked you to marry me," she said as she scooted away from the billowing fire.

"Now why would I wonder why an English-born blue blood would want to tie herself to a half-breed bounty hunter shunned by Polite Society?" he said as he rolled agilely to his feet to retrieve supplies from his saddlebags.

"Because you consider me an imbecile?" she ventured playfully.

Trey wheeled around to loom over her like a sleek, powerful wolf. "Let's get one thing straight, here and now, English. I don't think you're an imbecile."

"But you said—"

"Forget what I said. I'm inclined to think you are unbelievably courageous, even if you are also hopelessly optimistic and naive."

Violet eyes fixated on him. "Naive? In what way?"

Trey sighed audibly, then plunked down to rummage through his saddlebags for pemmican and hoecakes. He offered Jennifer a chunk of dried beef as he explained. "You see me as your chivalrous knight, or some such nonsense. But the fact is I'm nobody's knight in shining armor, so you can toss that silly notion out of your head right now.

"My business is depopulating the West of vicious riffraff who prey on society. I get paid a helluva lot of money to be deadly with guns, knives, and fists. I am not getting paid to be charming and charitable. No one expects me to be. And you better not, either, unless you thrive on disappointment."

"I am being naive to think there is more to you than quick, deadly reflexes?" she countered. "I am naive because I perceive you to be more man than I have ever met?"

Her compliments were stated as foregone conclusions. Trey had never met a woman who was so determined to look for the best in him. Jennifer seemed hell-bent on liking him, even when he had given her no reason. How was a man supposed to maintain his defenses when he encountered such genuine honesty and unconditional respect?

All he knew was that it was impossible to remain emotionally detached and immune to Jennifer's considerable charms. One kiss and Trey wanted her in the wildest, most intimate ways. And hell, as many times as he had practiced self-denial throughout his Comanche upbringing and his forays in the wilds, he should have had more control over himself. But controlling his unruly body was proving to be a battle royal where this adorable English aristocrat was concerned. And worse, Jennifer was oblivious to the profound effect she had on him.

"Just what is the point of this proposed marriage?" he demanded, interrupting his lascivious thoughts.

Jennifer bit into the pemmican and chewed on it before replying. "Three months ago, my father was ambushed, leaving me in charge of eighty thousand acres of pasture, several cattle herds, and a bunkhouse teeming with cowhands. I also oversee the raising of my fifteen-year-old brother, Christopher."

"And you want me to track down your father's killer," he presumed. "You don't have to marry me to do that."

"Finding the assassin will take time, given the present situation in West Texas," Jennifer elaborated. "Large ranchers have squared off against small farmers and rustling and robbery have escalated. Sweetwater Creek, the best water supply in two counties, runs through our property. My father allowed farmers and ranchers alike to water their livestock. Since my father remained neutral in the conflict, both sides tried to persuade him to join their cause."

"And because he wouldn't side with either faction he was eliminated," Trey speculated.

"It would seem so," Jennifer said morosely. "Since my father's death, I have been pressured by Jonas Rafferty, the leader of the farmer faction, and Quincy Ward, who is determined to force out nesters."

Jonas Rafferty . . . Trey went utterly still. The name triggered haunting memories from his past. Trey never knew what had become of Jonas. Last he heard, the son of a bitch had joined the Army. So the bastard was alive and well and had returned to Texas, had he? Too bad about that.

Jennifer smiled tremulously. "I find myself in a most frustrating situation. I am being actively courted by two men who want control of the property my brother and I have inherited. If any other man in Mobeetie mentions my name as a prospective bride he is soundly discouraged."

"Discouraged? How?" Trey prodded.

Jennifer grimaced. "Pistol-whipped and threatened."

"What? No knives?" As Trey recalled, Jonas was damned handy with a dagger. Trey had a long, unsightly scar on his belly to prove it.

"Since I'm handy with weapons I can withstand the pressures as your husband, is that it?" Trey knew there had to be a catch here. Ultimately, Jennifer wanted the same thing that everybody else wanted from him. He should have known she was too good to be true.

"You misunderstand. I have no intention of involving you

in what might become a deadly feud. I do not expect you to
risk life and limb, just because I want to keep the peace between
farmers and ranchers,'' she hurriedly assured him. ''Your legendary reputation will discourage Quincy and Jonas from
unwanted courtships motivated by greed and revenge.''

Greed and revenge? Hell! If Jennifer thought any man on
this earth pursued her for nothing more than that, she was sorely
mistaken. Her intelligence, sophistication, and beauty made her
quite a prize. Her prestigious pedigree and land holdings only
added to a very enticing package.

''I have no strong affection for either man,'' she went on to
say. ''All you need to do is sign the marriage certificate without
any further obligation to me. You can go your own way, just
as you have always done. I do not intend to make the slightest
demand on you.''

Trey was getting confused. He was also getting aroused,
speculating on what it would be like to share this alluring lady's
bed, discovering every luscious inch of her feminine body . . .

Trey scowled when his thoughts derailed. He tried to concentrate on the matter at hand—though it wasn't very easy.

''I'm afraid I don't follow you. How can taking my name
resolve your problems without the use of my guns?''

Jennifer smiled indulgently. ''The very fact that I am wed
to someone other than a man involved in this feud will resolve
my problem. Quincy and Jonas cannot use me as a means to
their selfish ends. I can remain neutral and continue my father's
policy of allowing farmers and ranchers to water livestock at
Sweetwater Creek. Then perhaps we can live side by side in
peace.''

The cynic in Trey scoffed at Jennifer's optimism.

''Neither Quincy nor Jonas, and I am not certain which one
is responsible for my father's death, will have the chance to
dispose of my new husband,'' Jennifer said. ''You will not be
within shooting distance. I intend to find out who killed my
father and see him prosecuted, but that is my responsibility.
This marriage is not meant to restrict or endanger you. I could
not live with myself if I did that!''

Now Trey was getting the gist of her scheme. Jennifer was definitely not stupid. She was exceptionally clever. Neither Quincy nor Jonas could make her a widow for their greedy purposes, if said husband was a notorious gunman. But there were other devious methods of twisting Jennifer's arm in order to gain her cooperation, Trey mused. Jennifer's young brother could be taken hostage until she agreed to cooperate.

"There is something else I have not told you," Jennifer confided. "Despite my grandmother's objections to my mother's choice of a husband—and I am sorry to say Gram had plenty of objections—my Grandfather Reynolds set up trust funds for my brother and me. I would not be surprised to learn that Grandpapa established the accounts, just to spite *Gram.* They did not get on well at all, you see. Their prearranged marriage was rife with arguments. When Grandpapa passed on, Gram claimed she outlived Grandpapa, just to spite *him.*"

"Charming family," Trey said, and smirked.

"My maternal grandparents delighted in getting each other's goats. My grandfather was a mite cantankerous, and Gram is a rather strong-willed kind of woman."

Trey suspected Jennifer was being respectfully polite. Gram sounded like a cranky old hag to him.

"According to the stipulations of the trust fund," Jennifer continued, "I cannot receive my inheritance until I wed, or celebrate my twenty-fifth birthday—whichever comes first. Because of so much cattle rustling in the area, I am short of ready cash. The money I set aside for supplies was stolen en route to Dodge. I suspect Quincy's hired guns, or Jonas's misdirected cohorts, stole the money so I would be at their mercy."

"Why don't you simply sell out and return to England?"

Jennifer stared at him with such sincerity and determination that Trey nearly drowned in her violet eyes. "This ranch is my father's dream. He wanted to begin a new life after my mother died of a long, debilitating illness. My father loved Mother so dearly that he could not bear to remain on the same continent with the memories.

"When English newspapers reported there was money to be made in the American West, Father saw his chance to leave the country. After the anthrax epidemic of the 1860's, cattle vanished from British hillsides. Since wealthy aristocracy had money to invest, they financed large ranches in Texas.

"It was said that a man could buy a calf in the forenoon, sell it in the afternoon, and make enough profit to pay for supper. Englishmen, my father included, were convinced the only way not to make money in the American cattle industry was not to enter the venture at all. For my father, it was the perfect escape."

Trey marveled at the naiveté of Englishmen who established syndicated ranches in Texas and New Mexico. "British newspapers forgot to mention the hardships of droughts, blizzards, robberies, and rustling, I take it."

"No, I daresay they did not," Jennifer confirmed. "But my father was restless. He sought a diversion, a challenge. He worked hard to make a success of our ranch, while other Englishmen sat back like royalty on their tufted thrones, allowing their businesses to crumble around them. My father hired good men to advise and assist him. He wanted to make a home for Christopher and me. He wanted us to belong, even though some of our aloof fellow countrymen still consider themselves too good to brush shoulders with hard-working cowboys they look down on as commoners."

"And what about you, English? Do you want to fit in?"

Jennifer smiled ruefully. "I am like you in a way. A novelty, an outsider. I have been labeled Duchess of the High Plains, and I am constantly reminded that I am English, not American, though I have tried to adapt to Western ways."

Trey realized he was as guilty as the next man. He had nicknamed her "English" and poked fun at her accent and manner of speaking. True, in her own way, she was as different as he was.

"I have tried to adapt the Western dialect, but I revert to

old habits as quickly as you revert to the Comanche language. But I do want to fit in," Jennifer insisted. "I want to fulfill my father's dreams and provide for my brother. Christopher is my responsibility now. I cannot disappoint my father or fail my brother.

"Perhaps I will never be accepted here, but my brother is young enough to learn Western ways. He can assume control of the ranch when he comes of age—if I can hold our investment together, without opposing factions of the feud trying to tear our ranch apart."

Jennifer tilted her head to a determined angle. "If you agree to give me your name, I can pay you generously, then purchase my supplies. I can acquire my trust fund to fence ranges that will provide routes to the creek. In short, our cattle will be well watered, and there will be fenced paths for neighboring livestock."

"Just how much is it going to cost to fence your ranges?" Trey questioned.

"Ten thousand dollars for wire and *bois d'arc* posts."

Trey whistled at the staggering amount. "Lord, English, that's a helluva lot of money, just to keep the peace!"

Jennifer nodded somberly, her beguiling features illuminated by the glowing campfire. "True, but I would give my entire inheritance to have my father back and keep peace. My trust fund will allow me to finance the endeavor, and Christopher's will be waiting for him when he comes of age."

Trey assumed the lady must be worth a king's fortune. If she didn't bat an eyelash at shelling out ten thousand dollars for fencing, she must be heir to phenomenal wealth. No wonder Quincy Ward and Jonas Rafferty wanted to marry her. They could control her inheritance, her ranch, and satisfy their lusts in one gratifying bargain.

"So you see, Trey—"

When Trey heard the growls and snarls on the edge of camp, he automatically reached for his six-shooters. When the wolves bounded toward the two men who crept from the thicket, their shotguns trained on Trey's chest, Jennifer vaulted to her feet and thrust herself directly in front of Trey.

"Damn it, English," Trey muttered as he hooked his arm around her and pulled her protectively behind him. "Don't ever put yourself between me and a loaded shotgun again!"

Three

"Those men are my friends. They won't shoot me," Jennifer assured Trey as she squirmed for freedom.

"Well, I might shoot you if you don't obey orders," Trey grumbled. "Let me handle this."

Flagrantly ignoring the command, Jennifer thrust herself between Trey and the two men who stared him down. "Jawbone! Sunset! Put those dratted shotguns down this instant. What can you be thinking?" Jennifer trumpeted.

Trey called off his wolves when the two men lowered the barrels of their shotguns.

Sunset eyed the circling wolves with wary apprehension, then cast a glance at Jennifer. "What the devil are you doing out here, Miss Jenny? We turned Dodge upside down looking for you. We were worried sick."

Jennifer sallied forth, fluffing the sleeve Trey had wrinkled when he grabbed her arm to shove her behind him. "As you can plainly see, I am in smashing good company."

Jawbone raised a dubious brow and scrutinized the brawny gunslinger who was dressed too indecently to be holding court with an English lady of quality. "Cavorting with Three Wolves ain't what I'd call the best company, missy—'' He shut his trap and flicked an edgy glance at Three Wolves, expecting to be shot for the insult.

"Jawbone, you are being deliberately rude and I simply will not have it,'' Jennifer scolded. "I daresay, Trey has been the perfect gentleman in my presence. We were having a nice chat before you interrupted.''

Jennifer motioned the cowboys forward to make formal introductions. "Mr. MacTavish, I would like you to meet Anthony Drake, or Jawbone, as he is affectionately called. And this is Reuben Greer, who goes by the name of Sunset.''

Trey stared at the outstretched hands that were half-heartedly extended to him, then he focused on the crusty cowboys. Jawbone's face was suntanned and leathery from years of relentless Texas sun. Blaring sunlight had put a squint in his eyes. Wrinkles creased his forehead like armadillo scales. He was stooped in the shoulders and he had a crook in his spine, compliments of riding too many wild broncs, Trey speculated. His Levis were tucked in the tops of dusty brown boots that were run down at the heels.

Sunset was the younger version of Jawbone. His leathery skin was dotted with a smattering of freckles. His eyes were pale green, his mouth too thin, and his ears too large for his narrow head. His brown Stetson couldn't possibly blow off of Sunset's fiery red head during a dust storm—not with those ears for anchors. There was also a tooth missing at the corner of his mouth.

When Trey refused to shake hands, Sunset and Jawbone dropped their arms awkwardly to their sides. Silence stretched out like a long shadow between the men.

"Did one of your friends agree to float you a loan?'' Jennifer questioned to break the silence.

"No, I'm sorry, Miss Jenny. Times are tough in Kansas, too,'' Jawbone replied.

"Then, how was your luck at the gaming tables?'' Jennifer asked.

"Not too good," Sunset mumbled. "We managed to save the money we started out with."

"In other words, you broke even," Trey paraphrased. "You're lucky, considering the caliber of the cardsharps in town."

"I was just explaining to Mr. MacTavish that we were a trifle pressed for cash after the robbery," Jennifer said.

"And *he* agreed to loan you money?" Sunset croaked.

Jennifer smiled enigmatically. "We were discussing an arrangement of sorts, yes."

Trey flicked Jennifer a glance. She obviously hadn't consulted these mother hens about her plans. That didn't surprise Trey. The lady seemed mighty independent and assertive.

"Well, excuse us for intruding, Miss Jenny, but it's getting late. Me and Sunset ain't had supper. Maybe you'd want to join us in town," Jawbone said hopefully.

"Yes, I suppose that would be best. I have intruded on Mr. MacTavish's privacy long enough already." Smiling, she turned back to Trey and extended her hand. "It has been a pleasure, sir," she said most politely. "I trust you will consider the terms of my arrangement. Could I perchance come around tomorrow for your answer?"

Sunset tried to object. "I don't think—"

"I could bring a picnic lunch," Jennifer broke in.

"Are you kidding?" Jawbone howled in dismay.

"That would be fine, Miss Templeton." Trey ignored the cowboys and clasped Jennifer's hand. "I'll give you my answer tomorrow."

When Jennifer was bustled off by her protective chaperones, Trey sank down beside the fire, lit his cigar, and watched the threesome fade into the darkness. He couldn't help but wonder if that lovely English lady had given a thought to what he might demand in exchange for the use of his name. She preferred to believe he was a gentleman.

She was living on assumption.

If "the good Mr. MacTavish" was going to take a wife, he

damned well intended to have a wedding night. Trey wondered how Lady Jennifer would react to that.

Trey smiled wickedly. He could almost hear her trying to convince him that bedding her wasn't what he really wanted to do. He chuckled, for he could easily picture himself convincing her that was precisely what he wanted in exchange for taking a wife . . .

Holy hell, what was he thinking? He couldn't marry that lovely, blue-blooded lady. She deserved someone with an upstanding reputation, someone who could live up to all her silly romantic expectations.

Trey was a bounty hunter, a gun for hire, the dark avenger of justice. No matter how high Jennifer's expectations were, he was what he was. Jennifer had seen him in action earlier that evening—though he hadn't allowed her to see him at his very worst. Still, she had begged him not to cripple Bob Yates completely. She didn't approve of his brand of justice. She preferred to overlook it.

But for just one night in her silky arms . . .

Trey cursed under his breath and bit down on his cigar. He wasn't good marriage material. There had to be another way to resolve her problems. As soon as his overactive hormones simmered down he would figure out a way to help her without damaging her reputation.

"Miss Jenny, pardon me for saying so, but going out to see that half-breed bounty hunter was a fool thing to do," Jawbone chastised.

"Oh, bother," Jennifer muttered as the horses clattered across the wooden bridge. She tightened her grip on Jawbone so she wouldn't bounce off the back of his mount. "I told you, Mr. MacTavish is a perfect gentleman."

"Three Wolves is as crafty and ill-termpered as the beast he's named after," Jawbone said with a snort. "A man who draws fighting wages don't know how to be a gentleman, and he sure as the devil don't know how to treat a lady like a lady.

Three Wolves ain't yer kind of folk, even if you take to calling him Mr. MacTavish. He's indecent and improper. Nothing is gonna change what he is—a hired killer with blood on his hands. You bargain with him and yer bargaining with the devil.''

"Rubbish!" Jennifer countered. "You are judging the man on hearsay. He possesses many admirable qualities."

"Jaw is right," Sunset chimed in. "You can't trust a wolf 'til he's been skinned."

"What is your point, Sunset?" she demanded impatiently.

"My point is that you can never tell when a Comanche wolf man will turn against you. You may think everything is hunky-dory, and wham! You say or do something that gets his dander up. Then you've got more trouble than you can say grace over."

"You've got to be as careful around that half-breed as a naked man climbing through a barbed wire fence," Jawbone said bluntly. "And that's perty damned careful in my book."

After the threesome crossed the sagebrush "plaza", Jennifer was deposited on the boardwalk in front of the hotel, thankful she didn't have to listen to another round of lectures.

"Me and Sunset will be upstairs later. You git to bed, Miss Jenny."

Smiling in amusement, Jennifer waved good night to her well-meaning friends and strode into the hotel. Those overprotective cowboys simply did not understand that the man they feared was the very man she needed most. Somehow, she would convince them that Trey MacTavish was deserving of their admiration and respect. Jennifer had every intention of dealing with Trey, because she was absolutely certain she could trust him.

When Jennifer entered the hotel, Jawbone stared somberly at Sunset. "Well, I guess you know what we gotta do, don't you?"

The red-haired cowboy nodded grimly. "Yep. Let's go have a powwow with that half-breed. I just hope he's inclined to listen."

* * *

Trey had just stretched out on his bedroll when the wolves bounded to their feet and growled. Reflexively, he grabbed his Winchester and aimed in the direction of the thrashing underbrush. He lowered his rifle when Jawbone and Sunset emerged from the thicket with their weapons held over their heads and white kerchiefs dangling from their rifle barrels.

"Don't shoot," Sunset shouted. "We just want to chew the fat. Call off them wolves, will you?"

A sharp command brought the wolves back to Trey's side. "Got a problem, boys? Didn't lose the duchess, did you?"

Jawbone snorted indignantly. "Hell no, we didn't lose her. We saw that she got back to the hotel safe and sound. But me and Sun thought we better 'splain a few things to you, just in case you got any wrong ideas about Miss Jenny."

Trey retrieved a cigar from his saddlebag and lit it over the glowing coals. He didn't usually share his stash of high-dollar cheroots, but he made an exception for these mother hens who seemed hopelessly devoted to Lady Templeton.

Jawbone blinked in surprise when Trey slapped a thick cigar in his palm. "Thank you kindly. I ain't had a cigar in a week."

Trey chuckled as he handed Sunset a smoke. "Because you've been traveling with English, I presume."

"Don't wanna offend the lady's delicate sensibilities," Sunset explained before he took a long draw on the cigar.

Trey didn't think these cowboys' perceptions of the aforementioned lady did her justice. Although Jennifer Reynolds Templeton had a delicate appearance, she was the boldest, most confident female Trey had ever encountered.

Take Jennifer's encounter with Bob Yates, for instance. Trey had expected her to scream her head off when the outlaw pounced on her. Instead, she kept her composure, even when that miserable son of a bitch put a gun to her head. Jennifer had displayed a rare brand of courage in that situation.

Jawbone puffed on his cheroot and lounged beside the fire. "We don't mean to sound disrespectful, but you know damned good and well what a man like you could do to a lady's reputation. And I suppose Miss Jenny told you she was a mite short on funds after the holdup. Me and Sunset were practically handcuffed when those three masked bandits jumped us south of Dodge. We couldn't draw our pistols without worrying about Miss Jenny catching a stray bullet.''

"Bad shots?" Trey questioned caustically.

"Well, hell no!" Sunset snorted, highly affronted. "We weren't worried about *our* bullets going astray. The bandits', of course!"

"I see." Trey blew smoky halos in the air and stifled a grin. "English seems to think the desperadoes who stole her money might have been working for the men involved in the Texas feud. What do you think?"

Jawbone blinked, surprised. "Miss Jenny told you that?"

"Yes. After all, we were having a *chat,* weren't we?"

"Are you gonna loan her the money to cover the cost of her supplies?" Sunset asked, flat-out.

"I'm considering it."

"And what sort of interest do you expect her to pay?" Jawbone asked, frowning suspiciously.

Trey broke into a scampish grin. "Just what is it you think I want in exchange for the loan?"

"You know damned well what we think you're thinking," Sunset muttered. "Miss Jenny is a beautiful woman, and you ain't the first man who's had designs on her. There ain't a man within a hundred miles of Mobeetie, Texas, who hasn't fantasized about her at one time or another."

"You included, I suspect," Trey put in.

Sunset jerked up his chin and glared at Trey. "The point is that she ain't that kind of woman."

"What kind of woman is she?"

"She's the best kind there is," Jawbone declared. "She's sweet and kind-hearted and we don't want nothing to happen to her. Since her pa got shot, we're all the protection she has from those two hooligans who keep trying to marry her. One or the other of them shows up on the doorstep every night, trying to git her to accept a wedding proposal. The main reason she came with us to Dodge was to git away from the pressure they were putting on her.''

''You don't approve of either man, I take it,'' Trey presumed.

''Nope,'' Jawbone said between puffs on his cheroot. ''I don't know where Quincy Ward came up with the money to buy in on that syndicated ranch owned by Scottish investors, but he had the cash when he needed it. I wouldn't be surprised to learn that it was stolen, considering the kind of hired guns he has working for him.

''As for Jonas Rafferty, he's been accumulating new calves faster than his piddly herd of cows can give birth. Truth be known, some of his livestock probably came from Templeton Ranch. I'm not sure I trust the motives of either man.''

''Me neither,'' Sunset chimed in. ''They ain't good enough for Miss Jenny. She oughta be married to one of them fancy, highfalutin dukes, but she's made up her mind to stay in Texas and keep the peace.''

''And just what do you expect me to do about the lady's offer?'' Trey inquired.

''If yer feeling generous, loan her the money for her supplies,'' Jawbone suggested. ''Just don't charge *interest.*''

''In other words,'' Trey said, chuckling, ''look but don't touch. The lady is too good for the likes of me, right?''

''Exactly,'' Sunset concurred. ''But don't take it personally. She's too good for most men in these parts.''

''I've got news for you, boys. English didn't exactly want me to float her a loan. Fact is, she asked me to marry her,'' Trey announced with great satisfaction.

Sunset and Jawbone choked on smoke and sputtered to catch their breath. Trey reached over to whack both men between the shoulder blades before they swallowed their expensive cheroots.

''She what?'' Jawbone wheezed, eyes bulging.

''You heard me. She wants to remain neutral between the two factions of the feud. English will gain control of her trust fund when she marries.''

"Marry *you?*" Sunset stared at Trey in disbelief.

"Marry me," Trey confirmed. "She says it is the *perfect* solution to her problems."

"Yeah, and a cow patty is the *perfect* paradise to a fly," Jawbone said with a disdainful sniff. "That's the craziest thing I ever heard."

Sunset stared somberly at Trey. "You ain't gonna accept her proposal, are you? Aside from the fact that yer mismatched, you would be signing yer own death certificate. Quincy and Jonas would cut you down before you knew what was coming. You may be exceptionally good with a gun, but you couldn't take on all those lead-pushers Quincy hired. Hell, the man practically has an army working for him!"

"Fighting her battles for her isn't part of the bargain," Trey explained. "According to English, I am to make myself scarce after the wedding ceremony."

Jawbone frowned pensively, then nodded in understanding. "That sounds like something Miss Jenny might arrange. She don't want nobody else to get hurt. Losing her pa was hard enough on her and young Christopher."

"So, what do you get out of this deal?" Sunset asked curiously.

"I get an estranged wife," Trey grunted. Though it shouldn't have mattered to him, the idea of being married to English without enjoying fringe benefits left a bitter taste in his mouth.

"Yeah, an estranged wife and a powerful hankering," Jawbone said perceptively. "So what are you gonna do, Three Wolves?"

"I haven't decided yet."

Sunset rose to his feet, then stared down at the brawny half-breed. "An honorable man would simply aid the lady in distress and then walk away like she asks."

"I'm getting damned tired of hearing what a decent, honorable man I could be," Trey grumbled. "Don't let that kind of talk get around. It would ruin my bad reputation."

Jawbone smiled faintly. "Me and Sun just want what's best for Miss Jenny and Christopher. We ain't got no grudge against you, you understand. We're just looking out for the lady's best interests.''

''Admirable,'' Trey told the bowlegged cowboys. ''Just don't get to thinking that we'll have these social chats around the campfire real often. I gave up powwows when I left the Indian reservation years ago, and what I decide to do is still between English and me. Don't poke your noses in places they don't belong, unless you want to risk having them shot off.''

Trey smiled coolly. ''Good evening, gents. Nice of you to drop by for a chat.''

When Jawbone and Sunset were dismissed, they tramped off through the thicket, accompanied by the pair of wolves.

''Do you think we accomplished a damned thing?'' Sunset questioned as he mounted his horse.

''Nope,'' Jawbone muttered. ''I've got the feeling that half-breed is gonna do whatever the hell he pleases.''

''I came away with the same feeling, Jaw. Thunderation, what can Miss Jenny be thinking? No matter what difficulties she faces, I can't imagine her married to that legendary gunslinger, even in name only.''

''I doubt there will be any *name only* about it,'' Jawbone said bleakly. ''Miss Jenny is dealing with a devil, no matter how she tries to sugarcoat the truth. Three Wolves is heap big trouble on his good days. I wouldn't want to tangle with him on one of his bad ones.''

Disgruntled, the cowboys rode back to town. They were pretty certain they had wasted their time trying to reason with Three Wolves. That left only one choice—trying to convince Jennifer to retract her proposal!

Cursing the air blue, Bob Yates slid off his winded horse and balanced on his good leg.

''You okay, Bob?'' Willie Yates questioned his brother, then inspected his own lacerated arm.

''No, goddam it, that son of a bitch slit my hamstring clean in two.'' Bob hobbled over to collapse on the bedroll that Russ

Trent had spread out for him. "I thought I had that bastard when I grabbed hold of the woman, but those goddam wolves chewed me up."

"Yeah, tell me about 'em." Willie scowled as he peeled off his shredded shirt to indicate his wounds. "Those wolves nearly took off my arm and leg." His gaze swung to Cousin Russ. "How'd you fair, cuz?"

Russ shucked his shirt and gestured toward the scrapes and bites on his chest and shoulder. "When I get my hands on that half-breed bastard I'm gonna carve him into bite-size pieces and feed him to his damned wolves!"

"You'll have to stand in line," Bob hissed, gingerly out-stretching his leg. "He crippled me for life. If it hadn't been for that woman, he would've sliced both my hamstrings . . ."

His voice trailed off as he cut away his breeches to pour whiskey on his wound. Bob grimaced when scalding pain shot down his leg. "The woman is the key. Three Wolves didn't do his worst because of her."

"You think she matters to him?" Willie scoffed at the absurdity. "That bastard doesn't give a damn about anybody. Any man who ain't afraid to die standing up—and keeps coming at you the way Three Wolves went after Edgar—doesn't have a heart, soul, or the least bit of fear in him."

"Maybe, maybe not," Bob muttered. "But Three Wolves tried to protect that woman. She's his only weakness, as I see it."

Bob took a swig of whiskey and eased back on his bedroll. "Tomorrow, the two of you are gonna ride into Dodge and drag that woman out here."

"I hope I don't have to do any shooting anytime soon," Willie grumbled, flexing his stiff gunhand. "My fingers are chewed all to hell."

"How about you, Russ?" Bob asked.

Russ plopped down on the pallet to pour whiskey on his injured shoulder, then howled like a coyote. "I can shoot if it doesn't have to be fancy. My shoulder is gonna be stiff for a few days. But I can sure as hell handle the woman."

"She shouldn't pose much problem," Bob predicted. "While Three Wolves isn't around, you can wrap her in a bedroll and toss her over the back of your horse. You'll have her out of town before that Comanche bastard knows she's gone."

"And then what?" Willie asked before he chugged a drink.

Bob smiled nastily. "Then we'll have bait for our trap. We're gonna give that devil wolf his due for killing our big brother and chewing us to pieces."

"Blast it," Jennifer muttered when she saw Quincy Ward standing at the bottom of the hotel steps. That rascal had followed her from Mobeetie. And truth be known, he was probably responsible for the robbery on the trail. Jennifer wouldn't put it past the domineering rancher. She suspected he had sicced his hired guns on her.

"My dear Jennifer, I'm glad to see you're all right. Word came down the trail that you and your cowboys were held up by bandits."

"My, word does travel fast, doesn't it?" Jennifer replied, flashing him an accusing glance.

When Jennifer reached the bottom of the steps, Quincy folded her arm around his elbow and escorted her into the adjoining restaurant. "Now that I'm here, your worries are over."

Not as far as Jennifer was concerned, they weren't.

"I'll pay for your supplies," he offered generously.

To Jennifer's chagrin, Quincy led her away. The long trip from Mobeetie, across No Man's Land, to Dodge had been wasted effort. Quincy had arrived to monopolize her time. She could not imagine how she could sneak away from town to confer with Trey without Quincy hovering a step behind her. Blast and be damned, how was she going to shake off this pesky Texan?

When Jawbone and Sunset saw Quincy towing Jennifer away, they stared grimly at each other.

"I reckon that bounty hunter does have his good points," Jawbone conceded as he led the way out of the hotel. "If we can persuade Three Wolves to ride into town to scare Quincy off, maybe that dad-blamed rancher will take the hint and leave Miss Jenny alone.''

Determined of purpose, Jawbone and Sunset hightailed it across the bridge to inform Three Wolves that one of the trouble-makers from Texas had arrived.

Exasperated, Jennifer found herself fed breakfast, then pro-pelled down the street to Rath and Company Mercantile Store. Quincy, boasting of his own magnanimous generosity, insisted on paying for the supplies Jennifer had ordered.

"I refuse to be indebted to you," Jennifer objected.

"Nonsense. You will soon be my wife and Templeton Ranch will be part of my responsibility. It only stands to reason that I should pay for your supplies since you had a stroke of bad luck.''

"Blast it, Quincy, you presume too bloody much—''

"Ah, there you are, English. I thought you were going to meet me at the hotel this morning.''

Jennifer's mouth dropped open when she pivoted to see Trey looming in the doorway. Her knight had arrived to save the day, bless him!

Dressed in a black Stetson, boots, shirt, and breeches, Trey sauntered up beside Jennifer to wrap a possessive arm around her waist.

"Take your hands off my fiancée!" Quincy huffed.

While Quincy glared menacingly at Trey, he sized up the bulky, six-foot rancher. "You back off before I—oooff!''

Jennifer discreetly gouged Trey in the ribs. If he didn't mind his tongue, he was bloody well going to instigate the kind of trouble she wanted to avoid. She had no intention of announcing that she had a husband until *after* he was miles away from possible danger.

"Quincy Ward, I would like you to meet Mr. MacTavish.''

"Trey," he corrected, his smoke-gray eyes bearing down on Quincy.

Jennifer rolled her eyes. Trey had resorted to that intimidating stare she suspected he used in showdowns. Blast it, there was not going to be one, not if she could help it!

"What business are you in?" Quincy asked, looking down his long nose.

"He is an expert in firearms," Jennifer replied hurriedly.

"A shopkeeper?" Quincy smirked.

"Traveling salesman," Trey responded. "When a man needs a good weapon, I supply one. That all right with you, Ward?"

A traveling salesman? Jennifer was surprised Trey had not introduced himself as a mortician at large. Drat it, she wished he would let her handle this!

When the clerk set Jennifer's bundle of supplies on the counter, Trey promptly paid her bill.

"Now wait a blessed minute, MacTavish," Quincy objected. "I'm paying for these supplies. Perhaps you don't hear too well. I said the lady is my fiancée."

Trey smiled at Quincy through the cloud of smoke that drifted up from the cigar he had clamped in his teeth. "I proposed to the lady last night and she accepted. Isn't that right, English?"

Jennifer swallowed a grin when Quincy's plain face puckered like a prune. "I am afraid you have not given me the chance to explain, Quincy. It was love at first sight, rather like what happened to my father and mother." She reached up on tiptoe to plant a kiss on Trey's lips—all the customers in the store gaped as if she had lost her mind. "Trey will be investing in the ranch when we wed."

"He can't do that!"

"Do what?" Trey's black brow arched curiously. "Invest in the ranch or wed the lady?"

"Neither! Jennifer belongs to me, damn it," Quincy hissed.

"Really? Maybe you'd like to put your pistol where your mouth—ouch—" Trey slammed his jaw shut when Jennifer kicked him squarely in the shin.

"Begging your pardon, Quincy, but Trey and I have arrangements to make." She clutched Trey's arm, steering him toward the door. "I will send Jawbone and Sunset around to load our supplies this afternoon."

Behind her, Jennifer heard Quincy's muffled curses. Clearly, he was not pleased with the turn of events. "Bloody hell," Jennifer muttered in Trey's ear. "I told you I did not expect you to fight my battles for me."

"You're welcome," Trey said as he escorted her onto the street.

Jennifer expelled an exasperated breath. "I did not mean to sound ungrateful, but I can handle Quincy. I do not want you hurt because of this situation I find myself in."

Trey chuckled in amusement. "Why, English, I didn't know you cared."

"Of course you did," she contradicted. "I just explained that it was love at first sight, didn't I? And where the blazes are Jawbone and Sunset? I need them to gather my supplies before Quincy decides to retaliate by swiping them!"

"Your cowboys are minding the wolves," Trey reported. "I'll collect your supplies and take them to my camp after I escort you to the hotel. Lock the door and don't let Quincy inside until your men return. I don't trust that sneaky bastard."

"You don't trust anyone," Jennifer pointed out.

"And that's the difference between us. You hope for the best and I plan for the worst." Trey pulled her to a halt in front of the hotel, his silver-eyed gaze narrowing on her. "And for your information, there is no such thing as love at first sight. I doubt Quincy Ward bought your story."

Jennifer's chin lifted a notch. "I say, that was spoken like a true cynic. For your information, my parents knew at first encounter that they were destined to be soul mates."

Ramsey and Eleanor Templeton had remained devoted to the very end, Jennifer reminded herself. They had both died, whispering of that special love with their last breath. The last word Jennifer's mother and father had spoken had been each other's names. And Jennifer knew without question that her parents had been reunited to spend eternity together.

A mist filled Jennifer's eyes as she recalled the night she

found her father lying beside his horse, suffering from a fatal wound. Ramsey Templeton had survived long enough to whisper to Jennifer before he closed his eyes that final time.

The miles and years had made no difference to Ramsey. He had carried Eleanor's memory in his heart and soul and he welcomed eternity, where she awaited him.

To her dying day, Jennifer would carry the vision of Three Wolves looming in the door of the mercantile store, the sight of him emerging from the smoke that rolled from the campfire. Never had a man made such a startling and profound impression on her. She could have loved this intriguing tumbleweed of a man long and well, if circumstances had allowed it. It was a shame that Trey had locked all tender sentiment deep inside him, letting it seep out only a drop at a time—and only then with reluctant hesitation.

Jennifer supposed Trey considered it perilous to nurture the gentler side of his nature. In his profession, he could not afford the luxury of tender emotion. He obviously considered it a weakness that might destroy him.

"More likely, what your parents called love at first sight was physical attraction and a lot of romantic foolishness," Trey contended.

Jennifer wiped away the tears that pooled at the corners of her eyes, then shook her head. "I don't think so, not when I remember the very last thing my father said to me before he died."

"What did he say?" Trey murmured as he traced her cupid's bow lips.

Jennifer shrugged, causing the corkscrew curls to bounce beneath her plumed bonnet. "You do not want to know. It might blow holes in your pessimistic philosophies. But do not try to impose your pessimism on me. I will continue to believe what I believe, and that is that."

Frustrated by her idealistic stubbornness, Trey wagged a finger in her face. "Just don't get any crazy ideas about falling in love with me. There is no such thing, not that I have ever seen. And don't start thinking I've turned into a gentleman just

because I came to your rescue. There are things you don't know
about me—things you don't want to know, things you could
not begin to understand.''

''Like what?'' Jennifer asked.

Trey waved off her question. ''There is only one thing you
need to know, here and now. If I decide to marry you there
will be a wedding night. I draw the line at taking a wife without
the traditional honeymoon. Now what do you have to say about
that?'' he challenged gruffly.

Jennifer stared up into his stony features, looking past his
hostile tone. She suspected he had upped the ante on their
bargain, expecting her to retract the offer. He was purposely
trying to pick a fight, hoping to frighten her off. But she was
not going to budge or renege. She had assumed her father's
crusade to keep the peace in Texas, no matter what the personal
sacrifice. And spending one night in Trey's arms did not frighten
her in the least. She knew how tender and gentle he could be.
He would never intentionally hurt her—the very fact that he
had arrived to save the day assured her of that.

''Well, English?'' Trey prodded. ''Are you ready to back
out?''

Jennifer looked him squarely in the eye. ''No, I am not. I
do not have the slightest qualm about meeting your stipulations.
When you are ready to marry me, *if* you decide to accept my
terms, I will be waiting in my room to accompany you to the
Justice of the Peace.''

When she turned on her heel and strode into the hotel, Trey
stared after her. His mind whirled at the speculation of sharing
her bed. He was so distracted by the tantalizing thought that
he was unaware that Quincy Ward had sneaked up on him.
The steel barrel of a six-shooter nudged Trey in the ribs. Oblig-
ingly, Trey strolled down the boardwalk—until he reached the
alley.

Without warning, Trey exploded into action, ramming his
elbow into Quincy's soft underbelly. When Quincy doubled
over reflexively, Trey's hand shot out to retrieve the pistol as
his knee caught Quincy in the groin. The Texan's legs folded

like a tent. Before Quincy knew what happened, he was staring at a dagger pressed against his throat.

"Who the hell are you?" Quincy chirped, staring cross-eyed at the knife.

"Most folks know me as Three Wolves," Trey said, watching shock register on Quincy's homely features. Smiling devilishly, he pricked Quincy's earlobe. "I told you Jennifer was *my* fiancée. You better learn to listen or you'll wind up a couple of ears short." His gaze narrowed into steel slits as he added in a venomous hiss, "And don't ever shove a pistol in my ribs again. It'll get you killed."

"And if you interfere with my plans, you'll be pushing up daisies, gunslinger."

Leaving Quincy hissing and cursing, Trey ambled down the street. He doubted he had seen the last of that sneaky Texan, but he was pretty sure he had made a strong first impression.

Trey had decided to make Jennifer's problems his problems. Besides, he had an ax to grind with Jonas Rafferty. Quincy and Jonas definitely hadn't seen the last of him, even if Jennifer planned to send Trey skedaddling off in the opposite direction.

Trey smiled to himself as he veered into the clothing store. He wondered how Jennifer would react when he informed her that he planned to accompany her to Texas and hang around long enough to establish the peace she had set her heart on between farmers and cattlemen. No doubt they would be having a nice, long *chat* about that, too.

After witnessing Three Wolves' row with the Texas rancher, Willie Yates ducked around the corner of the alley. In silence, Willie and Russ Trent watched the half-breed bounty hunter veer into one of the shops on Front Street. Willie didn't have a clue what business Three Wolves had in a fashionable clothing store, and he didn't much care. All Willie knew was that the coast was clear to sneak into the hotel to abduct the blond-haired woman they had met the previous night. Whatever business the gunfighter planned to conduct would detain him long enough for Willie and Cousin Russ to take their hostage and make a fast getaway.

"You bring the horses 'round back," Willie instructed. "I'll stand watch to make sure Three Wolves doesn't come this direction."

"If he's coming this way too soon, I sure as hell don't want to tangle with him," Russ muttered. "Did you see how damned fast that gunslinger downed the rancher?"

"I saw," Willie grunted.

"The son of a bitch isn't even afraid of a loaded gun stuck in his spine."

"Well, when Three Wolves comes to fetch the woman we're taking, I plan to be armed to the teeth. I just hope to hell my trigger finger doesn't stiffen up when we confront that savage." He flexed his hand as he craned his neck around the corner to keep an eye out for Three Wolves while Russ trotted off to get the horses.

That Comanche bastard was going to pay dearly for siccing those wolves on him, Willie promised himself. He had taken pleasure in killing several men the past few years, but nothing would be as gratifying as bringing down that headhunter. With the woman as bait, Three Wolves was going to get everything he had coming. Wolf bait, Willie promised himself. That was what that Comanche bastard was going to be when the Yates Gang was finished with him!

Four

Jennifer fluffed her skirt and stared at her reflection in the mirror. She wanted to look her best when Trey returned to escort her to the Justice of the Peace.

Smiling in anticipation, she smoothed the pink satin dress over her hips. This garment had been a birthday gift from Grandmother Reynolds. The duchess had turned her back on her daughter years ago, but Gram had not severed ties with her grandchildren. Jennifer dutifully wrote to the Duchess of Calverdon, keeping her abreast of the goings-on in Texas. Elegant gifts arrived regularly, compliments of Gram.

Jennifer rearranged her coiffure and pinned the recalcitrant strands in place. She wistfully wished she could enjoy a true marriage to Trey MacTavish. Whether he realized it or not, Trey needed her. He had been soured by life's trials and tribulations, and it would take time to draw from the well of emotion buried deep inside him. Though Jennifer knew it would not be easy, she would have tried—had circumstances been different.

Although Trey did not believe in love, because he had been shunned and ostracized by society, Jennifer knew love existed. She had seen it flourish between her parents, felt its radiance all around her. She could have taught Trey a thing or two, but she refused to endanger his life by allowing him to accompany her to Texas. She was just beginning to recover from the devastating loss of her father. Losing the man she sensed she could love forever would be more than she could bear . . .

The rap at the door jostled Jennifer from her thoughts. She lurched around, remembering Trey's word of caution. "Who is it?"

No answer, only another quiet rap.

"Quincy, is that you?" Jennifer demanded impatiently.

"No, ma'am, it's the hotel clerk. I was asked to deliver a message to you from Three Wolves."

Jennifer's satin-clad shoulders sagged in relief. She hoped to bypass Quincy until after the wedding ceremony had taken place. Once the deed was done, and Trey had gone on his way, Jennifer would deal with Quincy—armed with a marriage certificate that would discourage his unwanted attentions.

Jennifer opened the door, then stumbled back when two scraggly ruffians charged toward her. Before she could scream, a grimy hand clamped over the lower portion of her face, quickly replaced by a smelly bandanna. When she struggled to escape, the second assailant wrenched her arms behind her back. She was flung to the floor and rolled up in a quilt, despite her attempts to buck and kick her way free.

Jennifer found herself toted down the back steps of the hotel, then tossed over the back of a horse and tied securely in place. She swore she was about to lose the greasy breakfast she had consumed when the jolt of the trotting steed pounded against her stomach. Blood ran to her head in a sweltering rush. Jennifer tried to breathe, but nausea overwhelmed her. The bedroll smelled of whiskey and sweat, and every motion of the horse brought her ever closer to tossing her morning meal.

When the horse reached open road and stretched out into a gallop, Jennifer squeezed her eyes shut and fought down more waves of queasiness. Then with blood pooling in her head, and the thud of the horse jarring every bone in her body, she lost consciousness . . .

* * *

Before Trey left Dodge he purchased two gold wedding bands and a set of gentleman's clothes. He had decided to do the wedding up right, for Jennifer's sake. Even if she wasn't getting a conventional husband, Trey decided to dress the part—temporarily.

When he rode into camp, the wolves whined and sniffed at him as if he were a strange and curious creature. Dismounting, Trey retrieved a small mirror from his saddlebag to appraise his reflection. He scowled at the man staring back at him.

No wonder the wolves were sniffing around him as if he were a stranger. He didn't even recognize himself. And furthermore, he looked ridiculous in these fancy trappings . . .

When the wolves wheeled around and growled, Trey automatically grabbed his pistol.

"Holy jumping hell!" Sunset squawked as he emerged from a grove of trees.

Sunset and Jawbone halted in their tracks when they saw Three Wolves decked out in a white linen shirt and matching black jacket, breeches, and cravat. His hair was tucked beneath a bowler hat and a smoking cigar was clamped between his teeth. An ornately carved cane hung over his left arm.

Trey noted the cowboys' reactions and muttered under his breath. Now he was positively certain he looked as absurd as he felt. The cravat felt like a hangman's noose. The breeches chafed and the jacket was damned confining. He was far more comfortable in doehide or a breechcloth.

Truth be told, half-naked always suited him best. The Eastern school, where he and the other Comanche children had been shipped, had failed to convert him to white man's ways. Trey recalled those years with disdain. Garbing himself in these garments reminded him of those miserable years and turned his bad mood black as pitch.

"So you've decided to marry Miss Jenny," Jawbone muttered. "I was afraid of that. I've got serious reservations about this arrangement, I'll have you know."

''Reservations or not, I have decided to accept the lady's offer,'' Trey said as he holstered his pistol.

Jawbone cleared his throat and shifted awkwardly. ''About yer wedding night—''

''You aren't invited,'' Trey broke in, flashing the aging wrangler a warning glance.

''If you were a real gentleman you wouldn't force yerself on Miss Jenny,'' Sunset dared to say.

Trey grabbed Diablo's reins and swung into the saddle. ''I'm not a gentleman and I have no aspirations of being one. I thought I had already established that fact.''

Jawbone stared grimly at Trey. ''I'm not a man to make foolish threats, but I'm telling you that if you hurt that lady, you'll answer to me, just as if I were her pa.''

''And as if I was her older brother,'' Sunset put in. ''Miss Jenny deserves to be treated with courtesy and respect. Don't forget that when yer male juices start percolating.''

Trey muttered to himself. The overprotective instincts of these cowboys were as annoying as they were amusing. Next thing Trey knew, he would be treated to a lecture on the birds and bees. But no matter what, Trey would have his rightful due. Why shouldn't he enjoy a little pleasure for once in his life? He had a price on his head and a saddlebag full of bench warrants, not to mention a threat from Jennifer's would-be fiancé.

To make matters worse, these mother hens were squawking about being gentle and considerate to Jennifer. Well hell, they weren't about to nag his conscience into bowing out. Marriage and honeymoons went together like bows and arrows. What was the use of one without the other? Trey wanted Jennifer in his bed and that was where she would be. He had made up his mind, and nothing these two cowboys could say would change it.

Each time Jennifer had touched Trey, no matter how harmless and innocent the gesture, he had felt a burning on his skin, inhaled the fragrance of lilacs. When he kissed her and took her to the ground to prove his point the previous night, desire had exploded through him. The naive little innocent didn't have a clue what a profound effect she had on him, because Trey had denied himself. But he was not going to deny himself tonight.

"Three Wolves." Jawbone said tentatively, "I'm asking you as nice as I know how. Be gentle and considerate of Miss Jenny. Her mama gave up her title to marry Ramsey Templeton. The high and mighty duchess didn't approve of the match. In fact, she threw a fit. Lady Agatha Reynolds, Duchess of Calverdon, did all she could to break up the marriage, even threatened to disown her own daughter. But disowned or not, that makes Miss Jenny a descendent of dukes and earls."

Scowling sourly, Trey headed toward town. He was about to marry a potential duchess? There was no telling how much money Jennifer had inherited from the dukedom—or whatever you called those fancy folks' property.

And here he'd been spouting off about a wedding night. After what Jawbone told him about Jennifer's background, Trey's confidence was faltering. What if he couldn't live up to her fantasies? What if he couldn't awaken her desire? How did a man make a woman respond when she didn't have a clue where passion led? Would Jennifer's cheerful optimism crumble at the prospect of intimacy?

Well, the fact still remained that English would spend her wedding night with him, Trey told himself. That was what he demanded in exchange for his name. He was a man who didn't make idle threats, after all. He made promises—Comanche promises, the kind that were never broken. When a warrior gave his word he was honor bound to keep it. Jennifer Templeton *would* have a wedding night.

Trey hoped she would remember it fondly, because he was pretty sure he would never forget it.

Jennifer's grandmother would probably have a seizure when she received word that her granddaughter had married a half-breed Comanche. Lady Agatha la-di-da Reynolds would be shrieking so loudly in her English castle that Trey could hear her from here!

*   *   *

Trey adjusted his garments and rapped on the hotel door. "English?"

No response.

Trey rapped on the door again. He was impatient to conclude the wedding ceremony and then peel off these citified clothes. He had left Jawbone and Sunset outside with the wolves. Both men looked about as thrilled at the prospect of giving away their precious ward as if they were facing the gallows. And if English didn't open the damned door pretty quick, Trey was going to lose his patience.

"I'm coming in," he announced as he shouldered into the room.

He halted in midstep when he found the room vacant. Jennifer's sunny yellow gown was folded neatly over the back of the chair. A trunk large enough to hold a wardrobe for a six-month vacation sat at the foot of the bed. Jennifer had either changed clothes or left naked, Trey decided. And not under her own power, either, he mused as he surveyed the room a second time. Her purse and parasol were lying atop the dresser.

"Damn that Quincy Ward," Trey muttered.

Wheeling around, Trey stalked down the hall. He couldn't say he was surprised by this last-ditch effort to thwart the marriage. But if Quincy forced Jennifer into marriage, Trey would have the man's scalp!

"What's wrong?" Sunset questioned when Trey stormed outside.

"English is gone. Where is Quincy Ward staying?"

"We dunno," Jawbone replied. "This hotel is filled to capacity with cattle buyers from the East. We rented the last two rooms."

Trey strode to the nearest hotel to check the ledger. He found Quincy's name at the second hotel, then took the steps two at a time to reach the Texan's room. Trey didn't bother knocking, just rammed his foot against the locked door—and split the crotch of his fancy breeches.

"Where is she?" Trey growled. Before Quincy could bolt from his chair, Trey was looming over him. "And don't insult my intelligence by pretending you don't know who the hell I'm talking about."

"I haven't seen her." Quincy tried to glare Trey down—it didn't work. "Get the hell out of my room—" His voice dried up when Trey whipped out his dagger and laid cold steel against his hairline.

Trey grabbed a handful of Quincy's curly brown hair and glowered down into his terrified face. "Where's English? You either tell me now or I'll separate you from your scalp!"

"I don't know!" Quincy wheezed when a tuft of hair feathered onto his nose. "Damn it, I swear on my mother's grave I don't know where Jennifer is!"

Trey released his painful grasp on Quincy's hair and tucked the dagger inside his jacket. "You better be telling the truth, because if you aren't, you're going to taste every known Comanche torture," he said with deadly menace.

"You've made yourself a dangerous enemy," Quincy hissed through his teeth. "You'll pay for this."

Trey shrugged carelessly. "I've got dozens of dangerous enemies. One more isn't going to make a damn to me."

"Maybe not, but I swear you'll be damned sorry you tangled with me, Three Wolves."

Ignoring the snarled threat, Trey stalked out. With Jawbone and Sunset scurrying behind him, he retraced his path to the lobby of Jennifer's hotel to interrogate the clerk. When Trey described Jennifer, the clerk shrugged a bony shoulder.

"I saw Miss Templeton go upstairs a couple of hours ago, but I haven't seen her since—"

" 'Scuse me," an adolescent voice interrupted.

Trey wheeled around to see a young, smudge-faced lad standing behind him.

"I was paid two bits to deliver this package to the man who owns the wolves," the boy said.

"You just found him, kid."

Trey tore open the package and swore. When he saw the

canvas sack stamped with the insignia from First State Bank of Denver, sickening dread coursed through him. Trey knew who had paid the kid to deliver the parcel. It didn't take a genius to figure out *why,* either. The Yates Gang had decided to retaliate by taking Jennifer as bait. Trey was being lured into a death trap.

"What's going on?" Jawbone demanded anxiously.

"English has been kidnapped by outlaws," Trey reported grimly.

Jawbone looked like a man who had been gut-shot. Sunset looked even worse when his freckled face drained of color.

"How bad are these hombres?" Jawbone wanted to know.

"The worst."

Trey strode out the door to retrieve his horse. He had encountered enough cutthroats in his day to predict what was in store for Jennifer. Her chance of survival was decreasing by the minute. The Yates Gang wasn't in the habit of leaving witnesses around to testify against them.

"What are we gonna do?" Sunset asked Trey as he mounted up.

"I'm sure there will be a trail I'm expected to follow."

"*We* are expected to follow," Sunset amended. "We're coming with you."

"I work alone."

"When Miss Jenny is involved, you've got reinforcements, whether you want 'em or not," Jawbone insisted. "How many men are in this damned gang?"

"There's three left. I shot the leader in Colorado."

"And now they want yer head," Sunset predicted.

"Something like that."

Trey didn't impart the fact that the Yates Gang was notorious for leaving dead bodies in their wake. Jennifer's devoted body-guards didn't need to hear the gory details.

As Trey raced back to camp to change clothes and gather ammunition, his mind reeled with the bleak possibilities awaiting Jennifer. Nothing in her sheltered existence would have prepared her to deal with merciless men. If Trey managed to rescue Jennifer she may wish he hadn't bothered. He knew what those ruthless bastards could do—and had done—to women. Jennifer's idealistic illusions about love and justice were sure to be shattered.

Shaking off his dread, Trey bounded onto Diablo's back and thundered off. No matter what else happened, Bob and Willie Yates and Russ Trent were going to hell in a handbag made of their own worthless hides!

Jennifer tumbled from the smelly bedroll. She still did not have the vaguest notion why she had been bound up and toted away.

"I demand to know what this is all about!" she insisted when her gag was removed.

"If you know what's good for you, lady, you'll keep your mouth shut," Willie Yates snapped as he jerked her to her feet.

"What do you want with me? If it is money, I am without a bloody cent. I was robbed on my way to Dodge."

Russ Trent leered at her, then smiled the kind of smile that made Jennifer shiver repulsively. "You'll find out what we're gonna do to you soon enough, honey."

Jennifer refused to be intimidated by the scraggly hooligan's remark. She decided to employ her grandmother's tactics. "I daresay, after chewing on that kerchief, I need a drink of water."

Caught off guard, Willie Yates held the canteen to her lips.

"Thank you," Jennifer said with exaggerated politeness. "Now, if you will untie me I would like to revive the circulation in my arms and legs. There is no need to bind me up like a blasted mummy. This gown is restrictive in itself."

Willie stared at Jennifer as if she were a babbling idiot. That was the exact impression she was striving for. If she could pass herself off as a prissy, empty-headed twit, her captors might take her for granted and she could escape.

"Please untie my feet," Jennifer insisted. "I bloody well can't go anywhere in this dratted dress."

When Willie jerked on the hem of her gown, ripping off the

delicate lace of what was to be her wedding dress, Jennifer gasped in feigned outrage. "Devil take it, this is the most expensive garment I own. It was a gift from my grandmother. Her seamstress will be chagrined to see what you have done. And a temperamental woman she is, too. Second only to my grandmother. I shall make you explain to them both why you did that."

"Will you shut up!" Russ snapped while Willie draped the lace over a tree limb to mark the trail.

"Shut up? I should say not. There is no law in these States that prohibits a woman from speaking her mind—"

Jennifer's voice trailed off when she saw the cruel desperado who had tried to blow her head off during the fiasco in Trey's camp. Bob Yates's homely, unshaven face puckered in a sneer as he glared at her.

Suddenly, Jennifer understood why she had been taken captive—and by whom. These three men had tried to bushwhack Trey. He had built a fire to lure them in and Jennifer had botched his carefully-laid plans. Now she was the bait to entrap the legendary bounty hunter.

Bloody, blistering hell! She was in more trouble than she originally thought. But she could not change strategy after she had established herself as a dim-witted chatterbox. She had to keep up the pretense, hoping for a chance to escape from these scheming killers.

"I cannot fathom what this is all about," Jennifer prattled as Bob hobbled toward her, propping himself on an improvised cane. "I have told these men that I was robbed already. I barely have the money to purchase my own meals."

When Bob Yates halted in front of Jennifer, she met his glower without flinching. "You remember me, don't you? I thought you would," he said as he shoved her toward a horse, making her hop to keep from falling on her face.

"I hope this encounter proves to be more pleasant than the last. By the way, how is your leg?"

"It hurts like hell," Bob snarled at her.

"Those wolves are dreadful," Jennifer commiserated. "I had

my own trouble with them and that rude, obnoxious gunslinger. Why, I have never dealt with such insolence," she declared, improvising as she went. "I was trying to hire that cad to . . . track down my shiftless husband who abandoned me, but that bounty hunter expected me to pay an outrageous fee."

"I can see why your husband deserted you," Willie grunted as he knelt to untie her ankles. "You talk too damned much, lady."

"Do you think so? Well, maybe that is because my husband rarely spoke to me at all. I never could tolerate silence. And I am the first to admit our marriage was not a match made in heaven, but there are children to consider—"

"Goddam it, woman, shut your mouth!" Bob bellowed as he flung her onto the horse.

Jennifer levered herself into a sitting position, her bound fists clamped on the pommel. "You need not be so abusive," she chastised. "A *please* and *thank you* would have sufficed. My grandmother is a stickler for etiquette. You are fortunate Gram is not here to give you thirty lashes with her tongue."

Willie pulled his brother aside. "Are you sure this chit means something to Three Wolves? It doesn't sound like it to me."

"Three Wolves tried to protect her last night. I predict he'll try to do it again," Bob insisted. "We'll take her to the abandoned dugout the railroad crews used while they were laying track across Kansas. We need to have our trap set before dark."

"I just hope we didn't go to all this trouble for nothing," Willie groused. "Three Wolves might not bother to chase after this yammering twit."

Russ glanced back at Jennifer, undressing her with his eyes. "Even if Three Wolves don't show up, the night won't be a total waste. Not to me, at least."

Jennifer knew she was taking a great risk, but she wasn't sure she would have another opportunity to make a run for it. While the three men were milling around her—on foot—discussing plans as if she wasn't there, she gouged her heels into the horse. The steed lunged off, colliding with the two mounts in front of it. Curses flew as Jennifer plastered herself against the horse's neck to dodge oncoming bullets. And there were several of them sailing in her direction, she was sorry to say!

Gritting her teeth, Jennifer hung on for dear life and let the steed have its head. The thunder of hooves echoed in her ears as the steed scrambled up the hill and stretched out in a dead run across the open meadow.

"Blister it," Jennifer muttered when she saw the outlaws top the rise to give chase. The men had retrieved their horses sooner than she anticipated. Jennifer didn't know what she was going to do if the outlaws overtook her. She would just refuse to get caught, she decided.

Another shot zinged past her head.

Bloody hell, that was close! Another inch and she would have had a permanent part in her scalp.

The whine of a second and third bullet struck the horse beneath her. Jennifer was catapulted off the stumbling steed and rolled helter-skelter across the ground. Frantic, she scrambled to her feet to race toward the thicket of cottonwood trees.

She groaned in pain when Bob Yates rammed his horse into her, sending her cartwheeling in a tangle of petticoats and satin. Her head slammed against the ground with enough force to blur her vision. Before she could get her bearings, Russ Trent yanked her up by her hair and backhanded her across the cheek.

Tears sprang to her eyes as she stumbled back into Willie's waiting arms. He clamped his hand over her breasts, pinching painfully into tender flesh. When Jennifer tried to pull away, Bob clenched his fist in the front of her gown and jerked her to him, his snarling face inches away from hers.

"Next time you pull a stunt like that you'll wake up dead," he growled.

Pain crashed through Jennifer's skull when Bob Yates struck her on the back of the head with the butt of his pistol. Her last thought, before the world turned pitch black, was that Trey MacTavish had warned her that she was entirely too idealistic for her own good. There was no honor or mercy among thieves.

Now Jennifer understood why Trey had become a man driven by survival instinct, cynical of love and kindness.

As for Jennifer, she had the terrifying feeling that she was about to endure the kind of hell Trey had come to know—and expect. She was very much afraid that she had become one of the newly damned . . .

"Be careful with those trunks, you dolt!" Agatha Reynolds, Duchess of Calverdon, fussed. She whacked the hired lackey on the shoulder with her parasol to demand his attention. "The contents of those trunks are worth more than you earn in a year. Now set them down gently!"

Cursing the old dowager under his breath, the man did as he was told.

"I say, Simpson, how can my poor grandchildren tolerate such incompetence from these American servants?" Agatha grumbled to her devoted butler. "Why, the whole stinking lot of them are fumbling bumpkins."

Simpson nodded his gray head in agreement. "Indeed, Your Grace, our cross-country jaunt was nothing but an exercise in frustration."

"That is a bloody understatement," Agatha harumphed. "Kindly locate a decent inn so we can spend the night." When a gust of wind blew by, stirring up dust, she wrinkled her nose distastefully. "Good gad, this peasant village smells like a cow pen!"

"Begging your pardon, Your Grace, but with a buffalo hide factory at one end of Dodge City and cattle corrals at the other, this place *is* a cow pen." Bowing courteously, Simpson tramped off with an armload of luggage.

"Bloody everlasting hell!" Agatha blustered at the incompetent attendant. "I said . . . set those trunks down nice and easy. Pretend they are your bloody children!"

"Yes, ma'am," the attendant muttered.

"It is *Your Grace,* to you." Agatha took excessive pleasure in correcting the lowly commoner. "From prime British stock, diamonds of the first water, with blood as blue as the sky."

"Yes, indeedy," the train attendant smirked. "You're the very reason my ancestors left your country to avoid—ouch!"

The dreaded parasol struck again. Agatha may have celebrated her sixtieth birthday, but there was nothing wrong with her hearing.

The attendant dumped the remainder of the luggage on the ground and thrust out his hand. "That's the last of it, my grace—"

"*Your* Grace, you idiot!"

"That's what I said. My grace."

Agatha scowled, dug into her reticule, and paid the man more than he was worth. In her estimation, she was being excessively generous.

"Now see here, my grace, we agreed—"

"We agreed that you would unload my belongings carefully, which you most certainly did not do," Agatha snapped. "And until you stack those trunks properly, I am bloody well not paying you more money."

The attendant flashed Agatha a glare that could have curdled milk, but she ignored the peasant. When he stalked off, Agatha perched herself on one of the trunks and glanced around with visible distaste. She simply could not fathom why Ramsey Templeton had dragged his children—her grandchildren—to this godforsaken outpost on the edge of civilization. A country plagued with common stock—the whole bloody lot of them, as Agatha saw it. But she was duty bound to retrieve Jennifer and Christopher after receiving word of Ramsey's death.

Truth be told, Agatha had grown bored with merry old England, since Ramsey was no longer around to take the brunt of her criticism. She needed a purpose. Rescuing her grandchildren provided the motivation that had been lacking in her life.

When the sun beat down relentlessly, Agatha flicked open her parasol. What the devil was taking Simpson so ruddy long to fetch a wagon for their belongings? Lord, she would be glad when she finally reached that place called Texas and surprised her deprived grandchildren.

According to the train conductor, Mobeetie, Texas, was two hundred miles south of this crude, smelly cowtown in Nowhere, Kansas. Agatha was dreading the upcoming coach ride, but she had rented the entire space so she would not have to share quarters with these local yokels.

Simpson was company enough. His manners were impeccable and he could carry on intelligent conversations. He was as loyal and devoted as they came, the hallmark of gentlemanly behavior. He was also Agatha's only remaining contact with English protocol. Agatha and Simpson had been together long before the Duke of Calverdon's death a decade earlier. And speaking of intolerable and insufferable, Thomas Reynolds had been both. Their marriage had been a sojourn in perdition.

"It is about bloody time," Agatha grouched when Simpson showed up in a wagon.

"I am dreadfully sorry, Your Grace," Simpson apologized. "You would not believe the deplorable conditions we have to endure during our overnight stay in Dodge."

Agatha cringed. "It gets worse?"

"Decidedly worse." Simpson assisted Agatha onto the seat, then took up the reins. "I had to rent four rooms, just to have enough breathing space in the crude inn overrun with cow servants. I shudder to think what meager accommodations your grandchildren are tolerating on their ranch."

"A good thing I have decided to return Jennifer and Christopher to their rightful home," Agatha murmured as she wiped the perspiration from her brow. "Five years in that forbidden hell called Texas is five years too long!"

Trey yanked the piece of lace from the tree limb and studied the trampled tracks. Scattered hoof- and footprints indicated Jennifer had been dumped on the ground and then hauled to her feet. Trey also noted the tracks of a man dragging his crippled leg. Bob Yates had rendezvoused with his cohorts.

None of this bode well for Jennifer. Damn it, he had to find her—fast!

With Sunset and Jawbone at his heels, Trey followed the trail up the slope, then halted abruptly. "Jennifer was overtaken here after she tried to escape," he said before he trotted west.

"How does he do that?" Sunset questioned Jawbone.

"Dunno," Jawbone murmured. "I've heard it said that Three Wolves follows tracks as if they were printed maps. Must be the Comanche in him."

"I scouted some in the Army," Sunset commented. "Never saw anybody this good before."

"Yeah, and I bet Three Wolves can even tell us what those slimy bastards are thinking, if he had a mind to. Trouble is, I'm not sure I wanna know."

Trey paused again, and swore to himself. He could tell by the smeared prints and skidding heel marks that a scuffle had taken place on this rise. He had a pretty good idea who had skidded backward when those vicious outlaws overtook their fleeing captive.

If Jennifer had not yet been abused, she had been struck, Trey predicted. The thought made his blood boil, but he cautioned himself not to let emotion interfere with his reasoning. He had to proceed with cold, calculated revenge . . .

Trey's thoughts trailed off when the wolves sniffed the ground, whined, then trotted to the creek. A knot of anguish twisted in his gut as he followed the wolves. He found himself holding his breath as he glanced down the ravine—afraid Jennifer hadn't survived the first phase of her ordeal.

Trey's shoulders slumped in relief when he saw the wolves feasting on a dead horse—the one Jennifer must have been riding. The Yates Gang had shot her horse out from under her to stop her, he speculated.

"Good God!" Sunset croaked as he topped the hill. "Are you just gonna stand there and let them wolves devour that horse? That is disgusting!"

"I want the wolves well-fed when we confront the Yates Gang," Trey said somberly. "More than once, outlaws have poisoned meat with strychnine and left it for my wolves—the same way white men poisoned water holes to kill Indians.'' He glanced grimly at his companions. ''Have you ever seen a man die of strychnine poisoning?''

Sunset and Jawbone shook their heads, their gazes glued to the feasting wolves.

''Consider yourself fortunate,'' Trey murmured as he trotted Diablo westward.

Jawbone frowned when Three Wolves rode off. ''Yer leaving the wolves behind?''

''They'll catch up when they have eaten their fill. I want them to be ready to kill, not hungry enough to tarry when I need them.''

Sunset and Jawbone gulped uneasily as they trailed behind Three Wolves. They weren't sure they were cut out for this grisly business of tracking and disposing of cutthroats. Only one man was—a man who had ridden into hell so many times that dealing with the damned had little else to teach him.

Trey pulled his black stallion to a halt to survey the area around him. He knew this country like the back of his hand. The land of the High Plains—*Llano Estacado,* as it was known to the Comanche—flattened out like a shadow. Trees were sparse, except along creek beds. There were few places to hide in this area where Mother Nature was harsh and unforgiving. Trey knew of only two locations that would allow the Yates Gang to set a trap. It was imperative that he arrive quickly to thwart this conniving attempt to entrap him.

Trey grimaced, wondering if *quickly* would be soon enough to spare Jennifer the torments that would have her begging to die.

With fiendish haste, Trey thundered across the prairie. Instinct told him where the Yates Gang was headed. He hoped Bob Yates wouldn't be expecting him earlier than planned. Surprise would be necessary to save Jennifer—if anything could.

Five

Jennifer bit back a wail when Russ Trent jerked her from the saddle and dragged her toward the dugout that had been carved into a knoll near a tree-lined creek. Everything in her rebelled at the thought of the atrocities she had already suffered on the trail—and what would happen to her before this living hell ended. She had not been prepared for the beating she had taken after she attempted escape, or for the repulsive men who pinched and prodded at her as if she were a side of beef. Jennifer was accustomed to courteous treatment from men. Suddenly, all the rules had changed and she found herself subjected to the abominable behavior of outlaws.

The ideals she held dear were shattering around her so fast it made her head spin. If she survived this ordeal—and she doubted she would—she could never believe in the goodness of mankind again. She understood why Trey had become so cynical, so skeptical. She was tolerating the same filth associated with the lowest, most despicable forms of life. She also knew why Trey had no qualms about disposing of all the Yates Gangs in this world. They made life hell for anyone who encountered them!

When Russ shoved Jennifer inside the dugout and sent her sprawling on the earthen floor, she bit back a groan. She shrank away when she saw rats scurrying into the holes in the crumbling walls of her dungeon.

This was yet another level of hell, she mused as she curled herself into a ball. The torment she was suffering peeled away layers of her soul. Soon, there would be nothing left of her soul, or her mind. And then she would reach the horrific state when she no longer cared if she lived or died.

Jennifer smothered another cry of pain when Russ jerked her bound arms over her head to stake her down. He made no attempt to dodge her fingers as he hammered the metal stake into place with a heavy stone.

"Bastard," she hissed into his smirking expression.

"Call me what you want, but you'll be down to begging when I come back to take my pleasure with you, prissy lady."

"Russ!" Bob's bulky form filled the entrance of the dugout. "Hurry up in there. We've got things to do before Three Wolves shows up. I want plenty of fresh meat, laced with poison, lying around. I'll be damned if I'll let those fanged monsters chew us up again. You and Willie can shoot a few rabbits while I fetch the poison from my saddlebag."

Alone, Jennifer treated herself to a few foul curses. The thought of poisoning the wolves to lessen the odds incensed her. She did not see how she could possibly come out of this hellhole alive, and she prayed Trey had not followed her. She could die easier if she knew she was not responsible for his death.

The crack of a distant rifle caused Jennifer to wince. She could not sit here wallowing in self-pity, she told herself. She needed to pry herself loose and provide a distraction in case Trey did stumble into this deadly trap.

Resolutely, Jennifer dragged her knees beneath her to tug at the stake. It didn't budge. She cursed mightily and heaved upward again. Glancing around, she spied the stone Russ had tossed aside before he trooped outside. Jennifer stretched out her leg to draw the stone toward her, then scooped it up in her bound hands. Although the rope attached to her wrists did not permit much leeway to swing the stone at the stake, Jennifer hammered at it from all directions. The packed dirt gave way enough to allow her to wiggle the stake.

Several minutes later she was able to jerk the stake from the floor. A shot rang out as she vaulted to her feet. She had to think! How could she distract these cretins? Running had not accomplished a dratted thing earlier. She had lost her horse and suffered the painful blows of meaty fists, then found her head at the butt end of a pistol.

Jennifer felt a spark of hope when she noticed the rounded tunnel dug into the back wall. It seemed to be an improvised cooler to preserve food or store jars of canned goods. She peered into the shallow tunnel, dismayed that the nook was not deep enough to crawl into completely.

"Bloody hell," she muttered as she took inventory of the dugout.

Her gaze landed on a broken crate beside the door. If she could tuck herself into the niche and pull the crate in front of the opening in the wall, she might be able to convince the Yates Gang that she had sneaked off while they were setting and baiting poison traps. And if the Yates Gang did locate her, and tried to reach into the niche to grab hold of her, they would feel the sting of her makeshift dagger—the stake.

Those outlaws would have to shoot her out of her hiding place, Jennifer decided. Being dragged out—dead—would be preferable to living through untold horrors. Russ Trent's and Willie Yates's demeaning gropes had already made her skin crawl. She refused to tolerate that humiliation again.

Dear God! How did Trey MacTavish live with all the terror and atrocities he must have witnessed—and endured—during his forays into hell? He had undoubtedly been stripped down to the core of his soul a dozen times. She, like Trey, had come to believe in—and depend on—little or nothing.

Jennifer was learning things she did not want to know—things that destroyed her optimism and left her burning with hatred and a craving for revenge. Her cheerfulness had been transformed into spitefulness. Trey was right, she realized. She had been a naive fool, living in castles in the air, blithely ignoring cruel reality.

On that dismal thought Jennifer retrieved the crate and tucked herself into the narrow cubicle. She clutched the stake in her hand and waited, vowing to take at least one of those vicious bastards with her when she left this wicked world.

Russ Trent had a helluva time keeping his mind on hunting rabbits. His hands itched to pleasure himself with the woman staked in the dugout. Lust was eating him alive.

Since he'd already dropped two jackrabbits in their tracks, Russ figured he'd done his part to bait poison traps. He had more interesting things to do with his time.

While Willie Yates tramped off to look for more rabbits along the creek, Russ stared hungrily toward the dugout. He could sneak back, take his turn with the chit, and be back outside in a few minutes. His cousins would never know where he was. Besides, there was still plenty of daylight left. Russ didn't expect Three Wolves until dark. By then, the trap would be set and the Comanche bastard would be shot full of holes.

Giving way to temptation, Russ scurried upstream to where Bob was sprawled in the grass, giving his bum leg a rest while he contaminated the fresh meat with poison.

"Here's two more carcasses for you, cuz," Russ said, tossing the rabbits beside Bob.

"How many has Willie bagged?" Bob asked.

"Just one. He's still having trouble getting his trigger finger to function properly. He went downstream to hunt."

Bob thrust three skinned rabbits at his cousin. "Take these to the east side of the dugout. No matter which direction Three Wolves takes, I want his vicious pets to find our bait. We'll need at least a dozen carcasses for those killer wolves to feast on."

The bark of a distant rifle brought Bob's scraggly head around. "Sounds like Willie must be having some luck."

''Either that or he missed his target again,'' Russ snorted as he ambled off.

A wicked smile pursed Russ's lips as he tossed the poisoned rabbits around the dugout. He was going to enjoy bringing that snippy female down a few notches while she was sprawled beneath him. When he was through with her, she dammed well wasn't going to be looking down her nose at him. He'd make sure of that.

While Willie Yates was staring down the rifle sight, trying to bring down another rabbit, Trey inched closer. When the shot rang out, Trey pounced. The butt end of his pistol cracked against Willie's skull, and the outlaw crumpled to the ground in an unconscious heap.

The wolves prowled around Trey's legs as Trey retrieved Willie's long-barreled Barns 50-caliber pistol, the rifle, and the dagger tucked in his right boot. Trey glanced over his shoulder when he heard the crackle of twigs behind him. *White men,* he thought crankily as Jawbone and Sunset skulked from the underbrush. These cowboys may have been whizzes at herding livestock, but they weren't worth a damn at stalking murderers. They made too much racket.

''What are you gonna do now?'' Jawbone whispered as he watched Trey peel off his black shirt.

''Get Willie out of his clothes,'' Trey ordered, unstrapping his holsters.

''What for?''

''Because I said so, and hurry up about it,'' Trey snapped as he tugged off his moccasins.

''We don't have time to torture this scoundrel. We've gotta get to Miss Jenny before it's too late,'' Sunset insisted.

''Just do as you're told or ride off,'' Trey growled.

Quietly, Trey stuffed Willie's limp arms into the black shirt and pulled the buckskin breeches in place. In a matter of minutes Willie was decked out in Trey's clothes—complete with the bead and bone breastplate and leather strap that sheathed a dagger to his thigh. The deadly blade, however, was still in Trey's possession.

Garbed in his breechcloth, Trey towered over the unconscious desperado. He kicked Willie in the ribs, jostling him awake. When Willie pried his eyes open, then opened his mouth to shout a warning to his confederates, Trey crammed his heel in Willie's face.

"If you scream, I'll stick a knife in your gut, just deep enough to seep blood and tear your insides to shreds," Trey whispered coldly. "You'll die so slowly you'll have time to repent for every sin you've ever committed. Understand me? You yell and you'll find out all about Comanche torture."

This was the man Jawbone and Sunset had come to know by legend—the skillful avenger who showed no mercy to vicious desperadoes. Jawbone swore he was standing on the fringe of hell, watching the devil swear in another wayward soul.

There was a strange, unnerving presence about Three Wolves now. The air fairly crackled with menace. This man wasn't just a mass of smoldering coals; he was the flame itself— burning like an ice-cold fire. His silver-gray eyes had taken on a strange glitter that caused Jawbone to gulp apprehensively.

Willie Yates must have noticed, too, because he hadn't moved—hardly dared to draw breath. He just lay there, staring into those hammered-steel eyes that radiated deadly malice.

Three Wolves sank into a crouch, so close that he was like Willie's own shadow. The half-breed's features were so hard that Jawbone was sure they had turned to stone. The tension in the air caused the hair to stand up on the back of Jawbone's neck as Three Wolves' breath became as shallow and measured as Willie's. The bounty hunter hovered beside Willie as if he were the other half of his soured soul.

Beads of perspiration popped out on Willie's brow when the sharp tip of the dagger pricked the underside of his chin. Wide-eyed, Jawbone watched the downed outlaw succumb to the kind of lethal intimidation Three Wolves was famous for. Watching the half-breed in action assured Jawbone that everything he'd heard was true: when the dark angel of vengeance went after murderers and thieves, he *did* bring hell with him.

"Nice and easy, Willie," Three Wolves whispered so quietly that Jawbone wasn't sure if he'd *thought* the words or actually *heard* them. "If you make a sound as you get up, you'll never make it to your feet. I'll have both your hamstrings slit before you can draw another breath."

Willie levered up on a wobbly elbow, and Three Wolves moved in synchronized rhythm, the knife poised at Willie's throat. When Willie pushed upright, Three Wolves was right beside him. The only difference was that Jawbone could see Willie's pulse pounding on the side of his neck, while Three Wolves' heartbeat was barely visible on his sleek, bronzed chest.

The burning flames in the gunslinger's eyes kept Willie silent. He kept darting glances at Three Wolves, who remained only a hairbreadth away, refusing to let the outlaw make even one false move.

"Sunset, fetch Diablo," Three Wolves ordered in a hollow, echoing voice. "Jawbone, get Willie's rifle. He'll be needing it."

Jawbone didn't ask why. Because of the unnerving scene he was witnessing, he couldn't seem to find his tongue. He'd never known silence to be so intense, never seen a man command such respect in the simple use of body language. Hell, Three Wolves looked as if he could climb right inside Willie's skin if that had been his wont. It was as if this unique Comanche half-breed had transformed himself into a dangerous creature that wasn't quite human. Jawbone had the strange impression of smoke drifting around Three Wolves—as if he wasn't really there in flesh, yet he was.

Jawbone shook himself loose from the odd sensations and images floating around him and walked over to fetch the rifle. When Sunset tried to lead Diablo forward, the devil stallion laid back his ears and balked. A quiet word from Three Wolves made him cooperative.

"Put Willie's hat on his head," Three Wolves ordered as

he secured Willie's hands to the pommel. "Jawbone, hand me the rifle."

Jawbone swallowed hard as he watched Three Wolves attach a length of twine to the rifle trigger, then gently ease the weapon beneath the black shirt Willie wore. The scruffy outlaw sat there like a scarecrow draped on a broom handle, his eyes bulging with apprehension.

"If you move, Willie, if you even shift sideways in the saddle, this string attached to the trigger, and anchored to the moccasins, will take your head off," Three Wolves assured him in a hollow voice. "If you move your leg, either one of them, you'll be wolf bait before you can blink. Do you understand, Willie? No matter what else happens, no matter whether the woman you abducted lives or dies, you will never know what became of her. One reckless gesture and you'll be scattered from here to hell."

A shudder passed through Jawbone's soul, draining the color from his face. He stared at the shotgun—with its barrel braced against Willie's skull. Twine, like a fuse, trailed down the outlaw's legs to his ankles. Jawbone peered grimly at Sunset, then stared at the desperado strapped on Diablo's back. For sure and certain, Willie Yates was about to pay penance for the trail of blood he had left behind him.

"What if Diablo bolts?" Willie squeaked.

Three Wolves gestured toward the martingale—the leather strap attached to the bridle that prevented the horse from tossing his head upward when startled. "This will keep Diablo from throwing you off balance. It's up to you to hold your back rigid and keep your feet from shifting in the stirrup."

"What if—?" Willie wheezed.

"I don't advise doing more than breathing," Three Wolves told him in such a cold voice that Jawbone shivered.

Three Wolves clucked his tongue, cueing Diablo into motion. A quiet command in the Comanche dialect sent the wolves trotting off at the stallion's heels.

It dawned on Jawbone, just then, what Three Wolves had planned. He had dressed Willie in the familiar clothes of the bounty hunter, then booby-trapped him on Diablo's back. From a distance, in the waning light of sunset, the outlaw looked as if he had swapped identities with the Comanche, especially since the wolves accompanied the rider.

Willie's hat was the clue. It indicated Three Wolves had made short work of Willie Yates and was wearing it as a trophy as he rode to confront the remaining members of the gang.

Willie Yates was a dead man riding, Jawbone realized grimly. It wouldn't matter whether Willie tripped the trigger. No matter what, he was about to die as he had lived—in a blaze of gunfire and violence.

Russ Trent eased the warped door of the dugout shut and squinted as his eyes adjusted to the dim light. He cursed colorfully when he didn't see Jennifer staked to the ground. That little twit had managed to uproot the stake and escape!

Wheeling around, Russ stamped outside but there was no sign of her.

And then Russ heard it—that all-too-familiar muster call of the wolf, the signal he'd learn to recognize as Three Wolves' trademark. He had heard that eerie sound the night Edgar Yates went toppling off a cliff to his death. He had heard it the previous night when he and his cousins tried to ambush Three Wolves in his camp south of Dodge.

Realizing Three Wolves had arrived ahead of schedule, Russ went into instant panic. He snapped his shotgun into position on his shoulder, aiming one direction and then another.

His breath stopped in his throat when the devil stallion trotted toward him. The wolves were sweeping back and forth behind the horse like drag riders on a cattle drive. The half-breed was poised in the saddle, the brim of Willie's sombrero tipped downward to shield his face from the setting sun.

Russ broke into a cold sweat when he realized what the hat symbolized. Cursing foully, he braced his legs and squeezed the trigger, then pumped another cartridge into the chamber and fired again for good measure. The stallion bolted sideways and the rider screamed the most horrible sound Russ had ever heard.

The hauntingly familiar voice of Willie Yates rang in Russ's ears. Russ felt his belly flip-flop when a rifle blast exploded and the rider plopped against the stallion's neck. As the horse trotted forward, Russ realized he had shot his own cousin. The sombrero fell by the wayside, exposing the greasy strands of brown hair.

Russ shrieked in terror when the wolves broke into a run—headed straight toward him. Screaming Bob's name, Russ spun around to plunge into the dugout. When he scooped up the wooden crate to hurl it at the approaching wolves, he saw the trailing hem of pink silk.

Russ jabbed Jennifer with the barrel of his weapon. "Come outta there now," he hissed.

When she didn't budge, Russ thrust his arm into the niche, but Jennifer stabbed him with the stake before he could latch onto her.

The scratching of paws indicated the vicious wolves had arrived. Their growls seeped around the edge of the door, and Russ reached a wilder state of panic. If he didn't get his hands on Jennifer to use as a shield, that Comanche bastard would use him the same way he had used Willie!

Despite the sharp jabs to his forearm and hand, Russ got hold of Jennifer's gown and tugged. Although she braced her legs to keep from being yanked out, she slid on the loose dirt. She screeched furiously when Russ pulled her out into the open. Before she could gain her feet, he clamped his arm diagonally across her chest and hoisted her up in front of him like a shield.

When Russ crammed the shotgun barrel into the side of Jennifer's jaw, she froze, wild-eyed.

His hand grasped her breast, squeezing into her flesh, forcing her to hold still. Then he hooked his leg around hers, spreading her feet apart. Propping himself against the wall, he wound his left leg between her thighs so Jennifer couldn't twist away.

She tried to steady herself while she was held spread-eagle in front of him, suffering the gropes of his filthy hands. When

his boot heel dug between her legs, Jennifer winced in pain,
but she arched back in an attempt to squirm free.

"Hold still," Russ hissed in her ear. "I swear I'll do worse
if you resist."

Jennifer believed him, and she well remembered how he had
pinched and prodded at her while he had her straddled over
the saddle during their journey. A muffled sob tumbled from
her lips when she heard the howling of wolves and felt Russ
pinch at her bruised flesh. The pungent odor of sweat assaulted
her. Jennifer didn't care if she died, here and now, because she
was sure she would never feel pure and clean again.

God, just let it be over, she cried silently. Let Trey survive . . .

Bob Yates mounted his steed when he heard the shots coming
from the direction of the dugout. He emerged from the trees in
time to see Russ firing at Three Wolves—or so Bob mistakenly
thought. When Willie's sombrero tumbled to the ground, Bob
swore furiously. Three Wolves had seen to it that Bob had to
watch his cousin shoot his little brother.

The ultimate irony, Bob realized in outrage. Damn that Comanche headhunter!

Bob spotted the bare-chested savage riding toward the dugout, plastered to the side of Willie's horse for protection. Bob
couldn't get off a single shot to slow down that sly half-breed
as Trey headed for the dugout where the snarling wolves
scratched at the door.

Bob wheeled his horse around and took off for cover. With
brother Willie dead, and cousin Russ soon to be, he had no
choice but to save his own hide. But Three Wolves hadn't seen
the last of him, Bob promised himself. He would hunt down
the half-breed and take his full measure of revenge!

Three Wolves trotted the steed toward the dugout, then
dropped into the tall grass. He jerked up his head in time to

see Bob Yates thundering over the hill. As anxious as he was
to get his hands on Bob, Jennifer needed his assistance. Russ
would be using her as his shield, the scroungy coward.

Silently, Trey slithered toward the dugout. He breathed
slowly, deeply, focusing on the task at hand. It was a technique
his grandfather had taught him during years of rigorous Comanche training.

Black Wolf, shaman of the family clan, had instructed his
half-breed grandson to reach deep inside himself, until mind
and body performed in perfect unison. Now, Three Wolves
took the time to prepare himself for battle, calling upon the
powers bestowed on him when he was but a child.

He reached into his saddlebag to retrieve the bottle of whiskey
he had confiscated from Willie. Using one of Willie's shirts,
Three Wolves saturated the cloth to make a torch. Flames
billowed around the torch as Three Wolves came to his knees
beside the vent pipe on top of the dugout. Smoke filled the
dugout as Three Wolves sent up a howl, calling upon his Comanche guardian spirit . . .

Jennifer choked as the smoke rolled over her. She heard the
eerie howl, the scratching at the door, and prayed she would
not have to watch Trey gunned down right before her eyes.

When the door opened, a swirl of smoke appeared. She saw
the snarling wolves the instant before they pounced on Russ,
chewing on his legs as he screamed in pain. The barrel of the
shotgun swerved toward the door.

"Bastard," Russ sneered. "Damn you . . ."

Frantic, Jennifer flung herself sideways, hoping to misdirect
the shot, praying Trey would not step into view. Her attempt
to distract Russ earned her another thump on the head. As pain
exploded in her skull, a strange image materialized in front of
her—a cloud of smoke with pools of mercury for eyes. Jennifer
could not keep her wits about her long enough to decide if the
blow caused the hallucination, or if she saw what she *thought*

she saw. She slumped over Russ's arm, then collapsed in the dirt when he shoved her limp body away to fend off the wolves.

Panting for breath, Russ staggered to keep his feet, but the wolves were making a feast of him. And then he saw the rising shadow at the door and heard that hollow, echoing voice. Eyes as cold as ice bore down on him like some strange creature from a nightmare.

"Welcome to hell, Russ Trent . . ."

Russ wasn't sure, but he thought he saw the barrels of two Colts swinging up from the swirl of smoke that hovered at the door. Before he had time to react, muffled shots echoed around the dugout. A numbing sensation settled over him as he was knocked back against the wall.

The howl of a wolf echoed in his ears as he stared at the smoky image that rolled toward him to steal his last breath . . .

Trey breathed slowly, calling himself back from where he'd been, releasing the powers bestowed on him so long ago. Jaw clenched, he squinted through the fog of smoke to see Russ Trent slumped against the wall, staring sightlessly at the ceiling.

Jennifer lay in the dirt, her face so pale that Trey cringed inwardly, imagining the terror she must have endured. He tried not to notice her torn bodice, the sooty smears on her shoulders where grimy hands had trespassed. The humiliation and revulsion she experienced were only part of the torments she would suffer before she put this incident behind her—if she ever could.

Trey cursed when he saw the bruise that discolored Jennifer's cheek and dried blood caked at the corner of her mouth. Seeing Jennifer semi-conscious on the floor, her elegant gown in tatters, got to Trey as nothing else could. When he knelt down to nudge her gently, she came awake and sobbed quietly. Recognizing him, she clutched modestly at her torn gown and shrank away.

It was at that moment that Trey realized he still had a heart— and it went out to Jennifer. She'd had more than her legs knocked out from under her. Her beliefs and ideals had been shattered, and Trey wasn't sure how to go about restoring them.

Ever so slowly, Trey reached out to assist her to her feet. "English—"

"Don't touch me." Jennifer recoiled as tears rolled down her cheeks. "Please . . . don't touch me. I don't think I can bear it now. Maybe never again." Her tormented voice cracked like eggshells.

"We're getting out of here, English," Trey murmured. "All I'm trying to do is help you to your feet."

"I cannot go outside!" Jennifer wailed. "My gown is in shreds."

"I'll have Jawbone fetch one of my shirts."

"I don't want Jawbone and Sunset to see me like this," she said on a sob. "I cannot even bear the thought of you knowing what those bastards did. Just go away, please . . ."

"It doesn't matter," he assured calmly. "All that matters is that you're safe. No one sits in judgment when you go through hell. Survival is the best anyone can hope for."

Trey wasn't sure if it was the soothing tone of his voice or his words that finally sliced through Jennifer's tormented thoughts. Whatever the case, she suddenly flung herself at him. Her tears fell like raindrops on his shoulder when she buried her head against his neck and hung on to him as if he were her salvation.

He could feel the soft flesh of her breasts pressed to his chest, and he squeezed his eyes shut, forcing himself not to touch her. He wanted to hold her close, but he was afraid he would remind her of her ordeal with the Yates Gang. And so he simply slid his arm around her waist as she bled tears for endless minutes.

Damn, for a man who had disciplined himself against all emotion, Trey was having trouble coping. Jennifer's tears cut through him like knives.

Even the wolves seemed to be at a loss. They whined and sank down beside her, their ears twitching in response to her muffled sobs.

"I-I'm . . . s-sorry," she managed to get out between gulps. "I know t-tears aren't up your s-street."

"It's all right, English," he whispered against her bruised cheek. "I understand."

"No, you don't!" she burst out suddenly, hysterically. "You cannot possibly!"

"Don't I?" Trey combed his fingers through the tangled blond tresses in a soothing gesture. "I've been to hell dozens of times, English. I know how it feels to have your soul peeled away one layer at a time, until you aren't sure if there is anything left inside you except a deep, dark hole nothing can fill. I know what it's like to have burning hatred eat away at you. You curse anything that robs you of self-respect, but it is never enough."

Trey gathered her trembling body closer, nuzzling his chin against her forehead, rocking her comfortingly as he continued. "I know what it's like to reach that point where surviving is all you can understand, though you're not sure it's worth the effort. I also know how it feels to sink into depression after danger passes. I have been where you are plenty of times, English. That's where I *live.*"

Usually, after his dangerous forays, Trey countered his wild mood swings with sexual gratification—if only to reassure himself that he did feel something besides survival instinct. But he couldn't apply that policy now, not with Jennifer. She had suffered at the hands of merciless bastards. The Yates Gang had left this innocent woman with distorted impressions of intimacy, he suspected. They had destroyed her romantic fantasies in the course of one day.

What should have been sweet and tender to Jennifer was now considered dirty, repulsive. Her vibrant spirit and optimism had been crushed, right along with her starry-eyed dreams.

The sound of thundering hooves jostled Trey from his musings. "I'll get something for you to wear. Stay here with the wolves, English."

As much as Trey wanted to drop his gaze to determine how bruised and battered Jennifer actually was, he didn't dare. She was too self-conscious to be subjected to scrutiny right now.

Gently, Trey set her aside and stood up, staring at the air

over her head. A quiet order to the wolves brought them to her feet while she fumbled to cover her torn bodice with her grimy skirt.

Trey strode outside to see Jawbone and Sunset staring at him apprehensively. He answered their question before they gathered the nerve to ask it. "English is all right, or at least as good as can be expected."

When Jawbone dismounted and hurried forward, Trey snagged his arm. "Don't go in, not yet."

"Why not?" Jawbone asked. "Did they—?"

"I'm not sure what they did besides rough her up, but she isn't prepared to have you see her like this." Trey stared grimly at the concerned cowboys. "If you want to help her recover her pride and self-esteem, you'll back away until she has time to cope with what happened."

Trey retrieved a clean shirt from his saddlebag and then glanced at the cowboys. "Take the outlaws back to Sheriff Hartman and collect the bounty money. The cash will more than cover the losses of the robbery. Then take the wagonload of supplies back to Texas—I'll bring English home when she feels up to traveling."

"You can't come to Texas," Sunset protested. "Jonas and Quincy will be all over you like ticks on cattle."

"English needs time to heal," Trey insisted. "If you want what's best for her, you'll do as I ask."

"Well, of course we want what's best, but it don't seem right to abandon her like this," Jawbone said.

"Your pity could do more harm than good. You're too close to her to be objective."

Jawbone stared at Trey for a long, ponderous moment. "At first, I balked at the idea of Miss Jenny keeping company with you. But I reckon you understand what she's been through better than anyone. All we ask is the chance to say good-bye before we go."

"No," Trey said firmly. "Not even that. English is stumbling on the edge. Knowing that you know what she has suffered is difficult enough for her. I'll tell her that you wish her well."

Sunset heaved an audible sigh. "All right, but it don't seem proper to just trot off like we don't care."

"If you can give Miss Jenny back her spirit, then we'll be grateful," Jawbone murmured as he mounted up.

After Trey returned to the dugout, Sunset stared pensively at Jawbone. "Did you notice anything different about Three Wolves?"

"Do you mean while he was setting his trap for those scoundrels?" Jawbone asked as they rode off to retrieve what was left of Willie Yates.

"Yeah." Sunset glanced uneasily at his friend. "But I'm not sure I can explain what I saw happening."

"Me neither. I'm not even sure I wanna try. All I can say is I don't think the legends about Three Wolves are the figment of anybody's imagination. There's something spooky about the changes that come over him."

Sunset decided *spooky* was the precise word to describe the transformation. Whatever the hell Three Wolves was, he was damned sure no average man. This unsettling encounter with the Yates Gang sure proved that.

Six

Trey descended the steps to the dugout—and stopped dead in his tracks. Jennifer had propped herself against the wall, as far from Russ's lifeless body as she could get. Torn, stained petticoats formed a pool around her updrawn legs. She clutched her satin skirt to her chest to restore the vestiges of modesty.

The expression in her eyes held Trey immobilized. Jennifer looked like a very old soul who had aged decades in the course of one day. There was no smile on her puffy lips, only bleak acceptance. Recovering from her ordeal was going to take time and dedication on his part, Trey realized.

The traumatic experience had made her cynical and wary. To combat the side effects of Jennifer's encounter with the outlaws, Trey needed to be cheerful. He was going to have to rely on his sense of humor, too. It would be a dry sense of humor, he suspected, since he hadn't watered it for the past decade.

Trey wasn't all that certain he could exchange roles with Jennifer. Cheery optimism had never been his forte. But he was the reason Jennifer had been kidnapped by the Yates Gang. He was responsible for her plight and he was obliged to teach her to *feel* again. In order to do that, he was going to have to *feel,* too.

On second thought, Trey mused, maybe he should have handed Jennifer over to Jawbone and Sunset. Perhaps he wasn't the right man to restore her belief in the goodness of humanity. Trey definitely understood what Jennifer had endured, having been to hell so often himself, but he wasn't so sure he could restore that enchanting smile that had been so much a part of her. All he knew was that he had to try, wanted to try.

"Here, English. My shirt will be a few sizes too big, but it's clean," Trey said, offering the garment to her. "I'll be back to fetch you in a few minutes. I'm sending Jawbone and Sunset to Dodge to gather your ranch supplies before driving south. They told me to tell you not to worry about a thing. They'll handle business at the ranch until you return."

After Trey scooped up his fallen enemy and hauled him away, Jennifer fastened herself into the oversize shirt. The soft fabric soothed her bruised flesh, and she absently brushed her hand over the black garment she had come to associate with Trey MacTavish. It was oddly comforting to be wearing his shirt, to inhale its fresh, clean scent.

"English?"

Jennifer glanced up to see Trey dressed only in his loincloth, surrounded by the shadows of descending darkness. The image of this brawny giant reminded Jennifer of the previous night and this afternoon, when he had materialized from a cloud of smoke to rescue her from those filthy bastards who—

A shudder rippled through her as Jennifer struggled to stop her anguish. She was not going to think about Russ Trent and his merciless cousins. She would not let those despicable demons destroy her sanity! Although she would never be the same again, she did not have to deal with those horrible men because Trey had sent them to hell where they belonged.

Jennifer hadn't asked about Willie and Bob, because she didn't care to know how they had ended up—only that they were out of her life. She didn't care about much of anything at all. All that mattered was that Trey was here to protect her, that he had survived.

As Trey approached her, Jennifer glanced up, glassy-eyed, to see him stretch out his hand, waiting for her to grasp it. She wasn't sure she could. She was too tainted and filthy to touch anyone.

Once upon a time, Jennifer had wished she could give her innocence to this magnificent man, to restore his faith in humanity, to make him whole again. Now she was of no use to him. She had been pawed by hurtful hands and her illusions had been shattered. What Trey needed and deserved, Jennifer no longer possessed. It haunted her that his touch would not be the first, that he had seen another man's hands on her.

Jennifer wasn't even sure she could accept the touch of the only man she had ever desired. The prospect of intimacy was no longer welcome.

"Would you like to bathe in the stream?" Trey questioned while Jennifer stared at his hand.

"Why? I will never truly be clean again," she said dully.

Smiling faintly, Trey squatted down in front of her. "The water isn't all that dirty, English. I already checked. I also have soap in my saddlebag. Good stuff, soap. I use it every chance I get."

"That is not what I meant."

Trey tried another teasing smile—for all the good it did him. "You prefer to stay down here with the rats?"

"No."

"But you don't want to bathe."

"No."

"Then will you come with me while I bathe? I don't want you to stay here alone."

"I will not be alone. I have the wolves."

Trey called upon his patience, and all the tenderness he possessed. "Please, English. I really need to have you with me right now."

She stared at him curiously. "Why?"

"Because when I come down from highs and sink low, I

don't like to be alone. All I want is for you to be nearby while I'm bathing. Will you come with me?''

She accepted his explanation, understanding exactly what he meant about emotional highs and lows. Jennifer stretched out her hand, allowing Trey to assist her to her feet.

He led her outside, and she went with him trustingly. When Trey swung onto Diablo's back, then leaned down to grasp Jennifer's forearm to boost her up behind him, she recoiled. Trey cursed himself for his abruptness. He knew that sudden moves would put her on the defensive, triggering painful memories.

"I'm not going to hurt you, English," he murmured, meeting her anguished gaze. "If there is still one thing you believe in, I want it to be that."

Again, he stretched out his hand to her. After a moment, she clasped her fingers around his forearm, allowing him to hoist her up. When Diablo trotted off, Jennifer braced herself on the cantle of the saddle without touching him.

Damn those bastards, Trey raged silently. They had taken purity and innocence and ravaged it. If he did nothing else, he would teach Jennifer to trust his touch, assure her that he would never paw at her as Russ Trent had.

When Diablo halted beside the stream, Jennifer slid to the ground and moved away quickly. Trey sighed, wondering what to do in this frustrating situation. He would have to deliberately seduce Jennifer, because the longer she allowed herself to believe passion was painful and distasteful, that she was damaged merchandise, the more difficult it would be for her to regain her self-respect. Trey ought to know. He had so much blood on his hands that he had begun to believe the rumors that linked him with demons. But as he recalled, Jennifer was the one who proclaimed that he had many admirable qualities and that the gossip was rubbish.

Now, Trey would have to return the favor by reinstating her self-esteem.

Never having set out to seduce a woman, Trey was in unfamiliar territory. He wondered how good he would be at it. He decided he had better become an expert in a hurry.

"Would you fetch the soap from my saddlebag, English?" he requested with premeditated nonchalance.

Mechanically, Jennifer did as he asked. When she turned away from Diablo, soap in hand, Trey was gone. She heard the splashes, realizing he had already taken to the water, along with the wolves. Jennifer strode down the creek bank to hand him the bar of soap. When Trey waded ashore, Jennifer gasped in embarrassment. The water level receded to his knees, and her gaze dipped below his waist. Her face flushed profusely as she stared at Trey's virile physique.

"Thanks, English," he said as he plucked the soap from her hand, then re-entered the creek.

"Bloody hell," Jennifer grumbled when she finally found her tongue. "Why did you do that?"

"Because I wanted the soap and you said you didn't want to come into the water," he said reasonably. Trey lathered his chest and Jennifer's gaze helplessly followed the sweeping motion of his hand. "A man can't scrub himself clean without soap, now can he?"

"Devil take it," Jennifer muttered as she jerked off her skirt and petticoats. "I do want to be clean again."

"Wanna borrow my soap—?" Trey nearly swallowed his tongue when his gaze landed on the silky legs beneath the hem of his black shirt. Damn, how he ached to hold Jennifer, console her, caress her, but he had to proceed cautiously. One false move and she would lose the small bit of trust she had regained.

Once again, Trey asked himself if he was the right man for the delicate task of repairing Jennifer's pride and spirit. When he stared at the beguiling vision enshrouded in moonlight, his mind and body seemed to be at cross-purposes.

Trey called upon the mental powers Black Wolf had taught him. Trey had disciplined his mind and body on dozens of occasions, but this was definitely his greatest test. He would have to behave like a perfect gentleman.

Now *there* was a real challenge, especially when he stared

at Jennifer. Damn, and here he'd been sure hell had nothing new to teach him.

"Kindly turn your back," Jennifer requested as she unbuttoned the shirt.

Reluctantly, Trey did as he was told until a splash assured him it was safe to turn around. When he did, a jolt pulsed through the lower regions of his anatomy. Hell, there wasn't enough water in the stream to cool the slow, burning fire that inflamed him as he watched Jennifer sidestroke across the creek, spotlighted by swirls of glittering silver.

Her unbound hair drifted around her like a golden cloud. Bare arms and shoulders gave way to enticing glimpses of creamy breasts as she swam circles around him. With each revolution she came slightly closer, and Trey had the wildest urge to grab her, to pull her luscious body against his and devour those sweet lips. But that was exactly what Jennifer didn't need, even if he did—desperately! And so, he curbed his needs and scrubbed himself so vigorously that he nearly washed off his skin.

Water swirled around Trey as Jennifer came to her feet behind him. Only her head and shoulders were visible above the water's surface. Trey glanced back to survey the purple bruise on her cheek, and cursed under his breath. She hadn't deserved the cruelty she had received from the Yates Gang. Damn them! She had been bait for the trap set for Trey. Every time he reminded himself that he was responsible for her pain and anguish the thought turned him wrong side out.

"Give me your hand, English," Trey requested huskily.

Jennifer held up her palm, expecting him to hand her the bar of soap. When he pivoted to draw her hand to his chest, she tried to pull away, but he refused to release her.

"Do you mind touching me so much?" He drew her fingertips across the breadth of his broad chest in a skimming caress. "After returning from hell, I also need reassurance that goodness and tenderness really do exist. You once assured me that they did, remember?"

"I remember," Jennifer murmured. But those days of hope and optimism seemed a lifetime away now.

"And you don't mind touching me?"

"No."

Jennifer stared at the sleek expanse of his shoulders, marveling at the warmth that replaced the cold, empty sensations in the core of her being. At least she could touch Trey without feeling ashamed. She doubted she would find the encounter enjoyable if it was the other way around.

"Mmm . . ." Trey whispered. "I'm feeling better already." He grasped her hand as it swept from one male nipple to the other, then drew her fingertips to his lips. "A touch of heaven. That's what you are. I need this."

"I wish I were your touch of heaven. Once perhaps, but no longer."

Her lifeless tone broke his heart. "You still are," he said with perfect assurance.

When she shook her head, Trey replaced her hand on his chest, then slowly reached out to curl his index finger beneath her bruised jaw, lifting her downcast gaze. "You will always be my touch with paradise, English. To me, you are all that is pure and sweet in this world. Nothing will ever change that."

"Everything has changed." Her voice wobbled as tears misted her eyes. "I wanted to come to you untouched, untainted. If things were different, and if not for the difficulties on our ranch—" Her words trailed off into a sob.

"Sh . . . sh." The pad of his finger grazed her quivering lips. "Don't torment yourself tonight. Forget the past, the future. There is only right now, right here, the two of us together. We can heal each other, English."

Perhaps he was rushing her, but Trey wanted her lush mouth beneath his, wanted to counter the abuse she'd endured with a kiss of tender reassurance. He needed it as much as Jennifer did, even if she hadn't realized it yet. He had to make her relax, but she was still trying to hold her emotions in check.

Gently, Trey drew Jennifer to him. Reflex prompted her to

back away, but he was so careful with her that she allowed him to guide her body against his.

And suddenly, the walls came tumbling down. Jennifer felt Trey's raw, masculine power engulfing her—without exerting the slightest force. He cradled her to him while he kissed her— soft, playful nibbles at first, then slow, languishing caresses.

"Touch me, English," Trey rasped between feathery kisses.

"Where?"

"Here . . ." His hand folded over hers, bringing her fingertips against the hard curve of his hip. "And here, if you dare." He shifted her hand to the corrugated muscles of his belly . . . and then lower . . .

Jennifer forgot to breathe when she felt his aroused flesh against her hand. She hadn't expected to feel the warm pulse of his desire, when she had done nothing to invite it, hadn't a clue how to respond.

Trey chuckled at her startled expression. "Ah, English, you are still the naive little innocent I met in Dodge. It still amazes me that you're so oblivious to the effect you have on me. You're incredibly lovely and desirable. Don't you ever look at yourself in a mirror?" he teased playfully.

Wide, violet eyes peered at him, searching his face. "Even now? Even after—?"

"Always," Trey assured her as he moved against her hand, aching to feel her intimate caress. "You could bring me to my knees with your touch if you wanted to. You have that kind of power over me."

Jennifer quirked her brow, unsure what he meant.

Trey grinned wryly. "Most men like to be stroked and caressed, English. Did you think I was different, just because I've been called the hound from hell?"

Jennifer moved her hand experimentally and heard Trey's breath catch. She felt his body clench as he brushed against her, felt the pulsing need of his passion in the palm of her hand. Would she feel that same need if he touched her?

Jennifer discarded the thought. She already knew the answer. Her ordeal had taught her that a man's touch triggered revulsion and pain. She could never enjoy the same things Trey did, and she wondered how her mother had deceived her father into believing she found pleasure in his touch.

Jennifer supposed Eleanor Templeton had loved her husband so dearly that she tolerated Ramsey physically, just to satisfy him. Eleanor's unconditional love made concessions to a man's basest desires, but Jennifer didn't think she could be that generous—knowing what she knew now.

"May I touch you in return, English?" Trey questioned, fighting like the very devil to control the need churning inside him.

"I don't think I will like it. Not the way you seem to."

Trey moved her hand back to his chest, not because he wasn't savoring her caresses, but because the sensations had altered his breathing to such extremes that he was afraid to trust himself. He couldn't remain calm and rational for Jennifer's sake while he was burning up inside. Tonight belonged to this disillusioned beauty who needed and deserved to be loved with all the patient tenderness he could provide. His pleasure would come in her small discoveries, in her realization that passion didn't have to be distasteful.

Again, he cursed the vile men who had shattered Jennifer's ideals, and he wondered if they had raped her. But he couldn't bring himself to ask her—not yet.

"Are you absolutely sure you wouldn't like my touch, English?"

When she winced, Trey felt her fingers dig into his chest unintentionally. He could see her playing the ordeal over in her mind, and he hated those memories that tormented her.

"Don't you know I would never hurt you?" he asked softly.

"You did once," she reminded him.

Yes, and Trey could have kicked himself to Dodge and back for it. "At the time, I was trying to warn you away, because you're too good for me. I was trying to make a point, not make love. There's a vast difference between lovemaking and forcefulness."

"Is there?" She searched his face, smiling sadly. "It doesn't

really matter now, because I am not good enough. I am unde-
serving of a man like you after those beasts—''

He brushed his thumb over her lips to shush her and stared
into those haunted amethyst eyes that glistened with unshed
tears. "Do you trust me with your life, English?"

"You know I do. The only reason I am alive now is because
of you."

And now the burning question, thought Trey. "Would you
trust me with your body, if it was good for your soul?"

Jennifer tilted her face up to study his shadowy features. She
sensed that same indefinable something that separated him from
other men, felt the vivid physical attraction that even her ordeal
with the Yates Gang could not completely diminish. The magic
was still there, she realized, beneath the bitter memories.

When Jennifer had been a foolish romantic, she had believed
she had fallen in love with Trey at first sight—or at the very
least, it was hero worship. Trey had scoffed at her silly fantasies,
and then Russ Trent and the Yates brothers had destroyed her
self-confidence and shattered her dreams. Yet, Jennifer still
believed the touch of this one very special man could make
the difference—if only she dared to find out for certain. But
it would break her heart to discover she was wrong.

"I trust you, no one but you," she murmured.

Her words went through him with enough force to make him
groan. Never in his whole rotten life had anyone placed absolute
faith in him. Never had anyone looked for anything positive
in him. This lovely woman was incredibly good for his soul.

"Come with me, Jennifer," he whispered as he turned toward
shore. To his relief, she followed trustingly, but she didn't
emerge from the water when he led the way.

"Where are we going, Trey?"

"Ashore," was all he said.

Trey rolled out his pallet on the grass and Jennifer halted in
her tracks. Moonlight spotlighted Trey's nude body, glistening
with diamond droplets. Despite her newly discovered cynicism,
Jennifer still found herself admiring the fascinating sight. Muscles rippled with each lithe, fluid motion. His sleek body was

a monument to physical perfection. Seeing Trey in all his masculine splendor made Jennifer itch to touch him, to explore every sinewy inch of him, until she knew every muscular curve, column, and plane.

"Aren't you coming out of the water?" Trey asked.

"Aren't you going to turn your back?"

He grinned wryly. "I'd rather not. I might miss something."

Shades of embarrassment tainted Jennifer's cheeks. Joining Trey in the water had been one thing. Walking ashore bone naked was something entirely different.

"Does it offend you that I'm eager to feast my eyes on you?" he questioned.

"No."

Well, that was a start, he thought. Of course, at this rate, Jennifer would be shriveled up worse than a raisin by the time she gathered the nerve to come out of the water. By then, Trey would have been reduced to a pile of ashes.

"Come here, Jennifer. I didn't save your life so I could hurt you. Nothing will happen on this pallet that you don't want to happen. Do you understand?"

Jennifer stared into his eyes and stepped into the shallows. Trey felt one jolt after another as she approached. The water receded, inch by inch, revealing soft, dewy flesh and supple curves. It was like watching a forbidden fantasy.

God, she was perfection, and he was burning alive, just staring at her. Her pale golden hair clung to her shoulders and curled around her nipples in such an enticing manner that Trey had to swallow his groan. Only a few women possessed exquisite figures, delicate features, and mesmerizing eyes. This English aristocrat had it all. She was every male's fantasy.

"You're the loveliest creature I've ever seen," Trey breathed in awe.

Jennifer avoided his direct stare. "I don't feel pretty. I still feel . . . soiled."

And unworthy, Trey predicted. Those bastards deserved to burn in hell for an eternity. How was Trey to restore her beliefs, when he had been the first to scorn them?

Trey clasped Jennifer's hand, drawing her down to the pallet beside him. Although his body throbbed with desire, he restricted himself to light, feathery kisses—ever mindful of the swollen side of her mouth. He didn't touch her as he longed to do. Instead, he clenched his hands in the bedroll. He could not—would not—frighten Jennifer or betray her trust. It would probably kill him, but he wanted to restore her belief in him more than he wanted life itself.

"Tell me about this love you claim your parents shared," he murmured as his lips skimmed her cheek.

"I have had to rethink my previous beliefs," she admitted.

"How so?"

"I think my mother must have been an exceptionally good sport when it came to certain matters."

"You think she tolerated intimacy just to please your father," he guessed correctly.

Jennifer nodded, and silver-blond tendrils tumbled over her shoulder onto Trey's chest. Impulsively, he lifted the damp strands, letting them glide through his fingers.

"I think you're wrong, English."

"How would you know? You don't even believe in love, and I'm no longer certain it exists, either."

"All I need is your faith, trust, and a little cooperation so we can find out if it does."

My, wasn't he the cheerful optimist? Trey thought to himself. Well, somebody around here had to be. Since he and Jennifer had exchanged roles, he was making a conscious effort to counter her bitterness. He wished that restoring her positive outlook was as easy as the fairy tale princess who turned a prince into a frog with one kiss . . . or was it the other way around? He hadn't paid much attention to those idiotic stories while he was at Carlisle Indian School.

Reform school, he amended resentfully. Not that he had reformed or conformed to white society. He had only tolerated and endured until government agents allowed him to return to the reservation. And with his white heritage, and his supposed indoctrination of the white man's ways, he was allowed to venture off on his own without restrictions.

"You are wasting your time with me," Jennifer said, jostling Trey from his unhappy recollections. "I'm afraid I do not believe in a ruddy thing after—" Her voice faltered and her breath hitched.

When she backed away, refusing to meet his gaze, Trey trailed his finger over her tense expression. His hand drifted down her shoulder to circle the thrusting peak of her breast. Jennifer's first reaction was to shy away, expecting to be hurt, but Trey skimmed her bruised flesh like a butterfly hovering over a flower petal.

When his fingertips feathered over her beaded nipple, Jennifer shivered. Eventually, she would discover the difference between his tender touch and degrading gropes, Trey promised himself. Tonight Jennifer would re-learn the meaning of gentleness. If nothing else, he would teach her that not all men mistreated women.

True, a man more deserving should be Jennifer's mentor, but Trey was the only man available, the one man who understood how deeply she had been hurt—physically and emotionally.

"Do you find my touch distasteful, Jennifer?" he asked in a strained whisper.

To Jennifer's surprise, she didn't. She had expected to be repulsed, but that was not the sensation coiling inside her. Instead, she experienced the same heated response that assailed her when Trey had kissed her beside the campfire the previous night. She had presumed the thick layers of clothing were responsible for those hot flashes. Her naiveté made her giggle.

His hand stalled. "Am I tickling you?"

Jennifer glanced at him accusingly. "You should have told me why I felt so hot while we were nestled by your campfire last night."

Trey grinned, relieved that they were making headway. "I was amused by your innocence, the same innocence you still

possess. Still game, English? I told you I wouldn't hurt you
and I don't intend to.''

Jennifer suddenly felt very game. Trey's magical touch
melted away her haunting nightmare. His gentle caress was
nothing like Russ Trent's cruel gropes. She trusted Trey with
her life, and now with her body. He wouldn't hurt her, she
assured herself. He may have been hell on outlaws, but he was
her salvation, the answer to her prayers.

Jennifer stared into those entrancing silver eyes and drowned
in their fathomless depths. ''I do want to believe in something
again. I want to believe in you.''

Her sincerity filled Trey with an unprecedented sense of
pride and accomplishment. Jennifer was staring at him with
the same unfaltering trust he had noticed last night. At least
they were back to where they started when they met. The only
difference was that Trey wasn't such a cynic and Jennifer
wasn't such a hopeless romantic.

He suspected she still saw him as her gallant knight, but he
didn't mind quite so much now. In fact, he was flattered. No
one on this earth held him in the same high regard. To repay
her for her faith in him, he was going to restore *her* faith, he
vowed.

When Trey traced figure eights around the curve of her
breast, Jennifer's breathing altered and her skin tingled with
unexpected pleasure. She was stunned by the heat waves rippling through her as hands as gentle as the evening breeze
whispered over her skin. Heightened awareness of this intriguing paradox of a man, who could be the epitome of tenderness
and strength, cascaded over her. His lips grazed her cheeks,
her eyelids, and Jennifer sighed audibly. Trey was instilling
inexpressible longings inside her. His patience and gentleness
melted her inhibitions one at a time, leaving her receptive
to each wondrous sensation. She responded eagerly to Trey,
wanting more.

When his lips skied over her collarbone and his tongue flicked
at the aching tip of her breast, Jennifer felt her body arch to
greet him. Trey had taught her not to fear him, and an ever-

growing sense of trust and the burgeoning desire to explore this mystical realm of pleasurable sensations consumed her. His caresses were so light and unhurried that Jennifer trembled, burned, and ached in the most fascinating ways imaginable.

His lips returned to hers, teasing, appeasing, luring her deeper into his spell. Her mouth opened as their tongues mated, their breath merged, and the world spun away for a timeless instant.

When his hand swirled over her nipples, hot, aching desire overwhelmed her. Jennifer suddenly needed to touch Trey again, to return the burning pleasure that uncoiled inside her. But Trey clasped her hand and took it with him as he explored the indentation of her waist, the slope of her hip.

"Feel how good you feel to me," he murmured against her quivering flesh. "You're like silk and satin. You're the opposite of everything I am."

"*You* are like velvet," she said on a ragged breath.

He smiled roguishly, his eyes twinkling down at her. "Oh? Where's that, English?"

"There." Her free hand glided over the hard yet velvety length of him, then lingered.

"Only there," he murmured huskily. "To match the softest, most sensitive part of you. When a man and woman unite as one, they fit perfectly, meeting and greeting each other as gently as daylight blending into night."

She smiled at his eloquence. "Is that Comanche philosophy, Three Wolves?"

"Yes, English, and there's more."

"What might that be?"

"Patience, English," he whispered as he drew the quilt over her. "You need to rest now."

"But—"

He dropped a kiss to her lips, then turned away to grab his breechclout. "Rest," he insisted.

"Where are you going?"

"Not far, English. I'll be nearby if you need me."

Need him? She needed him now! Jennifer thought as she battled the erotic sensations still spiraling through her body.

She definitely needed something, though for the life of her she wasn't certain exactly what it was or how to acquire it. Trey's languid kisses and caresses had left her entire body pulsating, hungering for more of those splendid sensations.

Jennifer wanted to protest the abrupt end of Trey's intimate ministrations, but she couldn't find the energy to move or speak. As the sensations gradually ebbed, she became aware of how exhausted she really was. Even though her body longed for more of Trey's touch, she found herself sinking into a state of oblivion, savoring the memory of each pleasurable sensation.

Trey got to his feet and went into the darkness. He walked in circles, fighting the urge to double over and howl in frustration. He was discovering the meaning of self-torture while he tried to mend Jennifer's broken spirit without greedily indulging his own lust. Touching her intimately and feeling her response had aroused him to the extreme, but he refused to rush her and didn't trust himself to lie beside her another minute.

In exchange for his gentleness, Trey had been granted a foretaste of heaven. He had wanted Jennifer to know she was safe with him, that he would never take more than she was prepared to offer, but damn! He was going to need another cold bath before he lay down to sleep beside Jennifer.

Trey had made a silent pact with himself that he would take Jennifer back to Texas—well-healed, her spirits restored. He was doing it out of the goodness of his heart, because Jennifer was the only person alive who saw goodness in him and made him feel worthy and needed.

This aristocratic beauty filled the emptiness inside him with tender emotion. Despite the rumors and legends swirling around him, Jennifer tamed the wild, violent instincts that had kept him alive the last ten years. And when the time came to let her go her own way, Trey was certain he'd never be able to look at another woman without seeing Jennifer. Forgetting her would be impossible.

In fact, he suspected it would take dying to get it done.

Several minutes later, Trey returned to the pallet. Jennifer had drifted off to sleep, emotionally and physically spent. Trey smiled appreciatively as he stared down at her. Pale blond hair tumbled around her battered features like a cloud of sunbeams and moonlight. She was angel-like, he decided. Definitely the most beguiling woman he'd ever encountered.

Trey hoped his attempt to dissolve her fears and rejuvenate her spirit would succeed. Remembering the empty shell of a woman he had encountered in the dugout made his heart ache. He wanted Jennifer to be her old self again. He wanted her to know that he would never hurt her, would always protect her.

Once Trey had delivered Jennifer home, resolved her problems at the ranch, and settled an old score with Jonas Rafferty, he was going to track down Bob Yates. And next time, there would be no quick, merciful end for the surviving member of the Yates Gang. Bob would be dragging more than a bum leg along with him when he descended into the deepest reaches of hell!

Jennifer awakened to the feel of sunshine beaming down on her, heard the sound of panting wolves beside her. Reflexively, she reached up to pat the nearest head, surprised when the hairy creature nuzzled against her shoulder like a puppy. She pried open her eyes to see the other wolf crawling on its belly toward her, as if humbly requesting the same affection. Jennifer chortled at the gentle nature of the wolves . . .

The thought brought Trey instantly to mind, and Jennifer smiled, remembering. The previous night Trey had displayed his dry sense of humor, a touch of playfulness, and infinite tenderness. She had sworn she could never tolerate a man's touch after her ordeal, but Trey had shown her the difference between abuse and gentle seduction. The scintillating sensations he aroused made her want to give herself to him, even if pain was involved in the ultimate act of passion. With Trey, she sensed it would be worth it.

Jennifer smiled ruefully, wishing she were allowed to spend

her life with Trey, teaching him to love her. But she could not risk having him come to Texas for fear of retaliation from Quincy or Jonas. Trey's absence was all that would spare him. She couldn't bear to have his death on her conscience. She cared, and respected him, too much to endanger him. She had to deal with Quincy and Jonas by herself.

Jennifer made a mental note to keep a cautious eye on her brother Christopher—just in case Quincy or Jonas decided to use him as leverage against her. She wouldn't allow her brother out of her sight when she reached the ranch. Though he would probably grouse about her overprotectiveness, it was for his own safety.

Frowning curiously, Jennifer scanned the line of trees, wondering what had become of Trey. His stallion was nowhere to be seen. The wolves had obviously been ordered to stand guard over her.

Blast it, surely Trey hadn't gone hunting for Bob Yates! He had regretfully informed her last night that the scoundrel was still alive. Jennifer hoped she never had to see that brutal heathen again. Her mouth was still tender from Bob's vicious blows. The very thought of that man sent a shiver of icy dread through her. He was the worst of the lot. There was something dark and sinister about him, and Jennifer wished she hadn't prevented Trey from doing his worst that first night when Bob grabbed hold of her and put a gun to her head . . .

"Ready for breakfast, English?"

Clutching the quilt to her breasts, Jennifer twisted around to see Trey, dressed in a loincloth and moccasins, ambling up the slope. Her gaze roamed over him appreciatively. Last night, he had made her ache with newly discovered desire. He had touched her so gently, then bade her to sleep, leaving her oddly unfulfilled. Trey had left her wishing she knew how to pleasure him the way he had pleasured her.

"Hungry, English?" he repeated.

"Depends on what you're serving," she said lightly.

His dark brow quirked as he sank down cross-legged on the pallet. "Feeling better this morning, I take it."

''Much better.'' She peeked shyly at him through her lashes.
''Thank you.''

''For what?''

''For teaching me the difference.''

''That wasn't the only reason I wanted to touch you,
English,'' he assured her, his voice dropping to a husky pitch,
his eyes glowing down on her.

''No?'' Her gaze flitted over the sleek, bronzed expanse of
his chest. Ah, how she itched to explore him, to memorize the
feel of his powerful body beneath her fingertips, to know where
those tingling sensations he had ignited could lead.

''No, it wasn't,'' he said between bites of roasted rabbit.

''I'm glad,'' Jennifer confided. ''I couldn't bear knowing
last night was just your way of showing compassion.''

''English, last night had not a blistering thing to do with
pity,'' he said, mimicking her English brogue. ''You know I
don't have much of that, considering the kind of men I deal
with on a regular basis.''

He plucked up a piece of juicy meat and offered it to her.
''We're a day's ride from Dodge, but there's a place I would
like to show you before we head back to town to see the Justice
of the Peace.''

''You're still planning to marry me?'' she asked, staring
directly at him.

''Nothing has changed. I thought I'd made that clear yesterday.''

''Actually, no. You never came right out and told me so. I
was left to presume you would be back.''

''I announced my intentions to your friend Quincy Ward.''

''He isn't the one you're supposed to marry,'' she said,
grinning.

''True.'' He stared pensively at Jennifer. ''Are you sure you
want to get stuck with a husband with my kind of reputation?''

Truth was, she wished she could have this man for all times.
But if she became Trey's downfall, it would be worse than the
torment she had endured at the hands of the Yates Gang.

"I would be proud and honored to call you *husband*," she affirmed.

"Then it's settled." He offered her another bite of meat. "Why don't you take a swim while I gather the supplies and feed the wolves."

Jennifer nodded agreeably. She was sore and achy and would welcome another bath. Again, she would cleanse herself and try to forget her unpleasant ordeal. She would dwell on Trey's tenderness and the security she felt in his presence.

And blister it, if one citizen in Dodge dared to utter a snide remark about her marrying the legendary bounty hunter, she would give the fool a piece of her mind. Trey MacTavish was everything a woman could possibly want—and more. And if what she felt for him wasn't love, it was pretty close to it.

Trey MacTavish was a most remarkable man, she mused as she waded into the stream. And in the years to come . . . Jennifer winced when she realized there would be other women in his arms in those years. She would be his wife, but she had yet to be his lover—and might never have the chance. When the ceremony was concluded, she would be heading for Texas. Last night might well be as close to a wedding night with Trey as she would ever get. Too bad she hadn't considered that before she fell asleep in exhaustion.

Seven

"Good gad!" Agatha Reynolds snorted in disbelief when she spied the rickety Concord coach that was to transport her cross-country to Mobeetie, Texas.

The dusty vehicle, with its paint chipped from bullets and arrows, looked like something an English peasant might employ—certainly not a dignified duchess!

"Is this the best to be had in this god-awful country, Simpson?"

Simpson opened the door to reveal the cracked leather seats with their protruding metal springs. "I fear so, Your Grace. I let the manager of the stage line know straightaway that his vehicles were badly in need of repair."

"And?" Agatha prodded, peering at him through her wire-rimmed spectacles.

"His reply was a mite vulgar, Your Grace. You do not want to know what I was told to do with this coach. The bumpkin seemed highly offended that I dared to complain."

"His behavior appears to be typical of the commoners we have encountered during our journey. Backward country, is it not, Simpson?'' She lifted her hand, waiting for Simpson to assist her inside.

"Indeed it is, Your Grace," he agreed as he sank down beside the exposed seat spring. "The sooner we collect your grandchildren and return to England the better off we will all be."

Agatha had just situated herself on the seat when the coach lurched forward, slamming her head against the wall. "Bloody hell! Who is driving this broken-down heap? The village drunk?"

"Another bloody bumpkin," Simpson said, bracing himself. "Hold on, Your Grace. This is going to be a long, rough ride, I am told. I ordered a lunch prepared at the restaurant." He gestured toward the basket beside him. "The stage stations are reported to be no more than farm cottages and crude rest stops. Bacon and beans are served three times a day."

Agatha made an awful face. "Hell's teeth, how long did you say this jaunt will take?"

"Three days," he reported grimly. "It is more than two hundred miles from Dodge to Mobeetie. We will be traveling night and day, with stops for fresh horses and foul food."

Agatha groaned in dismay. "Oh, bother, can't these commoners do anything right in the States?"

"Apparently not, but what can one expect from a country populated with European rejects?"

In Agatha's opinion, Simpson had said a mouthful. She was not impressed with America. Foreign gentry were not accorded the respect they deserved. And certainly, traveling conditions were not up to snuff. Agatha could not wait to return to her sprawling estate, and her London townhouse, where proper social order prevailed. She would reinstate her grandchildren into Polite Society and bestow the titles she had withheld when her daughter Eleanor married Ramsey Templeton.

And blast it, Ramsey should have had more sense than to drag his blue-blooded children to a dusty outpost in Texas—of all places. That certainly verified the man's lack of intelligence, didn't it?

At the onset of the courtship between Ramsey and Eleanor, Agatha had insisted it was a disastrous mistake. But did Eleanor listen? No, drat it. The poor woman had claimed to be hopelessly and eternally in love with Ramsey.

Rubbish! Position and title were everything. Agatha had reminded herself of that throughout her stormy marriage to a man of equal bloodlines. True, one child was all Agatha could tolerate creating with her husband. She and Thomas were barely compatible, but they had come from royal stock which had to be preserved.

As soon as Agatha toted Jennifer back to England she would set about finding the girl a suitable mate. When the time came, Agatha would match Christopher to a young lady of true breeding. Both her grandchildren would have their rightful titles. Of course, Agatha was not ready to relinquish all her titles yet— a double duchess from both sides of her family. She still had a few good years left—if this jolting ride didn't bounce them out!

Agatha braced herself on the seat when the coach dropped into a rut. Blooming hell! If she had known how primitive the accommodations would be on this journey she might have hired a Bow Street runner to fetch her grandchildren home. But Agatha did not trust any man in Jennifer's company for weeks on end. The girl was too lovely by half—or at least she had been before her father carted her off to this backward country.

By now, poor Jennifer might have dried up like the leather seats in this coach. The girl would have to be soaked in mineral baths for six months to restore her peaches-and-cream complexion.

And poor Christopher! Agatha thought in dismay. The lad needed proper schooling. No telling what they were teaching boys over here—if anything at all.

Yes, Agatha bloody well had her work cut out for her. Jennifer and Christopher might even have lost their polished accents by now. But Agatha would restore her deprived heirs to their home in England and this unpleasant matter would be behind them.

War whoops resounded around the coach, causing Agatha to jerk upright. She glanced out the window to see bare-chested riders approaching. "Who the bloody hell is that?"

Simpson poked his head out to see five half-naked men on painted ponies gaining on the coach. "Cover your eyes, Your Grace," he squawked, appalled.

Agatha didn't cover her eyes. She gaped in stunned amazement. "Devil take it! Those must be some of Lady Godiva's long-lost relatives. Those men don't look as if they are wearing a stitch of clothes!"

"They are Indians," Simpson presumed. "I was told the government had herded the heathens onto reservations. Obviously some of the wilder bunches broke loose."

When the coach rolled to an abrupt halt, Agatha was launched into Simpson's lap. Muttering, she adjusted her bonnet and uprighted herself. She heard the dark-skinned warriors rattling in a foreign tongue before the door was jerked open. Agatha stared down her nose at the barbarians.

"I daresay, this is a private coach. Now be on your way." She shooed them off as if they were a flock of crows.

Another exchange of guttural conversation passed between the Indians before the door slammed shut. Agatha heard another whoop, a holler, and the thunder of hooves. She waited, expecting the coach to lurch forward, but it didn't.

"Simpson, go see what's holding us up," she ordered impatiently.

When Simpson returned a moment later, his face was the color of putty. "We seem to have a problem, Your Grace."

"That is all we have had thus far," she grumped. "Now what is wrong?"

"Our driver seems to have bailed out and two of your trunks have disappeared."

"What!" Agatha scrambled outside to see her unmentionables scattered on the rutted road. In the distance she saw the heathens making off with the trunks packed with her most expensive gowns. "Those scoundrels!"

"Our driver must have jumped off when trouble arose,"

Simpson muttered. "But never fear, Your Grace, I will take control of our stage."

Once the garments were repacked and tied in place, Agatha clambered into the coach. "Bloody, everlasting hell!" she muttered, scowling as she swept the dust from the sleeve of her gown.

This was definitely no place for her and her kind. God Himself did not approve of this forsaken country where thieves ran around naked. If He had approved, this country would still belong to England. Agatha had to retrieve her grandchildren and return home quickly. Every moment she delayed would make it that much more difficult to indoctrinate Jennifer and Christopher into Polite Society!

Jennifer smiled appreciatively when Trey called a halt to their journey and gestured south. Below the rolling hill lay a meandering stream shaded by a thick growth of trees. As Trey walked Diablo downhill, Jennifer noticed a knoll amid the trees. A natural mote encircled three sides of the shady clearing, and crystal-clear water gleamed in the sunlight.

A sense of serenity settled over Jennifer as Trey curled his arm around her, then gently set her on her feet. Birds serenaded her as she surveyed the peaceful surroundings. It was as if an oasis had been carved into the High Plains to grant weary travelers a taste of paradise.

"This spring is considered sacred ground to Comanches," Trey informed her as he unloaded the supplies.

Jennifer nodded mutely. It was not difficult to see why this location held great appeal for anyone who happened upon it. The wind seemed to whisper through the trees, as if Mother Nature herself was trying to communicate with mankind.

"The spring is tucked behind that clump of willows," Trey told her. "Why don't you fill the canteens and gather stones to place around our campfire while I hunt game for supper."

After Trey dropped a quick kiss to her lips and trotted away, Jennifer strode off to explore the spring, the wolves at her heels. She halted in front of the stone face of the hill, where water gurgled over a cascade of rocks, forming an inviting pool below. Smiling in pleasure, Jennifer drew the hem of her tattered gown between her legs and tied it in place with a piece of lace to form makeshift breeches. She waded into the shallows without having to worry about stumbling over her cumbersome skirt.

As she sidestepped up the staircase of stones beside the spring, the wolves frolicked in the pool, lapping up their long-awaited drink. Jennifer cupped her hands to sip the clear water, then perched on a throne of stone to peer through the tunnel formed by overhanging tree limbs.

She hadn't realized how much she needed this sojourn until Trey brought her to this isolated oasis. For three months she had battled grief, struggled to manage the vast ranch, and dodged Jonas Rafferty and Quincy Ward's aggressive pursuits. At long last she was granted the time and space to gather her thoughts and put the ordeal with the Yates Gang behind her. She sat there for the longest time, absorbing the peaceful setting, admiring the scenery, reviving her spirits.

"I see you found the spring."

Jennifer jerked upright, then blushed profusely when Trey stepped into view. "I'm sorry I got sidetracked. This is such a grand place that I got caught up."

Trey nodded in understanding as he knelt to gather an arm-load of stones. "The Comanche call it Spirit Springs."

"Because of the whispering breeze and babbling brook," Jennifer presumed as she inched down the cliff to help Trey gather rocks.

"It was once a common haunt for warriors on vision quests," Trey explained as he turned back toward the campsite. "Those who sought direction came here."

"Have you had a vision?" Jennifer asked curiously.

Trey smiled cryptically as he glanced through the tunnel of tree limbs that arched over the stream. "This is the place where I found the wolves."

Or rather, the place the wolves appeared to him after he left

the reservation in Indian Territory and heard the silent call that
compelled him westward. He had encountered the wolves years
earlier in a snow-blanketed ravine in Colorado, but Trey was
reluctant to confide those life-altering incidents to anyone
except his grandfather. It was a private thing that he could not
satisfactorily explain, especially not to Jennifer. For her, it
would be difficult to measure the unusual against the yardstick
of the familiar. It was easier for Trey to let Jennifer see what
she wanted to see in him and let it go at that.

"So this is where you found the orphaned pups," Jennifer
mused aloud.

"Not exactly." Smiling enigmatically, Trey squatted down
to unload his armful of rocks. "I'll show you how to build an
inconspicuous fire, then I'll clean the wild turkey for cooking."

Jennifer listened attentively while Trey instructed her to
arrange the stones against the slope of the creek bank in the
shape of a frying pan. He placed an iron grate on the narrow
neck so heated coals from the larger fire could be scraped back
for cooking. The campfire, he said, provided heat in the chill
of the night without sending up a thick curl of smoke that might
invite unwanted intruders.

Following Trey's specific instructions, Jennifer laid the circle
of stones in place, then hiked off to gather wood. By the time
she had the fire going, Trey returned with the turkey dressed
for cooking.

When Trey suggested Jennifer bathe before supper, she
eagerly accepted his offer. Bathing soothed her aches and
bruises, and the ritual of symbolic cleansing made it easier to
put yesterday's frightening ordeal behind her. Only when Trey
called out to her did she reluctantly leave the pool and return
to camp—refreshed, at peace with the world, with herself.

"I do love this place," Jennifer said contentedly. "If I could,
I would dig it up and transport it to our ranch in Texas."

"The Comanches would be upset if you did." Trey chuckled
as he sliced up the juicy meat and placed it on tin plates. "The
People wouldn't know where to find their sacred ground, if the

day ever comes when the government decides to release them from those concentration camps referred to as reservations.''

Jennifer could not fathom what it would be like to live where the almighty government decreed. The land that once belonged to American Indians had been stripped away. Was it any wonder that white settlements were raided, hoping to frighten the intruders off property that had belonged to the Indians since the beginning of time? Jennifer wondered if she would also experience that same need to fight to protect her land, then promptly assured herself that she would.

Undoubtedly, Templeton Ranch had once been part of the vast Indian stomping ground. It saddened her to think that she prospered because of someone else's misery, because the Indians had been unjustly confined. She could certainly understand why Trey felt resentment toward his white heritage. He was trapped between two opposing civilizations that did not begin to understand each other. He was the descendant of the victim and the aggressor, walking the line between two worlds and never finding his rightful place in either one.

Life could be very unfair, Jennifer mused. Cruelty, greed, and retaliation caused untold hardships; she had become painfully aware of that lately.

''I'll take my turn bathing,'' Trey announced as he rose to his feet after dinner. ''We'll call it an early night so we can break camp at dawn.''

When Trey ambled off, ordering the wolves to remain with Jennifer, she gathered the plates and cups and ambled downstream to wash them. She was a trifle disappointed that Trey had not invited her to join him, as he had last night. Truth was, she wanted to experiment with those erotic sensations he had stirred in her. Although he insisted he had not kissed and caressed her out of pity, he had made no move to instigate further intimacy between them tonight.

Had her inexperience caused his lack of interest? Was he simply being too considerate to come right out and say so? Or was he waiting for her to extend an invitation, to initiate the encounter?

Jennifer didn't know how to proceed, being entirely new at this sort of thing. But she did want to know where those marvelous sensations led, and distinguish the difference between tenderness and lust. How did a woman indicate to a man that she wanted to explore uncharted territory without inviting more trouble than she knew how to handle? If the encounter suddenly took a turn for the worse, would it be possible to stop?

Pensively, she stared at the two bedrolls Trey had placed near the fire, remembering how she had lain in his arms last night, marveling at the sensations he called from her, wondering how much more he could teach her if she had the courage to let him.

Would Trey call a halt if she asked him to? If, somewhere along the way, pleasure turned into the kind of pain she endured yesterday, would he back away?

Perhaps it was wiser to leave well enough alone, Jennifer decided as she peeled off her clothes and snuggled into the bedroll. Maybe she was better off harboring sweet imaginings than having her silly fantasies shattered. Nothing ventured, no dreams destroyed, she reminded herself . . .

Jennifer gasped in surprise when she glanced over her shoulder to see Trey hovering over her. "Blast it, how do you do that? I swear you have the silent tread of a cat. One moment you aren't here and the next second you are."

"I didn't mean to startle you, English," Trey murmured as he shucked his breeches and slid into his bedroll. "I guess it's just a habit I developed over the years."

Jennifer stared up at the dome of stars and wispy clouds that played hide-and-seek with the moon. She waited, wondering whether to reach out to Trey or stay where she was. This, after all, could be their last night together. Truth be told, she had not even expected to have this much privacy with him. She presumed he had intended to break camp and ride back to Dodge before dark. But Trey had granted her extra time to heal, to regenerate her spirit. The extra hours had been a godsend that helped to restore her energy and self-esteem.

"English?"

"Yes?"

"Good night," Trey whispered.

Oh, drat it, thought Jennifer. For better or worse, she *did* want to fall asleep in Trey's arms one last time, to feel the sizzling sensations brought on by his kisses and caresses. If things went awry . . . well then, she would deal with that when and if the time came, she decided.

A trifle unsure of herself, Jennifer eased onto her side to see Trey studying her with those hypnotic silver eyes that seemed to bore right into her very soul. Instantly, instinctively, she put her trust in him. He said he would never hurt her and she honestly believed him. He had proved that with his words as well as his deeds. Since they met, he had devoted his time and effort to helping her, protecting her. He was her knight, after all. Even though the rest of the world feared him, she felt safe and secure.

Trey swallowed a groan when Jennifer closed the small space between them to press her lips to his. Damn, he was pretty certain he could survive on the sweet taste of her alone. She satisfied every sensual craving he had ever experienced—not to mention the ones he secretly imagined.

The fact that Jennifer initiated the kiss gave him hope that she believed he was no threat whatsoever. They were definitely making progress here, Trey decided. Within twenty-four hours, Jennifer's trepidation had become a timid but noticeable quest for intimacy.

Trey closed his eyes and savored her—one tender kiss at a time. When his hand glided down her hips to trace the sensitive flesh of her inner thigh, he bit back a groan. He could feel the heat of her desire, and he ached to bury himself in the warmth of that secret fire he felt burning so near his fingertips.

He was afraid to find out how Jennifer would react if he dared to caress her more intimately than he had the previous night. If he alarmed her, frightened her away, he would never forgive himself. But if he didn't dare to touch her he was going to drive himself completely insane!

He dared, telling himself he could deal with the consequences—somehow—if he unintentionally betrayed the trust she had placed in him.

When his caress skimmed over her belly and he brushed the pad of his thumb over the dewy nub of passion, her breath broke on his name. His body coiled into a hard, aching knot as he traced the very essence of her femininity with his fingertip and felt Jennifer's wild, sweet response.

When he gently glided his fingertip inside to stroke her, arouse her, he felt her burning like a liquid flame. Over and over again, he caressed her with thumb and fingertip while his lips hovered over the beaded crests of her breasts. She was shimmering around him like starlight, blinding him to everything but the sound of his name on her lips.

"Trey . . . Dear God . . ."

Jennifer shuddered uncontrollably as he caressed her, showering her with featherlight kisses. He had sensitized every nerve, every inch of her flesh. He had mesmerized her, until the wildest sensations she had ever experienced expanded inside her, converging and intensifying. The ache became so pronounced that Jennifer wondered if she could possibly bear the profound pleasure. She could barely draw breath. It was as if his skillful caresses were no longer enough to satisfy the monstrous need that consumed her.

She clutched at him desperately, her nails digging into his muscled forearms, needing to anchor herself against the overwhelming feelings that sent her spinning completely out of control.

"No . . ." Jennifer gasped when another tidal wave of mind-boggling sensations crested over her like floodwaters rushing over a crumbling dam. "Oh . . . my—"

His lips slanted over hers, silencing her wild, astonished cry. He felt her shimmering around him, felt her clinging to him in breathless desperation. And when she melted in his arms, climaxing so unexpectedly, Trey experienced an indefinable sense of satisfaction. Jennifer was learning—one erotic lesson at a time—that lovemaking was not to be dreaded. And when the time came to consummate their vows, he wanted Jennifer to come to him, aching as he was now, longing to know complete fulfillment.

Only after Jennifer had recovered from the onslaught of unprecedented sensations did Trey withdraw his fingertip. When he traced the moist heat of her desire over her parted lips, her eyes flew open and her flushed face blossomed with even more color. He smiled at the intimacy he shared with her, then bent to taste the passion that he ached to share even more intimately.

"Sleep well, English," he said huskily. "We have a long ride ahead of us tomorrow."

Damned near impossible though it was, Trey eased into his bedroll. He lay there for what seemed a century, silently howling at the moon and thanking Black Wolf for teaching him the art of self-control and self-denial. Trey had relied upon those practiced techniques so often the past few days that he should be an expert at it. He was that, he supposed. Now he knew what it was like to ache to the very core of his being while the man in him was cursing him soundly—repeatedly—for being so damned noble.

For Jennifer's sake, Trey intended to wait until after their wedding to ease this monstrous need that threatened to swallow him alive. He was going to do it up properly. It was the one decent thing he was going to do in life—proper conduct befitting a man who planned to marry a proper, blue-blooded aristocrat.

Jennifer cuddled inside her bedroll, her body burning with the aftereffects of sensual pleasure, baffled by the intense sensations that besieged her when Trey caressed her so intimately. Sweet mercy! There for a moment she was not certain if she could survive the white-hot pulsations that sizzled through her like a lightning bolt.

Sleep well, Trey had said. Not bloody likely! Jennifer was sure her sleep would be constantly interrupted by dreams that took up where he'd left off. Passion, she was beginning to think, was sweet torment, not painful torture. Trey had left her aching for him, craving more than the caress of his hands, the

light touch of his lips. She needed him to fill the empty ache
that echoed through her body and whispered into her lonely
soul.

My, but her perspectives had changed drastically again,
hadn't they? She was no longer hesitant about discovering
where these new sensations led. She was sure she was being
deprived of pleasure. Perhaps when the wedding vows were
spoken, Trey would linger long enough to teach her all there
was to know about passion.

With Trey, lovemaking would be magical—she was positively certain of it. She wanted him to make love to her fully,
completely, even if he could never actually fall in love with
her before he went his own separate way. A pity that, because
Jennifer was certain she was never going to feel this way about
any other man. Trey could have been her soulmate if fate would
have allowed them to meet at another time and place.

Jennifer thoroughly enjoyed the journey back to Dodge and
she regretted seeing it come to an end. Simply being with
Trey had become pleasure in itself. He had told her about his
background, and she, in turn, had shared memories of her own
childhood. For certain, her life had been heaven compared to
Trey's nomadic wanderings and the massacre that killed his
mother, father, and grandfather. He mentioned his forced atten-
dance at Carlisle Indian School in Pennsylvania and his distaste
with the schoolmaster's philosophy of killing the Indian in the
child to save the man.

Although Trey hadn't gone into detail, he mentioned a trip
to Texas to seek help from his white relatives. She could tell
by the tone of his voice that whatever happened had been
anything but pleasant.

Trey wouldn't discuss his forays to track down criminals.
She suspected he had spared her the details because of her
dealings with the Yates Gang. For that, she was grateful. The
memories were too fresh in her mind to imagine what it was
like to deal with cruelty every day of one's life.

When Jennifer and Trey reached the campsite south of town, her belongings awaited her—compliments of Jawbone and Sunset. She donned a blue satin gown that Trey laid out for her and then whirled around to see him wearing the fancy trappings of a gentleman—right down to the bowler hat that concealed his long raven hair.

"You look wonderful," Jennifer complimented as Trey sat her atop her steed.

"I'm choking to death in this damned cravat," he grumbled as he mounted his stallion, ever mindful of the ripped crotch he had yet to mend. "As for this ridiculous hat, I'm going to lose it as soon as the ceremony is over. There's nothing practical about this hat. Its narrow brim provides no shade. It's a waste of perfectly good money and I don't know why I even bothered with it."

Jennifer bit back a grin as he squirmed uncomfortably in his citified clothes, but she said no more on the subject. Clearly, Trey had no appreciation for fancy trappings.

"Are Sunset and Jawbone meeting us for the ceremony?" she inquired.

Apparently, Jennifer had been too distraught the night of her abduction to register the information Trey had given her. Neither did she seem to recall the drastic changes that came over him when he entered the dugout to send Russ Trent to hell where he belonged. If Jennifer didn't remember, Trey wasn't about to remind her. He preferred that she remain ignorant of the transformation he underwent when dealing with deadly desperadoes.

"Your cowboys had other tasks to attend," Trey said evasively. "I'm afraid you'll be stuck with only me."

"I would never consider myself *stuck* with you," Jennifer assured him. "I consider myself extremely fortunate. You are head and shoulders above any man I have ever met, Trey MacTavish!"

Trey smiled inwardly at Jennifer's gusty declaration, feeling inordinately pleased. He had spent the past few days trying to rebuild her pride and spirit, but *she* had done wonders for his self-image since the day he met her. It was pleasing, yet humbling, to be the object of this aristocrat's praise.

Every so often Trey had to remind himself that there could be no fairy-tale ending to his encounter with this almost-duchess. Despite Jennifer's unrealistic, romantic notions, she and Trey were—and would always be—civilizations apart. He was the night—the darkness of life—and she was the light. She was the symbol of fresh, spring sunshine ... and he was the icy winter wind. Not even Jennifer's returning optimism was going to change that fact. She had yet to see him at his *very worst*.

Trey prayed Jennifer would never have to, either. Her belief in him would shatter if she did.

May the Great Spirit spare this idealistic angel from encountering *El Lobo Diablo*, Trey thought with a grimace. He wasn't sure he would be able to bear Jennifer's fear and disillusionment.

The wedding ceremony turned out to be a very simple affair. The minute the ink dried on the certificate, Jennifer stashed it in her purse. When Trey escorted her down the street, the newlyweds drew considerable notice. The accompanying wolves left no doubt as to Trey's identity, in spite of his dandified attire.

The townsfolk stopped and stared at Jennifer, silently admonishing her for cavorting with a notorious gunfighter, presuming *he* was responsible for the bruises on her cheeks. When Jennifer opened her mouth to respond to one old hen who flung up her nose in distaste, Trey clutched Jennifer's elbow and towed her back to his side.

"Don't bother," he told her quietly.

Jennifer had no intention of letting the old biddy think Trey had laid a hand on her. "I will not have that woman saying—"

Trey pressed his index finger to her pouting lips and grinned. "Retract your claws, English. I don't give a damn what people say about me."

"Well, I bloody well do," she huffed.

"Learn not to," he advised as he guided her toward the lawyer's office. "Go finalize the paperwork for your trust fund while I pick up the rest of your belongings."

"But what about—?" Jennifer muttered under her breath when Trey strode off, the wolves at his heels. She had hoped Trey would remind her that she owed him a proper wedding night—as if she could have forgotten the terms of their agreement. But apparently, he had opted to send her on her way without that. From the look of things, Trey was hurrying off to locate Jawbone and Sunset so she could depart for Texas immediately.

Disappointed, Jennifer hiked off to Benjamin Brice's office, marriage certificate in hand. She hadn't wanted Trey to be eager to get rid of her so soon. Had the last two nights been nothing more than pity for her? Though he had denied it, she suspected he felt sorry for her and had tried to heal her emotional scars.

The thought that Trey didn't find her appealing enough to insist on a true wedding night crushed Jennifer's confidence. She wanted him to feel something special for her—something besides compassion and pity.

Setting her dispirited thoughts aside, Jennifer marched into the lawyer's office. As the lawyer promised, the funds were credited to her account with one stroke of his pen and a quick trip to the bank. Instantly, Jennifer became a woman of independent means. She also had a husband who had held her, touched her, out of sympathy . . . and married her because she proposed to him. Now, all she had to look forward to was a long ride to Texas with Jawbone and Sunset feeling sorry for her the whole time.

That sounded like grand fun, Jennifer thought glumly. There was also a chance that Quincy's hired guns would be waiting to frighten the daylights out of her again. Blast and be damned, she was dreading the journey home already.

Stop feeling sorry for yourself, Jen. You have your inheritance and a husband whose name and reputation can keep the Texas feud at bay, she reminded herself. *You should be satisfied that you had the opportunity to know Trey. You are probably the only person in four states who knows how kind, tender, and protective he can be.*

You knew from the onset that Trey MacTavish could not be a part of your life without endangering his. You have what you want, so consider yourself fortunate and stop whining about the could-have-beens. You have a mission, remember?

Jennifer tilted her chin to a resolute angle. Although she had come to care deeply for Trey, she had to bid him farewell and continue her crusade to preserve peace between the farmers and ranchers in Texas.

That was what her father had wanted—peace. It was up to Jennifer to pacify both factions and protect her brother. Her personal sacrifice was leaving behind the one man she would have delighted in spending the rest of her life with.

"What do you mean Sunset and Jawbone are gone and so is the rest of my luggage?" Jennifer demanded, staring incredulously at the carpetbags Trey had draped over the two horses.

"I told you two nights ago that your cowboys headed south. Naturally, they took what we couldn't carry on horseback."

"*We* cannot carry on horseback?" Jennifer's gaze narrowed accusingly. "You know bloody well I was in no condition to digest information that night. Blast it, you tricked me!"

Yes, he had—for her own good. That's why Trey had told Jennifer of his plans while she was too rattled and distraught to protest.

She was not too rattled and distraught to protest now.

"You are *not* accompanying me to Texas and that is that. We cannot arrive together—"

Trey swept Jennifer up in his arms and deposited her on her horse. Her chin went up. "I will take the bloody stage home," she insisted.

"You can't. Some highfalutin muckamuck paid for the private use of the coach. There isn't another stage due out until tomorrow afternoon.''

Trey led Jennifer across the "Plaza" toward South Side. She played tug-of-war with the reins for a good five minutes before her next outburst. "You are not coming to Texas with me!" she yelled when they reached the outskirts of town.

"Give over, English," he grumbled as he loosened the hated cravat. "If you'll just let me do what I do best—"

"You have already kept your end of our bargain. This part is non-negotiable." She dug into her reticule to retrieve the cash she had withdrawn from her account. "You have been paid in full. Now I can go my way and you can go yours."

"I don't want your money," Trey told her as he leaned over to tuck the bank notes in the brim of her bonnet.

"And I cannot accept your company!" Jennifer huffed. "I have told you time and again that I do not wish to see you hurt because of my crusade. I have already lost my father because of the Texas feud and I refuse to lose you."

"Well, you're stuck with me, English," Trey said firmly. "We are traveling to Texas together."

The way Jennifer had it figured, she would have to discourage Trey from this madness by behaving badly. When he had had his fill of her grousing he would go away. She didn't have much practice at being mean and nasty, but she had seen enough of Grandmother Reynolds in action in years past to know how it was done. Gram could find fault with every little thing.

Blast and be damned! Jennifer was trying to spare Trey's life and he was ignoring her. She would become so disagreeable that he would dump her at the nearest stage station.

"Well then, have it your way, as usual," she said loftily. "But do not expect me to speak to you during this trip."

When her chin went airborne again, Trey stifled a grin. Although Jennifer was trying to be snippy and mean-spirited, she simply couldn't pull it off. It wasn't her nature. Her behavior did more to entertain than annoy him.

"I don't plan on getting myself killed," Trey assured Jennifer as he led her off the beaten path.

"Most of us do not," she contended, forgetting her vow of silence. "I doubt my father had a deadly ambush on his last day's agenda."

"What kind of man would I be if I sent my new bride into trouble?" Trey asked reasonably.

"An intelligent one. Obviously you are not as bright as I had originally thought. If you had any sense—which you apparently do not—you would ride off in the opposite direction."

"Thank you for the insult, English."

"My pleasure. You should know that each time your comments or actions do not meet with my approval I shall be calling it to your attention."

Trey bit back a chuckle. "I thought you said you weren't going to speak to me for the duration of the trip."

"I changed my mind," Jennifer declared. "I will not hesitate to lambaste you if you insist on accompanying me to places I don't want you to go."

"It won't work, English. I've made up my mind."

"So have I." Jennifer met his stubborn stare with equal intensity. "I daresay, this is the last you will hear from me—except when I voice complaints."

Trey knew this spirited aristocrat couldn't keep her mouth shut indefinitely. She was entirely too talkative and highly amusing all trussed up in her noble crusade to spare his life. Damned touching, he thought. No one had ever given a fig what happened to him. Of course, Jennifer probably wouldn't either, once she abandoned this ridiculous fantasy of gallant knights and distressed damsels. Once he resolved her problems in Texas, she would be eager to be rid of him, he predicted.

Jennifer was one of those people who felt the need to "fix things". If there were problems, she negotiated solutions. She had gotten it into her head that she had to save the ranch for her younger brother, no matter what personal sacrifice was required. Trey admired her for that—in an exasperated sort of way. But no way in hell was he going to let her jeopardize her life because of that damned feud between nesters and ranchers.

If Jennifer wanted to give Trey the cold shoulder, fine and dandy. He was accustomed to that kind of treatment when he ventured into white society. But he would be damned if he'd let his wife ride off when she needed his help.

Wife . . . the word hummed through his mind as he rode south. Who would have thought a man like him would ever be married to an English beauty like Jennifer. It just went to show how unpredictable life could be, Trey mused as he glanced at his sulking bride.

Bob Yates eased down on his pallet and tipped up the whiskey bottle, intent on numbing the nagging pain in his leg. Seething rage ate at his gut when flashbacks of the incident at the dugout sprang to mind. Damn that Comanche bastard! One by one, Three Wolves had destroyed the last of Bob's family. His older brother Edgar had been the first to fall under that bounty hunter's gun. His younger brother Willie met with disaster while Bob watched in helpless fury. And then Cousin Russ met his bad end.

That half-breed headhunter would come gunning for Bob next. Damn it, there had to be a way to stop that man. Everybody had an Achilles' heel, even Three Wolves.

Bob chugged another drink and stared at the gray clouds gathering in the night sky. He could head north—where he wasn't known by sight—but he reckoned he'd spend the next few years looking over his shoulder, dreading the inevitable confrontation with that human wolf and his man-eating pets.

Better to take the offense than defense, Bob decided. He had doubled back to Dodge for supplies and heard the rumors flying about Three Wolves marrying that prissy Englishwoman. She was definitely that Comanche bastard's weakness, just as Bob had first thought.

The only way Bob could avenge his family was to strike Three Wolves where he was most vulnerable. This time Bob would take nothing for granted, never let his guard down. He'd be more cautious. He sure as hell wasn't going to follow so closely that the wolves caught his scent. And with any luck, Three Wolves would be too distracted by his new bride to notice he was being watched.

Bob stretched out his maimed leg and swore foully. He would catch a nap before the brewing storm blew in. Then he'd trail after Three Wolves and his prissy bride. Once that half-breed was dead and left to the vultures, Bob could get on with his life. This death wish would be fulfilled, Bob vowed fiercely. His family couldn't rest in peace until it was!

"I daresay, Simpson, you have managed to get us lost," Agatha grumbled. "We have not seen a stage station since those half-naked heathens stole our belongings. And if I ever lay eyes on that cowardly driver who abandoned us, I plan to have him hung!"

Simpson assisted the duchess from the coach and sank down in the grass to munch on the last of the rations in the picnic basket. "I do not know how I could possibly have gotten off track when I took over driving the coach," Simpson said as he handed Agatha a chunk of cheese.

"Well, you obviously took a wrong turn," she muttered between bites.

Undaunted, Simpson surveyed their surroundings. "We must be somewhere in the place called No Man's Land. Texas has to be south of here. I was told that there are five trails leading south from Dodge. There is the Rath Trail, Jones-Plummer Trail, Tuttle Trail, Tascosa Trail, and the Palo Duro Trail. We will happen onto the right one eventually."

"The paths are not well defined at all," Agatha groused. "I do not consider cow chips and horseshoe prints satisfactory markings. It goes to prove this country is populated with incompetent dimwits."

Agatha finished her meal and sighed tiredly. She glanced up to note the clumps of clouds that piled up like vaporous mountains on the southwestern horizon. "It looks as if the fog will be rolling in soon. This desolate land will be as soupy as London by dark.''

"Indeed, Your Grace. But with luck, we will come upon a stage station to ward off the chill. Perhaps we can hire another driver.''

Each passing hour of inconvenience and frustration made Agatha even more determined to tote her grandchildren back to England and familiar surroundings. The last leg of this journey was proving to be an intolerable ordeal.

Grumbling, Agatha helped Simpson fold down the coach seat into a narrow bed. She doubted she would get much sleep—not on this hard pallet, surrounded by chilling fog.

Gad, thought Agatha, it was going to be another long night!

Eight

True to her word, Jennifer held her tongue, unless she was complaining about the long hours in the saddle and lack of food and drink. She even made an attempt at whining, like many of the dames of English court were prone to do when they did not get their way. Jennifer had never been an accomplished whiner, but she gave it her best effort in hopes of annoying Trey.

She had predicted he would lose his temper and deposit her at a stage station. Unfortunately, that did not happen. She probably should not have announced her intentions, she mused. When she voiced complaints he merely grinned and kept riding.

"Blister it!" Jennifer exclaimed after an hour of deliberate baiting that achieved none of the desired results. "You have the hide of a rhinoceros. Does nothing bother you?"

Chuckling at the pout on her lips, Trey lifted Jennifer from the saddle and set her on her feet. "Sorry, English, I've heard so many insults that they roll off like water down a goose's back. You'll have to try harder."

Thunder rumbled in the distance, and Jennifer glanced skyward. The sun had disappeared into the angry clouds. She had experienced full-blown storms in West Texas often enough the last five years to know they were in for a stretch of rough weather.

A lightning bolt punctured the gray clouds and struck the ground like a hurled spear. Jennifer instinctively buried her head against Trey's shoulder. She well-remembered losing cattle in electrical storms, recalling the smell of singed hide and the terror of stampedes.

"We'll make camp here," Trey announced as he set Jennifer away from him and began to gather firewood.

"And what are we going to use for shelter, may I ask?" Jennifer flicked a glance at the shallow creek lined with cotton-woods and locusts. She had never weathered a storm on the open plains, and she did not expect to enjoy it. She would make certain Trey knew when she was miserable and uncomfortable.

"You can unroll the packs behind your saddle while I set up a wood frame," Trey told her before he strode toward the cluster of trees. "We'll have adequate shelter in half an hour."

Jennifer stared warily at the blackening sky. "I am not sure we have thirty minutes to spare."

"We'll have forty-five minutes' preparation," Trey said matter-of-factly. "I'll have plenty of time to make camp."

Jennifer gaped at Trey, then appraised the threatening sky. How could he predict the time the storm would descend? Probably because he had spent so much time dealing with Mother Nature. Braving storms was nothing new to Trey MacTavish, she imagined. He took danger and inconvenience in stride, while she sent silent prayers winging heavenward, hoping she would not encounter a lightning bolt that had her name on it.

By the time Jennifer unrolled the canvas tarp, Trey had already fashioned one side of the framework. Using braided weeds and grass as twine, he lashed seedlings together to form a structure that looked like a cross between a tent and a tipi. Following his instructions, Jennifer secured the canvas and gathered the bedrolls.

By the time Trey hobbled the horses and fed the wolves, darkness had descended on the *Llano Estacado*. Gusty winds replaced the eerie calm. Jennifer stood outside their improvised shelter, watching the crab-like fingers of lightning claw at the roiling clouds.

"I'm afraid it's going to be a bad one, English," Trey predicted. "Smell the dust in the air?"

Jennifer nodded. "England has nothing to compare to these storms."

"Thinking of going home?"

Her chin snapped up. "Texas is my home now. I have problems there."

"*We* have problems," he amended. "And what happened to your silence? Forget again, English?"

"Thank you for reminding me." She wheeled around and ducked under the flap.

Trey burst out laughing at her melodramatics. "Come on, English, you know silence doesn't suit you. Give up this nonsense. It hasn't had any effect on me. This is our honeymoon, after all. I thought brides usually granted new husbands a week's grace before trying to change everything about them—including their minds."

Jennifer flounced down on the pallet. Her gaze rose to the brawny man who had switched back into his favorite attire— a breechclout. Her heart twisted in her chest as she stared at the magnificent giant, wanting him in ways she never thought she could want a man.

Trey was right, Jennifer realized. This was their honeymoon—such as it was. She had spent the entire day trying to convince him to leave, but he would not budge. She simply did not have the heart to go on being unkind to her handsome knight. She would be an absolute fool to miss a few days of pleasure since it was proving impossible to shoo Trey on his way. When they reached the ranch, she would demand that he leave Texas, she decided.

"I have changed my mind," Jennifer announced when Trey entered the makeshift tent.

He stretched out on his pallet, linked his fingers behind his head, and cast her a curious glance. "Changed your mind about what, English?"

"About complaining my way through our honeymoon."

"We're going to have one, then?" he asked with a roguish grin and waggle of eyebrows.

Jennifer's heart melted when Trey flirted openly with her. In the course of a few days he had taught her there was nothing to fear from him, that he was here to protect her.

His tenderness had left her craving so much more.

"If you want a true honeymoon, I have no objections," she murmured, her face flushing at the memories of his kisses and caresses.

Trey nodded his shaggy head. "I *would* prefer a truce to your sulking silence."

"But do not expect it to last," she warned. "Your safety is tantamount, and I really must insist that you leave when we reach the ranch."

"Of course you must," Trey replied. "I expect nothing less from a martyr."

"Thank you. I appreciate your understanding in this matter. And forgive me when I become an irritating shrew again, should you balk when I ask you to leave for your own safety and well-being."

Trey swallowed his laughter when Jennifer stared gravely at him. "Certainly, English. I realize it's nothing personal. Just the principle of the thing, right?"

Jennifer's brows drew together when his lips kicked up at the corners and he muffled a snicker with a cough. "You are poking fun at me, aren't you?"

"No." What he was doing was trying very hard not to burst out laughing at his entertaining wife. He had never met a woman so utterly adorable when she was trying to be peevish and pushy.

Jennifer did not believe him for a minute. The man was not taking her seriously—but he would very soon, she decided. She was going to consummate this marriage and make it legal in every sense of the word.

The prospect put an impish smile on her lips.

Trey regarded her warily. "*Now* what scheme are you contemplating, English?"

Jennifer smiled to herself when a brilliant idea struck her. She would take this handsome knight to the limits of his willpower, just as he had lured her to the edge of her own self-control. And somehow, she would make him promise to leave Texas before hell broke loose.

It was a manipulative thing to do, she admitted shamefully. Seduction was dishonest. But blister it, Trey's future was at stake here! She had to find a way to wrench a promise from him. He did not understand how much he meant to her. He did not realize she was fighting for his life. And furthermore, she wanted to make love with him—only him, because she was pretty certain she was already falling in love with him. She would like to enjoy being in love, if only for one night.

Before Jennifer could put her plan in motion and enjoy her wedding night, the wind kicked up and thunder boomed overhead. The wolves scurried inside to whine and pace. That was not a good sign, Jennifer realized. The animals' keen senses anticipated danger. She waited, wondering how well this shelter would stand up against pelting rain and fierce wind. The canvas was already popping and snapping like the sails on a storm-tossed schooner.

Rain pounded the ground and drummed on the canvas tarp. If Trey hadn't taken the precaution of digging a trench around the shelter, Jennifer was sure they would have floated away. When she poked her head outside to survey the snarling clouds, she squawked in fear. Twin tails dangled from the clouds, spotlighted by bright flashes of lightning.

"What's wrong?" Trey questioned as he crouched behind her.

"Twisters," Jennifer chirped.

"Damn."

Trey shouldered past her, but Jennifer grabbed his arm. "Where do you think you are going?"

"To free the horses. They'll need a fighting chance if we end up in the path of one of those monsters."

"You cannot go out there—"

He was gone before she could even reach for him.

Despite the drenching rain, Jennifer monitored Trey's dash toward the jittery horses. Diablo was prancing in his hobble, tossing his head at the barrage. The instant Trey unhooked the ropes, the stallion flung his tail in the air and took off at a dead run. The bay gelding followed at his heels.

By the time Trey returned to the shelter, hail was pattering the leaves of the overhanging trees and thumping the canvas. Jennifer was certain hailstones would have crashed through their tent if Trey hadn't fashioned tree branches and grass to support the roof. As usual, he had prepared for the worst, while she had simply hoped for the best.

Twice, Jennifer thought they were goners. The howling wind jerked the stakes from the ground. Trey lurched forward to grab the snapping end of canvas before it flipped back to let the driving hail and rain inside. While he pounded the stake back in place, Jennifer held down the adjacent corner of the tarp.

This frightening battle with Mother Nature reminded Jennifer that she should relish every moment to its fullest—just in case the worst happened. If she and Trey survived this ordeal she was going to love him to death—

"Bloody hell!" The wind ripped the tarp from her fists and she bounded to her feet to grab hold before the canvas was torn to shreds. Trey moved her aside and yanked the canvas in place. Jennifer tripped over the wolves and expected to have her neck bitten off. Instead, the wolves snuggled up against her, and she patted them comfortingly while Trey battened down the tent.

"Don't do that, English," Trey said as he sank down on the damp pallet.

She stared at him, bumfuzzled. "Don't do what?"

"Don't try to tame creatures of the wild. They aren't meant to be domesticated."

She wondered if he was referring to himself as well as the wolves. "Don't love them? Don't comfort them?"

"No." His tone was sharp. "They have been trained to perform certain tasks for me. They won't obey if all they crave is love and compassion. It will make them weak and useless."

Jennifer had the unshakable feeling that Trey's Comanche training fueled his comments. Earlier in the day, when she lapsed into silence, Trey had spoken of his life with his father's tribe, his training with Black Wolf. He had told her it was the duty of a boy's grandfather to instruct him while his parents hunted, cooked, and protected the clan.

He had told her that he had been tied on a horse at the tender age of two and taught to ride. At age six he was handed a bow and arrow and ordered to practice. When he was nine he was put in charge of his father's horse herd. At thirteen, being large for his age and strong enough to perform the necessary tasks, he accompanied older warriors on raids.

Trey had been taught to withstand pain, hunger, and thirst to protect his family. But the Comanches had not been able to withstand the overpowering Army that massacred Indians and herded the survivors to the reservation near Fort Sill in Indian Territory.

He had gone into more detail about his ordeals in Carlisle Indian School, describing it as a prison ruled by a harsh warden. But Trey had clung to his deeply-ingrained beliefs that a Comanche warrior could never be tamed and had convinced himself that affection invited vulnerability—and that was dangerous.

Trey cared for his wolves—Jennifer knew he did, though he never petted or soothed them. She had an idea that Trey had received very little affection in life and he didn't know how to deal with it, much less express it. The dear man—he needed her love more than he could possibly imagine!

Jennifer moved her hands away from the wolves and waited until the wind died down before trying to speak without having to compete with the storm. "How is it that you know so much about weather conditions and such?'' she asked conversationally.

Trey settled himself on the bedroll, keeping a watchful eye on the canvas. The small tallow candle, surrounded by a circular wall of stones, cast honey-gold light on Jennifer's lovely features. Damn, but she was breathtaking. And she belonged to him—for a time, at least.

The thought was oddly comforting. Trey had never spent so much time in a woman's company, learning her moods, her needs, sharing her innermost thoughts. Although he knew he would probably regret it later, he relished these private moments. He had confided in her already—telling her things he hadn't told another living soul.

Although Jennifer had maintained her silence all afternoon, he knew she had been listening attentively while he talked away the long hours. And he kept talking, because it was the first time in years that anyone had ever bothered to listen to what he said. And now, once again, Trey found himself explaining life in the Comanche camp with the Wolf clan. His lifestyle seemed to fascinate Jennifer, who had grown up in wealth and luxury.

"Comanche children are taught to be self-reliant. My grandfather taught me to hunt with caution, silence, and infinite patience. Using vegetation as cover, we literally sneaked up on prey by keeping downwind. Black Wolf instructed me to read nature's signs on the open prairie, to determine where water sources lay and how to emulate the habits of wild creatures."

Trey gestured toward the wolves that bookended Jennifer, content where they lay. "Take these animals, for instance. Before and during the brunt of the storm, they were restless and uneasy. They caught the scent of danger in the wind and remained on the prowl, alert and prepared for flight. But now they've settled down."

Jennifer glanced down at the wolves as they rested their broad heads on their oversize paws. "The worst appears to be over for the night, judging by their behavior."

Trey nodded. "Comanches are taught to react as instinctively as wild animals, to mimic their survival techniques. I've weathered enough storms in the wilderness to gauge their speed and intensity by the height and color of clouds. The Comanche warrior respects thunder and lightning as great forces of power. No self-respecting warrior would take a storm for granted. The whites have a tendency to wait until after the fact to take precautions. They are never prepared when the worst happens.''

"We are not as attuned to nature as we should be," Jennifer paraphrased.

"Exactly. Comanches don't think white men have good horse sense. And so lacking, they never have the sense to rely on the horse.''

Jennifer laughed lightheartedly. "You truly are a marvel. I wish my brother had the chance to profit from your vast knowledge. Christopher would like you immensely, I think.''

Her smile faded. Christopher would never be privy to such information because Trey could not remain at the ranch. A pity, that. Christopher could have used a skilled, capable mentor like Trey.

"Something wrong, English?" Trey asked, watching her closely.

Jennifer shrugged evasively as she stared through the waving tent flap, watching the storm vent its fury on the plains.

"Good gad, Simpson, what is that?" Agatha gaped at the churning, funnel-shaped cloud illuminated by lightning.

An unfamiliar rumble shook the earth while Agatha and Simpson stared out the window of the coach. The stage rocked on its suspension belts when the wind swirled around them. The churning cloud was less that a quarter of a mile away, bearing down on them like a locomotive.

"I haven't the vaguest idea, Your Grace," Simpson murmured. "I have never seen—"

Marble-size hail thudded against the coach. Agatha shrank away from the window before pebbles of wind-driven ice cracked her spectacles. She squealed at the top of her lungs when a ferocious gust of air lifted the coach and plunked it down on its side. Agatha felt the wind sucking at her as she toppled on Simpson. The twosome landed in a tangle of arms and legs and held onto each other for dear life.

"Your Grace! Are you all right?" Simpson questioned after the roaring wind swirled past.

Agatha smoothed her hair back in place—it had been standing on end. "Bloody hell, Simpson, what kind of country is this?"

"The devil's playground, I would guess," he said as he assisted her to her feet. He stared at the door that was now overhead. "A positively dreadful place, Your Grace. A regular hell on earth."

"I hoped you secured the horses," Agatha said as she braced herself inside the overturned coach. "If not, we will be lost and afoot . . ."

Her voice trailed off when she heard the thunder of hooves, indicating the horses had left without them. Blast and be damned, what else could go wrong? This journey had already become her worst nightmare!

After the storm blew over, Trey ordered the wolves outside and tramped off to check on the horses. Two loud whistles brought Diablo back. The bay gelding followed obediently behind the coal-black stallion. After Trey had hobbled the horses for the night he returned to the shelter—and stopped dead in his tracks.

Jennifer had peeled off her damp gown and let down her hair. The flickering candle glowed molten gold on the bare, silky arms and shoulders protruding from the edge of the bedroll. Everything in Trey responded. He wanted Jennifer like hell blazing, but he refused to approach her, refused to frighten her. But if he wasn't mistaken, he was being issued an invitation.

Problem was, he wasn't sure he had the kind of patience required to teach her where the previous night's kisses and caresses could lead. One false move and he could trigger terrify-

ing memories in her. Trey would cut off both his hands before
he let that happen!

"Are you going to lie down or do you intend to sleep standing
up?" Jennifer teased.

The loincloth concealed very little. Trey was definitely aware
of her. Jennifer struck a pose that would have done Cleopatra
proud. Although she was a novice at seduction, she wanted to
entice Trey, to make him want her the way she had wanted
him when he'd left her aching and unfulfilled.

"English," Trey said as he tied down the canvas flap. "I
hope you know what the hell you're doing lying there like
that."

"You know perfectly well that I do not know what I am
doing. After all, this is the first time I have attempted to seduce
a man. How am I doing so far?"

"Incredibly well." He quirked a brow as his gaze wandered
hungrily over her, not quite certain what to make of this.
"Should I be honored or wary?"

Violet eyes twinkled at him as he stretched out beside Jennifer. "You should be patient," she requested. "I do not expect
to become an expert at this sort of thing overnight." She lifted
her hand to trace the whipcord muscles that curved over his
shoulders and rippled down his body. "Do you find my touch
pleasurable, Trey?"

Trey's breath hitched when the pads of her fingers cruised
over the corrugated muscles of his chest and traced the leather
strap of his loincloth. The fabric suddenly seemed a mite too
tight for comfort.

"Pleasurable, compared to what?" he croaked.

"Compared to what you are used to," Jennifer said as she
explored the planes and contours of his brawny body.

"I am definitely not accustomed to this," Trey wheezed.
His body knotted beneath her roaming hands, burning as if
branded. Instinctively he reached for Jennifer, only to have her
set his hands away from her. "Why not, English? Is this some
kind of torture you have designed, because I didn't give you
your way about this trip?"

Her hand stalled and she blinked at him in dismay. "You think this is punishment? Bloody hell, am I that bad at this seduction business?"

His throttled laughter eased the tension claiming his body. "No, English, I'm extremely sensitive to your touch. You would have to be blind not to notice what you do to me. And I would have to be dead a week not to react to you."

"Why? Because I am a woman?" Her hand strayed off again, gliding up his forearm to measure the expanse of his shoulders.

He frowned, groaned, and struggled to maintain his self-control while his heart bounded around his chest like a caged grasshopper. "What is it you're asking, English?"

"I am asking if I could be anyone else and you would react the same way you are now," she clarified.

"I wouldn't know," he said honestly. "I've never let another woman touch me the way you're touching me now."

Jennifer was both pleased and befuddled. How was she going to learn how and where Trey liked to be touched if she was all the experience he had at this sort of thing? And why wouldn't any woman who had lain with him not want to caress him, feel that sleek, muscular power beneath her prowling fingertips? Was she the only one who felt the urge to touch Trey so familiarly?

"What is wrong with me, do you suppose?" she mused aloud.

"Wrong with you?" Trey chirped, his vocal cords as constricted as his body.

"Why do I feel the obsessive need to touch you when your other lovers have not?"

Trey tried to smile through the hunger that throbbed through him, but his muscles were so clenched with restraint that he couldn't relax enough to grin. "I never let anyone touch me like this before," he admitted. "I didn't want them to."

Her luminous eyes peered at him. "Whyever not? I thought you liked it."

"From you, yes. From them, no."

"How many other *thems* were there?"

"None who mattered," he whispered.

"Why?"

"Damn it, English. I don't know. It's just different now."

"Because we are married?"

It was a safe out. Trey decided to take it. "Yes."

The answer was a devastating disappointment to Jennifer. She hoped to hear him say that *she* mattered—just a little—to him. Well, she would make an effort to teach him to care by returning the pleasure he had given her.

To that end, Jennifer called upon her ingenuity. She remembered how wildly vibrant she had felt when Trey's gentle hands skimmed her body, when his sensuous lips feathered over her flesh. She longed for him to know—and understand—how she felt, how she ached for him.

Jennifer bent to press a kiss to his brow, his cheek, his parted lips. The tantalizing scent of him clouded her senses, commanded all her thoughts. She wanted to love Trey, and have him love her in return—fully, completely, as her parents had loved.

Trey stifled a groan when her soft lips skimmed his jaw and drifted over his collarbone. Impulsively, he reached for Jennifer and, again, she stilled his hands.

"Please don't," she murmured against his taut nipples. "When you touch me it stirs such wondrous sensations that I cannot concentrate. I want to become as good at this as you are."

Trey squeezed his eyes shut and prayed for more willpower. This woman's sincerity was eating him alive. "Why are you trying to seduce me?" he managed to ask.

She lifted her head, and a waterfall of blond hair tumbled across his chest. "To pleasure you."

"English, I don't think I can—"

Her lips came back to his, shushing him in the most tantalizing manner possible. "Don't think," she murmured as she nibbled at the corner of his mouth, "just feel."

He was already feeling maddening sensations that boiled his

blood. This was torture, pure and simple. Trey could not only hear her softly-uttered words drifting over his shoulder, but he could feel them vibrating on his skin.

He was entirely too aware of this woman, that was a fact. He couldn't breathe without inhaling the scent of lilacs, couldn't move without feeling her silky flesh brushing provocatively against his. He was being treated to the most exquisite form of torment anyone ever devised—and he was loving every minute of it.

The instinct to press Jennifer to her back and bury himself in the soft essence of her body was nearly overwhelming. But she had asked for his patience while she experimented. Sweet mercy! He hadn't realized what it was going to cost to lie here while Jennifer treated him to languid caresses.

"Trey?" she whispered against the muscles of his belly.

"What?" His voice had rusted. He must've stood out in the rain too long.

"You are enjoying this, aren't you? I am not botching up too badly, am I?"

"Bloody hell, English," he groaned, unaware that he'd borrowed her favorite phrase. "You're turning me into a jellyfish."

"I am?" She smiled as she untied the leather strap that held his breechcloth in place. Her hand brushed against the doehide fabric that covered his aroused manhood, and she chuckled throatily. "I beg to differ. You definitely do not feel like a jellyfish to me."

When she drew the breechcloth aside and trailed her forefinger down his pulsating length, Trey let out his breath with a ragged sigh. To his shock and dismay, he felt himself arching toward Jennifer's inquiring hand. When her fingertips closed around him, his heart slammed against his ribs—and stuck there.

"If you don't stop what you're doing, I may not last the night—"

Trey stopped breathing altogether when her lips grazed his most sensitive flesh like the fluttering of butterfly wings. When her moist tongue flicked at him and her fingers contracted, he clenched his fist in the pallet to prevent clutching her to him. Unappeased desire bombarded him from all directions while his new wife drove him wild with pleasure.

Lord, he wasn't going to survive! He could handle anything but this all-consuming need. Outlaws, he could face unafraid. But this amethyst-eyed beauty was dismantling his willpower and filling his body with sensations that left him shaking with desire.

Jennifer explored Trey's body with a newfound sense of wonder. His responses gave her confidence in her ability to arouse him. She longed to make him burn with the kind of intense pleasure he had given her.

She measured him from base to tip and felt him quivering beneath her lips, heard his breath tear out on a gusty sigh. Jennifer tested his strength, his satiny softness, awed by the remarkable contradiction of the man. The secretive pleasure of knowing him so intimately aroused her just as surely as it aroused him.

When her caresses drifted over his thighs, Trey's fingers flexed in the cape of blond hair that spilled over his chest. Jennifer traced the throbbing length of him, and another uncontrollable shudder snaked through him. "Jennifer! I can't hold myself in check when you do things like that—" Sharp talons of need clawed at him when the mischievous little imp did things *exactly like that*—again. "Stop it!"

She did stop, but to Trey's surprise, the hungry ache got worse! "Don't . . . stop," he moaned in utter defeat.

"I thought you said—"

"Never mind what I said. I'm damned if you do and damned if you don't. Just—"

Trey felt heat explode inside him when her sweet mouth closed over him, tasting the pearly drop of need he couldn't contain. She suckled at him, stroking him until she called forth yet another dewy response. The pleasure he experienced was more intense than any pain he had ever endured—and he had never welcomed it more. Jennifer was dragging him along the jagged edge, leaving him teetering on the brink of oblivion.

Jennifer cherished her intimate knowledge of this magnificent man, reveled in the power she commanded over him. This famous bounty hunter, whose name struck fear in the hearts of renegades and desperadoes, did not frighten her in the least. She admired him, respected him, wanted him. Trey could conceal his feelings from the rest of the world, but not from her, not at times like this. She could see the silver flames flickering beneath the fringe of black lashes, hear the heavy thud of his heart beating like hailstones against the night. He couldn't hide the sensations he was feeling behind a mask of indifference. Not now, not when she held his very essence in her hand and touched him with exquisite care. She was spreading her love over him, feeling the echo of his need vibrating through her. He desired her and she knew it.

"You want me," she whispered against his aching flesh.

"Like hell burning," he rasped. "Come here, Jennifer."

"Only if you promise me . . ." She twisted sideways, her hand gliding over his rigid flesh while her lips drifted up his chest to skim his lips.

"Anything," he answered all too quickly.

Her thumb brushed his blunt tip, calling forth another moist response. "Promise me you will leave me before I cost you your life. I couldn't bear it, Trey. I swear I couldn't. I love you and I refuse to lose you. Promise me."

"No." He bit back a tormented groan when she caressed him so tenderly that his nerves shattered and all thought disintegrated.

She straddled him, the heat of her own need brushing against him until he moaned aloud. "I want to make love with you, but not without your promise." Her sultry gaze bore into him as she glided over him provocatively, holding him in the palm of her hand, caressing him tenderly. *"Comanche promise,* Three Wolves," she implored. "I want to love you and go on loving you with all my heart and soul, until you have to go away. Promise me this and I will ask for nothing more."

"Damn it, English—"

Trey felt himself arching toward her, so hungry for her that his self-control skittered off like a leaf in a cyclone. But he couldn't give in, even if it damned near killed him—and it was about to.

"Comanche promise," she repeated before she leaned down to take his lips beneath hers. The velvety peaks of her breasts caressed his chest, her hips moved against his hard, aching flesh. "I love you, Trey. Don't you know that? I need to know you will be safe from any misfortune I could bring down on you."

Her whispered words, the feel of her satiny flesh were doing impossible things to his mind and body. Suddenly, nothing seemed as vital as burying himself inside her until these wild, hungry needs subsided.

"Comanche ... promise ..." He heard himself say, then tried to take it back. But it was too late. He had given his word and the aching desire demanded to be appeased.

Nine

With a hoarse groan, Trey rolled sideways, taking Jennifer down to the pallet. He braced himself above her—and saw the trusting look in her eyes, wondering if she would trust him so thoroughly when the inevitable moment arrived.

"Remember what I said about never hurting you?" he murmured as he guided her thighs apart with his knees.

"Yes, and I believe you," she whispered.

"I . . . might have lied," he said hesitantly. "You might feel pain this first time."

"You picked a fine time to tell me."

Trey wanted to laugh, he wanted to sigh with relief. He also wanted to scream in frustration. Though Jennifer had inadvertently assured him that she hadn't been raped by the Yates Gang, he wasn't sure he could trust himself to be as gentle as she deserved. He was already shaking with a need so great it was torture to hold himself in check.

"If I hurt you, it's only because there is nothing I can do to prevent it. It's Mother Nature's cruel trick."

"Well, she ought to be shot for it. Bloody hell, Trey, are you going to make love to me or not?"

His body surged toward hers as he hooked his arms under her knees. He felt Jennifer wince as he came to her and he tried not to do what came naturally.

"Oh, God!" she gasped, wide-eyed.

"I'm sorry!"

"You are apologizing for this?" Her violet eyes twinkled impishly up at him as she relaxed, adjusting to his masculine invasion.

"You're okay with this, English?" he asked, returning her infectious smile.

"I will let you know when we are finished ... We aren't finished yet, are we?"

Trey shook his head and grinned rakishly. "No, English, this is just the beginning of the best part of all—"

He lowered himself to her, inch by inch, his lips descending the instant he took complete possession—and found himself possessed.

Jennifer ignored the initial pain and gave herself up to this one special man who had her heart, her body, and her soul at his command. She could feel the lightning spearing through her, flinging her into an indescribably pleasurable dimension. The storm she and Trey were brewing was more powerful than the one Mother Nature had hurled at them. This wild tempest blew the stars around and left Jennifer reeling in ecstasy. Each deep, penetrating thrust took her higher and higher, until she clung to Trey in a careening world, matching him, hungering for him in breathless desperation.

Trey struggled to draw breath when Jennifer moved with him in perfect rhythm, causing the incredible passion coursing through him to intensify. It was unnerving to be so lost, so utterly possessed by a woman. Jennifer was a unique kind of danger that he had never before confronted. She triggered an outpouring of emotion he hadn't realized he had in his shriveled soul. He could no more restrain the wild pulsations that whipped through him than he could tame the thunderstorm that had churned over the High Plains.

He swore the earth was wobbling on its axis, sending him

cartwheeling through space. His heart nearly beat him to death as red-hot need sent him plunging into her, harder, deeper, seeking release. His arms instinctively contracted around her as desire exploded through him like a holocaust of flames that blazed out of control.

Heaven help him! He wasn't sure there was any possible way to appease these phenomenal needs that he and Jennifer had awakened in each other. He wasn't even sure if a lifetime of making love with her would be enough to satisfy him. Trey had never experienced anything like this; he couldn't stop trembling as all-consuming passion riveted him. Helplessly, he surrendered body, mind, and soul to unparalleled pleasure . . .

Ripples of inexpressible joy washed over Jennifer when Trey shuddered above her and held her to him as if she were the other half of his pounding heart. Ah, if only she had the chance to teach him to love her as much as she had come to love him. Perhaps someday he would reflect on this short-lived marriage and realize that there was such a thing as love. It was the one gift she wanted to give him. She longed for him to accept her affection without question. She wanted him to know that wherever he roamed he would be in her thoughts, her heart—forevermore.

Trey battled through the numbing rapture that surrounded him. He was angry with Jennifer—angrier with himself. He had never been so vulnerable, so out of control. For the first time in his life he had been mastered by someone else's will. Ironically, he had been overpowered by such loving gentleness that he had no means to battle it.

He, who had learned to second-guess his enemies, had been defeated by his own reckless desire. He had melted in Jennifer's hands like butter, and she had used her newly-acquired skills very well indeed. She had asked for a promise and he had given it. She had tricked him, damn it.

Trey was beginning to think he didn't have any control whatsoever over this lovely siren. Only once, he amended. Only when he had touched her, giving all of himself to satisfy and reassure her. And tonight, they had all but destroyed each other with their unique brand of passion.

"Trey?" Jennifer murmured against his chest. "I know you are probably upset with me, and I know you have a right to be. But I love you too much to see you hurt."

"Blister it, English," he muttered, unaware that he had borrowed her second-favorite expression. "I'll never forgive you for wrenching that promise from me while I didn't have enough sense to argue with you."

Jennifer smiled at his poignant expression. She wondered if he realized that he had all but admitted the extent of her power over him. But *she* knew, and she would treasure that knowledge always.

"And I will never forget you, never forget this night," she whispered. "Love is everything I hoped it would be."

"Damnation, woman, stop saying you love me!" he blurted in a burst of bad temper.

"You want me to lie to you?" she asked, affronted. "I have never lied to you and I never will."

"Yes, I want you to lie . . . I mean no!" Trey sighed, exasperated, then stared at the canvas wall. "All I want you to do is admit that what we have here is a severe case of mutual attraction. It will fade when the newness wears off."

"My instincts tell me that is not the case," she said with great conviction.

"Well, your instincts are all out of whack, English."

Jennifer snickered at his scowl. Men shrank from this skilled pistolero when he lost his temper. She, however, found it highly amusing. "I cannot help the way I feel about you. You are simply going to have to live with it."

"The hell I will." Trey propped up on his elbows and glared sternly at her. "Now you listen to me, English, and listen well. What we just shared wasn't reality, no matter how good it felt to both of us. Reality is what you encountered with the Yates Gang, what you will face with the feuding Texans. My fighting skills are what you need most. I want you to give me back that damned promise!"

"I bloody well will do nothing of the kind! You gave me your word and I am holding you to it, Trey MacTavish."

Trey rolled away, muttering. He didn't know how to handle this dainty but determined female. She beat anything he had ever seen! When she made up her mind to something the idea was etched in that rock she called her mind. If he couldn't get past her stubbornness, then he would find a way around the promise.

He was not about to walk away from Jennifer while she was caught in the middle of two feuding factions. Furthermore, he would not have her deluding herself into believing she loved him. No one loved him, not anymore. Those who had borne and trained him were dead, cut down by Army rifles. Trey was accustomed to hatred and prejudice, not unconditional love.

On that thought, Trey fell asleep. First thing in the morning he would do everything he could to drive Jennifer away from him. She would realize she had mistaken infatuation for love. And she would retract that cursed promise. No matter what, he would find a way to make Jennifer take that promise back!

It did not take Jennifer long to realize Trey had resorted to her previous tactics of grousing and complaining in hopes of driving her away. But it was not going to work any better for him than it had for her. He could snap and growl until hell wouldn't have it, but she would continue to love and protect him.

A Comanche promise was as binding as a legal document to a man like Trey. No matter how he aggravated her, she would never be angry enough to let Jonas Rafferty and Quincy Ward fill his handsome hide full of buckshot. The poor man had too many criminals to contend with already!

Trey had become purposefully inconsiderate in his campaign to win back the Comanche promise. He bossed Jennifer around every chance he got. He barked at her to saddle her own mount, then ridiculed her when she floundered with the fifty-pound saddle. He laughed himself silly when the saddle cinch came loose and she plunked on the ground in an unladylike heap.

With absolute determination, Jennifer got to her feet to brush the clumps of mud from her skirt. She tightened the girth and mounted up to follow Trey, who had not bothered to wait for her. She was not going to succumb to his baiting, she promised herself—repeatedly.

Twice, Trey left her with the wolves while he scouted their route, forcing her to spend hours in solitude. Undoubtedly, he expected her to hurl insults at him when he returned. But Jennifer simply shook her head at his every attempt to discourage her. She knew he was uncomfortable with her affection. He did not know how to deal with love, did not consider himself worthy of it—not when the rest of the world loved to hate the legendary bounty hunter whose fearful reputation—

The crack of a pistol jostled Jennifer from her musings and put the wolves on full alert. Fearing for Trey's safety, she galloped headlong over the hill. To her utter disbelief she saw him sitting atop Diablo—well out of pistol range—staring at the horseless stagecoach that lay on its side. The stranded travelers were taking pot shots at him!

Jennifer trotted up beside Trey and frowned at the twosome who had taken cover beside the upturned coach. There was something faintly familiar about the two individuals. Jennifer nudged her steed forward to have a closer look, but Trey snatched the reins from her and steered her back beside him.

"Leave them alone, English. I don't think those fools want our help. They tried to shoot me out of the saddle once already. You wouldn't look good with your head blown off."

"Nonsense," she objected, tugging on her reins. "They are probably frightened half to death after suffering through the storm and losing their horses. I will ride down and chat with them."

Trey scowled at her. "Damn it, haven't you learned anything? There aren't all that many good and decent folks in this world. Most of them will cut you down to get what they want.

That's the golden rule—every man for himself and to hell with everybody else.''

There it was again—Trey's cynical view of humankind. Although he had pretended to be cheerful for her benefit after her ordeal, he still had no faith in his fellow man. All he saw was the worst excuse for humanity, because he dealt with vicious criminals. Jennifer refused to believe evil men were the rule, even though the outlaw gang had temporarily distorted her perspective.

"They are not going to hurt me," she assured him.

"That's what you thought about the Yates Gang and look where it got you," he muttered sourly.

Jennifer ignored the grim reminder. Trey had restored her faith, and somewhere deep inside him he did believe in goodness, she convinced herself. She simply had to show him how to trust again.

When Jennifer jerked the reins loose and trotted boldly toward the overturned coach, Trey muttered and clutched his rifle. He was prepared for a bad reception, even if Mrs. Optimist expected to be invited to tea and crumpets. Hell's bells, if Jennifer got herself shot trying to play the Good Samaritan, he would strangle the woman.

Another wild shot zinged over Trey's head, striking an overhanging tree limb. When he snapped his rifle to his shoulder, Jennifer clamped her hand over the end of the barrel.

"Don't shoot!" she yelled at the twosome who had squatted down beside the coach. "We only want to help you locate your horses. We've been through the storm ourselves."

A feminine screech erupted from under the coach. Bemused, Jennifer stared at the bundle of black skirts.

"Bloody, blooming hell! Is that you, Jen?" Agatha waved her free hand in an expansive gesture. "Get away from that barbarian before he scalps you, or whatever those bloody savages do!" Wheeling about, Agatha scuttled back to wrest the pistol from Simpson's hand and turned it on the brawny, half-naked giant who sat upon his devil stallion while wolves circled around him. "Get away from him while you can, Jen! I will cover you!"

A stray shot hissed through the air and thunked in the tree, indicating Agatha's lack of marksmanship.

Jennifer sat there, her jaw scraping her chest. "Gram?" she bleated in disbelief.

"You know that idiotic female?" Trey stared in disgust at the shrimp of a woman in black velvet and lace.

"That is my Grandmother Reynolds. Duchess of Calverdon. And her faithful butler, Simpson, is with her. What the bloody hell are they doing in America?"

"Your grandmother . . . the duchess?" Trey choked out.

Nodding affirmatively, Jennifer gouged her steed in the flanks and trotted off. Trey and the wolves lagged behind.

Agatha dashed forward, yanking Jennifer from the saddle in her haste to get her granddaughter behind cover before the half-naked heathen abducted her again. Agatha glared at the sinewy giant, whose bronzed flesh gleamed in the sunlight. The barbarian sat atop a horse as black as midnight, looking like some all-conquering lord of the plains, flanked by ferocious wolves.

And didn't that just about say it all? thought Agatha. This man was as wild and vicious as his four-legged pets. The scoundrel had obviously taken poor Jennifer captive, then abused her, molested her—only God knew what else! One look at Jennifer's disheveled blond hair, bruised cheek, and muddy skirts testified to her mistreatment.

Agatha was fit to be roped and tied. No one abused her blue-blooded granddaughter and lived to brag about it!

Whipping the pistol up in front of her, Agatha took aim, intent on blasting a hole through the savage's bead-and-bone breastplate—clean through to his wicked heart.

Trey reflexively grabbed his Colt and fired at the dowager in black. The pistol flipped over her wrist and landed in the grass. Her shocked shriek sent Simpson dashing to her rescue.

"Your Grace! Are you all right?"

"That barbarian tried to shoot me," Agatha howled in out-rage. "He tried to shoot a bloody duchess. Is he mad?"

"Lady, you aim a pistol at me again and I'll take your hand off, one finger at a time," Trey snarled at the old battle-ax.

Agatha blinked in astonishment. "The blooming savage speaks English?"

"Gram, for God's sake, if you would only let me explain—"

Jennifer was not allowed to say another word. Agatha shoved her to the ground, leaving her muttering in the grass.

"Do not interfere, Jen. I shall handle this. Now that I am here, we will see justice served. This wolf pack will be hanged as soon as I can locate a bobby."

"What the hell is a bobby?" Trey demanded.

"An English policeman," Jennifer interpreted as she crawled onto her hands and knees.

Simpson thrust himself in front of Agatha like a shield. "How dare you fire at a duchess! I demand that you apologize to Her Grace at once!"

"Sorry, Grace." Trey's voice was anything but apologetic.

"Not *Grace,* you dolt," Agatha sputtered. *"Your Grace."*

"My name sure as hell isn't Grace," Trey said, and snorted.

Jennifer could not contain her laughter. The cultural gap between Trey and Agatha was downright hilarious. They both spoke English, but they definitely did not speak the same language.

Agatha frowned at her giggling granddaughter. "Hell's teeth, Jen, your ordeal with this ignorant savage must have addled you." She glowered at Trey. "Now get away from here. You are not laying another hand on this poor child. And I will bloody well see you punished for what you've done, and do not think I won't!"

Trey stared at the old woman whose gray hair protruded from the brim of her lopsided bonnet like snow drifts. Snapping blue eyes shot flaming arrows at him. Her sagging bosom heaved with each huffy breath.

Now here was a true shrew, Trey decided. The duchess was spoiled rotten, and full of her pompous self.

Trey couldn't believe the old harridan was Jennifer's grandmother. Jennifer was sweet, kindhearted, cheerful, and too optimistic for her own good. But Grace—or whatever the hell she wanted to call herself—was a shriveled up old hag with the disposition of a wounded buffalo.

"Three Wolves cannot leave yet," Jennifer insisted, stepping between Trey and Agatha. "He is the only one around here capable of retrieving the horses and restoring your coach to proper working order. And where is your driver anyway?"

"He jumped ship the moment we were attacked by this savage's cousins," Agatha replied, flinging Trey an accusing glance.

"Small wonder," Trey smirked.

"You were robbed?" Jennifer gasped in dismay. "Are you all right, Gram?"

"Of course I am not all right!" Agatha blustered. "Those thieving heathens stole my best clothes. I thought the American government had penned up those vicious savages—"

"Now look here, Grace," Trey cut in, offended. "I don't give a damn who you think you are, but I won't have you referring to Indians that way."

"*Your* Grace," Agatha snarled.

"English, kindly tell this old bat that my name isn't Grace," Trey insisted.

Jennifer burst out laughing again.

Agatha glanced sharply at Jennifer and frowned. "You are obviously suffering from hysterics after losing your father and enduring a horrifying ordeal with this ignoramus in a loin-cloth."

Trey glared at the old battle-ax. "Look, Grace—"

"Why don't you call me Duchess and leave it at that," Agatha broke in, her nose in the air. "And what name shall I have placed on your tombstone after you have been hanged for molesting my granddaughter?"

Trey had been talked down to for as long as he could stand. This highhanded old witch needed to be knocked down a notch—or three. "For your information, Grace, your grand-daughter happens to be my wife." There, let the old prig stick that up her snooty nose and see if she suffocates on it.

Agatha screeched like a banshee as she stared at the matching gold bands Jennifer and Trey wore. Her face turned pasty white as she wilted on the grass in an unconscious heap.

It was the first peace and quiet Trey had enjoyed in a half hour.

Jennifer knelt down, while Simpson fanned Agatha's peaked face. To his credit, Simpson was totally devoted to his employer of forty years. Jennifer well remembered how loyal he had been to the duchess when Christopher and Jennifer made their semi-annual visits. Simpson constantly inquired as to Agatha's comfort and catered to her every whim. Jennifer wondered if Gram fully appreciated her true and devoted friend.

Jennifer had always suspected the butler was in love with the duchess, though he would never overstep his place. Simpson tended to overlook Agatha's obvious faults, excusing her because she had lived a life of royal pampering. Agatha had endured a contracted marriage to a man she had never loved— which Jennifer thought was probably the reason for her grand-mother's irascible disposition.

Simpson glanced up from his crouched position to glower at Trey. "That tears it, you scoundrel. If you say another word to upset Her Grace you will answer to me!"

"Now there's a terrifying threat if I've ever heard one," Trey mocked. Ignoring the butler, he focused on Jennifer. "I'll fetch the horses while you're reviving Grace."

Jennifer watched Trey trot off, the wolves at Diablo's heels. In her opinion, he had gone out of his way to be unsociable— not that Simpson and Gram had been courteous to him. But they had an excuse, Jennifer allowed. After all, Gram and Simpson were completely out of their element, and had just been through one terrible calamity after another.

Jennifer had the unmistakable feeling that Trey would use this situation to convince her he was all wrong for her. He would receive no objection from Gram and Simpson. And naturally, Trey had considered that, Jennifer suspected.

Well, she would simply have to sing Trey's praises and convince Gram and Simpson that Trey was not only worthy of her love, but also their respect. What Jennifer did not need was to find herself in the middle of a family feud while she was trying to resolve the ongoing feud in West Texas!

"Bloody, blooming hell . . ." Agatha groaned when she regained consciousness. "Tell me I am having a nightmare, Simpson."

Simpson patted Agatha's hand consolingly. "I would if I could, Your Grace, but I fear I cannot."

"That heathen said what I thought he said?" Agatha bleated. "He is Jen's husband?"

" 'Fraid so, Your Grace."

When Agatha began to feel faint again, she inhaled slowly, deeply. "Where is my granddaughter? That rapscallion didn't abscond with her again, did he?"

"No, Your Grace, Lady Jennifer is right here." He gestured to Jennifer to stand at Agatha's feet. "There, you see? She is safe and sound, just as I said she was. Now, do you wish to stand up or do you prefer to lie down a trifle longer?"

"Perhaps sitting will revive me. It is not helping matters that I have had nothing to eat."

Jennifer wheeled around to fetch the pemmican and canteen strapped to her horse. When she strode back to the shade tree where Simpson had propped Agatha up, lively blue eyes zeroed in on Jennifer.

When she offered Agatha a stick of what looked to be shoe leather, she shrank back distastefully. "What in God's name is that?"

"Dried meat," Jennifer explained. "As you have undoubtedly discovered, there are no roadside inns in the area, only sparsely-scattered stage stations that serve meager meals. Overland travel in the West requires such staples as pemmican, hoecakes, and jerky. Taste it, Gram. It is not as bad as it looks."

She handed a stick of dried beef to Simpson. He stared at her as if she had offered him a three-day-old dead fish. Finally,

Jennifer bit off a chunk and chewed on it. Reluctantly, Simpson tasted the trail rations.

"Edible," he assured Agatha. "Not up to English standards, but perhaps it will regenerate your strength, Your Grace."

Simpson's testimonial prompted Agatha to sample the dried beef. Although she made an awful face, she did chew and swallow.

"Hand me a drink to wash this down," Agatha choked out.

After Agatha took a sip from the canteen, she peered somberly at Jennifer. "Now tell me that the savage lied to me, Jen. He isn't really your husband, is he?"

"Yes, Gram, he is. And I daresay, he is the finest, most competent man you will ever meet."

Agatha smirked, then bit into the pemmican.

"It is true," she insisted. "He is a legend in these parts." That much *was* true. Jennifer simply neglected to say what kind of legend and reputation preceded him wherever he went. "Three Wolves is half Comanche—"

"And all ornery devil," Agatha put in sourly.

Jennifer ignored the snide comment. "He is the American version of Camelot's gallant knight."

"Oh, please, Jen!" Agatha sniffed in disdain. "I will not have you comparing that naked barbarian to our knights in shining armor."

"You are quite right," Jennifer agreed. "Three Wolves is heads and above English knights, for he needs no armor to protect me, or himself. If you had seen him in action, as I have, you would not doubt his capabilities. Why, he rescued me, singlehanded, from a gang of outlaws, and he walked away without so much as a scratch. I cannot say the same for the cretins who mistreated me. But if not for Three Wolves, I would not be alive today."

"Good gad! Outlaws?" Simpson croaked. "You poor child. Life in these States is worse than we imagined. What of young Christopher? Was he captured, too?"

"No, he is at the ranch," Jennifer reported. "I was abducted while purchasing supplies in Dodge City."

"And that savage demanded that you marry him in exchange for saving your life?" Agatha asked, appalled.

"Actually, Gram, I was the one who asked Three Wolves to marry me."

When Agatha looked as if she were about to faint again, Jennifer poured water from the canteen onto Agatha's monogrammed kerchief and dabbed it on her pallid face.

"Blast and be damned. Why would any woman in her right mind want to wed that heathen? There are men all over England who would leap at the chance to marry you, Jen."

"But none would suit me as well as Three Wolves does."

"He does not suit you well at all," Agatha said with great conviction. "We will have this ridiculous marriage annulled as soon as possible."

"We cannot. I need Three Wolves."

"Rubbish. I cannot fathom what you need with the likes of him. Eve needed a naked man because that was all that was available. You are not that desperate, young lady. I will find you a proper match in London—a nice young man who knows how to dress and speak without offending, one who realizes what *Your Grace* means. You and Christopher will be reinstated in society, and no one will have to know about your absurd marriage to Hiawatha. I can guarantee that Simpson will not breathe a word about this. He is unswervingly dependable."

"I do not want another husband, because I happen to love the one I've got—Gram? Don't faint again!"

"Then don't say such things," she muttered between gasps for breath. "You cannot possibly love that man. He is only two legs short of a wolf, for God's sake. If you crave a pet, I will have Simpson buy you a dog."

"I want Three Wolves."

"Fine, then we will get you three wolves, whatever color you prefer. We will pen the beasts up in a kennel where they belong."

Jennifer sighed in frustration. "Gram, you seem to forget that I am twenty-two years old. I am perfectly capable of choosing my own husband. It will ease your mind to know that

Three Wolves will only be accompanying us until we reach the ranch.''

"Hallelujah! I hope you had the sense to avoid the marriage bed, or wedding camp—whatever those savages call it. It will be most inconvenient if you find yourself with child because of this mismatched union. And worse, if you created a child who resembles that heathen, we will have a devil of a time grooming the wildness out of him. I suppose if we start young enough, we can make him a proper Englishman, even if he does have red blood rather than blue.''

"Gram—''

"And we can invent some tale about your deceased husband to satisfy your prospective suitors in London,'' Agatha went on.

"Gram—''

"With your inheritance and title, your beaus will overlook your unfortunate past.''

"I do not have any titles,'' Jennifer reminded Gram when she finally paused for breath.

"You bloody well will have. Who do you think will inherit the duchies when I pass on?''

Jennifer blinked, stunned. "You are planning to give the titles and estates to Christopher and me? But you refused to accept my father and disowned my mother.''

Agatha resituated her crumpled skirts and averted her gaze. "Yes, well, I thought your mother would come to her senses eventually and leave the man she fancied herself in love with. I cannot fathom where Eleanor got that crazed notion that love was more important than titles and position. Marrying Ramsey, whose inherited estates were small potatoes compared to three duchies, was as preposterous as your marrying that Prince of Wolves. Really, Jen, why did you think you needed that savage?''

Jennifer finally lost her temper. She could tolerate no more derogatory remarks about Trey. "I married him so I could keep the peace in this feud between my Texas neighbors, but I—''

"Well, that explains it.'' Agatha patted Jennifer's rigid shoulder. "You probably had to lie and say you loved that scavenger, just to appease his pride. I realize that does not solve your problem of an unwanted husband, but it helps me understand why—"

"I happen to love him!" Jennifer all but shouted in exasperation.

"Of course you do, my dear girl," Agatha patronized and winked conspiratorially. "As soon as we shoo the savage on his way, we will gather your belongings and set off to England. Why, in six months, you will forget your stressful ordeals and your Prince of Wolves."

Jennifer wanted to explain—in extensive detail—but Trey returned with the team of horses. Agatha ordered Jennifer to leave her alone for a few minutes of rest. Grumbling over Agatha's ill-conceived notions, Jennifer stamped off with Simpson at her heels. She contemplated rehashing the conversation with Simpson, but the man was so devoted that he would believe whatever Agatha wanted him to believe. In that, they were like one steel-minded trap—British-born and English stubborn.

"Where's Grace?" Trey questioned as he dismounted. "Still unconscious, I hope."

"I heard that, you rascal!" Agatha flung at him.

Trey shot a mutinous glance in the old hag's general direction. "The horses were scattered all over creation. And how the stage got so far off the main route I can't imagine."

"Because I was driving without a map," Simpson spoke up.

"That explains it." Trey appraised the stuffy Englishman, whose chest swelled up like a bagpipe. "What's-a-matter, Butler, you couldn't figure out which way was south?"

"My name is not Butler."

"Right, and the old witch isn't Grace. How can I keep forgetting?"

"That tears it!" Simpson assumed his pugilist stance. "Put up your dukes—"

"We've got dukes around here, too? Where *are* the old chaps, by the by?" Trey mimicked his challenger. "Maybe the lot of us should have a chat."

Simpson growled in outrage as he thrust out his right arm, intent on wiping the smirk off Trey's face. Trey caught the extended arm and simultaneously hooked his heel behind Simpson's stork-like legs. The man went down like a felled tree, grunting in pain when he landed flat on his back.

Trey loomed over Simpson with the infamous glower that put the fear of God in men. "I'll tell you the same thing I told Grace. Don't mess with me, Butler. My wife is all the amnesty you've got from me. If you keep taking pot shots at me, I'll be carving epithets on your tombstones. And if you think I'll bother hauling your cocky English asses home for proper burial, better think again. My wolves would love to get a taste of your arrogant British hide."

Trey barked an order in Comanche and the wolves were at Simpson's throat in the time it took to blink. Simpson whimpered fearfully as Trey stalked off to work on the coach.

Despite Trey's order not to show the wolves any kindness, Jennifer squatted down to coo at them. The wolves left their appointed post to nuzzle against her.

"Damn it, English, I told you not to pamper those wolves," Trey muttered at her.

Jennifer smiled, noting that the glitter in his eyes was less intense than it had been when he was looming over Simpson. "Sorry. I keep forgetting."

"Like hell you do," was all Trey said before he fastened a rope to the coach and hitched up the horses.

Simpson shook his head in amazement. "Have you no fear of these vicious creatures? How can you be so cheerful when you find yourself wed to that surly devil?"

"I told you, I love him."

"Right. Don't we all," Simpson snorted as he clambered to his feet. "I feel no obligation to be nice to that peon, Lady Jennifer. I will leave you to deal with your half-naked knight while I check on Her Grace. Hopefully we can be on our way soon. I am counting the hours until we reach the ranch and that wolf man goes his own way!"

Ten

"Wake up, Grace. We're burning daylight."

Agatha stirred like an overturned beetle on the fold-down seat of the coach. Her fuzzy gaze landed on a looming silhouette against the faint light of dawn. Mostly, all Agatha could see was the glint of his silver eyes, glaring down on her like pinpoints of starlight.

"Rot, it is not even morning yet," she muttered grumpily.

"Close enough," came Trey's gruff reply.

Agatha gnashed her teeth and propped up on an elbow to sharpen her tongue on the insolent savage. "In England, the gentry do not rise until late morning," she informed him with a haughty snort. "If you were even half civilized you would know that."

"This ain't England, Grace. If you had half the intelligence you think you do, *you* would know that."

Agatha clenched her fists in the blanket, wishing she had a stranglehold on this heathen's thick neck. "You are insufferably obnoxious," she hissed. "The only reason I have tolerated your disrespect is because of my granddaughter. But I do not intend to endure your ruddy presence indefinitely. You will not be married to Jen any longer than it takes for my solicitor—''

''Your what?'' Trey interrupted.

''My lawyer to nullify this preposterous marriage,'' she finished nastily.

Trey took an ominous step forward, his white teeth gleaming in the faint light. Agatha was abruptly reminded of the wolves that traveled with this two-legged beast. The man looked utterly predatory, his eyes glittering, his teeth bared, his half-naked body poised to pounce.

''The only reason I'm tolerating you is because of English,'' he gritted out. ''And there's something else you better know, Grace. I'm the only one out here in the wilds who's keeping you and Butler alive. If I decide to ride off without you, all you'll have for protection is your rapier tongue. Shooting off your mouth won't keep you alive in these parts.

''As far as my marriage is concerned, you can have your highfalutin solicitor dissolve it anytime you please. I only intend to stay married to English long enough to resolve her problems in Texas. Whether you believe it or not, I have her best interests at heart. It's her uppity family that I can't stomach,'' he added with a sententious glance.

That said, Trey lurched around and stalked over to where Simpson lay sprawled beneath a tree. A swift kick in the hip brought him awake. ''Get the team of horses hitched up, Butler. I'm ready to leave.''

Accompanied by Agatha and Simpson's curses, Trey strode off to locate Jennifer. He found her lingering in the clump of trees by the creek, eavesdropping on his conversation. The wounded look on her face had Trey scowling to himself. He hadn't meant for Jennifer to hear that part about dissolving their short-term marriage, or how he felt about the persnickety duchess and her stork-legged butler.

On second thought, maybe that was one way of destroying Jennifer's silly illusions. The sooner she lost her temper and abandoned her absurd notion of falling in love with him, the better off she would be. The greatest favor Trey could do for her was to end the Texas feud, then get the hell out of her life—for good.

With only a slight nod of greeting, Trey strode off to feed the wolves, leaving Jennifer to stare after him. To say she was disappointed that he had not asked her to sleep by his side the past two nights was an understatement. Since they had happened onto Agatha and Simpson, Trey had gone out of his way to be unpleasant and unsociable. His remote attitude reminded her of the first day she had met him on the streets of Dodge.

Once again, Trey had shut her out of his life. She didn't want to admit that his irascible disposition was getting to her—but it was. Jennifer had bitten her tongue a number of times when Trey purposely baited Gram and Simpson. And it hurt to be avoided and ignored.

Dispirited, Jennifer ambled over to the coach to help Gram adjust the coach seat where they had slept.

"I daresay, Jen, if we were in England I would pull a few strings and have your insufferable husband shipped off to Australia. And blast it, he is so ignorant that he keeps calling me Grace and referring to Simpson as Butler. How stupid can the man be?"

"Trey knows your names," Jennifer assured Gram. "He is only trying to annoy you."

"It is working too bloody well," Agatha harumphed as she fastened the buttons on her black gown. "The mere sight of him in his skimpy loincloth sets my teeth on edge."

Seeing Trey in his loincloth set things besides Jennifer's teeth on edge. She rather suspected that even Agatha was not immune to the display of brawny masculine flesh, though Gram would cut out her tongue before she admitted any such thing. Gram, after all, was more bullheaded than Trey MacTavish ever thought about being. Gram had had decades of practice.

Simpson trudged toward the coach, working the kinks from his back. His salt-and-pepper hair was standing out every which way and his eyes boasted dark circles. Apparently, bedding down on the hard ground was not agreeing with him.

"I swear that man is the devil's own son," Simpson muttered

as he massaged his aching back. "He picks and prods me all the bloody time. He barks orders as if I were his personal lackey. Begging your forgiveness, Lady Jennifer, but how could you have married that man?"

"I have asked her the same question a dozen times myself," Agatha grumbled. She glanced around the campsite. "Where is that scoundrel anyway? He got me up at this ungodly hour and now has disappeared into thin air."

"He is feeding his wolves," Simpson reported. "He left orders for me to see that we have eaten our travel rations and are prepared to depart when His Majesty returns."

Jennifer had to give Trey credit. He was doing a bang-up job on Agatha and Simpson. He was using their dislike for him to aid his cause. She was forced to listen to Gram and Simpson grouse—as if their low opinions of Trey would rub off on her. They would not! She refused to let them.

Rallying her optimism and determination, Jennifer hiked off to fetch the last ration of pemmican, jerky, and hoecakes. She had one night left before Trey would have to keep his promise. No matter how furious he tried to make her, Jennifer vowed to enjoy one last night in his arms—one sweet memory to tide her over in the lonely years to come. When he left Texas, her thoughts would always be with him, no matter how far he roamed. Nothing he did could destroy her tender feelings for him.

Not that he believed it. Ah, how Jennifer wished she had a lifetime to convince him!

Dust rolled into the stage like fog, showering the three occupants with another layer of grime. Agatha clamped her hankie over her face and muttered.

"What was that, Your Grace?" Simpson inquired, brushing away the dirt on his sleeve.

Agatha removed her kerchief and said, "I swear that heathen is doing everything possible to make us uncomfortable. He refuses to let us stop to stretch our legs, and we are forced to wait until the horses need water before we take a break. He puts the needs of the livestock and wolves above ours. Good gad, how much longer will we be on the road before we reach the ranch?''

"We should arrive by noon tomorrow." Jennifer stared across the thick grasses that tumbled into a broad range of winding gullies and ravines capped with rocky peaks and dotted with cedars, junipers, and cottonwoods. The prairie had opened into canyons that were once the haunts of the Comanches. The rugged stone embankments and deep arroyos made grand hiding places. This area of Texas reminded Jennifer of the rough terrain on Templeton Ranch. It also reminded Jennifer that she would soon be home—and Trey would be gone.

When the stage finally ground to a halt at dusk, Agatha and Simpson piled out, flashing Trey their customary glares of disapproval. Not to be outdone, he scowled back.

"Butler, unhitch the horses and take them down to the river for water," Trey ordered crisply. "Grace, you can unfold the coach seat to spread your pallet. We're making an early night of it."

"Blast it!" Agatha flared irritably. "I am not taking orders from you. I am a duchess and you will refer to me as *Your Grace,* if you must speak to me at all!"

Trey swatted away the tip of the parasol aimed at his bare chest. "I'm part Comanche, lord of these wild plains. You can call me Three Wolves. Now make your bed, Grace, or you'll go hungry tonight. I'm the only one around here who knows how to hunt and cook. Unless you want to dine on your royal fingernails, you'll see to your designated duties while I see to mine."

"Insufferable, intolerable, insolent—oh!"

"Come along, Gram," Jennifer broke in when Agatha raised her arm to whack Trey with her parasol. "I will help you."

"No, you won't," Trey objected. "You'll have to gather firewood while I'm hunting."

"You expect your wife to fetch and heel?" Agatha hooted.

"In this rough, unforgiving country, we all have to pull our weight. Titles don't mean a bloody damn around here, Grace."

"Now see here, Three Wolves—" Simpson tried to protest.

"Take care of the horses," Trey snapped, then stalked off with the wolves at his heels.

"Jen, we are not waiting until we return to England to have this ludicrous marriage negated. We will have it done in Texas, first chance we get."

"No, Gram, that would defeat the entire purpose. And I would appreciate it if you would be civil to my husband."

Agatha sniffed disdainfully. "Why would I want to do that?"

"Because I asked you to."

"Make any other request," Agatha muttered before she pivoted on her heels to fold down the coach seat. "That one is impossible."

Jennifer rolled her eyes heavenward. These constant confrontations were wearing on her cheerful disposition. There was much to be said for solitude, Jennifer realized as she trooped off to gather wood.

Trey kicked at a clump of grass on the bank of the Canadian River, then cussed under his breath. Supper had been another unpleasant affair. Agatha had been at her obnoxious best and Simpson had been the old hag's echo. The pompous duchess had wolfed down her food and then inquired as to what kind of meat she had consumed. When Trey announced she had partaken rattlesnake steak, Agatha flung herself into a coughing spasm. She swore Trey was trying to poison her.

The thought had crossed his mind, he had to admit.

Simpson, devoted to the end, upbraided Trey for upsetting the duchess. One thing Trey did have to admit was that the old gal gave as good as she got. Trey didn't like her one whit, of course, but he admired her spunk. He hoped he lived to be as cantankerous as Grace.

What really grated on Trey's nerves was his own attitude toward Jennifer. He had pretty much ignored her, hoping to dispel her knight-in-shining-armor fantasy and provoke her into retracting that blasted promise. But nothing was working. She refused to lose her temper with him.

He ambled down to the river and leaned leisurely against a tree to smoke a cigar. Purposely hurting and disappointing Jennifer was taking its toll. She didn't deserve the lack of consideration he had dished out. The poor woman already had Agatha for a grandmother. That was punishment enough!

The splash of water, and ripples sweeping downstream, drew Trey's attention. He glanced north, watching the channel sparkle like a ribbon of mercury. When he saw Jennifer gliding through the water, desire hit him like a doubled fist.

Keeping his distance from her was driving him crazy. Forbidden memories came rushing back, tormenting him. He really should return to camp to fence words with the old battle-ax. It would take his mind off wanting to wade into the water to make love to Jennifer one last time before they parted company . . .

"Trey, is that you?" Jennifer called out.

He bit into his cigar and cursed colorfully when he saw her coming ashore. He grimaced uncomfortably when she reached for the chemise to cover herself. As if that mattered, thought Trey. The image of her shapely body was emblazoned on his mind for all eternity.

Trey crushed the cigar under his heel. He had to be strong and persistent. He had to convince Jennifer he no longer wanted her so she would abandon her mistaken belief that she actually loved him. For sure and certain, he had given her no reason to.

"Stay the hell away from me, English," Trey grumbled as she walked toward him. "I'm not in a good mood."

Jennifer refused to be rejected—not tonight. She would make him want her, somehow. She would refuse to let him deny either of them the pleasure they could offer each other.

"I want you, Trey," she murmured as she came to stand in front of him.

"Well, I don't want you, English," he said gruffly. "I've had you once. I prefer variety."

Jennifer told herself he was being deliberately cruel—but she would not let him dissuade her. "Fine, then just pretend I am someone else," she countered.

There was only one way to break this spell Jennifer was operating under, Trey decided. He would offer her lust, not lovemaking. Only then would she realize that what she believed was love was an idealistic delusion.

"You want my body, English?" he asked as he loomed over her.

"Yes."

"Then you'll have it."

His lips came down hard on hers, his tongue thrusting into her mouth to rob her of breath. He hooked his arm around her waist, pulling her against him with rough impatience. He expected Jennifer to protest and retreat, but she didn't. She surrendered trustingly, and Trey felt another door in the cavern of hell opening to grant him entrance. He was going to hate himself for doing this, he just knew it. And yet, he could think of no other alternative.

His free hand grazed the taut peak of her breast, and he felt her flinch at his hurried touch. His palm folded around the soft mound before his caresses swooped down to settle on her inner thigh. When she instinctively resisted his impatient fondling, Trey forced himself to become more persistent—and hated himself all the more for it.

"Open for me," he demanded.

He cupped her, his fingertips moving swiftly downward while he insinuated his leg between her thighs. Jennifer was forced to straddle his leg when he clamped hold of her hips and shifted her backward to take her mouth greedily once again. His hips thrust toward hers, shoving her farther up his bent leg until she was riding his thigh and her knee was pressed against the hard length of his manhood.

"An even trade, English, my body for yours," he ground out against her mouth. "It's all I have left to give. The first time I patronized your innocence, but I don't have the time, or inclination, for anything except my own needs.''

His gruff words cut through Jennifer like a knife. She had given herself unselfishly to Trey, and he was hell-bent on mating like creatures of the wild. Tears of hurt and disappointment fogged her eyes as he plundered her mouth with the kind of rough urgency she was not accustomed to receiving from him. His fingers gripped her hips, pressing her against his leg, crushing her breasts against his chest.

Suddenly, the memory of her ordeal with Russ Trent buffeted her. She could see Russ's satanic smile in the shadows of her mind, feel his disrespectful gropes. Trey was trying to link thoughts of him to that horrible outlaw, and Jennifer could not bear for him to have her dream shattered, not when this was all she would have left of him before he went away. She would not let him turn her loving fantasy into a nightmare!

Jennifer braced her hands on Trey's chest and pushed away. He caught her to him, but with a small cry, she jerked loose and dashed back to the river.

"Come back here," Trey snapped. "You don't get a man hungry then saunter away."

Before she could wade into the stream, Trey latched onto her hand and swung her around to face him. "You wanted this, English," he growled at her. "Aren't you woman enough to—?"

His voice evaporated when he saw the tears streaming down her cheeks. When she muffled a sob, Trey's heart twisted into a knot. He had never been immune to Jennifer's tears. She stared at him the same way she had the night Russ Trent broke her spirit and humiliated her.

God help him, he couldn't be cruel to Jennifer—no matter how honorable his ultimate intentions. When he gave her reason to cry it was like thrusting a spear through his own chest and bleeding one drop at a time—one drop for every tear that fell.

"Aw, English, I'm sorry . . ."

Ever so tenderly, Trey brushed his thumb over her flushed cheek and then sipped salty tears until he had kissed them all away. His lips skimmed her trembling mouth, feeling her shuddering breath wash over him, eroding another layer of calluses that had never been thick enough to protect him from his bewitching wife. Somewhere along the way, he had become the echo of Jennifer's emotions. He had become too aware of her needs, too damned attached to her for his own good—and hers.

Trey scooped her up in his arms and walked into the water. His gaze never left those mesmerizing amethyst eyes as he peeled away her chemise and unfastened his loincloth.

"Please don't hurt me," she whispered brokenly. "I cannot bear that from you. You taught me the meaning of gentleness. Don't shatter that sweet memory. It is all I have, Trey. Don't you understand that?"

"This time," he murmured against her honeyed mouth, "this last time, you'll have the sun, English. You'll burn for both of us, and I'll be your flame."

"Comanche promise?" Her teary gaze riveted on his chiseled face.

"Comanche promise." Trey sealed the vow with the gentlest kiss.

Jennifer felt her bones melt and her flesh sizzle when his tender caresses erased the impatient touches of moments before. His moist lips glided over her nipples while his fingertips gently kneaded her breasts. Her body instinctively surrendered to the gentle giant she had come to love, though he was still too cynical to believe what she felt for him.

Over and over again, his hands coasted over her sensitive flesh, until every nerve tingled. His sensuous lips skied over her shoulder and flicked down her ribs, counting them one by one as he cradled her in his arms, holding her suspended in the water.

Inexpressible need coiled in Trey's body, and he groaned as he inhaled the sweet, clean scent of her. His gaze swept over her luscious body, memorizing each silky inch, thrilled by her generous responses. He felt sensual lightning spill through him as he smoothed his hand over the thrusting crests of her breasts.

He heard her raspy moan as his hands swirled over the flat plane of her belly to trail over her inner thigh.

Beguiled, Trey watched Jennifer arch up to greet his caresses each time his hand paused. He marveled at her ability to shed all inhibition when she was in his arms. She made him feel all-powerful, as if his touch was the gift she had waited a lifetime to receive. When his fingertips shifted to test her moist, sensitive flesh, he heard her breath hitch, saw her eyes widen in response to the waves of pleasure sweeping over her.

Her lashes fluttered downward like butterfly wings to rest on her checks when he caressed the delicate nub of passion. He felt her sultry heat spilling onto his fingertips and stifled a groan of pleasure.

"Don't close your eyes," he whispered as he traced her with the greatest of care. "I want to see the fires flickering in those beautiful eyes when I touch you."

Jennifer's lashes swept up and she focused intently on his tender smile. His hand moved, lingered, teased and aroused. She moaned helplessly as pleasure ribboned through her. His dark brow rose when he felt her shiver around his fingertips, and he grinned when she blushed at their shared intimacy.

"You burn with the most incredible fire," he said in awe.

His mouth descended on hers, his tongue penetrating in synchronized rhythm with his gliding fingertip. He stroked her, excited her, until frissons of heat consumed her body, burning all thought from her mind, drawing sounds of pleasure from her lips.

"Mmm . . . do that again," he requested huskily.

"D-do what?" she whispered shakily.

"Purr for me."

"I—"

Her voice broke as he caressed her with thumb and fingertips. He felt her fiery desire burning against his hand, and he quivered in response to her need. He saw passion flare in her eyes, felt her body calling to him, compelling him to become part of her. But Trey restrained his own hunger. He longed to bring Jennifer to the edge—again and again—to share her every response before he came to her.

"One last time, we'll share the kind of passion that can burn down both ends of the night," he whispered to her.

When he inserted two fingers inside her, Jennifer all but came apart in his arms. Wild, riveting sensations expanded, then contracted, until she forgot to breathe and could not remember why she should have to. His lips feathered over the throbbing tips of her breasts, her belly, her thighs. Jennifer cried out his name as his sensuous mouth hovered, his tongue flicking at her sensitive flesh.

Jennifer whispered unconditional love for Trey, certain these were the last words she would ever speak. She didn't think it possible to survive such indescribable pleasure, because each time he took her to a high plateau of ecstasy he stole another slice of her soul. There was nothing left of her but the wild, shimmering essence defined by his gentle, erotic touch. She had become what he made of her—an uncontrollable flame burning hot against the night, a flame that all the water in the river couldn't extinguish.

"Trey, please . . ." she gasped.

"I thought I was," he teased her.

"Yes, but I can't—"

Her words trailed off into a breathless moan when sensations so profound and intense channeled through every part of her being.

"The sun," he murmured as his lips grazed her thigh. "Did you find it, English?"

"No." Jennifer groaned in torment when his kisses and caresses drew another shivering response.

"No?" He felt the silky heat of her desire contracting around his fingertips, caressing him so sweetly, so secretively. "Are you sure?"

Jennifer stared at him, need so visible in her eyes that Trey groaned aloud.

"You are my sun," she assured him. "I can't find it without you. I love you . . ."

Trey was hopelessly lost. Entranced, he shifted Jennifer in his arms, gliding her legs around his hips. He saw the hint of a smile as she wrapped her legs around him and glided toward him. He smiled back as he bent to take her mouth at the exact moment he took her body—and lost his own existence.

The passion Trey had so valiantly held in check burst like the sparkling chips of a kaleidoscope—swirling, changing form, creating a new design with each penetrating thrust that sent ripples undulating around them. He felt an odd transformation claim him as desire catapulted him into infinity. This was far different from the kind of change he underwent while confronting ruthless outlaws. He felt like an eagle in flight, drifting on updrafts—diving, soaring, spiraling in splendor.

White-hot flames burned, consumed. Ecstasy sent him orbiting through space. He was suspended in a dimension of time where pleasure defied description. Trey muffled a wild cry that ached to fly free, but he feared the wolves would come running. He wanted no one else to see him as he was now—hopelessly consumed by sensations that nothing in his life had prepared him to defend against.

And later, when Jennifer whispered her love for him before she walked off into the darkness to bed down in the coach for the night, Trey told himself he was every kind of fool for creating a memory even more potent than the first time they made love.

In the lonely years to come, he knew he couldn't let himself remember what paradise was like, not without driving himself bloody, blooming mad . . .

Agatha came awake when Jennifer eased down quietly on the pallet. The duchess cursed under her breath, for she knew exactly what had detained her granddaughter. No bath took that long!

"Jen?"

Jennifer gritted her teeth. She had hoped to bed down without rousing her grandmother, but Jennifer obviously had not perfected the art of moving with the silence of a shadow. Only Trey had accomplished that amazing feat.

"Yes, Gram?"

Agatha rolled sideways to stare at Jennifer. "Just answer me one question."

"What question is that, Gram?"

"What the blazes can you possibly see in that man?"

Jennifer smiled wryly. "The sun, Gram. I see the sun."

For a long moment, Agatha stared into the lovely face that reminded her so much of Eleanor's. Drat it, Jennifer was as much the romantic as Eleanor had ever been.

Agatha shook her head in dismay and turned her back. She would permit the poor girl her silly fantasy for one more day. Then things would change drastically, because that annoying half-breed would be leaving—thank God! Agatha would find a suitable duke for Jennifer to marry. And when Three Wolves was out of sight, Agatha would do her level best to assure Jennifer that she was better off without that heathen.

This nonsense definitely had to stop! That mongrel heathen was not worthy of a blue-blooded aristocrat like Jennifer. She was meant for the glitter and glamour of English court life, and Agatha would see that she had it. Having Jennifer properly wed would become Agatha's new crusade. Not even the devil himself—who was presently prowling the night with his two bloodthirsty wolves as companions—was going to stop Agatha Reynolds, Grand Duchess of Calverdon!

Eleven

As Trey led the procession to Templeton Ranch, he noticed two separate groups of riders trying to remain inconspicuous by hiding in the arroyos and canyons that cut through West Texas. The wolves had picked up the scents, and Trey had watched three flocks of birds take to their wings when riders intruded into their domain.

Trey suspected Quincy Ward and Jonas Rafferty were keeping surveillance, because he had laid claim to the woman who owned the property both men coveted. And there was another sinister presence lurking in the distance—one that Trey had noted four days earlier. He had felt it since he and Jennifer left Dodge. That was why Trey scouted the route constantly. An old enemy had been trailing behind him.

Bob Yates hadn't given up his personal vendetta. Smart man, thought Trey. That wily desperado knew Trey hadn't forgotten about him. Seemed the last survivor of the Yates Gang had decided to strike before Trey struck. Yates was out there waiting for his chance to attack. Good—that would save Trey the trouble of tracking down the son of a bitch. Nothing like having all his ducks in a row, Trey mused as he stared into the distance.

From atop the stage, Trey saw Jawbone and Sunset riding out to meet Jennifer and her snobbish family. Several other wranglers had joined the welcome committee.

Trey spotted young Christopher Templeton instantly. The fifteen-year-old boy was the spitting image of his sister. The lanky lad had refined features that denoted his aristocratic breeding. Judging by Christopher's handsome features, Trey predicted the kid would be a lady-killer by age eighteen. With his deep, intense blue-violet eyes and lopsided smile, Christopher was also destined to become the duchess's pride and joy.

The prospect of young Christopher being shipped off to England with Agatha and Simpson put a scowl on Trey's face. The kid was doomed to be a dandy. Too bad. Trey would have liked to get his hands on him before the duchess sank in her royal claws.

"What the devil are you doing with a stage?" Jawbone questioned as he reined up beside Trey.

Trey hitched his thumb over his shoulder. "You've got guests on board, the kind who rent a stage for their own private use."

Jawbone frowned, bemused. "Visiting dignitaries, you mean?"

"Something like that," Trey grunted sourly. "Polish your manners, Jaw, or the Grand la-di-da Duchess of Calverdon will cut you to ribbons."

"The duchess is here?" Sunset wheezed, staring owl-eyed toward the window of the stagecoach.

Christopher straightened himself from his casual position on the saddle. "Gram is here?"

The kid didn't look all that thrilled, Trey noted. Apprehensive was more like it. It was just as Trey suspected. Dear old Grace had made a lasting impression on her grandson. No doubt, the old hag had nagged Christopher to death about his posture and manners when he paid his compulsory visits.

Agatha poked her head out the window and zeroed in on her grandson. "Good gad! Where are your proper clothes, boy? Don't tell me these cow servants have already corrupted you."

Christopher's smile vanished abruptly. The boy definitely

needed a man's guidance, not Agatha's churlish condescension. Trey made a mental note to draw the kid aside and teach him the kind of self-confidence and self-reliance needed to withstand his domineering granny.

When Sunset eased up beside the coach, Trey knew what the wrangler intended to ask before he even posed the question. Concern flickered in Sunset's hazel eyes and put a frown on his leathery features.

"English is her old self again," Trey assured Sunset quietly. "The worst is over and forgotten, so let's leave it at that."

Sunset's shoulders sagged in relief. "Thank God. After that ordeal with the Yates Gang—"

"Drop it, Sunset," Trey cut in, staring meaningfully at the concerned cowboy.

Sunset nodded his red head and reined around to convey the message to Jawbone, who tossed Trey a grateful smile. It was the last smile seen on the man's wrinkled face for several minutes. Agatha unleashed her criticism at the cluster of dusty cowboys who hadn't taken time to bathe and spruce themselves up before greeting Jennifer and her dignified family.

When Jawbone cast Trey a sidelong glance, unsure of how to take the cantankerous duchess, Trey grinned. "Charming lady, the duchess. I've encountered snakes with less venom."

Christopher overheard the comment and glanced up at Trey. Clear blue eyes wandered assessingly over Trey's breastplate and breechcloth. Oddly enough, Trey saw a little of himself in the boy. There were plenty of times when Trey had felt out of place—a stranger trying to fit into two worlds. Christopher was never going to be accepted by Westerners, not if his grandmother got her hooks into him. The kid had been in the States long enough to want to adapt—hence the Levis, red bandanna, and Stetson. But he needed guidance and Trey vowed he would have it.

Agatha wasn't going to stuff this kid into a frilly shirt and itchy breeches. Come to think of it, Trey suspected that's probably why those English dandies strutted.

When Trey chuckled at the thought, Christopher smiled at

him tentatively. Trey winked and gestured his head toward the coach. When Christopher glanced at his grandmother, she immediately ordered him not to slouch. But this time, Christopher's grin remained intact, because Trey encouraged him with a scampish smile.

Trey felt a natural affinity with the boy. Maybe it was because Trey was exceptionally partial to the kid's beautiful sister. Maybe it was because he felt Christopher looking to him for direction. Whatever the case, Trey intended to take the boy under his wing before he kept that damned Comanche promise to Jennifer and left the ranch. Their time together would be short, but productive, Trey vowed.

If the duchess realized what Trey was up to she would have a conniption. Let her . . . It would be worth a laugh.

When the coach rolled to a halt in front of the house, Jennifer bounded down—and found herself surrounded by loyal ranch hands who commiserated about the robbery. When Christopher dismounted, Jennifer rushed over to squeeze the stuffing out of him. At her quiet prompt, he removed his hat and walked over to assist the duchess from the stagecoach.

With Simpson leading the way, formally introducing the Duchess of Calverdon to the peasants, Agatha made her regal descent.

While Agatha held court on the front lawn, Trey hopped from his perch and called to the wolves. Apparently, Jawbone and Sunset had forewarned the ranch hands of Trey's arrival. The two cowboys had obviously put in a good word for Trey, because the wranglers greeted him respectfully. That was a switch. Trey was accustomed to being ignored or treated with wary trepidation.

While Agatha made her stately entrance into the three-story mansion on the plains, Simpson enlisted the assistance of several ranch hands to lug in the duchess's trunks and satchels. Simpson wasted no time in instructing the cowboys how to address the duchess. As for Trey, he had no intention of adhering to all the ''Your Graces'' and ''Her Graces'' that Simpson insisted upon. Trey enjoyed watching Agatha puff up like an offended toad when he treated her as his equal, not his better.

"Sir?"

Bookended by the wolves, Trey pivoted to see Christopher ambling cautiously toward him. When the wolves growled, the boy froze in his tracks.

"Do they bite?" he asked warily.

"Only grouchy duchesses," Trey said, grinning wryly. When he spoke to the wolves in Comanche, the animals trotted up to sniff Christopher's ankles. "They need to be fed. Would you care to join me while they hunt?"

Christopher perked up, then slouched. "Gram will expect me to join her for tea."

"I'll clear it with English."

"Who?"

"Your sister," Trey translated. "Knowing the duchess, it will take her a couple of hours to get settled in. She'll have to read the riot act to the household staff before she takes tea."

"How long have you known Gram?" Christopher questioned curiously.

"Too long," Trey mumbled as he untied his stallion from the rear of the coach. "Why don't you find some feed for Diablo while I speak to your sister."

"Yes, sir."

"And don't call me *sir*," Trey insisted. "The name is Trey, or Three Wolves, whichever you prefer, but keep the *sirs* to yourself, kid."

Christopher took the reins and stared at Trey pensively for a moment. "Is it true that you married my sister?"

"Yes. Any complaints?"

"No, s—" Christopher caught himself, then grinned. "No, I'm just a tad surprised is all."

"So was the duchess. Not enough spit and polish for her tastes."

Christopher snickered at he turned on his heels. "I will be in the barn with your stallion."

"I will be in the house with the witch and my wife."

Christopher burst out laughing as he ambled away. With the wolves at his heels, Trey hiked off to find Jennifer. He hoped he could bypass the witch.

No such luck.

"Get those mangy varmints out of this house!" Agatha howled. "And for God's sake, put on some decent clothes."

When Trey issued a quiet command, the wolves showed the fuming duchess their full set of teeth. Leaving Agatha backed into the corner, Trey strode off to find Jennifer. He poked his head inside three elegantly-furnished rooms before he located her in the downstairs bedroom. She was bustling around, rearranging furniture to accommodate Agatha's mountain of luggage.

Trey propped himself negligently against the doorjamb to watch Jennifer buzz here and there. "English?"

Jennifer wheeled around to stare at him. "You aren't leaving already, are you?"

"No, not yet. I just came by to tell you that Christopher is coming with me to feed the wolves."

"Christopher?" she repeated blankly.

"Your brother. You do remember him, don't you?"

Smiling, she picked up the rocking chair and repositioned it in the corner. "I remember him well. I only hope he is not making a nuisance of himself."

"No, I invited him along so I can get acquainted with my brother-in-law."

Jennifer eyed him dubiously. "And?"

"And what?"

"That is what I want to know."

Trey grinned broadly. "I'm going to corrupt him, of course. Grace will be outraged. Maybe you shouldn't tell her," he said as he pivoted to disappear down the hall.

Jennifer smiled at Trey's wry sense of humor, wishing with all her heart that she would have the rest of her life to encourage that playful side of his nature. But that simply could not be, not without putting Trey's life in jeopardy.

She did not doubt for one minute that Jonas Rafferty and

Quincy Ward were already making arrangements to dispose of her new husband. Jennifer could not bear the thought of Trey being gunned down like her father. She had to send Trey on his way before the leaders of the feud set their plans in motion.

"Is this to be my room?" Agatha questioned as she stepped into view.

"Yes, Gram." Jennifer frowned when she noticed her grandmother's face was the same color as the fresh white sheets she had placed on the bed. "What's wrong, Gram?"

"That infuriating husband of yours sicced his wolves on me," she burst out in bad temper. "Bloody, everlasting hell, Jen, when is that savage going to make himself scarce?"

"In a day or two, I expect. Trey intends to remain here just long enough for everyone in the area to realize that I actually have a husband."

Agatha flounced on the bed. "I suppose I can endure, if I must. Now let me rest," she said, dismissing Jennifer with a flick of her wrist. "It has been a long, trying journey. After I recuperate for a few days, we will return to England where we all belong."

"Gram—"

"Do not argue with me," Agatha broke in. "I have made up my mind." With that grand declaration, Agatha rolled over and fell into an exhausted sleep.

Under the pretense of letting the wolves hunt game, Trey scouted the pastures and canyons on the ranch. The wild tumble of ravines carved into the High Plains were a spectacular sight, with their caprocks of reddish-brown mudstone. Above the reddish layers, known as "Spanish skirts", were various shades of orange, green, and brown sandstone. Stone-gray escarpments made an eye-catching foreground against the backdrop of endless blue sky.

Templeton Ranch, with its panoramic view dotted with cedars, junipers, and cottonwoods, was truly a marvelous sight to behold, Trey mused. It was little wonder that Rafferty and Ward coveted this sprawling property—and its bewitching heir.

He made note of the partially-fenced path that led to Sweetwater Creek, where neighboring cattle herds quenched their thirst when water was scarce during droughts. He also noticed the stretches of fence that had been clipped, then patched after rustlers had come and gone.

"Are you really as good with a gun and knife as Jawbone and Sunset say you are?" Christopher blurted out as he followed in Trey's footsteps.

"Good enough, kid."

"Would you show me how to use those weapons?" Christopher asked eagerly.

This was the opportunity Trey had hoped for. Retrieving his dagger, he placed it in the boy's hand. After a few basic instructions Christopher hurled the knife—and struck the nearby tree. While Christopher beamed with pride, Trey instructed him on the finer points of handling the weapon.

Trey wasn't surprised the kid was an easy teach. Christopher was as bright and quick-witted as his sister. Lanky though the boy was, he possessed quick reflexes. Trey discovered that when he taught the kid a few hand-to-hand combat tactics.

Christopher's eagerness to learn and his natural ability combined to show great promise. Although Trey's size, stature, and superior strength made it difficult for Christopher to compete, the kid bounded back to his feet each time Trey cut his legs out from under him.

"I would give anything to be as skilled as you are," Christopher said, panting for breath. "How do you keep upending me when I know what you are going to do before you do it?"

Trey walked Christopher through the moves in slow motion, indicating vulnerable points on the body that could be preyed upon, if needed. Things were going splendidly until Christopher tried one of his new moves—and caught Trey in the groin rather than the underbelly. Trey went to his knees, gasping for breath.

"I'm sorry!" Christopher apologized frantically. "I didn't mean to—"

Trey held up his hand for silence as he sucked much-needed air. "That was lesson number four," he choked out. "You just got a little ahead of yourself, kid. When all else fails, hit a man where he can be hurt the worst."

"My sister will never forgive me for injuring you there—" Christopher's face flamed bright red when he realized what he had said.

Trey chuckled as he staggered to his feet. "You know about such things already, do you, Chris?"

The boy blushed profusely. "I have watched livestock breed, after all. I am not totally ignorant. Besides, the cowhands talk about their visits to the brothels in Mobeetie. I figure my time is coming pretty quick. I could use some advice—man to man, if you don't mind. So . . . what is it like?"

Trey blushed for the first time in living memory. "Don't ask, kid. You're too young to know."

"I will be sixteen next month."

"Good for you, but you're still too damned young."

"How old were you the first time?" Christopher persisted.

Damn, Trey had planned to teach the boy self-defense, not give a dissertation about the birds and bees. But then, he reminded himself that, until very recently, Jennifer had not known a thing about sex and she wasn't in a position to answer her brother's questions.

"I was older than fifteen," Trey said belatedly.

"How old?" Christopher wanted to know.

"Thirty."

"Thirty?" Christopher gaped at Trey as if he had antlers sprouting from his head.

"I was thirty before I discovered the difference between sex and lovemaking," Trey elaborated, shifting awkwardly from one foot to the other. "If you're smart, you'll wait until you know the difference instead of fumbling around with meaningless flings like I did."

Christopher eyed him perceptively. "So you are saying you are in love with my sister."

Trey retrieved the pistol and knife that had fallen by the wayside. Damn, the kid was as relentless as his sister. "That's none of your business. What's between a man and his wife is personal, so don't ask." He placed the Colt in the kid's hand and said, "Time for target practice."

"On the birds and bees?"

When Christopher grinned playfully, Trey swallowed a smile. "Smart-ass remarks like that will get you in dutch with the duchess. She thinks I'm a bad influence."

Christopher raised his arm and stared down the sight on the pearl-handled Colt. "I am going to grow up to be just like you, even if Gram doesn't approve."

Trey felt a strange knot coiling in his gut. No one ever wanted to be like him. Hell, he never considered himself a worthy role model—least of all for an aristocratic kid with a blue-blooded pedigree as long as his arm.

"Christopher, there are things you don't understand about me. Not many people do. You don't know what I become when—"

The boy lowered his pistol when Trey hesitated. The look in the kid's eyes held the kind of admiration and respect that nearly knocked Trey's legs out from under him.

"Jawbone and Sunset said you were more man than they have ever met. My sister must think so, too, or she would not have married you. No one else around here has taken time to teach me to take care of myself. The ranch hands treat me like a child, always watching out for me, and all."

He nodded his blond head and his lips compressed into a determined line that reminded Trey of Jennifer. "Yes, sir, I am going to be as bloody competent as you are one day. Just see if I'm not."

Trey dropped the subject and concentrated on teaching Christopher to aim and fire in one fluid motion. Christopher caught on quickly, emulating Trey's skills with smooth precision. Trey marveled at the boy's adeptness. He could imagine how Agatha would react when she learned Trey had instructed her grandson. The thought made him grin devilishly. Annoying Agatha had become one of his favorite pastimes. He derived wicked satisfaction in ruffling that old dowager's royal feathers.

"Where the blazes is my grandson?" Agatha demanded as she sank down at the table for the evening meal.

"Christopher is doing his chores," Jennifer hedged, shaking out her napkin. "We will proceed without him."

"Chores?" Agatha sniffed distastefully. "Really, Jen, that boy should not lower himself to menial tasks. He was bred to command, not tackle the work itself."

"Cattle ranching demands involvement," Jennifer explained as she watched the ever-present Simpson scurry over to pass Agatha the bowl of fried potatoes. "The reason many of the British syndicated ranchers in Texas have faltered is because of their lack of participation. One poor chap discovered, too late, that his foreman was stealing him blind. He was forced to sell out, because his investors received no profit. Quincy Ward took over the ranch when Sir Charles Lindamen returned to England with his tail tucked between his legs."

"Sir Charles?" Agatha blinked. "Why, to hear him tell it, he was doing a smashing good job, but he tired of the dust and blizzards and craved the civilized society of his native homeland."

Jennifer shook her head. "Sir Charles should write fiction. The truth is that his highhanded manners rubbed his ranch hands the wrong way. He made it clear that Britishers and Westerners did not think the same way or speak the same language. Charles refused to mingle with his hired help, or the other ranchers, because he considered them beneath him. His cowboys began mavericking calves right under his nose. They drove the cattle to the stockyards and sold them. Charles never knew what happened to his missing cattle. He never had a clue that his own foreman was in charge of rustling stock and dispersing the money equally among the ranch hands."

"Well, young Christopher will not have to fret about that sort of thing," Agatha said as she munched on the potatoes. "I will see that he is enrolled in the finest schools so he can complete his formal education."

"Formal education?" a voice howled from the doorway.

Agatha swiveled in her chair to see her grandson poised beside that pesky, half-naked half-breed. Ignoring the brawny giant, Agatha motioned Christopher to take his seat.

"Of course, m'boy. I am taking you and your sister to England. We will be leaving after I recuperate from the long trip."

Christopher's shocked gaze flew to Jennifer. "You are leaving your husband behind? But I thought—"

"Come sit down, Christopher," Agatha ordered—as only Agatha could.

"I'm not hungry," he muttered before he lurched around and stalked outside, leaving Agatha staring at him, open-mouthed.

"Damn it to hell," Christopher scowled as he stared up at the vast expanse of night sky.

"I was about your age when the Army shipped me off from the Comanche reservation to be schooled in Pennsylvania," Trey murmured from out of nowhere.

Startled, Christopher spun around. "How do you do that?"

"Do what?"

"Appear from nowhere." He glanced at the ominous shadow lurking by the door, then stared at the wolves that bounded onto the porch to sit at Trey's heels.

"Old Comanche trick," Trey said with a chuckle.

"I bloody well wish I knew how to do it," Chris grumbled. "I would disappear into thin air so Gram couldn't pack me off to London. I was uprooted and toted off to Texas and it took me years to adjust. Now Gram wants to do it all over again. Hell's teeth, I am never going to figure out where I belong. And blast it, I have enough education to suit me already."

"I had plenty of education myself," Trey mused aloud. "But not the kind the government thought a Comanche boy needed. The Indian schoolmaster whacked off my hair and stuffed me into a suit, taught me to read and write, and tried to convince me that white men knew best.''

''Did you adjust?''

Trey barked a laugh. ''Do I look like I did?''

''Half way,'' Christopher replied. ''I won't fare much better. I like it here in Texas. I don't want to go back to England.''

Trey knew it was a waste of time to sulk. Besides, he had things to do and he needed Christopher's assistance. Trey's evening plans would take the kid's mind off the dear ole duchess's announcement.

''Come on, kid,'' Trey said as he strode off the porch. ''Saddle your horse. I have an errand to do and I need you to give me directions.''

Christopher eagerly followed Trey into the barn, imitating his long, swaggering strides. ''I really like you, Trey, I really do,'' Christopher murmured as he saddled his mount.

Trey chuckled quietly. ''I like you, too, kid. But don't let your grandmother know we're friends. She'd have a fit of the vapors.''

''Good, then I can sneak off before she totes me to England. I am not going and that's that. I like it just fine where I am.''

Trey made a pact with himself, there and then, to resolve the problems at the ranch so Christopher and Jennifer could remain where they were without fearing for their lives and their property. This was one job Trey planned to complete. Even though this could never be his home, he wanted Jennifer on the same continent, needed to know she was safe. As for Agatha, she could hightail it back to England—and stay there!

Jonas Rafferty returned from his late-night rendezvous with his rival, Quincy Ward. Until today, Jonas wasn't sure Quincy was telling him the truth, but Jonas had seen Three Wolves with his own eyes, and he cringed at the memories of that day sixteen years earlier when he had first encountered the half-breed. The memory stood out vividly in his mind, and Jonas wondered how Three Wolves would react if he discovered Jonas was in the area. Jonas doubted Three Wolves had forgotten his visit to Texas those many years ago. Damn, of all the men in the country, why did Jennifer have to marry that man!

Jonas strode into the barn to unsaddle his horse. He yelped in surprise when he was slammed up against a steel-hard body and felt a dagger prick his throat. Sweet Jesus, Jennifer must have mentioned Jonas's name to Three Wolves!

"Long time no see, Jonas Rafferty," Trey growled down his neck.

"What do you want?" Jonas squeaked.

"Information about the death of Ramsey Templeton will do for starters."

"I didn't do it!" Jonas squawked.

Christopher Templeton lurked in the shadows of the barn while Trey pounced with the silence of a wolf. Christopher didn't have a clue why Trey asked him to lead the way to Rafferty's farm, and he hadn't realized these two men knew each other, either. But there was no mistaking the deadly menace in Trey's voice—or Jonas's terrified reaction.

If there was one thing to be said about Trey it was that he wasted no time in his fact-finding. He used unique, abrupt methods to dig up the truth.

"Don't lie to me," Trey hissed, pricking the underside of Jonas's chin. "You ought to know by now that I would just as soon slit your worthless throat as look at you. You know how we Comanches are—bloodthirsty bastards with no morals, no conscience."

"I was just a kid myself when you came to find my mama," Jonas chirped, afraid to move for fear he would end up holding his severed head in his hands. "I only did what she told me to do!"

"And you enjoyed doing it, didn't you?" Trey snarled.

Christopher shrank deeper into the shadows—watching, listening. He could understand why Jonas was quaking in his boots. There was something utterly terrifying about Three Wolves when he was on the attack. It was in the strange resonance of his voice, his crouched stance, that supernatural aura that swirled around him like a black, hazy cloud.

Christopher shook off the unnerving sensations. Lord, he would like to intimidate his bossy grandmother like that! Maybe she would back off and leave him in Texas where he wanted to stay.

"Look, Three Wolves, if you came to settle old scores—" Jonas's voice dried up when the edge of the blade sliced across his skin.

"If you'll provide the answers I want, I'll overlook old grudges. You decide if you want to live or die. It doesn't make a damn to me."

"I didn't kill Ramsey, I swear to God I didn't," Jonas wheezed. "I'll admit I've clipped a few fences, stole a few head of cattle and discouraged some of Jennifer's suitors, but I didn't kill the old man."

"Then who did?"

"I don't know. It could have been anybody. It could have been a mistake, but I didn't make it!"

Trey didn't release his vise-like grip on Jonas. He wanted to make double damn sure he was getting the truth. There was nothing worse than not knowing your enemy. Men got killed when they made that mistake. If Jonas was guilty, Trey wasn't cutting him any slack whatsoever.

"How well do you know Quincy Ward?" Trey demanded.

"Good enough not to like the sneaky bastard."

"Then why were you meeting with him tonight?"

Jonas gulped, and Trey felt the shiver of apprehension skitter down Jonas's spine.

"Setting traps, Jonas?" Trey hissed in his ear. "For me perhaps?"

"I—"

"Careful what you say." Trey slid the blade along the pulsating column of Jonas's throat. "I've been in the bounty hunting business long enough to detect a lie when I hear one. It won't be the words I'll be listening and reacting to. It will be the body language you can't control. In fact, it's like reading braille.

I can feel the truth, Jonas. Be very sure that's what you're giving me.''

Jonas was scared stiff! He had heard gruesome tales of this legendary gunslinger—and there was this old grudge between them, too. With each prick of the blade, Jonas saw another phase of his life buzz past his eyes. If he gave the wrong answer he was a dead man.

"Quincy got in touch with me the day he returned from Dodge with the news that you planned to marry Jennifer. He thought we should join forces to dispose of you," Jonas explained.

"Go on," Trey demanded, tightening his grasp.

"We were keeping surveillance on you so we can pick you off when you least expect it."

"Whose idea was it?" Trey's voice was as sharp as the steel of his dagger. "Yours or Quincy's?"

"His. I didn't know you planned to marry Jennifer until he told me. He sent me a message to meet him at Cutthroat Gap two days ago. Quincy had it all planned out and asked for my help."

"You're a fool, Jonas," Trey hissed in his ear. "Don't you know a set-up when you hear one?"

Jonas blinked. "What do you mean?"

"Who do you suppose will be singled out to take the rap for my murder? Quincy will point an accusing finger at you and send out his hired guns to capture you. You'd be lucky if you make it to jail alive. Once Quincy's rival, and Jennifer's unwanted husband, are out of the way, Quincy will have exactly what he wants. From what I've learned from Sunset and Jawbone, the big-time rancher is good at that sort of thing.

"If you're going to make any deals, I suggest you try to make one with me. I'm a helluva lot more straightforward and to the point than Quincy Ward."

"What am I going to get out of this deal?" Jonas asked.

"You get to live. You will also be granted rights to water at Sweetwater Creek during dry spells. Quincy will be allowed the same option, if he isn't responsible for Ramsey Templeton's death. If he is, he'll answer to me. Now, do we have a deal, Jonas?''

"Yes."

"Thought so." Trey moved like streak lightning. By the time Jonas stumbled forward, the pearl-handled Colt rested in Trey's free hand.

Hands held high above his head, Jonas turned around—very slowly. It was then that he noticed the dark figure in the corner of his barn. "Who's with you?"

"My witness or my alibi, whichever I need," Trey replied. "In case you get shot, I'll have someone to corroborate that I wasn't at your barn this fateful night. If I let you walk out of here alive, I'll have a witness who can testify to this conversation and present the evidence to proper officials. Problem is, you won't know who my witness is."

Jonas scowled. "You're a real bastard, Three Wolves."

"A *live* bastard," Trey clarified. "I didn't get that way by accident. I've learned not to trust folks who would shoot me in the back if I gave them the chance."

Jonas kept his hands held high. "All right, Three Wolves, what do you want me to do?"

"Play along with Quincy for the time being. I'll make it easy for him to monitor my activities. When he decides when the ambush will take place, you'll deliver the message to me at the line camp shack three miles north of Templeton Ranch." Trey took a menacing step closer, looming over Jonas like a thundercloud. "If you double-cross me, it will be the last thing you ever do. You understand, don't you, Jonas?"

Jonas nodded grimly.

"Not good enough. Say the words, Jonas, I want to hear if you actually mean what you say."

"You have my word. I'll get the message to you as soon as I know when Quincy plans to make his move. But it may be a while."

"No, it won't," Trey contradicted. "I intend to become very visible and predictable." He gestured his pistol toward the

entrance of the barn. "Now, why don't you go to the house
and take a load off your feet."

Jonas did as he was told, and he never looked back. The
way he had it figured he was damned lucky to walk out of the
barn alive. Three Wolves was one deadly predator who wasn't
known for his compassion.

Twelve

Christopher kept his mouth shut for the first mile of the return trip to Templeton Ranch. Obviously, that was as long as the boy's curiosity allowed, Trey decided.

"Do you really think Jonas was telling the truth about my father's death? He could have lied to save his own neck, you know."

"He could have," Trey agreed. "But I don't think he did."

"How can you be so certain?"

"It's a gut feeling that comes with experience. Some things you just know, even if you aren't sure how you know it."

"A hunch," Christopher paraphrased. "Did your hunch have anything to do with the grudge you mentioned?"

"Yes." Trey gnashed his teeth. He had the unmistakable feeling the inquisitive Christopher was going to pry into his past. And maybe it was time Trey dealt with some of those deep-seated emotions. If Jonas did try to double-cross him, Christopher needed evidence and background information to make sure Jonas stood trial.

"How do you know Jonas Rafferty, when you didn't know where he lived?"

"He's my cousin."

"What?" Christopher hooted. "You really would have cut your own cousin's throat?"

"Why not? He once tried to slice off my hide with a butcher knife."

Trey spoke quietly to the wolves, sending them trotting off to scout the unfamiliar area—just in case Jonas decided to bushwhack him first chance he got. "When my mother was killed during an Indian massacre in New Mexico, she made me promise to find her family in Texas, hoping they would take me in so I wouldn't have to be confined to the reservation. I sneaked away while the soldiers were counting bodies and gathering prisoners. I trekked east across *Llana Estacado* until I reached the family farm near Fort Griffin."

"Was that where your white mother lived before she was captured by the Comanches?"

Trey nodded slightly. "My mother was still living with her parents at the farm when she was abducted by my father's raiding party. Her older sister, Rachael, had recently married Silas Rafferty. The two of them had ridden off to the sutler's store at the fort to gather supplies. My mother never knew that her parents had been slaughtered. It was Rachael who found the mutilated bodies that night.

"When I came to Texas to seek refuge with my white grand-parents, I encountered my aunt. She came at me with a knife, and when I knocked it away, she screamed at Jonas to attack me. Jonas managed to take a few ounces out of my hide while Rachael hurled things across the room and screeched like a banshee."

"My God," Christopher whispered.

"Yeah, it was one helluva family reunion," Trey agreed. "Although I managed to run from the house, I lost a lot of blood because of the knife wound and passed out. Jonas rode to the fort to inform the troops. I was hauled to the reservation to heal before I was shipped off to school in the East. I have Jonas and his loony mother to thank for the scar on my belly and my indoctrination into white society."

"I'm sorry," Christopher murmured. "I guess I sounded like a spoiled child when I complained about being uprooted and dragged back to England. Compared to being attacked by your own family, I guess I don't have it so bad."

"None of that matters now," Trey said coldly. "I can't change the past and neither can you. It's the future we have to think about." He flashed the lad a quick glance. "And speaking of the future, I don't want you to breathe a word about any of tonight's events or conversations to your sister. I don't want to be peppered with questions from English. She has a tendency to try to fix things, and I don't want her involved in this."

Christopher frowned thoughtfully. "Just why are you risking your life to find my father's murderer and resolve this feud?"

"Because that's what I'm paid to do, and that's what I do best."

"My sister paid you to find my father's killer?" Christopher queried, stunned. "But what about your marriage?"

"It's a long story."

"It's a long ride to our ranch."

Trey sighed audibly. "Damn, kid, did anyone ever tell you that you ask too many questions?"

"No."

"Well, you do. All you need to know is that English and I have a private arrangement."

"Right, and I am not supposed to wonder how you really feel about my sister," Christopher grumbled. "Well, I've got a hunch you care about Jen. If you didn't, you wouldn't risk your hide to find my father's killer and keep the peace so we can retain our property."

"You also talk too damned much, kid," Trey muttered.

"That is because Jawbone took me under his wing when my father died."

"That explains it. Little wonder how the crusty old cowboy came by his nickname."

"Trey?"

"Now what?" he said, exasperated.

"You may consider me a nuisance, but I am honored to have you as my brother-in-law."

"Too bad most of my acquaintances don't share your opinion."

"My sister does," Christopher contended. "I can tell. If a woman ever looks at me the way she looks at you, I hope the bloody hell I know what to do about it. And I would, if someone would take the time to explain how to go about dealing with girls—"

"We are not discussing your prospective love life right now," Trey snapped, grinning in spite of himself. No doubt about it, Christopher was every bit as persistent as his sister.

"When then? If you are waiting until I get those urges, it's too late. I already have them."

Trey groaned aloud. "Well hell, what is it you want to know?"

Christopher proceeded to pose questions in specific detail. Trey was thankful for the darkness of night. If the heat in his face was any indication of the effect Christopher's pointed questions had on him, Trey suspected his complexion had turned crimson.

But he did answer Christopher's intimately personal questions. Trey was probably giving Agatha another reason to despise him—not that she needed more reason, or that he cared. Trey wasn't the least bit fond of the old prig and her Old World conventionalism.

Jennifer paced the parlor, then paused to glance at the grandfather clock in the corner. Muttering, she paced some more. It was a quarter past midnight, and Trey and Christopher had not returned from wherever they had gone.

Agatha and Simpson had collapsed in bed hours ago, and the servants had retired for the night. Jennifer was the only one keeping vigil. She told herself everything was fine, but shadows of doubt were clouding her customary optimism. Surely Jonas or Quincy had not swooped down like vultures to—

The creak of the front door sent Jennifer lurching around. She was poised to rush to greet her brother, but something stopped her when Christopher stepped into the lighted hallway. He seemed different. There was a new confidence about the boy since he had spent the afternoon and evening with Trey. My Lord! She had predicted Trey would have a positive influence, but she had not expected such an immediate change.

Then Jennifer reminded herself of how quickly Trey had healed her spirits and soothed her fears after her ordeal with the Yates Gang. In less than two days he had restored her optimism and taught her to trust again.

"Sorry I'm late, Jen," Chris apologized as he swept his hat from his blond head. "And I'm sorry I lost my temper with Gram."

"Gram can be very trying," Jennifer conceded. "I considered strangling her myself a couple of times this evening. Luckily, Simpson was here to protect her." She eyed her brother curiously. "Why were you out so late?"

"I was learning to be a man," he said, sporting an enigmatic grin.

While he swaggered up the steps, Jennifer appraised him curiously. When she turned around, Trey was looming directly behind her. Jennifer blinked, startled. It was a constant marvel that a man of Trey's size and stature could move like a disembodied spirit when he wanted to.

Desire hit Trey like a doubled fist as he stared down at Jennifer. The lamplight spotlighted her unbound hair, making it glow like a river of honey. Her flimsy nightgown did more to entice than conceal, and Trey found himself looking through the sheer fabric to savor her luscious curves. This woman, with the body of a siren and the face of an angel, was absolutely irresistible.

Trey stood there telling himself he should make camp on the perimeters of the ranch and establish a predictable routine to deceive his enemies, but throbbing need played hell with his common sense. He was fully aware that he had never made

love to his new wife in a real bed. At the moment he could
think of nothing he wanted to do more.

"What have you been doing, Trey?" Jennifer questioned as
she reached up on tiptoe to press her lips to his.

"Wanting you," he said huskily.

The comment made Jennifer smile in satisfaction. There was
that, at least, she consoled herself. *Wanting* might be as close
as a man like Trey ever came to actually loving her. And after
a frustrating evening with Agatha and her staunchly devoted
butler, Jennifer was anxious to forget everything except the
feel of those sinewy arms around her.

Just once more, Jennifer prayed silently. *God, grant me just
one more sweet memory with this incredible man before he goes
away. Let me love him once again—for always and forever.*

Trey framed Jennifer's enchanting face in his hands and met
her unblinking gaze. At first touch, he felt powerful sensations
pounding through his blood. "Damn, English, I never thought
it possible to starve to death for the want of a woman."

The humbling admission was well worth the radiant smile
Jennifer bestowed on him. She gave in to him so generously,
so sweetly, that Trey had to brace himself against the emotional
blow that turned his scarred heart into putty.

"I love you," she whispered softly and sincerely. "I will
always love you. That is the one constant in your unpredictable
life that you can depend on."

Trey muffled a groan as his mouth came down on hers,
drinking her response like a desperate man quenching his thirst.
Damnation, this lovely aristocrat was tearing him apart. He
didn't want to hear those words of love, because he was a non-
believer. But whether Jennifer's love was real or imagined, he
had heard those three little words so often lately that his resolve
was starting to crumble. He was letting her get to him. *Letting*
her, he reminded himself. He knew better than to nurture a
vulnerability, a delusion. It could become suicidal.

Well, he would risk the dangers for just one more night in
her arms, he decided. He would share one last night with her,
then put her out of his mind and concentrate on resolving her

problems. He would feed this fire—gorge himself in it. He would get Jennifer completely out of his system this one last night.

Funny, Trey thought as he scooped Jennifer up in his arms and tread quietly up the steps. He swore he had said the same thing each time he had made love to her. It was beginning to sound like *famous last words*.

The wolves padded at Trey's heels as he reached the landing. He stifled a groan when Jennifer's fingers combed through his mussed hair, when she smiled up at him in sensual promise. He wanted her in bed now—touching her, cherishing her until he couldn't tell where his body ended and hers began.

Impatiently, Trey veered into the room at the top of the stairs. It was a mental miscalculation on his part. If he were living in this house, his room would be atop the mountain of steps—like a guard tower where he could see all that went on around him.

"That's—" Jennifer closed her mouth and blushed to the roots of her hair when Trey opened the wrong bedroom door—to find Christopher standing barefoot and bare-chested.

Trey inwardly groaned at the picture he presented to his fifteen-year-old brother-in-law, whose urges they had recently discussed—in extensive detail. Trey felt his face flush when he met Chris's knowing grin. Damn, he could see the kid speculating on everything he and Jennifer were about to do.

"Jen's suite is the second door on the left," Christopher directed, grinning broadly. "I did not realize my sister had sprained her ankle and had to be carried to her room."

Without a word, Trey pivoted around and strode down the hall—the wolves were still at his heels. He stopped in his tracks when he opened the door to survey the spacious room. Trey had never seen anything so elegant and yet cozy, never visualized himself in such resplendent surroundings.

Masterfully crafted walnut furniture graced the sitting room that opened into the bedroom. A lantern flickered invitingly beside the canopy bed. It was like walking into a lavender-tinted paradise. The elegantly furnished room contrasted with everything Trey was. It was too lush and refined for such a rugged, earthy man. Jennifer was too sophisticated and well-bred for him, too. He knew that—he just kept ignoring it because of his obsessive desire.

When Jennifer left his arms, Trey retreated apace. He knew he should leave. He was only feeding her fantasies, as well as his own. He should make it known to Christopher that he hadn't spent the night here. He should . . .

The feel of gentle hands unfastening his bead-and-bone breastplate caused his good intentions to take a flying leap out the second-story window. The feel of her fingertips tripping lightly down his chest caused desire to throb heavily in his lower extremities. When Jennifer's palm glided down his belly. Trey realized that what he should do, and what he was going to do, did not coincide. He listened to the insistent calling of his aroused body and ignored the sensible urgings of his brain.

Jennifer sensed Trey's hesitation. She knew what he was thinking while he appraised the room Ramsey Templeton had designed for his young daughter who had been whisked away from English refinement to the wide-open range of Texas. But Jennifer refused to let Trey leave, as he had promised—without reassuring him that her love was not a whimsical fantasy. He would stay this last night with her—in this house, in her room. If she could not earn his love, she would have at least this much from him.

"I haven't thanked you properly for what you did, however it was that you managed to do it," Jennifer murmured as she drew feathery circles around Trey's nipples.

"What did I do?" Trey asked, his voice wobbling noticeably.

"You made a man of the boy in the course of a day," Jennifer replied as her fingertips skied over sleek, masculine flesh. "But I daresay, I am not surprised. You made a woman of me in one night."

When she peeked up at him through long, sooty lashes and smiled impishly, Trey felt his legs turn to marmalade. Every time she grinned at him like that he was lost.

When her hand drifted over the washboarded muscles of his

belly to unfasten his breechcloth, he knew he wasn't going anywhere except to that delirious world of sheer passion. She was simply irresistible. Hadn't she wrested a Comanche promise from him, even when he had no intention of giving it?

Trey was always lost at first touch, first kiss. This fire Jennifer ignited inside him was too intense to be denied—or controlled. She was the kind of woman who destroyed his strength of will—and made him like it.

When she slid her hand into his and led him to bed, Trey went with one thought in mind: after tonight, only distance would save him from being entangled in her silly fantasy. She wanted him to believe in everlasting love, though he knew better. His mother had never loved the Comanche warrior who abducted her. Glenna MacTavish had tolerated and endured because of Trey. But when he was with Jennifer she made him believe in forbidden dreams come true.

Trey felt himself stepping over the threshold into an unfamiliar culture. He was surrounded by keepsakes from an unknown world beyond the sea. All of England's elegant finery was in this room—porcelain trinkets, priceless treasures that had once belonged to Jennifer's mother. But when Trey stared at Jennifer, he stopped noticing that he was completely out of his element, stopped comparing himself to fancy dukes with blue-blooded pedigrees.

When Jennifer pivoted in front of him to unfasten her gown, letting it flutter to the floor in a pool of daffodil-colored silk, Trey felt his heart stampede around his chest. He beheld Jennifer's astonishing beauty, knowing that he alone had been granted the privilege of holding her, savoring her, loving her.

Another bittersweet memory to torment me in days to come, Trey thought to himself as he watched Jennifer stretch out on the satin sheets in this palatial room. Whenever he closed his eyes he was positively certain he would see Jennifer lying there with that mass of silky blond hair flowing across the pillow where he once slept, her eyes shining up at him like amethyst stars. He would remember every last moment of tonight—and he would be aching all over.

Heaven, Trey mused. And being anywhere else was going to be hell. But he should be accustomed to that by now, shouldn't he? Hell just hadn't been such sweet, maddening torture until now—until Jennifer.

She leaned over to douse the lantern, and Trey found himself instinctively moving toward her. He longed to hold this beguiling beauty in his arms, to feel her petal-soft lips opening to his hungry kiss. He wanted her so badly that his hands shook as he reached out to her.

In fact, he wanted her so damned bad that his need shook the whole damned bed—or so he thought. When Jennifer burst out laughing, Trey blinked. Then he heard the heavy panting that could have been his—but wasn't. Trey swiveled around to see his wolves poised on the foot of the bed. Damn, he had forgotten about them. It seemed they were as eager for a taste of luxury as he was.

At Trey's brusque command, the wolves dropped their heads, bounded to the floor, and slinked into the sitting room. The matched pair plunked down on the carpet in the doorway and stared up at Trey like whipped pups. Muttering, Trey rolled off the bed to shut the door.

Jennifer's amused giggle met him halfway across the room. "I think they envy our soft bed." She stretched sensuously as Trey came back to her.

He groaned when Jennifer struck a seductive pose and smiled invitingly at him. He couldn't rejoin her fast enough to suit himself. He wanted to devour her, but he refused to give in to lusty impatience, not when this was his final good-bye. He wanted to savor each tender sensation, to pleasure Jennifer— and himself—slowly, thoroughly.

Trey began by pressing his lips to hers, tasting her fully before his kisses skimmed her jaw to hover over the accelerated pulse beat in her throat. His hands glided over the taut crests of her breasts and descended to swirl over the flat plane of her stomach.

Jennifer's quiet sigh was all the encouragement he needed. When she whispered his name and arched toward his hungry mouth and roaming hands, his control slipped another notch. When her fingertips folded around the place where he was most a man, stroking him, teasing a silvery drop of desire from him, Trey knew his willpower would never last.

Jennifer was coaxing him to her with an urgency his body eagerly answered. She was driving him, overpowering him with her gentle touch. Wanting her was becoming such a tangible thing that Trey felt himself reaching out, reaching deep within himself, to give her all of what she made of him when he was with her . . .

That was the last thought to skid through his mind before he felt his body glide over hers, felt himself become the wild flame burning inside her, for her, because of her. He heard her name tumble from his lips as she took him over the edge into mindless oblivion. He felt the all-encompassing powers of passion surging over him like a rolling tide.

He heard the howl of the wolf echoing through his soul as ecstasy claimed him—and her—simultaneously.

"Again . . ." Jennifer whispered as she moved evocatively beneath him, generating energy when Trey swore there was nothing left of him.

"How do you do this to me?" Trey asked raggedly as he propped up on his forearms to peer down into that exquisite face.

She smiled adoringly as she traced his lips with her forefinger. Gently, she brought his head back to hers. "When? When I fell in love with you. How? Because I love you. Again, Trey, love me once more before you go away . . ."

Trey groaned when her velvety lips melted beneath his. He felt his body clench with renewed desire. He made love to her as if there was no tomorrow. And in the darkest hour before dawn, while Jennifer slept peacefully beside him, Trey marshaled the will to leave her bed. He said his silent farewell to Jennifer and her fantasies of dashing knights and love everlasting. But Trey hadn't realized how empty and alone he would feel . . . until he walked away.

It was as if he had left his very soul behind. He hadn't even

thought he had a soul left, not after dozens of treks through
hell to battle its resident demons. But Trey had a soul, all right.
Oddly enough, he had discovered that—just in time to lose the
very essence of what he was to a woman who was everything
he could ever want ... and far more than a man like him
deserved.

Jennifer awoke, feeling an aching emptiness in the pit of her
stomach. She turned her head to see a pale yellow rose lying on
the pillow where Trey had slept. Although he did not consider
himself the least bit romantic, Jennifer found his farewell gift
so touching that it brought tears to her eyes.

A hound from hell, they called him? The dark angel of
vengeance? No, Jennifer assured herself as she lightly traced
the thorn that accompanied the elegant beauty of the wild rose.
For, like the rose, Trey could be fierce or gentle, depending
upon what part of him people wanted to see. Most folks saw
him as the prickly thorn, but there was far more to the man—
something beautiful, something deserving of love and devotion.

Over and over, Jennifer consoled herself by remembering
that Trey's leaving would keep him safe from harm. Yet, all
Jennifer's optimistic pep talks didn't soothe the longing inside
her. She already missed his dynamic presence in her life—and
he'd only been gone a few hours.

Agatha, on the other hand, was delighted to rouse at a late
morning hour to note that the half-breed had taken his devil
stallion and ridden off into the sunrise. Agatha had stated,
innumerable times, that Jennifer was better off without her ill-
bred, discourteous husband underfoot.

When Agatha insisted on taking the rented stagecoach to
Mobeetie, Jennifer enlisted two cowboys to accompany Gram
and Simpson to town. Jennifer predicted Gram would enjoy the
bustling activities that centered around court week in Mobeetie.

The frontier town—the first community established in the
Texas Panhandle—had once been a buffalo hunter's camp
known as Hidetown. Now, Mobeetie was the headquarters for

the thirty-fifth judicial district. The community was the home base for the District Judge and District Attorney responsible for dispensing justice in the twenty-six panhandle counties. The law officials traveled to Tascosa and Clarendon, then returned to mete out sentences to the unruly riffraff and drunken, disorderly soldiers from nearby Fort Elliot.

Although gamblers and drifters gave the community a reputation equal to Dodge City's, most of the population cleaned up their acts during court week. There were scheduled celebrations, social affairs, and horse races that could provide plenty of entertainment for Agatha and Simpson. Many of the Englishmen who managed the syndicated ranches in the area stayed in town to socialize with each other. Knowing Gram, she would introduce herself to her fellow countrymen and enjoy a few Old World customs while she had the chance.

Jennifer was relieved to have Gram and Simpson out from underfoot for a few days. She had been away from the ranch for over two weeks, and spring roundup was scheduled to begin. Now that she was head of the household, she had to oversee the branding and separating of calves for the trail drive to the railhead in Dodge City.

When Jennifer strode out to the corrals, Sunset met her with a barrage of questions about Trey's unexpected departure.

"Trey has obligations elsewhere," Jennifer reported.

"But I thought Three Wolves would stay more than a day."

"I never had any intention of letting him get caught up in this feud," she insisted.

"We could have used another gunhand. There has been more trouble on the ranch while we were in Dodge," Sunset informed her. "Fences were cut and more cattle stolen. Don't be surprised if the calf numbers are down from yer projected estimates. The sooner the cattle are rounded up and driven to Kansas, the better off we'll be. We won't have to fret about losing calves until after the new crop is on the ground this fall."

"While the cattle drive is underway we can begin the fencing projects. The wire and posts should be arriving from Dodge within two weeks."

''We're gonna have to hire more men,'' Sunset said as he mopped his perspiring brow with his bandanna. ''We can't take riders off their posts while rustling is still a threat.''

''How many men will we need?'' Jennifer questioned.

''Ten should do it. There's always dozens of cowboys looking for work after spring cattle drives. Me and Jawbone will hire some dependable workers for you.''

Jennifer frowned curiously while she watched her brother approach one of the colts being trained for use on the cattle drive. The horse had been roped and lay on its side in the dirt. Christopher knelt to blow his breath in the horse's nostrils. Five other colts were tied in a similar fashion, looking as if they were carrying on confidential conversations with five ranch hands.

''What the devil is Christopher doing?''

''Three Wolves taught your brother the Comanche technique of gentling wild horses,'' Jawbone explained as he moseyed up beside Jennifer. ''According to Chris, after the horses accept man as master and git accustomed to our scent, they are left tied long enough to make them sluggish. Phase two is just beginning over there.'' He pointed toward the south end of the corral.

Several horses were blindfolded, then nudged to their feet. The disoriented colts didn't move a muscle when saddles were strapped to their backs.

''Well, I'll be damned . . . er . . . darned,'' Sunset chuckled as he studied the unique procedure. ''I never saw a wild bronc accept a saddle that easily before.''

''Me neither,'' Jawbone seconded. ''I've been breaking horses for twenty years, and I never saw a horse stand still for saddling, much less the first ride. But the blindfolded colt Christopher mounted during his demonstration didn't buck, not even once. Darnedest thing I ever saw. Them Comanches sure know how to gentle a horse.''

Jawbone leaned against the corral and chuckled as the blindfolded colt followed cautiously behind one of the cowboys. ''When I was a roughstring rider, I crawled on the backs of the wildest mounts you ever saw. They'd kick the lid off and come undone under me. There were spinners that bucked in tight circles and high rollers that leaped up and bucked in midair.

"I've ridden weavers that never stuck ground in a straight line, sunfishers that twisted their bodies into crescents, and windmillers that swapped ends in midair. I've ridden hundreds of wild horses that got rid of me so fast that I wrinkled my spine when I hit the ground. I could've saved a lot of wear and tear on these old bones if I'd known about this technique years ago."

Jennifer marveled at the efficiency of this new method of training horses. In the past, she had seen several men hurled through the air to slam into fences. Indeed, this procedure was safer for horse and rider.

It also placed young Christopher in a position of authority, Jennifer realized. Thanks to Trey's guidance, he was gaining self-confidence and rapport with the experienced ranch hands.

Trey MacTavish had not stayed long, but he had definitely left his mark on Christopher. Trey had also carved his initials on Jennifer's heart. She would never forget him. Each time she closed her eyes she would see him rising up like a shadow from a swirling cloud of smoke, see him bending over her, his silver eyes glowing with intense passion.

"Would you look at that!" Sunset hooted.

Christopher removed the colt's blindfold, then handed the reins to one of the roughstring riders. The colt swung its head to sniff at the man on the saddle, then took a few tentative steps around the corral. Not once did the colt object to being ridden.

"We'll have mounts broken to ride for the roundup twice as fast as usual," Sunset added. "Beats anything I ever saw."

Fascinated, Jennifer watched the procedure from beginning to end, amazed that what usually took days—not to mention a string of salty curses and bruised bodies—had been accomplished in a few hours.

When the procedure was complete, Christopher requested

that all ten colts be harnessed to mules and put out to pasture. The sturdy mules, according to Chris, would make certain the colts were broken to lead without wasting the cowboys' time.

Another half dozen colts were brought into the pen and quickly gentled. Astonishing! thought Jennifer. At this rate, she could sell their extra horses to the soldiers at Fort Elliot and enjoy a tidy profit.

Quincy Ward could never force Templeton Ranch out of business if she sold gentled horses as well as cattle.

"Sunset, would you be so kind as to saddle my mare? I should like to ride to Fort Elliot to have a chat with the commander."

Nodding agreeably, the red-haired cowboy strode off.

"What's the rush to reach the fort?" Jawbone questioned.

"We are going to sell our well-mannered mounts to the Army," Jennifer announced. "And perhaps our beef can also be contracted for sale, if negotiations go well. Quincy monopolized last year's contracts for cattle, some of which I suspect were stolen off this ranch. If we are going to provide soldiers with beef, we might as bloody well enjoy the profit, instead of Quincy."

Jawbone frowned warily. "You might rile Quincy if you undercut him on the fort contracts. He's none too happy about your marriage and he won't like this any better."

"A pity that," Jennifer said, unconcerned. "Free enterprise is a trademark of the United States, is it not? And if all goes well, I might be able to negotiate the sale of beef to Camp Supply and Fort Sill in Indian Territory. It would save us from making the long cattle drives to Dodge City."

When Jennifer swung onto the saddle and trotted away, Sunset stared after her curiously. "What the hell is she gonna do at the fort?"

"Make Quincy Ward furious," Jawbone grumbled. "Miss Jenny has taken it into her head to supply beef and horses to the forts. I expect the commander will prefer to do business with her instead of Quincy."

"That will put Quincy in a foul mood for sure," Sunset prophesied. "He lost his fiancée, and now maybe his livestock contracts. I hope he don't take it out on Miss Jenny by rustling a few more of her calves. Seems to me that man has been gathering cattle faster than cows can naturally give birth.''

''We'll place extra guards in the pastures, just in case Quincy decides to have his revenge. Knowing him, I doubt he's gonna take the news about his contracts sitting down.'' Jawbone predicted.

Thirteen

Quincy Ward propped himself against a tree beside the creek and surveyed the camp pitched on the far end of the pasture. For the better part of four days Three Wolves had lounged around his campsite, taking target practice at regular intervals. Quincy didn't have a clue what the half-breed gunslinger was up to, but he suspected the newlyweds had a spat and the groom had been ordered out of the house.

Good. That would simplify matters. Quincy hoped Jennifer had finally come to her senses. Quincy was anxious to dispose of that shootist—permanently. The sooner Three Wolves was dead and gone, the sooner Quincy could get on with his plan to marry the young widow.

If all went according to expectation, Jonas Rafferty would be accused of the murder. Once the leader of the small-farmer faction became an example to his cohorts, this area of Texas would be rid of those pesky nesters.

Very soon, Three Wolves would belong to eternity, Jonas would be awaiting hanging, and Quincy would have control of Templeton Ranch. There was no sense dillydallying, he decided.

"Yancy!" Quincy called to one of his new hired guns who had come up from Abilene. "Take a message to Jonas and tell him to meet me at the line shack tonight. Have Bernie Giles keep watch on Three Wolves while I ride over to the fort to talk to the commander."

The scraggly-haired gunman nodded before reining his steed toward the group of riders keeping surveillance on Three Wolves on the eastern front.

Smiling in anticipation, Quincy headed for Fort Elliot. Everything was falling neatly into place. He silently thanked Jennifer for ousting her husband from the house. She had facilitated the upcoming ambush, and Jonas would get blamed for doing the dirty work.

Quincy's good mood lasted until he reached the fort. He was outraged to learn that Jennifer had arrived earlier in the week to undercut his contract to supply beef to the soldiers. In addition, he discovered that Templeton Ranch would also be supplying mounts for the cavalry. Damn it, he wondered, how could Jennifer promise to deliver so many trained horses so quickly?

To Quincy's further frustration, he was informed that Jennifer had asked permission to drive her cattle to the nearby forts in Indian Territory. He was definitely going to have to marry that female—or go broke underbidding her. If he was forced to put large cattle herds on the trail to Dodge, he would run the risk of rustlers. Damnation, things had been simpler when *his* men were doing the rustling!

Agatha Reynolds beamed in supreme satisfaction. Her three-day sojourn in Mobeetie had been extremely productive. She had hired a lawyer by the name of Phinneus Albright to draw up divorce papers, releasing Jennifer from her absurd marriage to that Comanche heathen. Using the power of her rank and position in British society, Agatha saw to it that the signatures of the bride and groom were not required before she bustled the document through court. Having herself declared legal guardian of her grandchildren resolved Agatha's concerns in one whale of a hurry.

Mission accomplished, Agatha's grand mood escalated. She and Simpson participated in the activities of court week in Mobeetie. She had rented rooms at a local hotel, which was owned by an Englishman named Mark Huselby. The man was exceptionally accommodating when he learned he was renting space to a duchess. Servants hopped to do Agatha's bidding. It was reminiscent of being in England where she was accorded the consideration and respect entitled to a woman of her magnanimous social stature.

Now, all Agatha had to do was find a buyer for Templeton Ranch. Her grandchildren would have no choice but to return to England, instead of remaining in Texas to deal with this ridiculous feud. Jennifer and Christopher did not need the headaches of running a ranch.

Selling it would not be difficult, Agatha predicted. From what her lawyer said, Templeton Ranch was the hottest property in West Texas. Agatha could sell it at rock bottom price to get out from under the whole situation and be packed to leave for England within a week—two at the most.

As Agatha hoped, Phinneus Albright put her in immediate contact with a man who was eager to take the ranch off her hands. Delighted, Agatha returned to the lawyer's office to meet the prospective buyer and draw up the contract.

Lucky thing Agatha had made this trip to the States, she decided. When she was ruling the roost, things got done in a hurry!

"You shouldn't be here," Trey hissed when Christopher trotted into camp an hour after dark.

"Why not? I'm part owner of this ranch, you know."

"That's not what I meant, kid," Trey muttered.

Christopher dismounted and smiled proudly. "I just wanted you to know that I followed your advice about breaking horses," he said, gesturing to his steed. "I did exactly what you showed me, and then I harnessed this gelding to a mule for a full day so it would be broken to lead. The ranch hands think I'm a bloody genius. Got any more Comanche tricks to teach me?''

"Yes.'' Trey grinned reluctantly. while Christopher stood there bursting with pride.

"What's next?'' Christopher enthused.

"You're going to learn to disappear into thin air. Quincy's men are keeping around-the-clock watch on me. I don't want them to mistake you for me.''

"But what about my lessons in self-defense? I need more practice, and you are the only one who can teach me.''

"Go practice your techniques on some of the cowhands,'' Trey suggested as he plucked up a cigar and lit it over the campfire.

"Can I try one of those?''

Trey glanced up to see Christopher gesturing toward the flaming cigar. "No. You're too young.''

"That's what you said about me and women,'' Christopher grumbled. "I think I should be allowed to try one or the other. There are girls at Mac's Dance Hall who are reported to break in boys who—''

"Take the damned cigar,'' Trey muttered, retrieving another cheroot from his saddlebags. "Now, about the other night—''

"You sure took a long time telling my sister good-bye,'' Christopher broke in as he sank down to light the cigar over the fire. He coughed, wheezed, and then grinned when Trey avoided his gaze.

Trey squirmed self-consciously. "Yeah, well, some things take time, kid.''

Christopher took another tentative drag, then blew smoke rings in the air. "You never mentioned anything about carrying a woman off to bed. Is that standard procedure?''

"Damn it, kid—''

"Well, when my time comes, how am I supposed to know how to proceed if I don't ask questions? You said a man was supposed to treat a lady with respect while having s—''

"Geezus! I swear you have a one-track mind. I thought I answered all your questions days ago."

"I've thought of a few more since then. For instance—"

"Smoke the damned cigar and shut the hell up," Trey ordered gruffly. "Then we'll sneak down to the creek to polish your self-defense."

Christopher beamed in anticipation, then recoiled when Trey stabbed a lean finger into his chest. "Afterward, I want you to hightail it back to the house and keep an eye on your sister. She could use the company. Spending a full day with your grandmother would drive anybody batty."

"Gram and Simpson have been in Mobeetie all week," Christopher reported. "It's court week and Gram decided to stay in town. Jennifer has been bustling around, making arrangements to sell cattle and horses at Fort Elliot. She undercut Quincy's price and got the contracts to Fort Elliot and the forts in western Indian Territory."

"What?" Trey hooted, owl-eyed.

Christopher nodded his blond head. "Quincy doesn't appreciate it, but that's too bloody bad. Jen says we won't risk as many losses on short drives, especially if we're moving livestock in different directions at the same time. Quincy's hired men will have to divide forces to rustle our cattle."

Jennifer was definitely a shrewd businesswoman, Trey decided. But she wasn't going to have to contend with Quincy Ward, because Trey intended to deal with that sneaky bastard himself.

"Can we practice self-defense now?" Christopher asked impatiently.

Trey snuffed out his cigar and strode into the underbrush so the posted lookouts couldn't see what he and Christopher were doing. Trey had never known anyone so anxious to learn. The lad was agile on his feet and quick with his hands. Of course, his sister had become exceptionally good with *her* hands—

"Ugh!" Trey cursed himself for getting sidetracked by tempting thoughts. While shadow-boxing with Chris, he had spun around and caught a doubled fist in the belly before he knew what hit him—he had walked right smack-dab into the punch, in fact.

When Trey staggered on his feet, Christopher stared at his own fist in stunned amazement. "Bloody hell, I'm better at this than I thought!"

"Never give yourself so much credit that you aren't ready for the unexpected." Trey wheeled around, cutting Christopher's legs out from under him. The boy landed with a thud and groan. "Now get back to the house, kid. I plan to lose my shadows so I can meet Jonas at the line shack."

Christopher dusted himself off and limped away, escorted by the wolves. "I'll be glad when this is settled so you can come back to the house to stay."

"I'm not coming back, kid." Trey's voice was hard, final.

Christopher wheeled around. "Why not? I know you care about Jen, and she cares for you. You should see her trying to busy herself, just to keep from missing you."

"Make yourself scarce, kid," Trey ordered, shooing the boy on his way. "I've got places to go and things to do."

Muttering, the lad stalked uphill. Damn, Trey thought to himself. He was going to miss that kid—almost as much as he'd miss Jennifer. No one had idolized him the way Christopher did. And no one had ever loved him the way Jennifer did—

Trey scowled to himself as he slipped off into the darkness. He had damned well better pay attention to business instead of mooning over a woman he couldn't keep. If not, he would catch more than a fist in the midsection. Next time, it might be a bullet.

Christopher grumbled under his breath when he stepped out of the house after lunch to see his grandmother and Simpson rolling down the dusty path in a buggy. Since Jennifer had ridden off to finalize the arrangements with the commander at Fort Elliot, Christopher was left to entertain his grandmother. It was going to be a long afternoon.

"Do not slouch," Agatha ordered as Simpson assisted her

from the buggy. "I daresay, resuming your formal education and polishing your manners will not come a moment too soon."

Christopher gnashed his teeth and strived for a polite tone of voice. "Did you enjoy the festivities of court week, Gram?"

Agatha buzzed toward the house with her usual vim and vigor, adjusting her expensive bonnet as she went. "I found a few activities to amuse me. A jousting tournament, depicting English life in the early centuries, was refreshing. The horse race, however, left much to be desired. Why, those nags cannot hold a candle to our fine British thoroughbreds. But then, I suppose they're the best to be had way out here on the fringe of civilization."

Simpson halted beside Christopher. "It might be courteous of you to offer Her Grace a drink to wash down the dust, Your Lordship," he prompted quietly. "A proper gentleman is always attentive to a lady's needs, you see."

Christopher took his cue and offered to fetch Gram a drink. Tea, of course, Christopher mused as he strode off to locate the cook. Gram had a fetish about her bloody tea.

"Simpson, find Jen for me, will you?" Agatha requested before plunking down on the couch in the parlor. "The sooner my grandchildren are informed of the arrangements I have made, the sooner we can begin packing."

"As you wish, Your Grace."

Agatha lounged on the sofa and smiled in satisfaction. Her journey to Mobeetie had been so productive she could scarcely believe it. She had removed that infuriating savage from Jen's life with the stroke of a pen and then sold this ranch without complications. As soon as the deed and contract were signed and delivered to the buyer, Jennifer and Christopher would have no excuses, no choice but to resume their positions in London society. Any moral obligation they felt to their departed father would become nonexistent.

"Your tea, Gram." Christopher set the tray on the table and dutifully sank down to keep her company.

"I made a few arrangements while I was in town." Agatha

spooned sugar into her teacup and took a sip. "As soon as Simpson locates Jen we will discuss them."

"Jen isn't here," Christopher informed her. "She is negotiating the sale of livestock at the fort. Two of our ranch hands went with her to deliver the first string of horses."

"Very well then, I will discuss the matter with you and brief Jen later." Agatha took another sip of tea, then proceeded. "First of all, I have negated your sister's ridiculous marriage to that dreadful barbarian."

"What!" Christopher came out of his chair as if he had stepped on a rattlesnake.

"Sit down, m'boy," Agatha demanded. "Surely you did not think I would permit Jen to remain tied to that rapscallion— he doesn't even have the decency to wear a full set of clothes! And anyway, the marriage was nothing more than Jen's attempt to resolve her problems with this ranch."

"Jen happens to be in love with her husband," Christopher all but shouted. "You had no right to break up the marriage."

Agatha waved off his irritation with the flick of her wrist. "It was only a temporary fascination at best. You are entirely too young to understand about such things. Besides, the heathen has come and gone from her life."

Simpson strode stoically into the room, then nodded respectfully. "Your Grace, I have failed to locate Lady Jennifer."

Agatha motioned Simpson into a chair. "I will deal with Jen later." She turned back to her grandson, whose hands were clamped around the arm of his chair in a stranglehold, his face red with fury. "Now then, Christopher, the second order of business is the guardianship I have established to protect you and Jen. Once this property is sold—"

"We are not giving up our father's land," Christopher objected—loudly. "We have sweated and sacrificed to carve a place for ourselves here in Texas!"

"Do not use that blustering tone with me, young man," Agatha scolded, wagging a bony finger in his fuming face. "You and your sister are not supposed to sweat and sacrifice. You have wealth, position, and proper social connections. You are supposed to hire servants for that sort of thing. Prospective dukes and duchesses have to maintain a certain image. It is beneath you to mingle with the servants. If your formal education had not been so shamefully neglected you would know that."

"I happen to like sweating and toiling," Christopher muttered.

"Bloody, blooming hell! I do not wish to hear any more of your back talk." Agatha glowered at her grandson, who glowered right back at her.

"You have no right to run our lives, Gram," Christopher spouted as he bounded to his feet.

Simpson surged out of his chair to stand in front of Agatha like a human shield. "Master Christopher, cease speaking to the duchess in such a rude manner. You have been so corrupted by the lack of protocol that you have forgotten proper etiquette. We do not raise our voices to titled English ladies."

"Sit down," Agatha snapped at Christopher. "I did indeed have the right to see to your future, and your future is in England." She whipped out the document and waved it in Christopher's face. "I have signed the contract and deed to the ranch. Quincy Ward will arrive at five o'clock to pay the agreed-upon twelve thousand dollars and sign his name to the document."

"Quincy Ward! Twelve thousand dollars!" Christopher howled at the top of his lungs. "Blast it, Gram, he is one of the men Jen was trying to keep from getting his hands on our property."

"Well, it will be his very soon, and you have no say in the matter—"

Agatha gasped in shock when Christopher snatched the deed and contract from her hand and ripped them to shreds. To her further outrage, he shook the torn papers in her face—along with his clenched fist.

"We are not dealing with the man who might have murdered my father!" Christopher shouted. "That bastard has bloody well done everything in his power to gain control of the property. But he will not have it, I tell you! I will not let him!''

"He murdered your father?" Agatha plopped back on the sofa to stare goggle-eyed at her grandson. "Are you sure?"

"I am reasonably certain of it, yes," Christopher seethed. "But proving it has been impossible. Now you practically laid our ranch in his greedy hands. I will not stand for this." Lurching around, Christopher stormed toward the front door. "I'm taking what is left of this deed to Quincy, and I bloody well intend to tell him what he can do with it."

"Simpson, stop Christopher this instant!" Agatha commanded.

When Simpson tried to barricade the door, Christopher called upon the skills Trey had taught him. With one lithe move, Christopher took Simpson's legs out from under him and left the butler sprawled on the floor. Simpson smacked his head on the doorjamb and slumped in an unconscious heap.

"Christopher! Have you gone mad!" Agatha howled.

Christopher spun about, his face contorted with fury. "I am never going back to England and I will not give up this ranch. It is my home. And for your information, Trey MacTavish has not come and gone. He is camped out on the north range and I have been in contact with him every bloody damned day. He is the one who taught me to protect myself."

"I should have known," Agatha muttered.

"If you hadn't interfered, Trey would have dealt with Quincy and that scoundrel would have gotten his just reward."

When Christopher stepped over Simpson's sprawled body and stalked outside, Agatha scurried over to pat the butler's ashen cheeks. "Simpson, wake up this instant, do you hear me? Bloody, everlasting hell, you know I cannot function without you beside me. I need you!"

Simpson groaned groggily when Agatha jostled him for the fifth time. "I daresay, Your Grace, that hot-tempered grandson of yours is as skilled at pugilistic techniques as that wolf man Lady Jennifer married."

"Oh, Simpson, I am so sorry!" In an uncharacteristic burst

of sentimentality, Agatha flung her arms around Simpson's neck and burst into tears.

"Your Grace?" Simpson blinked, astonished. Still, the duchess did not loose her fierce hold on him. "My dear Agatha . . ."

The temptation was too great for Simpson to resist. He gathered the duchess in his arms and held her close to his heart, living his secret fantasy. For the first time in forty years of impeccable, devoted service, Simpson stepped over the line, allowing his pent-up affection to pour out. He kissed Agatha squarely on the mouth—and she kissed him back with equal enthusiasm. They clung together for a long moment before the creak of the front door forced them to come up for air.

"What the devil is going on in here?"

Jennifer froze in her tracks when she saw Simpson lying spread-eagle on the floor, with Agatha half-sprawled on top of him. The twosome were entwined so tightly there was barely enough space for a flea to turn around.

Agatha clambered to her feet, her wrinkled features flushed with embarrassment. "This is all your brother's fault. He went berserk and knocked out poor Simpson."

"Christopher did this?" Jennifer asked in amazement.

"Of course Christopher. How many brothers do you have?"

Jennifer reached over to steady the butler, who swayed on his feet when he stood up. Bracing himself against the doorjamb, he gingerly inspected the goose egg on the side of his head.

"Why on earth would Christopher clobber Simpson when it is you who—" Jennifer slammed her mouth shut so fast that she clipped her tongue.

"You may as well say it," Agatha muttered. "I know what you were going to say."

"Begging your pardon, Gram, but you have made a habit of insulting Christopher. And forgive me for pointing this out, but he inherited your quick temper."

"Yes, well, I fear I really set him off today. He thrashed out of here like a mad cow."

"Like a mad bull," Jennifer corrected.

Agatha retrieved her hankie to dab at her eyes. "I made

some arrangements to which your brother violently objected—poor Simpson caught the brunt of his wrath.''

Agatha tugged her black gown back into place and raised her chin. ''You may as well know what put your brother in a snit. But I pray you will not throw any punches at Simpson that you secretly want to direct at me. He has suffered enough for one day.''

''What arrangements?'' Jennifer asked warily.

''I established a guardianship and had your marriage dissolved.''

Jennifer stumbled back as if she had been struck. Blister it! Her marriage was what kept this feud from blowing up like a keg of dynamite. ''You didn't,'' she whispered, involuntarily brushing her thumb over the gold band she wore proudly on her left hand.

''I bloody well did, and for your own good, my dear girl. I also made plans to sell the ranch so we could quit this place. But Christopher told me that I made a very bad error by dealing with Quincy Ward.''

''Quincy Ward!'' Jennifer parroted in disbelief.

''He offered me twelve thousand dollars for this—''

''Only twelve thousand dollars!'' Jennifer broke in wildly. ''You took twenty cents to the acre for land that is worth one dollar and a quarter?''

''Well, how should I know how to count this foreign money?'' Agatha muttered in self-defense.

''My God, you let him steal you blind, Gram. If he gets hold of the water rights he will ruin every small farmer within miles of Mobeetie. Their land will not be worth a penny without access to Sweetwater Creek. Quincy will buy up every tract at a fraction of its worth.''

''I daresay, I will not be selling to Quincy after all. Christopher ripped the deed in half before he stamped off to tell the man that the deal is null and void. I will simply sell to someone else.''

''You let Christopher ride off to Quincy's ranch in a rage?''

Jennifer cringed at the thought of her brother confronting Quincy—and his hired guns—single-handed.

"I could not very well stop the boy after he knocked Simpson out cold, could I?" Agatha huffed. "I had to tend to poor Simpson."

Grumbling, Jennifer lurched around. She had to run interference for Christopher. He had obviously gone off half-cocked to undo the damage Agatha had done. Christopher was likely to get himself hurt if he was forced to answer to Quincy and that army of hired guns.

"Where the blazes are you going?" Agatha demanded as Jennifer rushed off.

"To smooth over the situation with Quincy before someone else gets hurt," Jennifer threw over her shoulder.

"Drat it." Agatha flung up her arms in frustration. "I fear these five years in Texas have ruined my grandchildren."

"Your Grace?"

Agatha glanced over to see that Simpson had turned pea green. She was at his side in a flash.

"Could I impose on you to fetch me a drink? I am feeling a trifle queasy. Dreadfully sorry for the inconvenience, Your Grace. I would not think to make such a request if I was not a bit under the weather."

"Think nothing of it." Agatha shepherded Simpson to the sofa and forced him to lie down. "I had no idea I would have to pad your salary for combat pay. This is positively disgraceful. That grandson of mine will apologize for this or I shall cut him off without a shilling."

"Judging by the wallop Master Christopher packs, I would be careful about inciting his temper in the future. And if his behavior is any indication, threatening to strip him of his title and fortune will not matter a jot or tittle. I fear the boy has his heart set on being a cow servant."

Agatha cringed, appalled. Then she tramped off to fetch Simpson food, drink, and a cool cloth to ease his discomfort.

                            * * *

Although Jennifer galloped cross-country to overtake her
brother, she reached the stone archway that led to Quincy's
ranch without catching sight of Christopher. Her brother's
mount, branded with a Rocking T, was tethered to the hitching
post beside the corral.

Jennifer dismounted and strode determinedly toward the
house. The door was guarded by three men who wore scruffy
boots that looked suspiciously like the ones belonging to the
thieves who had stolen her money en route to Dodge. Jennifer
had the unshakable feeling that the money she had lost had
become these hooligans' drinking money. Either that, or these
scoundrels had turned over the stolen cash to Quincy for the
down payment on Templeton Ranch.

Blister it, Agatha had complicated what Jennifer had so carefully resolved by marrying Trey . . .

The ruggedly handsome image that popped to mind caused
Jennifer's spirits to deflate. It was silly, she knew, but she had
wanted to remain married to Trey, even if they had to be
separated. Knowing he belonged to her eased her sense of loss.
Now she had nothing but a few precious memories.

Damnation, Jennifer would have liked to punch her grandmother right in the nose for negating her marriage. Of course,
Simpson's mouth would have undoubtedly gotten in the way.
He was so unselfishly devoted to Agatha that he would have
taken the blow to protect his beloved duchess.

Jennifer suspected Simpson had been Christopher's scape-
goat. And where, she wondered, had Christopher learned to
fight? Had Trey taught the boy in the short time they spent
together?

Flinging aside her unproductive thoughts, Jennifer drew up
in front of Quincy's human guard dragons. "Please inform
your employer that I wish to speak with him—now," she
demanded with an air of authority that would have done Agatha
proud.

Bernie Giles nodded curtly, then swaggered inside. To Jennifer's dismay, she was ushered in the door by Yancy Wyatt and Frank Irving. It looked as if she was not going to have a private audience with Quincy. The big coward was afraid to talk to her without his armed men hovering around him.

Quincy was seated at his office desk. Bernie Giles, the tallest of the three guards, loomed beside him. Yancy and Frank took their places on either side of the door. Although Quincy was sporting a smug grin that made Jennifer gnash her teeth, she marshaled her bravado and forged ahead.

"I have come to collect my brother," she announced.

Quincy lounged in his chair and regarded Jennifer for a long moment. "Your brother doesn't have your manners, I'm afraid. My men had to lock him away until he calmed down. If I feel inclined, I could press charges against him for attacking me."

"I am sure Christopher regrets his burst of temper." Truthfully, she doubted her brother was the least bit sorry. *Furious* was probably closer to the mark. The boy was obviously on a rampage after dealing with Gram and her highhanded meddling. "I'm sure you have realized by now that my grandmother has thought it over and decided not to sell our ranch."

"I presumed as much when Christopher arrived to hand-feed me the document he had torn to pieces," Quincy replied sarcastically.

"He's young and impulsive," she said in her brother's defense. "Diplomacy is not one of his strongest virtues—yet. Now, if you will kindly hand Christopher into my care I will be on my way."

Quincy smiled nastily. "I'm afraid neither of you is going anywhere until your grandmother arrives with a new deed and contract. She agreed to sell the ranch to me and I intend to hold her to it."

Jennifer lifted her chin to look down her nose at the homely rancher. "Am I to understand that we are being held hostage?"

"You understand perfectly." Quincy rose to his feet and walked over to growl down at her. "You could have made it easy on yourself by marrying me, but you chose to wed, and bed, that vicious gunslinger. Now you can trot back to England

with that stuffy grandmother of yours or you can accept my
marriage proposal. If you have any sense, you'll marry me and
beg my forgiveness for sleeping with that half-breed killer!''

That did it! Jennifer, who had spent years behaving in a
dignified manner, lost her good disposition. She had been forced
to deal with her persnickety grandmother for a long, endless
week. That had been a constant challenge. She had lost the
only man she would ever love, and now this shrewd scoundrel
had taken advantage of a foolish young boy who had tried to
become the man of the house after his father had been killed—
probably by Quincy or one of his henchmen, if the truth be
told.

''I daresay, Three Wolves is more man than you or these
foppish gunmen could ever hope to be!'' Jennifer hissed at
him. ''I knew Three Wolves was the man I wanted the first
time I clapped eyes on him. I would not have married you if
you were the last man in Texas, or in these United States! And
you will bloody well have the fight of your life on your hands
if you think I will allow you to control our ranch, even if you
do force Gram into signing that bloody deed. You might find
a range war on your hands, Quincy Ward, and I will be leading
an army of my friends and neighbors against you.''

Jennifer inhaled deeply and raved on, venting her roiling
temper. ''And don't think for one minute that I do not know
who stole the cash for my supplies, and who ordered our cattle
rustled. It was you and these three goons. You are going to
find yourself investigated for the murder of my father, too. I
have tried to keep the peace, but I will see you financially and
socially ruined if you dare hold me hostage. You might even
find your own hired guns bought out from under you.''

''Get her out of here,'' Quincy snarled.

Jennifer struck like a coiled snake, employing the tactics she
had seen Trey use on the two men who took potshots at his
wolves in Dodge City. Frank Irving received a swift kick in
the crotch of his breeches. The unexpected blow stole his breath
and knocked him to his knees. Yancy Wyatt received a hatchet
chop that sent his pistol skidding across the floor.

Although Jennifer dived for the weapon she came in second. A boot heel crunched her fingers. She retaliated by taking a bite out of the leg attached to it. Bernie Giles howled in pain and lifted his six-gun. The pistol butt clanked against Jennifer's head with enough force to blur her vision instantly.

Blinding pain was the last thing Jennifer remembered before the world turned black. She collapsed against the boot that mashed her left hand into the floor.

"Toss her in the cellar with her hot-tempered brother," Quincy snapped as he stared at the unconscious body littering his office carpet.

Quincy had presumed a lover's spat had resulted in Three Wolves' departure from the ranch house, but apparently that was not the case. Jennifer had rushed to that bastard's defense in one helluva hurry. Of course, she could have been bluffing, Quincy thought to himself. But there was a strong possibility that he would have to deal with Three Wolves—whether Agatha had dissolved the marriage or not.

If Quincy's luck held, he could send off a note demanding that Agatha draw up another contract and deliver it in person— immediately. That pompous old harridan wouldn't risk endangering her grandchildren's lives because of a deed to a Texas ranch she didn't want or need.

On that happy thought, Quincy jotted a message to Agatha. While he awaited her arrival, he would assemble all his men to make sure they were well-armed and well-prepared, just in case Three Wolves got wind of the turn of events and came to retrieve his ex-wife.

Or better yet, Quincy decided, he would send out some of his men to bushwhack Three Wolves and then let Jonas Rafferty take the heat. Might as well resolve all his problems in one night. Three Wolves had gotten the best of him once, but it damned well wasn't going to happen again. That savage gunslinger was as good as dead and Jonas was going to hang for the murder.

Fourteen

Jennifer moaned miserably when she regained consciousness. Her head was pounding something fierce. Musty smells penetrated her disoriented senses. When she tried to roll over, anchors—or something equally heavy—restrained her. Jennifer pried her eyes open to find her wrists bound and lashed to the rickety banister in the cellar beneath Quincy's home.

"Jen?"

Jennifer half twisted, startled to see her brother trussed up and tied to a chair in the far corner. The dim light from the window slanted across his face, outlining one swollen eye and puffy lips caked with blood. His shirt lacked buttons, and one sleeve had been ripped off.

"Dear God, Christopher, what did they do to you?"

Christopher breathed cautiously, grimacing at the pain in his ribs. "I tried to cram that blooming deed down Quincy's throat, but his guard dragons came to his rescue," he said bitterly. "I could have taken that cocky bastard, I know I could have, if not for those burly henchmen."

"You should not have confronted Quincy alone," Jennifer chastised him. "That was stupid."

"Well, I was mad."

"So Gram said. You will have to apologize to Simpson for leaving a knot on his head. Gram is particularly fond of the man, you know."

"Damn her," Christopher burst out resentfully. "I can't believe she tried to sell the ranch to Quincy, of all people! And I'll be damned if I'll go back to England, no matter what Gram decrees. I'll run away first!"

"Gram will have to sell the ranch to Quincy now, because we're being held hostage." Jennifer tried to sit up, then thought better of it. Her head was spinning like a windmill. "I came to rescue you, but I have made matters worse, I fear."

"I'm sorry, Jen. I should not have stamped off in a fit of temper."

"No, you definitely should not have," Jennifer agreed. "You could have accomplished the same thing by tearing up the contract and taking *Gram* hostage. Now Quincy has a distinct advantage."

"I truly am sorry," Christopher murmured.

"Well, we will simply have to devise a way to untangle ourselves from this pickle, won't we?"

"I may be a little hot-headed, but you are entirely too optimistic. Always were. We do not have an icicle's chance in hell," Christopher said defeatedly.

"I would rather be known as an optimist who died trying," Jennifer contended.

"I wish you would use some other cliché," he mumbled as he stared despairingly at the dingy walls of their prison.

Trey frowned at the absence of lookouts surrounding his camp the past few days. Using his spyglass, he surveyed the countryside, miffed by the lack of interest he was suddenly receiving from Quincy's hired guns.

Something had happened, or something was about to happen, he predicted. Not knowing what was going on made Trey uneasy. He could only hope Jonas hadn't double-crossed him. If Trey had misjudged his cousin, he would be a sitting duck.

Mulling over the possibilities, Trey made an effigy of himself in his bedroll and propped it against his canvas lean-to. He left Diablo grazing peacefully in the pasture and called to the wolves. If an ambush was about to take place from all directions at once, he decided to be conveniently absent.

Crouching in the clump of grass that surrounded the lean-to, Trey crawled on his belly as his grandfather had taught him many years ago. The technique of burying himself in grass and underbrush was a tactic practiced by the Comanche and Apache. Trey had purposely set up camp beside the clumps of grass that led down to Sweetwater Creek, where thick vegetation made disappearing into thin air not only possible but simple.

Trey had accomplished the feat with less cover to work with plenty of times in the past. He would have to remember to teach young Christopher this vanishing act. The kid was hungry to learn all sorts of Comanche tricks.

After checking for intruders, Trey rose to his feet and strode along the edge of the creek. Instinct told him something was definitely wrong. He'd found himself in too many precarious situations in the past not to smell trouble—or the lack of it—in the wind.

Following the meandering stream, Trey trekked southwest, ever conscious of the shadows of the trees and cliffs above him. He headed toward the ledge that led to another winding gully and ravine where the isolated line shack was located. He hoped like hell that Jonas was waiting for him there. He didn't let himself depend on that, though. He knew he could be walking into a trap.

Trey halted on the east creek bank when he noticed the footprints left in the damp sand. A feeling of dread coiled on his spine as he squatted down to take a closer look. A man's smeared boot print skirted the shallows of the creek, mingling with hoofprints that indicated a horse had been watered and led away. Trey had seen similar prints beside the stream west of Dodge City earlier that month.

Bob Yates, dragging his crippled leg, had been here recently. Damn! Trey didn't need to contend with Bob right now. He wondered if Bob's arrival had anything to do with the lack of guards around his camp. Maybe Bob hadn't been able to launch an attack because of Quincy's hired guns—or had gotten his filthy hands on Jennifer . . .

That unsettling thought prompted Trey to scramble up the steep incline to follow Bob's trail. Bob's bum leg had given out on him once during his trek up the eroded slope. Too bad his mount hadn't trampled him when he fell. It would have saved Trey a great deal of trouble.

Raising the spyglass, Trey scanned the open area before emerging from cover. He needed to circle to the back of the line shack so he could scout the labyrinth of ravines to make sure he wasn't walking into an ambush. Nothing would have pleased Trey more than for Bob to hole up in the line shack and be mistaken for Trey. Of course, if Bob was riddled by Quincy Ward's hired guns, Trey would enjoy very little satisfaction.

When Trey got his hands on Yates, the outlaw was going to find himself nursing more than just a slit hamstring. Bob had a high price on his head, and Trey wanted to be the one to bring that murdering bastard down. After Yates mistreated Jennifer, Trey had vowed to kill the man—slowly.

Clinging to the shadows of dusk, Trey inched up the slope, then darted into the steep ravines and arroyos that cut a rugged gash through the High Plains. The wolves were circling, making wide sweeps, returning to heel when Trey sidestepped down the crumbling stone break north of the line shack.

Crouching beside a scraggly juniper, Trey surveyed the dilapidated shack in the shadows of the towering stone ledge to the west. Using his spyglass, he located the horse tethered beside a clump of cedars. Bob Yates's mount, Trey guessed. Jonas wouldn't have bothered hiding his horse. If Jonas was setting a trap to double-cross Trey, there would likely be a whole string of horses hobbled in the cedars.

Trey slid his pistol from the holster and eased down the

slope, shielding himself in the gray shadows cast by the over-hanging stone ledge. When he reached the point directly above the shack, which was built into the side of the ravine, he heard the thunder of hooves approaching from the main trail that lay due south.

Trey scowled when he recognized the rider. Jonas Rafferty's timing was terrible. If Bob Yates was ensconced in the cabin, Jonas might find himself shot out of the saddle and left for the buzzards. Whether Trey could trust Jonas or not, he needed his cousin alive. Jonas was Trey's only link to Quincy Ward.

A moving shadow near the window of the shack brought Trey's senses to full alert. A rifle barrel slid across the window-sill, pointed in Jonas's direction. Trey scrambled for position to get off a clean shot, but he was well out of range. The rifle barked, echoing around the deep chasm like a rumble of doom.

Trey swore under his breath when Jonas tumbled off his horse and sprawled facedown in the dirt. The horse clattered off, leaving Jonas an easy target in the patch of sunlight that streamed down to the floor of the ravine.

Trey waited, watching the rifle barrel withdraw from the window. A moment later, Bob Yates appeared in the doorway—his weapon trained on the body that lay below the steps. Bob limped down the stairs, pausing now and then to be sure his victim wasn't playing possum.

While Bob inched toward Jonas, Trey stalked closer. Without warning, Trey sent off a shot that took Bob's good leg out from under him. He howled in pain when his right knee folded and he tumbled down the last five steps. His rifle skidded down the slope to lodge in a prickly pear cactus.

Bob groped for the pistol tucked in his belt. He swung the weapon in every direction, trying to figure out where the shot had come from. Taking careful aim, Trey fired again. Bob's six-shooter flipped out of his hand.

"You sorry son of a bitch! Come out where I can see you!" Bob snarled as he cradled his bloody hand against his belly.

Trey squinted into the sunlight, watching Bob closely. The bastard was as twitchy as a coiled snake—and he was also armed to the teeth. If Bob had two visible weapons, then he was likely to have four concealed in his clothes. Trey didn't have time to tangle with Yates, not when Jonas needed medical attention. But Trey sure as hell wasn't about to let Yates off with a quick bullet through his black heart, either.

Terror flashed in Bob's eyes when he heard the howl of a wolf echoing around the V-shaped chasm. Frantic, he rolled to his belly and grabbed the derringer tucked in his boot.

Bob heard the muffled growls before he saw the deadly eyes, those fanged jaws open like hell's gate. Spouting foul oaths, Bob swung the snub-nosed pistol up to fire at the lead wolf, but the pistol leaped from his hand and searing pain immobilized his fingers. He didn't have time to bellow a curse at the man who had targeted him with three unerring shots—he only had time to scream before the wolves pounced on him.

Trey skidded down the slope to call off the wolves. Why he called them off, he didn't know. Considering all the innocent lives lost at this butchering thief's hands, Trey should have let the wolves chew Yates to pieces.

Bob's hands and legs were bleeding from wolf bites, but he was more than capable of spouting unprintable curses when Trey stuffed a moccasined foot in his belly. Snarling, Bob snatched up the dagger concealed inside his shirt, only to have it knocked from his bleeding fist.

"You miserable Comanche bastard," Bob seethed.

He spat at Trey, trying to provoke him into issuing a quick death. It didn't come. Trey had no intention of letting Yates off easily. Without a word, Trey retrieved a strip of leather from beneath his breastplate and bound Bob's wrists. Then he relieved him of the rest of his concealed hardware. While Trey secured Bob to the railing on the steps, Bob snarled vulgar curses. Trey ignored him and walked off to check on Jonas.

"How bad are you hit?" Trey questioned as he knelt beside his cousin.

Jonas shifted slightly and lifted his red-blond head. "I caught a bullet in the shoulder, but I was afraid to move for fear of inviting another one. Who the hell is that son of a bitch anyway?''

"Somebody I used to know," Trey murmured as he eased Jonas onto his back to cut open the bloody shirtsleeve.

Breathing raggedly, Jonas lifted his pained gaze to Trey. "You saved my life."

Though dazed with pain, Jonas noticed Three Wolves' icy facade thaw slightly. There was a hint of warmth in what had been a cold, unrelenting expression seconds earlier.

"Are you complaining, cuz?" Trey tore off a strip of fabric and tied a tourniquet around Jonas's upper arm.

"Hardly. I'm just surprised, is all. After what I did to you back then—" He met his cousin's unblinking stare. "Why did you spare me, Three Wolves?"

Trey smiled wryly, then responded as Jennifer would have had him do. After all, according to English, Trey was a good and decent man who had been sorely misunderstood.

"Bloody hell, Jonas, I couldn't let you die, now could I? You're the only family I've got left."

Jonas quirked a bushy brow and regarded his half-breed cousin for a moment. "I spent half my life in fear, wondering if you would track me down to repay me for pacifying my hysterical mother, who was having difficulty coping with the recent loss of my father. She made me take a knife to you when she couldn't do it herself. To tell the truth, I regretted it for years. And now you've saved my life, because I'm your family?" he asked incredulously. "I swear, I will never figure you out."

"Don't bother trying," Trey advised. "I'm not sure why I did it. It must have been something Jennifer said to me."

"What did she say?"

"That I have many redeeming qualities that nobody bothers to notice."

Jonas choked on a laugh. "Damned if I don't think she's right. A week ago, I thought I was a dead man when you held your knife to my throat. Now, you're coming to my rescue."

"Yeah well, you're my good deed for the decade, cuz, but don't go getting all sentimental about it."

While Trey applied pressure to stop the bleeding, Jonas stared somberly up at him. "I was telling the truth when I said I didn't kill Ramsey Templeton. He let me water my livestock when my creeks and ponds dried up. And as for Jennifer, well, what man wouldn't want her?"

"Is that what you rode out here to tell me? That you want my wife more than you want her property?" Trey asked as he wrapped a makeshift bandage around the wound. "Why did Quincy pull off his guards?"

Jonas grimaced as he levered into a sitting position. "Because Quincy is planning on coming at you tonight. He has what he wants and he plans to tie up the loose ends in one convenient knot."

Trey frowned warily. "Meaning what?"

"Meaning the high and mighty Duchess of Calverdon drove to Mobeetie to have herself declared guardian of her grandchildren." Jonas braced himself on his good arm, blinking rapidly when the world tilted on its axis. "Then the duchess had your marriage annulled and she sent out word that she wanted to sell the ranch."

Trey muttered several salty curses at Agatha.

"Quincy was the buyer," Jonas reported grimly.

"Damn that meddlesome old witch! Can't she keep that hooked nose of hers out of anybody's business?"

"Apparently not. She claims her grandchildren don't need the ranch because they have British titles."

Trey wanted to wring the dowager's neck. Jennifer had made all sorts of personal sacrifices to keep the ranch, and Agatha had signed the place over to Quincy with one stroke of her royal pen. How could she be so inconsiderate and oblivious to her grandchildren's needs? Jennifer and Christopher deserved a say in the matter, damn it!

"I'll fetch your horse," Trey volunteered, anxious to walk off his mounting frustration.

By the time Trey retrieved Jonas and Bob's horses, Jonas

had managed to stagger to his feet. Although his face was as pale as the limestone ridge that gleamed in the fading sunlight, he was determined to walk to his horse.

"I'll take you back to Templeton Ranch to dig out that bullet," Trey insisted.

He was also going to have a "chat" with Grace—the kind in which he did the talking and she did the listening. As for strangling the old prig, he might still do it after he raked her over flaming coals.

"What are you going to do with our friend over there?" Jonas panted after Trey eased him onto horseback.

Trey pivoted to see Bob Yates sprawled in the dirt while the wolves prowled around him. "You head for the ranch. I'll catch up with you in a few minutes."

Jonas nodded weakly and nudged his steed into a walk—and he didn't look back.

Bob Yates cringed when the long, hazy shadow fell over him. He squinted into the setting sun, seeing nothing but the brawny outline of *El Lobo Diablo*—the devil wolf—condensing from a fog. The bounty hunter's features were no longer clear, because of the blinding light behind him. Bob vividly remembered that flinty look in those gray eyes, the clench of the jaw, and the grim line of that chiseled mouth.

An eerie sensation slithered down Bob's spine, mingling with the throb of wolf bites and bullet wounds. He could smell the coppery scent of blood . . . and smoke.

He glanced up quickly as the haze of black fog swirled toward him. Holy hell! What kind of man was this headhunter? he wondered frantically. It was as if Bob could suddenly see right through this dangerous predator whose menacing eyes bore down like pinpoints of silver in a spinning swirl of smoke.

Bob gulped as he watched the strange apparition retrieve the Colt .45 from the cactus. Apprehensively, Bob watched Three Wolves slowly, deliberately empty the cartridges from the pistol—save one bullet.

The cloudy figure came to stand at Bob's feet. The burning

sunset at Three Wolves' back forced Bob to stare up into the blinding light surrounding the darkest of silhouettes.

"There are two wolves and one bullet, Yates," Three Wolves told him in a strange, hollow-sounding voice. *"You can use the bullet on one of the wolves, if he doesn't get to your throat first. But if the first wolf doesn't get you, the second one will. I'm giving you the choice of how you want to spend your last bullet."*

Bob stared at the inky black silhouette framed by streaming sunlight, feeling the eerie aura radiating around him, wondering if he had heard the voice whispering to him or if he'd imagined the words. A strange calm settled over the smoky figure, causing Bob to shiver in cold dread.

"You bastard," Bob hissed. "Devil wolf—"

"I recall a case two years ago when one daring outlaw vowed to take one of my wolves with him when he died," came that chilling voice.

Bob couldn't stop shaking, couldn't stop looking at the spooky cloud that appeared to be changing forms right before his eyes. "Yeah? So what did the son of a bitch do?"

"You still see the two wolves, don't you?"

To Bob's horror, the silhouette began to change forms again, gathering inside itself. Bob screamed a wild curse when the pistol dropped beside his fingertips and the cloudy apparition retreated.

"This is your judgment day, Bob Yates. You decide how you want to end it . . ."

Bob's hoarse shriek echoed around the canyon as he watched the two gray wolves bound toward him with teeth bared and eyes as black as the pits of hell. Frantic, he yanked up the pistol.

Trey opened his eyes, concentrating on the sound of his pulse drumming in his ears, feeling the coldness slowly ebb. He mounted Bob's horse and turned toward the trail leading south. The call of the wolf was still echoing around the canyon walls.

A pistol blast reverberated off the bare stone cliff, lingering, fading, disintegrating into empty silence.

Moments later, two wolves trotted from the arroyo to dutifully follow their master . . .

"Bloody, everlasting hell!" Agatha crowed in outrage.

She muttered several curses unbefitting a duchess, then re-
read the note delivered by one of Quincy's henchmen. Wheeling
around, Agatha waved the message at Simpson, who was reclin-
ing on the sofa, battling a queasy stomach.

"Do you believe what that weasel has done? He has taken
Jen and Christopher hostage and refuses to disregard our bargain. The nerve of that bumpkin! He expects me to trot back
to Mobeetie and have another set of documents drawn up,
signed, and delivered before he will release my grandchildren!
What am I to do?"

Agatha paced the floorboards. "If I do not submit to that
blackguard's demands, there is no telling what might happen
to my grandchildren. And if I do knuckle under, Jen and Christopher will never forgive me for selling their precious ranch to
the very man they suspect of killing their father. I may not
have approved of Ramsey, but he was still their sire. They were
devoted to him, though to this day I cannot fathom why."

Simpson tried to lever upright, then wilted back to the couch,
groaning miserably. "I believe you know what you must do,
Your Grace," Simpson bleated. "You will not like doing it,
of course, but we both know this sort of thing is not up your
street. This calls for professional expertise."

Agatha lurched around to glare at Simpson's chalky visage.
"Devil take it, you know it's going to kill me to do what you're
suggesting. I would rather cut out my own tongue than ask *him*
for assistance."

"I realize that, Your Grace, and I am dreadfully sorry it has
come down to this," he commiserated. "But your grandchildren's lives are at stake. One does what one must do at
times like these, including swallowing one's pride and begging
for help from those one would prefer not to associate with at
all. But under the circumstances, you have no bloody choice."

Agatha sighed dramatically. "You are quite right, of course." She peeked at Simpson over the rim of her spectacles. "Will you come with me while I humble myself to that insolent heathen? I will need moral support."

"Would that I could come." Simpson grabbed his stomach when it pitched and rolled.

When the door whined open, Agatha scurried to the hall, hoping beyond hope that her grandchildren had miraculously escaped Quincy's clutches. She was disappointed—and yet relieved to see Three Wolves looming in the doorway, garbed in his uncivilized attire of breastplate and breechcloth. He was supporting a man Agatha had not met. Thankfully, Three Wolves had arrived, saving her the trouble of searching for him.

"Thank God you're here!"

Trey arched a dark brow and stared at the dowager in astonishment. Agatha was thanking God that he had arrived? The old gal must have lost her grasp. In his haste to put Jonas to bed, Trey ignored Agatha and assisted his cousin down the hall.

"What are you doing?" Agatha sputtered when Trey eased Jonas onto her bed.

"He's been shot."

Agatha flung Trey a withering glance. "I can see that for myself. Why did you shoot him?"

Trey rolled his eyes ceilingward, requesting divine patience to deal with the old witch. "Tell English to fetch hot water and sterilize my knife. This bullet has to come out."

"Jen is not here." Agatha wrung her hands, tried to speak, then cleared her throat as if she had a chicken bone stuck in it and said, "I need—"

"Then go tell the cook to bring the supplies so I can doctor Jonas," Trey cut in impatiently. "Or have Butler do it."

"My butler is under the weather."

"Nobody is above the weather, Grace," Trey snorted sarcastically. "Except you, of course. You're above damned near everything," he couldn't help but add.

Agatha had that coming, Trey told himself. She had sold the ranch out from under her own family. He wasn't going to cut the old prig any slack since she had complicated the situation so badly with her highhanded dealings.

"Now see here, you rapscallion, I do not have to tolerate—"

"Just get the damned supplies and be quick about it," Trey barked, slapping the knife into her hand.

"Brave soul, aren't you?" Agatha smirked, staring at his bare chest as if a target were pinned on it.

"Do your worst, Grace, and see where the hell it gets you," he dared her.

Muttering, Agatha spun toward the door and nearly tripped over the wolves. "Get those monsters outside at once. These fleabags will infest the whole blooming house!"

A quiet word from Trey had the wolves crouching and snarling.

"Drat it, just forget I asked," Agatha grumbled.

"You didn't ask, you demanded."

When the wolves retreated, Agatha stamped off, muttering something Trey didn't have the time or inclination to ask her to repeat.

Several minutes later, Agatha returned with fresh bandages, water, and the sterilized knife. The sight of Jonas's wound had her gasping and wincing while she obeyed Trey's order to cleanse the injured flesh.

"Good gad, when you shoot somebody, you do make a mess of it," Agatha groused.

"I didn't shoot Jonas."

"I'm his cousin," Jonas said weakly.

"You have my sympathy, young man. We all have our crosses to bear."

Trey's fingers coiled to form a choke necklace one size smaller than the snippy duchess's throat, but he resisted the urge. Once Jonas was resting comfortably, Trey would allow himself the luxury of unleashing his fury on this harridan.

"Keep the damp towels coming," Trey instructed as he shouldered his way in front of Agatha to remove the bullet.

He handed Jonas the leather sheath that held his dagger and ordered him to bite down—hard. "Brace yourself, cousin. The less you move the sooner I'll be finished."

Nodding in grim compliance, Jonas clamped his teeth around the sheath and stared at the ceiling. When the probing knife touched tender flesh, Jonas turned white as cottage cheese and grimaced, but he didn't move a muscle. Beads of perspiration popped out on his forehead as Trey performed primitive surgery.

"Done," Trey announced. "I'll send Christopher to the fort to fetch the army surgeon."

"Christopher is not here, either," Agatha piped up.

"Where the hell is he?"

"The same bloody place Jen is."

As Trey bandaged the wound, he glanced over his shoulder to note Agatha's pallid countenance and her deflated airs. It was the first time he recalled seeing the duchess without her confidence. That did not bode well.

"Where's English?" Trey asked with wary trepidation.

Agatha retrieved the message she had tucked in her pocket. She presented it to Trey with shaky hands. "I need your help," she said humbly. "In fact, I know of no one else competent enough to undo the damage I have done."

Trey did a double take. He stared into those misty blue eyes that usually glittered with condescension but were now wide with desperation. Trey grabbed the note, read it, and then frowned curiously at Agatha.

"When I told Christopher I had made arrangements to sell the ranch to Quincy Ward, he exploded. He tore up the contract and stalked off to inform Quincy that the deal was off. I was not aware that Quincy was suspected of killing Ramsey, and I had not a blooming clue that this property was worth more than twenty cents an acre—"

"Twenty cents!" Jonas croaked. "You sold this ranch for twenty cents an acre? Good Lord!"

"Well, I was *going* to," Agatha amended. "Quincy had yet to sign the contract and make his payment. When Jen learned

that Christopher had charged off to confront Quincy, she went
after him. Then this message arrived, informing me that if I
don't draw up a new set of documents and sign the bill of sale,
my grandchildren will be the price I pay for reneging.''

Trey scowled in disgust. Agatha had made a horrible mess
of things. When Trey went up against Quincy and his army of
hired guns, it would be like storming a well-fortified castle.

"He would not dare dispose of my grandchildren . . . would
he? Surely that scoundrel knows I would have him shot, stabbed,
and hung!''

"You'll have to drive into town to rewrite the contracts,''
Trey told Agatha.

"But I cannot sell him the ranch now. My grandchildren
will never speak to me again. You have got to do something.
Jen maintains that no one is as adept at this sort of thing as
you are. I desperately need your help!''

"What are we going to do, Three Wolves?'' Jonas questioned
groggily. "You know Quincy will be ready and waiting if the
duchess doesn't make that trip to town. And he will probably
be expecting you, after his attempted ambush falls through.''

Trey glanced grimly at Agatha. "Get Butler to drive you
into town. I want Quincy's men to see you leaving before it's
too dark to make a positive identification.''

"Simpson is recuperating.''

"I am feeling better now, Your Grace.''

Agatha lurched around to see Simpson propped against the
door. "Simpson, go lie down before you fall down!''

Trey appraised the staggering butler, who had latched onto
the doorjamb for additional support. "What happened to you?''

"Master Christopher lost his temper when I tried to prevent
him from going up against that sneaky blackguard.'' He glanced
at Agatha. "I am going with you and that is that.''

Trey lifted a mocking brow. "Butler is giving you orders
these days, is he? And you are begging me for assistance?
Bloody, everlasting hell, Grace, what is this world coming to?''

"Do shut up, you ornery rascal,'' Agatha harumphed. "Just
because I have to humble myself—to barely tolerable

extremes—to gain your assistance does not mean I actually like you. I may be desperate, but I have not taken leave of my senses, you know.''

''Actually, Three Wolves is a good and decent man,'' Jonas said on Trey's behalf. ''He saved my life.''

Agatha snorted at the pale-faced patient. ''You do not look all that saved to me. I happen to think you are delirious from shock, truth be known.''

Despite her gruff words, Agatha's gaze swung back to Trey. Her eyes locked and clashed with his, then she looked at him with what Trey deciphered as grudging respect—very grudging. Trey also thought he saw the slightest hint of a smile appear momentarily on those pinched lips. But he wouldn't want to have to swear to that.

''If you save my grandchildren from this wretched mess I have made, you can name your own price,'' Agatha said magnanimously.

''And if I don't come out alive?''

''Then I shall award you with a dignified English title and have your crest carved on your headstone.''

''Thanks, Grace. Just what I always wanted,'' Trey said, and smirked.

''Very well then, if you make the supreme sacrifice on my grandchildren's behalf, I shall have *myself* shot. That should make you immensely happy.''

''Your Grace!'' Simpson objected loudly.

''Bloody hell, Simpson. I was only jesting,'' Agatha said with her customary hauteur intact. ''Who would rule the world if I were gone? The entire social structure would crumble.''

Trey smiled to himself. Who would have thought he liked Agatha's airs better than her humility? She simply didn't fit the meek, humble role. ''Just one more thing before you go, Grace. There is a stipulation to our agreement.''

''Good gad, I should have expected as much from you,'' she grumbled, but her tone wasn't as critical as it had once been. Trey was sure the stressful situation had taken the starch out of her.

"If English and Christopher are safely returned to you, then I want your promise to let them choose where they want to live." Trey's silver eyes bore into Agatha. "I mean it. No interference. I want your word as a duchess, or whatever the hell you Britishers swear on."

"You rascal, you are twisting my arm a dozen different ways."

"That's the deal," Trey insisted. "Take it or leave it."

"Bloody, blooming hell!" Agatha fussed, stamped, and snorted. "Oh rot, have it your way then. No interference from me. And blast it, I shall always hate you for making me agree to this!"

Agatha took herself off, muttering the words *insufferable, intolerable,* and *insolent*—to name only a few.

Jonas frowned, bemused, when Agatha and Simpson disappeared from sight. "I'm not sure how to take the duchess."

"In small doses," Trey said, and smirked.

"The duchess is full of spit and fire, isn't she?"

Trey didn't bother to reply. His thoughts had turned to Jennifer and Christopher. "I need you to draw me a sketch of Quincy's ranch."

"What are you planning?"

Trey shrugged evasively.

"Whatever you decide to do had better include me," Jonas insisted. "You can't take on Quincy and his army by yourself."

"You aren't going anywhere. If I don't come out alive, someone has to be around to make sure the duchess keeps her word."

"You know what I think?" Jonas asked wearily.

"What makes you think I care what you think?"

Jonas grinned. "I think you and the duchess have a lot in common. Your barks are worse than your bites."

"Think again, cousin." Trey hitched his thumb toward the wolves at the door. "My bite can be very effective when it needs to be."

He patted Jonas's good shoulder, as much surprised by his impulsive display of friendship as Jonas was. Trey had undergone a change that he was at a loss to understand. Although instinct and training still controlled his actions in times of danger, Jennifer's influence had brought out gentler aspects of his personality. His association with her had put him back in touch with emotions he believed to be dead and buried decades ago. She had breathed life back into his soul.

Trey hoped they both survived so he could thank her—or curse her. Being kind and sentimental definitely felt awkward and unnatural after years of bottling up his feelings and isolating himself from the world.

Fifteen

"Is anybody ever gonna tell us what the hell is going on around here?" Jawbone muttered when Trey strode off the front porch.

"The duchess and her butler flew off to town, and I haven't seen Miss Jenny or Christopher for hours," Sunset said worriedly.

"One of the cowboys came back from getting supplies for the cook and said the ranch had been sold!" Jawbone jerked off his hat and slapped it against his thigh. "Damn it, Three Wolves, what happened?"

Trey quickly explained the situation, in between Sunset and Jawbone's hisses and sputters. "If I'm not back by dawn, the two of you are in charge of a strike force to storm Quincy's headquarters. You better start devising a plan and gathering your posse," Trey advised.

"You don't mean to take on that stronghold, all by yerself, do you?" Jawbone asked. "Hell's fire, everybody knows Quincy has an army of sharpshooters protecting him."

"How many?" Trey wanted to know.

"Ten quick-draws packing all sorts of hardware, and ten

burly brutes who tear up Mobeetie every Saturday night for pure sport.''

"That's not counting the twenty toughs who ride herd on the cattle. They ain't exactly the kind of men who go right home to their mamas, either,'' Sunset put it. "Then there are those three new hoodlums, the ones I suspect robbed us on the way to Dodge. According to rumor, they escaped from jail somewhere south of here, before Quincy hired them on, but nobody has proof and the sheriff hasn't got the nerve to go find out with all those hired guns around the ranch.''

Trey had the unmistakable feeling the three names on the bench warrants that Sheriff Hartman had handed to him in Dodge fit the descriptions of the men riding with Quincy's pack. No doubt the marshal in Abilene would dearly like to know what became of the men who killed his young deputy, Trey mused.

"Jawbone, I want you and Sunset to ride to the north range to fetch my gear and horse from my campsite. There are three bench warrants in my saddlebags. Take a close look at them. I expect the descriptions fit Quincy's new gunmen. When you return, leave Diablo and my gear beside the back exit of the barn.''

"And what are you gonna be doing while we're running errands?'' Jawbone wanted to know.

"Feeding the wolves,'' Trey said as he strode away.

"At a time like this?'' Sunset crowed in frustration.

"Exactly at a time like this,'' Trey threw over his shoulder.

"Damn it to hell,'' Sunset muttered as Trey and the wolves disappeared into the shadows of the night. "How can he be as calm as a toad in the sun at a time like this? My nerves are tangled in jittery knots, wondering if Miss Jenny and young Chris are all right.''

"That's why you herd cattle for a living and Three Wolves tracks desperadoes,'' Jawbone insisted.

"Well, if Miss Jenny and Christopher aren't back here by dawn, I'm gonna change professions real quick,'' Sunset declared as he bounded onto his horse.

"I'm feeling the calling myself," Jawbone seconded as he rode off to tend his errand.

Trey took the wolves down to Sweetwater Creek, allowing them to hunt while he focused his thoughts and energies on the difficult task ahead. His gaze followed the skulking wolves, remembering the first time they had appeared to him.

As a young boy, Trey had been ordered by his grandfather to leave their campsite to hunt alone. He had gotten lost in the thickets when a Blue Norther blew down from the mountains. He had been ill-prepared for the icy temperatures, and had fallen asleep, shivering from the cold, never expecting to wake up, praying to the spirits his grandfather spoke of so often. Over and over, Trey had called to the powerful totem that Black Wolf insisted would be there to guide and protect him.

At dawn of the third day, Trey had awakened to find a pair of gray timber wolves flanking his shivering body, providing the warmth that had allowed him to survive the blizzard. He had known the moment he looked into those fathomless eyes, and heard the silent howl echoing in his mind, that Black Wolf's prediction had come true.

The Comanche shaman had repeated constantly that the power of the spirit world would appear to him when the time was right. Black Wolf instructed him not to be afraid, but to accept and embrace the power source—*puha*—that was his to command.

For two more days Trey had slept beside the wolves, waking to communicate with them in ways white civilization failed to understand, in ways he himself was at a loss to explain at such a young age. During their time together, Trey had become one of them, a creature of instinct and habit, a predator of the wilderness.

The wolves had taught by example, relentlessly searching to find food, prowling the snowdrifts, always on guard. And Trey had learned things from them, things difficult to explain to anyone except Black Wolf.

When the Comanche shaman came searching for Trey, the wolves had sent up their mournful howls, leading Black Wolf to his grandson. While Black Wolf stood at a distance, the wolves had circled, then disappeared into a haze among the trees.

With an understanding nod of his gray head, Black Wolf had opened his arms and called Trey to him. "The lobos have chosen you, sought you out, extended their great power to you. You have met your allies, and where there were two wolves now there will be three, Wolf Prophet," the old Comanche shaman murmured as he wrapped Trey in the warmth of the buffalo robe.

Eight years later, when Trey returned from the eastern school, he was granted his walking papers because of his white heritage. Led by the silent call of the wolves that had rescued him that cold, desolate night of the blizzard, Trey had followed the instinctive calling to Spirit Springs. There, the wolves appeared to him again, and he had fully embraced the powers bestowed on him . . .

Trey breathed deeply, feeling those familiar sensations seeping into him as they had so often the past ten years. It was an inexpressible communion of body, mind, and spirit that Trey had never been able to explain to Jennifer—never wanted her to see for herself.

Jennifer had been oblivious to the changes he had undergone during his attack on the Yates Gang at his campsite near Dodge, because Trey had been careful to come back into himself enough to communicate with her. And after the merciless outlaws took her captive, she had been semi-conscious when he brought his wrath down on Russ Trent in that dugout. But Jennifer might get a good look at *El Lobo Diablo* before this night was out. If he managed to save her, he would have to let her go forever, because she might not be able to cope with what he became when he battled life's worst evils against difficult odds.

Trey had warned Jennifer once that she didn't know him as well as she wanted to believe she did, but she had refused to listen. But tonight, she might become intimately acquainted with the Wolf Prophet—just as Bob Yates had before stark terror prompted him to turn the gun on himself.

To save Jennifer from Quincy, and his pack of hired guns, Trey might have to lose her respect and admiration, lose *her* forever . . .

This dark side of him, the deeply ingrained part of his Comanche upbringing, was the real reason why Trey could never be part of Jennifer's world. She didn't understand—only Comanches knew of the mystic revelation that altered the course of Trey's life two decades ago. And yet, this part of him was what Trey had to call upon, rely upon, to save Jennifer and keep the fragile peace she held so dear.

If Jennifer saw what he became, she would be terrified, repulsed by him. The love she claimed to feel for him would die in that moment. She would see him for what he truly was when Trey *called in the wolves* . . .

Trey's troubled thoughts trailed off when muffled snarls, and a rabbit's last cry—a shrill, haunting sound—hung in the damp night air. He could feel the spiritual powers of his guiding totem gathering in the night like an approaching storm. He focused absolute concentration on the mission that awaited him. To battle the demons he had to become the crafty, cunning wolf.

El Lobo Diablo, the devil wolf . . . Trey cleared all other thoughts from his mind. There would be no mercy, no hesitation. He would rely solely upon swift, unerring predatory instinct. He could not be the good and decent man Jennifer optimistically believed him to be, not while he stalked on the dark side.

This is what the white man referred to as ''the last resort''. This was what had inspired the legends of his feats against desperadoes.

Jennifer maintained that the tales were preposterous rumors. She had yet to realize that the incidents that spawned the wild rumors were closer to the truth than she could possibly imagine.

As for Quincy Ward, he was about to encounter the devil wolf, born of smoke, fed by flames . . . and thirsting for revenge.

When Trey immersed himself in those deep, dark recesses of the mind and called to his guardian spirit as Black Wolf taught him to do, there would be no turning back. The avenging spirit of justice fought fire with fire, and smoke with smoke.

Resolutely, Trey called the wolves to heel. Together, they moved silently along the creek, evanescent in the swaying shadows, rising in the silence of the night to move with the wind . . .

The "muster call" of the wolf caught on the breeze and swirled around Jawbone and Sunset as they gathered the belongings that had been riddled with bullets at the campsite. From the look of things, Quincy's henchman had attacked, filling the effigy of Three Wolves with buckshot before riding off into the night.

Jawbone grimaced when he heard the eerie sound rolling toward him. He had heard that "muster call" in the past, while riding night hawk on cattle drives. He had heard it said that there was a certain howl that summoned the scattered members of a wolf pack together for attack. Jawbone had witnessed such attacks in the past. Every ranch in the area had lost cattle and sheep to the predators on occasion—after all, Wolf Creek in West Texas hadn't been named for nothing.

Jawbone well remembered seeing a longhorn bull attacked by four wolves on a remote section of Templeton Ranch. Having made the disastrous mistake of wandering from the herd, the bull had jerked up its head from grazing to find itself surrounded. When the wolves pounced, the bull slashed its horns at the swarming enemy, but the trailing wolf snapped the tendon on the back of the bull's hock and rendered it immobile—much like Three Wolves had sliced Bob Yates's hamstring.

Jawbone had ridden hell-for-leather, firing his pistol in an attempt to scatter the wolves before they tore open the bull's flanks and cut the jugular vein with those razor-sharp teeth. But in the span of one minute it had been too late. Clips from those powerful jaws left Jawbone gaping in amazement. There was no defense against wolves mad with hunger and vicious enough to stop man and horse from interfering with their killing and feasting.

The haunting call of the wolf rose again when Jawbone tethered Diablo near the back exit of the barn—as Three Wolves instructed. Jawbone glanced out the doorway to see the full moon beaming down like a shiny silver dollar.

Comanche moon—the only light source needed to illuminate the way, cast exactly the kind of light that enabled predators to prowl in the darkness.

Sunset rubbed the back of his neck as he led his steed to its stall to remove the saddle. "I've got a bad feeling in my bones, Jaw. Something is different tonight. Something eerie."

From the adjacent stall, Jawbone glanced around apprehensively. "Reminds me of taking night watch on cattle drives. Every sound is amplified until it starts working on yer nerves and yer imagination."

"I hope it works on Quincy's imagination," Sunset grumbled. "Miss Jenny is so sweet and kind that the thought of anything happening to her tears me up inside—"

"What was that?" Jawbone spun around, reflexively reaching for his six-shooter. To his shocked amazement, the black stallion he had tethered beside the back door of the barn had vanished into thin air.

Another "muster call" of the wolf caught on the wind and distant howls—dozens of them—came rolling in from all directions at once.

"Geezus!" Sunset shivered in his boots when an icy breeze swept through the barn. "It sounds like he's calling in the wolves!"

Jawbone peered through the open door, watching darting shadows condense and swirl away. He swallowed hard, then glanced uneasily at his companion. "Do you remember the day Three Wolves took on the Yates Gang and we thought there was something strange about him?"

Sunset's red head bobbed, recalling that unnerving feeling that overcame him while he watched Three Wolves in action.

''Yeah, it gave me the willies the way his voice and eyes changed, the way that smoky aura kept whirling around him. But damn, this is ten times worse!''

''Lord . . .'' Jawbone breathed, rubbing the goose bumps that pebbled his skin. ''I'm glad I ain't Quincy Ward tonight. I got an itchy feeling all hell is about to break loose in West Texas.''

''Yeah,'' Sunset murmured. ''And I got a feeling yer right.''

Christopher blinked in surprise when he saw his sister's trim silhouette pass through the scant beam of light that filtered through the cellar window. It was obvious that Jennifer had managed to wrest her hands loose from the binding rope. ''How'd you do that, Jen?''

''Old Comanche trick,'' she said, smiling triumphantly.

''You sound just like Trey,'' Christopher mumbled.

Jennifer's smile vanished as she carefully negotiated around the clutter of cans, wooden crates, and jars to untie her brother. Time had not dimmed her vivid memories of Trey. She had hoped the pain of loving him so deeply would ebb, but Trey MacTavish was not an easy man to forget. Jennifer had let herself love him with her entire being, because instinct told her she could never feel that special emotion for any other man.

Even now, here in the darkness, she could see his striking image floating above her, see those entrancing silver eyes staring at her like the moonlight beaming through the window.

Jennifer had memorized every detail about Trey. She could almost feel his dynamic presence beside her. Hardly unbelievable, she thought as she knelt to untie Christopher's feet. When a man took up residence in a woman's very soul, it was small wonder that scents and sounds triggered certain sensations.

She also recalled that powerful aura of self-confidence that radiated around Three Wolves when he was his most dangerous, most predatory. Jennifer tried to emulate that sense of power and strength of will in her escape attempt. Trey had once told her that the Comanche learned from the habits of wild creatures to move undetected.

She also remembered the symbolic feather woven into the braid in Trey's raven hair. The tail feather of the eagle, which carried a bird silently in flight, was Trey's constant reminder to proceed with the silence of shadows.

Jennifer intended to use that technique—just as she had used the cold dampness of the root cellar, and the whiskey in the jug beside her to make her skin contract so she could slide her hands loose from the rope. Of course, she smelled like a brewery after spilling half the contents of the jug on her wrists, but the cool liquid had served its purpose.

"Take off your boots, Christopher," Jennifer instructed.

"What? Why?"

"I want you to tiptoe up the steps and peek through the keyhole," she whispered. "Find out how many guards are standing watch."

While Christopher reconnoitered, Jennifer removed her shoes, then stacked crates against the stone wall of the cellar to form a makeshift staircase to the window. With her fingertips she traced the wooden frame of the window that held the glass in place. As if she were wiggling a loose tooth, she jostled the warped frame, drawing the faintest rattle of glass.

"I only see one guard," Christopher murmured. "It's the same one who tried to rearrange my face while his cohorts held me down. I think I can take him."

"Through a locked door? I daresay we are not mistaking confidence for foolhardy arrogance again, are we?"

Christopher gnashed his teeth. "I'm a man now, Jen. I can take care of myself when I need to."

"I am glad to hear it," she said, distracted. "Now kindly hand me your pocketknife so I can remove this glass. Perhaps you have decided to knock down the door and make mincemeat of the guard, but I prefer a quieter exit that will not draw attention. Quincy has too many men prowling around for us to take them on, unarmed."

Christopher tiptoed down the steps to hand his sister the

knife. "You will never be able to remove the glass without breaking it. That will make as much racket as ripping the door off its hinges—"

"An excellent idea. Glad you thought of it. See if you can slip the bolts from the hinges, and then set a few booby traps on the steps. Use the rope, jars, and crates to trip up the guard if he comes barreling inside. If I make a racket removing the glass, our fumbling guard might not be able to reach us before we crawl outside."

Christopher groped around to locate anything—and everything—that might serve as an obstacle in the guard's hasty flight down the steps. Within a few minutes he had gathered a stockpile of crates, jars, and tin cans from the shelves.

Once Christopher had set his booby traps, he grabbed four pickle jars to use as grenades and missiles—just in case. He sincerely hoped the bully of a guard came tumbling down the staircase and landed in a heap. Christopher would like to enjoy a little revenge on that big ape who had blackened his eye and bloodied his nose.

Mission accomplished, Christopher followed the dim shaft of light to the window where Jennifer worked with painstaking care. "Any luck yet, sis?"

"Minimal progress," she reported. "I pried one side loose."

"How much longer?"

"I don't know. Have patience."

"I have patience aplenty. It's time we may be a trifle short of."

Christopher eased down onto a chair-size crate and waited, then waited some more.

"Hell's teeth! Open this blasted door!" Agatha crowed impatiently. "Phinneus, wake up. I am on a desperate errand here. This is no time for you to be gadding about in bed. You were bloody well paid to be at my beck and call!"

"What the hell is—?" Phinneus Albright, garbed in his long nightshirt, stepped back apace when he whipped open the door to find the Duchess of Calverdon and her ever-present butler standing on the stoop. "Your Grace, what is wrong?"

"Everything!" Agatha barged inside without awaiting invitation. "You must draw up another contract for the sale of the ranch. The price per acre will now read three dollars."

"Three dollars?" Phinneus croaked, wide-eyed. "Your Grace, that is outrageous."

"So is taking my grandchildren hostage to blackmail me into a sale that I have decided not to make," Agatha harumphed.

Phinneus staggered back another step. "Quincy Ward kidnapped your grandchildren?"

"Indeed, and I am filing a formal complaint against him. As my solicitor, I expect you to see that rascal jailed, shot, and his carcass hung out to dry. Your client is a sneak, a murderer, and a thief. I advise you not to represent him if you are partial to your law practice. I will have you blacklisted in every state in this nation if you do!"

Snatching the lantern from Phinneus's hand, Agatha breezed into the study. "Get some paper and let's get at it, Phinneus. Time's a-wasting. If Quincy Ward intends to buy the ranch, then he will bloody well pay through his blooming nose! And if he declines, then it will be his option. I mean to have his head for this, one ruddy way or another!"

Phinneus scurried to his desk to fetch pen and paper. Within a few minutes he had a handwritten document signed and witnessed—according to Agatha's specifications.

"First thing in the morning—no, first thing *now,*" Agatha amended as she tucked the folded document in her reticule. "I want you to contact the sheriff and file complaints of kidnapping, blackmail, extortion, and whatever else you think will apply. Stretch it, Phinneus. Quincy Ward will not battle a duchess and win. I daresay it goes against the very laws of nature!"

"Do you want a posse to handle this dreadful affair, Your Grace?" Phinneus questioned.

Agatha sniffed at the preposterous suggestion. "My good man, I have already enlisted a posse of one. I hardly need a gaggle of sleepy-eyed geese botching things up."

Phinneus blinked like a startled owl. "One man, Your Grace?"

"Well, I only have one problem, don't I? I have enlisted the services of the one and only man capable of getting things done."

When Agatha blew off like a cyclone, Simpson opened the door for her and followed her outside. "Begging your pardon, Your Grace, but are you aware of what you just said?"

"Yes, yes, Simpson. I am vividly aware of what I said."

Agatha flounced onto the buggy seat and snatched up the reins. It was a new experience for her. She had never driven herself anywhere in her entire life, much less climbed aboard a carriage without assistance.

"But I have to give that devil wolf man due credit, don't I? And Jennifer seems to think that positive mental powers can be projected into workable solutions. I have decided to give it a whirl."

"Good gad, Your Grace, if I did not know better, I would say you have actually come to like that ornery barbarian," Simpson said with a teasing chuckle. "When did this happen?"

Agatha hadn't thought it possible for that sinewy mountain of a man to have a tender bone in his body, but she had been very much impressed by the way Three Wolves gentled in Jennifer's presence. Of course, Agatha would never actually comment about that in front of the insolent galoot. Couldn't have the man thinking she actually respected him, now could she? After all, he was stairsteps below her station in life.

"So you are saying that you do like the man?" Simpson persisted.

"Of course not," Agatha snapped as she popped the reins on the horse's rump. "I will never appreciate my ex-grandson-in-law. He is so much like me that I can barely tolerate the rascal."

Simpson squawked when the buggy lurched forward, flinging his head against the back of the seat, causing his sensitive stomach to heave. "Perhaps you should let me drive, Your Grace."

"Nonsense, Simpson. I can handle this nag—whoa!"

"Holy hell! What was that?"

The night watchman on the west range of Quincy's property jerked straight up in the saddle and stared every which way at once. The rider who had come to replace him shifted uneasily on his mount as it sidestepped skittishly beneath him.

"What the devil is the matter with this damned horse?" the second watch muttered.

Both steeds threw their heads and pranced backward, drawing foul curses from their riders.

"It must be the wind," the first rider said.

"Wind doesn't yap ... Hell, that sounds like a pack of wolves!"

"Damn it, if those varmints stir up the herd, these cattle will be climbing all over us—"

The two night riders felt the earth rumble beneath them. In the distance, blue sparks flickered in the darkness. But it wasn't harmless fireflies skipping across the sprawling pasture. It was the light given off by the friction of long horns clanking together as the frightened cattle leaped to their feet and charged off, serenaded by the howls of circling wolves.

"Stampede!" the second night watch shouted in alarm.

A sea of blue sparks floated above the rumbling earth. It looked as if every herd of longhorns grazing in every pasture for miles around had converged, driven by a plague of wolves. Unsettling howls mingled with the sound of bawling cattle and pounding hooves. Barbed wire coiled and fence posts cracked and fell beneath the thundering hordes that churned their way across the prairie.

Darting shadows were everywhere, and the eerie howls penetrated the night air. Fanged creatures scrabbled up from the stony arroyos and cedar-choked ravines, causing the frightened cattle to circle, then split apart to escape the vicious bites of powerful jaws snapping at their heels. Mayhem erupted, and the pistols of night riders flared like torches, then vanished in the billowing cloud of dust.

And the wolves kept coming . . .

Sixteen

From his advantageous position on the balcony, Quincy stared across the pasture. Sounds reminiscent of thunder, and sparks like lightning, fanned out in all directions. Shadows swirled in the full moonlight.

"What the hell is happening out there?"

"Sounds like the world is coming to an end," Bernie Giles said uneasily.

"It's the cattle!" Quincy realized suddenly. "Hightail it to the bunkhouse and rouse the rest of my men. Something spooked my cattle herds."

When Bernie jogged off, Yancy Wyatt moved a step closer to convey the message delivered a few minutes earlier. "The watch guards said to tell you that the duchess and her servant raced off to town just before dark."

"Good—that old bat should be at the lawyer's house, drawing up a new contract." Spellbound, Quincy stared at the gray fog that hovered above the flinty sparks. "What about Three Wolves? Did the men make short work of him at his campsite?"

Yancy shifted uneasily as he peered at the swirling shadows on the perimeters of the cloud of dust. "Afraid not, boss. We came down on him with pistols blazing, but when we checked his bedroll he wasn't there. He must have slipped away without us realizing it."

"Well, damn," Quincy hissed.

"Our watch guards spotted him at Templeton Ranch just before dusk. He took his wolves for a walk. Nobody has seen him since he disappeared into the cottonwoods beside Sweet-water Creek. I guess that's good news, eh, boss?"

"No, that is the worst kind of news," Quincy grunted as unsettling sensations skittered down his backbone. "I don't trust that half-breed bastard, whether I can see him or not. He must be out there somewhere."

Yancy chuckled recklessly. "Surely you don't think one man is responsible for this gigantic stampede."

"Stampede?" Quincy half turned to glare at the cocky gun-man. "Does that look like any stampede you've ever seen? The dust is rolling in from all directions. You would have to have a hundred skilled riders on a hundred well-trained horses to set off a stampede of this magnitude. And it will take three hundred expert horsemen to stop it!"

"Templeton Ranch doesn't even have a hundred hired hands," Yancy replied. "I know because we've got guards posted around the place. All the hired hands are present and accounted for. So what could have possibly started ten stam-pedes at once?"

"Hell if I know."

Quincy fixed his gaze on the spooky blue sparks and ominous dust cloud. A chorus of eerie howls wafted toward him, becom-ing more distinguishable with each passing second. Quincy erupted in furious curses when he saw orange flames crawling up the walls of the barn, spreading like golden fingers across the roof.

The shrill whinnies of terrified horses split the air. Darting silhouettes poured from the bunkhouse. Shouts rose to the bal-cony, and Quincy's well-armed brigade was suddenly scattering like retreating troops from battle. The ranch headquarters had become mass chaos. He could hear the horses screaming as they pounded their hooves against the stalls to escape the fire. Ranch hands dashed around madly, trying to rescue the prize animals before they were fried alive.

The world Quincy had commanded and controlled was crumbling before his very eyes. His last stronghold was the house— protected by only three bodyguards, one of whom had charged off to the bunkhouse minutes earlier. Where Bernie Giles was now was anybody's guess. But thankfully, Frank Irving was still guarding the cellar door so the hostages couldn't escape.

A nerve-shattering howl caused the hair on the back of Quincy's neck to stand on end. The "muster call" of wolves came from everywhere at once—like a haunting chorus of demons echoing through the night.

"Three Wolves is here. God Almighty," Quincy muttered as he lurched toward Yancy Wyatt. "Bring Jennifer to my office."

"What about her brother?"

"I want to keep him separated from Jennifer. I'm not going to make this any easier for that half-breed gunslinger than I have to. If he wants to burn this house down around me, I'll damned well take the Templetons with me."

With a pistol clamped in each fist, Yancy scurried off. He prepared himself for attack from any direction as he inched down the staircase to the ground floor. A hazy shadow passed in front of the screen door, and Yancy gulped apprehensively. He could have sworn Quincy had left a lantern burning in the foyer. Either the flame had gone out . . . or someone had snuffed all the lanterns in every room on the ground floor.

Cautiously. Yancy craned his neck around the corner of the parlor. Someone had definitely been prowling around. Damn it, what the hell was going on?

Swallowing hard, Yancy inched along the wall toward the entrance to the cellar. He was anxious to get his hands on Three Wolves' pretty ex-wife, so he could use her as a shield. Surely Three Wolves wouldn't go through Jennifer to get to him . . . would he?

The sound of muffled footsteps caused Yancy to spin

around—his index finger poised on the trigger of his Colt. Yancy half collapsed against the wall when he recognized Frank Irving's familiar silhouette in the faint light from the moon. It was sheer luck that the two men had recognized each other before they blew each other to kingdom come.

"Damn it, Yancy, you scared ten years off my life," Frank hissed through clenched teeth. "Who turned off all the goddam lights?"

"I thought maybe you did," Yancy whispered. "Hell, I was hoping you'd done it."

"Wasn't me. I've been guarding the cellar door, but damned if I know why. I haven't heard a peep from our hostages in two hours."

"Well, you won't have to guard the door any longer." Yancy drew a steadying breath and surged down the hall. "Quincy wants Jennifer where he can keep a close eye on her. He's certain Three Wolves is around here somewhere."

"What's going on outside? It sounds like another Civil War broke out," Frank mumbled uneasily.

Yancy scanned the shifting shadows cast by the burning barn. "I'm beginning to wish I'd stayed in jail in Abilene and thrown myself on the mercy of the court."

"Stop talking crazy, Yancy. You know you'd be weighting down a hangman's noose by now. That marshal and his pal, the judge, weren't offering any mercy."

"Well, serving a prison sentence for killing that young deputy might be better than coming face-to-face with the legend of Three Wolves," he whispered. "I've been hearing lots of tales about that bounty hunter lately. Folks are saying that he is indestructible, and Quincy thinks Three Wolves is responsible for the stampede and burning barn."

Frank snorted carelessly. "We've all gotta die sometime, even the almighty Three Wolves. Besides, there's a small army outside that's packing enough hardware to stop a whole war party of Comanches. How's one man gonna get through all our reinforcements?"

"Our army has scattered like quail to fight battles on all

fronts,'' Yancy growled. "If you ask me, that one-man war party is turning out to be one man too many—" His voice dried up when haunting howls mingled with screams of torment. Shadows swirled past the windows—shadows that were starting to look like the dark silhouettes of man-eating wolves!

"Damn, Frank. It sounds like Three Wolves has definitely arrived—and he brought hell with him.''

Like a shot, Yancy darted toward the cellar to retrieve Jennifer. Suddenly, he didn't have the slightest objection to hiding behind a woman's skirt—especially if the skirt belonged to the woman the legendary wolf man had been married to.

"What is that?" Christopher questioned. "Is this what an earthquake sounds like?"

Jennifer pried the last corner of glass, feeling it vibrate in her hands. "I don't know, but it looks as if the world has gone up in flames." Finally, she managed to slide the glass from its frame and peek outside. "The barn is on fire!"

She handed the glass to her brother, then gestured for him to help her down from the stack of crates. "You will have to climb out the window and pull me out after you," she insisted. "I'm not tall enough to hoist myself up and out."

Steadying his hands on Jennifer's shoulders, Christopher scaled the wobbly crates. He braced his elbows on the narrow window ledge and heaved himself up until he was half in and half out of the window. Using the crates beneath him as a springboard, he surged upward. The stairsteps of crates tumbled down behind him.

"Bloody hell," he muttered.

Alarmed, Jennifer wheeled toward the door and heard the rattle of the key in the lock. The door crashed onto the landing and obscene curses filled the cellar like a fog. Frantic, Jennifer restacked the fallen crates while Christopher wormed through the narrow opening.

Another round of expletives filled the air when Yancy Wyatt and Frank Irving stumbled over the booby traps Christopher had left in their path. The men tumbled down the steps, then crawled onto their hands and knees while Jennifer balanced on her shaky pyramid.

"If we don't stop her, Quincy will have our heads," Yancy said and scowled as he crawled toward the shaft of light.

Jennifer tried to find a foothold on the wall, but there was nothing to aid in pulling herself up to reach Christopher's outstretched hand. If her brother tried to help her escape, she feared he would get himself shot. Jennifer refused to put Christopher's life in jeopardy.

"Run, Chris," she shouted urgently.

"But—"

"Blister it, run!"

Jennifer shrieked when Frank grabbed the hem of her dress and yanked her off her unstable perch. Crates clattered and tumbled, and Jennifer smacked her head against the stone wall as she fell. Gritting her teeth against the pain, she came up swinging, determined to provide enough distraction for her brother to make his getaway.

"Ouch! You little bitch!" Yancy hissed when sharp fingernails slashed across the side of his face. "You'll pay for that— ooff . . ."

Jennifer's elbow caught Yancy in the soft underbelly, sending him stumbling over the scattered crates. When Frank latched onto her sleeve, she bit a chunk out of his knuckles. As he recoiled, she kicked him squarely in the crotch, and Frank began howling like a dying coyote.

Although woozy from the second blow to the swollen knot on her head, Jennifer pushed away from the wall and bounded over the downed men. If Yancy hadn't rolled onto his belly and snaked out his hand, Jennifer might have made it up the steps, free and clear. But Yancy's fist closed around the trailing hem of her skirt. Groping for an improvised weapon, Jennifer plucked up a nearby crate and konked Yancy atop the head. She tried to bound off, but her legs entangled in her skirts as she scrabbled over the jars and cans that littered the steps.

Frank flung himself toward Jennifer before she could reach

the door, yanking her backward by the hair. "I've got her, Yancy! Get up here and help me before she squirms loose."

Yancy scrambled up the stairs to hook his arm around Jennifer's waist. When he crammed the barrel of his pistol between her ribs, Jennifer muttered in defeat. She found herself bookended by the two henchman and propelled down the darkened hall.

At least Christopher had escaped, she consoled herself as she felt the dizzy sensations whirring around her. She would be eternally thankful if one Templeton heir managed to come out of this calamity alive. And thank God she had not involved Trey in this, she mused. She would never be able to forgive herself if that had happened. Wherever Trey was, she hoped he would remember her fondly . . . if this turned out to be the last night of her life . . .

"Jen . . ." Christopher muttered to himself as he watched his sister being led away. He hadn't run, as she had told him to do. He had waited, hoping to offer her a helping hand, but she had opted to dash up the steps—and found herself overtaken by Quincy's henchmen.

Cursing silently, Christopher climbed to his feet and backed away from the window. Startled, he slammed into an object as solid as a stone wall and as cold as the arctic. A steely hand clamped over his mouth before he reflexively let out a yelp.

Christopher shuddered uncontrollably, sensing that whatever had a hold on him was not quite human. The harsh breath against his neck was like the chill of death.

"Don't turn around, and don't make a sound . . ."

The voice was so hollow and distorted that Christopher couldn't decide if he had heard the words or thought them in that moment of petrifying fear. He couldn't see who—or what—stood behind him, engulfing him like the tentacles of an octopus. The scent of smoke penetrated his nostrils.

"When you have been released, run straight toward the

grove of cedars. Three horses are tethered there. Take one of them and ride home."

When the icy arms fell away, Christopher glanced sideways, seeing what appeared to be a living shadow looming behind him. The hazy outline was like a pocket of black against a backdrop of darkness. It was . . . like an inky-black mirage— a pool of cold, lethal power roiling up from the ground. Not quite a fog of smoke, for the . . . thing . . . had an eerie structure about it. It lived, breathed, but it wasn't . . .

"Don't look back."

Christopher couldn't help himself. Gulping, he stared at the indescribable being—something beyond the realm of his comprehension. "Dear God," he wheezed as he staggered on his feet.

When the glint of mercury flickered within the whirl of stationary smoke, Christopher felt a mild jolt of recognition. Yet, it was so vague that he wasn't sure he should trust what he thought he saw—and felt.

"Trey?" His voice warbled on a gust of breath. "Three Wolves?"

There was no answer. The foggy object—creature, whatever it was—faded momentarily, then darkened until it was as black as a chunk of coal.

"They've got Jen," Christopher burst out. "I couldn't get her out of the cellar."

"I know." The voice was no more than a distant echo—a hollow, desolate sound, as cold as a tombstone.

Icy fingers of darkness curled around Christopher's forearms, sending a chill right to his soul, freezing his tongue to the roof of his mouth. He tried to speak, but no words came out as he stared over his shoulder at the creature hovering behind him.

"Go home. Tell Jawbone to bring his men to the house now. Quincy's henchmen won't pose much threat while they're dodging stampeding cattle and fighting the fire."

Christopher felt himself jerked backward by a force of indefinable strength when thudding footsteps heralded the approach of a lone gunman. It was as if the gunman didn't notice him standing there. The man darted past—not ten feet away from where Christopher stood.

As if propelled by a force other than his own, Christopher moved toward the clump of trees. When two stalking wolves appeared from the underbrush, their eyes reflecting the golden flames from the fire, Christopher sensed that it had been Trey that he had been talking to.

The cold vacuum of smoke retreated, looming just above the carpet of grass. *"Did you tell English I'm still here?"*

"No, you told me not to," Christopher chirped, squinting at the churning swirl of smoke and eerie darkness. "Trey? Is that really you?"

Christopher felt the pocket of cold air sweeping over him—like a damp chill settling over a river valley at night.

"Beware of the lobos . . ."

Christopher turned and ran toward the horses when he heard the wild howl. He didn't look back. He rode hell-for-leather to deliver the message to Jawbone and Sunset.

When Christopher disappeared from sight, *El Lobo Diablo* let himself be thoroughly consumed by the icy darkness. He knew he had terrified young Christopher, and before the night was out, he knew he would alienate Jennifer as well. But that was the price to be paid when he took full command of the Comanche guardian spirits that guided him, accepted the ominous power entrusted to him. When he called in the wolves, there was no turning back.

"I daresay, you do not have to wrench my arm out of its socket," Jennifer complained to Frank Irving.

"Just shut your mouth and keep walking," Frank growled.

She halted abruptly when she saw Quincy seated behind his office desk. The flames from the burning barn glared through the line of windows on the south wall. Burnished light slanted across his angular features, puckered in a furious scowl.

Jennifer watched the two henchmen check the windows and

lock the door. When the room was secured, Quincy shoved her into a chair and tied her in place.

"I cannot fathom what you hope to accomplish," Jennifer muttered at Quincy.

"I'm going to have the deed to Templeton Ranch," he informed her as he glanced cautiously around the room.

"I do not have any property now that Gram decreed herself my guardian. I am afraid you have run amuck here—"

"Will you shut up, woman, or I'll do it for you!" Yancy sneered menacingly.

"I cannot. I have a tendency to chatter when I am nervous."

When Jennifer heard the scratching at the locked door she blinked, startled. Dear Lord, it couldn't be the wolves! She had wrested a sacred promise from Trey that he would vacate the area before trouble erupted. A Comanche promise—the binding kind that no self-respecting warrior dared to break. Curse that man. She would not let him get killed on her behalf! That was the whole blessed point of making him leave West Texas.

How had Trey known where she was? The man must have the nose of a bloodhound, in addition to all his other talents. Was he responsible for the chaos around the ranch? Was that why Quincy kept flicking glances at the door, why his henchmen were shifting uneasily?

When the unearthly howl filled the room, Jennifer tensed. She had heard that sound before—immediately before an attack. It suddenly sounded as if hundreds of wolves were pawing at the door, scratching like demons seeking entrance to collect the souls of the damned.

A lone wolf bayed again, and a chorus of haunting replies rose up outside the house. Jennifer felt her hair stand on end as a cold chill rippled down her spine. *The reckoning,* she caught herself thinking.

Quincy and his henchmen must have sensed the eerie phenomena as well. They whirled around, eyes wide with apprehension, pistols trained on the shadows that milled beyond the windows like swarming phantoms.

Trigger-happy Yancy Wyatt cursed foully and fired his pistol.

Glass shattered and eerie shadows flowed into the room like
rolling smoke billowing against the ceiling, then sinking down
the walls. Lobos bayed like wretched souls sending up tortured
cries from the darkest reaches of hell.

Jennifer shivered uncontrollably when the sounds of wolves
intensified, overriding the crackling flames that devoured the
barn. The scent of smoke caught in the wind and drifted through
the broken window. Hazy shadows swept back and forth across
the lawn, then flooded across the room, bringing a draft of
frigid air that seemed out of place on this warm spring night.
In the distance, thundering hooves rumbled like the aftershocks
of an earthquake.

Mercy! When Three Wolves set the stage for his arrival, he
did it up too bloody well, Jennifer noted. She was getting a
bad case of the jitters. She had no fear whatsoever of Three
Wolves—or at least she hadn't until now.

Swirling apparitions materialized outside the broken window, and Yancy wheeled to fire again. More glass shattered,
and Quincy cursed his gunman. Now the panting of the circling
lobos was easily detectable through the broken windows. The
sound intensified until Yancy lost patience and fired at the
smoky shadows drifting around the room.

When the scratching at the office door struck up again, all
heads turned. The insistent pawing seemed to rise up the door,
inching upward while howls seeped into the room.

Cursing and scowling, Frank Irving blasted the door with
rapid-fire shots. The door crashed open and a pack of wolves,
their eyes glowing like silver fire, bounded into the room.

Jennifer knew what to expect, having seen these agile predators twice before. But the effect was no less terrifying, especially
when there seemed to be a smoky haze churning around the
vicious beasts.

Frank's bloodcurdling shriek resounded around the room
when the lead wolf sprang into the air and attacked. Screaming,
Frank flung up an arm to protect his face and throat, but the
oversize beast knocked him to the floor.

Yancy scrambled for his life, literally trying to climb up the bookshelves to avoid snapping jaws. When sharp teeth clenched around his boot, Yancy screamed bloody murder. Wildly, he hurled books at the growling creature, but he was dragged down to the floor to be set upon by a host of snarling, smoke-engulfed lobos.

Jennifer gasped in disbelief when a dark shadow of smoke materialized in the hallway. An icy draft of wind crept across the room, causing the temperature to drop a quick ten degrees. It struck her just then that the ferocious leader of the devil wolf pack had entered the office. It was as if he floated in with the wind, enshrouded in smoke that condensed like a ghastly nightmare.

The foreboding shadow, with silver flames for eyes, spiraled toward Quincy. Screeching in horror, Quincy stumbled back against the windowsill, struggling to unholster his pistol. Jennifer could see the enlarged whites of Quincy's eyes, feel the stark terror rippling from him like waves on the sea.

Hardly daring to breathe, Jennifer glanced at the ominous shadow that was no more than a pool of black embedded with pinpoints of glowing silver. Immobilized, she stared at the ghostly specter, afraid to trust what she thought she saw, what she felt, what she believed to be real.

"Drop the gun, Quincy Ward."

The voice was so cold and barren that it hung in the air. An eerie coil of apprehension knotted in Jennifer's stomach.

Gasping for breath, staring at the looming swirl of smoke as if entranced, Quincy let the pistol slip from his fingers and fall to the floor.

A hushed command brought the wolf pack around the corner of the desk to surround Quincy. Frank and Yancy whimpered as they lay curled up on the floor, shivering in the cold pocket of air that had descended on the room.

The ropes fell away from Jennifer's arms, but she didn't move—couldn't move. She was too mystified by the destruction that lay around her, too enthralled by the unrecognizable voice that seemed to echo down a long, winding, corridor.

There was nothing comforting about the dark shadow loom-

ing behind her. Although she was vividly aware of the icy
presence, nothing about this ghoulish specter reminded her of
the man she had come to love. Indeed, *El Lobo Diablo* was
not human. The only emotions she detected were fury, vengeance, and imminent death.

When something cold and oppressive settled on her shoulder,
she shrank away, avoiding the terrifying touch. Despite her
attempt to keep silent, a wild shriek erupted from her lips.

*"Leave the room, Jennifer, but do not go outside. Not yet.
It's not safe . . ."*

Odd tremors shook her body when the eerie voice came from
so close behind her—if one could call it a voice at all. It was
more like a thought than a detectable sound.

This was definitely not a safe night to be out and about,
Jennifer thought, trembling helplessly. Vicious lobos lurked
everywhere, forming a forbidden ring around this condemned
house, constantly circling, scratching, howling down the night.

"Do as you're told, now . . ."

Jennifer swiveled in her chair, and then recoiled at the
unnerving sight behind her. The giant beast, its jaws rimmed
with razor-sharp teeth and eyes like burning mercury, stared
at her. Yet, the beast had no clear outline in the darkness. It
breathed, seethed . . .

Shrieking, Jennifer bounded from her chair, stumbling over
the man who lay sprawled on the floor. Hypnotized by the eerie
sight, Jennifer floundered for her footing. When cold fingers
reached out to steady her, she snatched her arm away and
wheeled around, unable to stare at the apparition a moment
longer. The spire of living smoke and ice assured her that there
was nothing left of the man she knew. There was only a dark
shadow within the shadow, a seething entity like nothing she
had ever experienced.

Jennifer felt the cold force descend on her again, guiding
her faltering footsteps toward the door. Wildly, she wondered
if she would ever see Trey again. Had he taken that final step
into the dark abyss?

El Lobo Diablo's haunting call exploded in the room, and

Jennifer dashed blindly into the foyer. The snarl of wolves was deafening, drowning out Quincy's horrified scream. Jennifer knew without question that Quincy Ward was staring death in the face—a ghastly face that offered no mercy. He was seeing the legend come to life, feeling the force of avenging darkness devour him.

Jennifer collapsed on the floor of the foyer as the door closed behind her. She couldn't stop shaking, couldn't regain her composure. Her head was pounding like a tom-tom from the blows she had sustained earlier.

As the howls rose up and Quincy's unnerving screams shattered the night, Jennifer lost consciousness. Something seemed to be sucking the very air from her lungs, filling her with a chill so frigid that she curled up in a tight ball in hopes of finding a smidgen of warmth.

Then the icy darkness swallowed her, and the last thing she heard was a bellowing howl that faded into deep, endless silence.

Seventeen

"Holy jumping hell!"

Sunset jerked back on the reins to keep his steed at a safe distance from Quincy's darkened house. Smoke and flames rose in the night, and shadows circled like floating specters.

"Hell's aflame, for sure and certain," Jawbone wheezed, staring at the eerie sight.

Christopher sat behind the thunderstruck cowboys. As desperate as he was to locate his sister, he was leery of crossing that imaginary line that separated him, and the other hired men, from what looked to be the underworld. Shadowy images of wolves, their eyes reflecting the golden light from the flames, surrounded Ward's headquarters.

So far, the rescue brigade had met no resistance. Quincy's men had fled from the plague of lobos. The place looked deserted, save the lurking phantoms of the night—hundreds of them. Christopher had heard the howl of wolves before he left the ranch to summon Sunset and Jawbone, but he hadn't actually seen the unearthly shadows . . . until now.

"What in God's name . . . ?" Agatha's voice trailed off as

she sat in the buggy beside Simpson, whose face was still chalky-white after the wild ride to and from Mobeetie.

A haunting call rose from the house and spread with the wind—a sound that seemed to carry a message that the circling lobos understood and obeyed.

Jawbone blinked, astonished, when the murky shadows of wolves vanished into the rolling smoke. The howling gradually ebbed, and an unnerving stillness, broken only by the crackling flames, settled over Quincy's ranch.

"It's safe now," Christopher heard himself say—and wondered how he knew it. It was no more than a feeling that tapped at his thoughts. He had the odd sensation that his words were the echo of a distant whisper.

The wary procession approached the house. Jawbone suggested drawing straws to decide who would go inside first to scout out the house, but Christopher boldly took the lead.

The house loomed in the darkness. Faint whimpers filled the foyer. Summoning his courage, Christopher followed the sounds to see Jennifer curled up in the corner, shivering.

"Jen?" Christopher called softly.

"Where is my granddaughter?" Agatha burst out as she elbowed her way through the crowd of cowboys standing on the stoop.

"Jen? Are you all right? Are you hurt?" Christopher questioned as he squatted down on his haunches.

Jennifer didn't respond, even when Christopher gave her a gentle nudge.

Agatha scurried up behind him to see Jennifer trembling as if she were suffering from frostbite. "Put the poor child in the buggy," she ordered. "Somebody fetch a doctor. You do have qualified physicians in these parts, don't you?"

Two cowboys trotted off to retrieve their horses and ride to Fort Elliot to summon the army surgeon. Simpson scuttled around to help Christopher hoist his semiconscious sister into the carriage. Agatha was still shouting instructions as she rumbled off in the carriage, leaving Jawbone and Sunset to handle whatever was left.

Sunset located a lantern and led the way to the office. "Holy jumping—"

"—hell . . ." Jawbone finished for the tongue-tied Sunset.

The cowboys surveyed the demolished room with its strewn books, broken windows, and maimed bodies. Frank Irving and Yancy Wyatt lay in their respective corners. Neither outlaw was capable of getting to his feet—ever again. Quincy Ward was nowhere to be seen. Jawbone wasn't sure he wanted to find what was left of Quincy—if these two outlaws' condition was anything to go by.

"Where's Three Wolves?" Sunset murmured.

"Don't know," Jawbone said quietly. "For sure, *El Lobo Diablo* has come and gone. That's all anybody needs to know. Seems to me there are things that are better left alone."

Jawbone had heard all the eerie legends circulating about that half-breed bounty hunter. Hell, Jawbone had even repeated them a few times himself. Now, he was absolutely certain that every story was true. Although Miss Jenny constantly maintained that Three Wolves was a good and decent man who had been misunderstood, there was definitely a dark, avenging side to that Comanche gunslinger that was infinitely more dangerous than the killers he tracked down.

The thought caused Jawbone to shiver uneasily. He glanced around the room, wondering how one man could have wrought so much destruction against such overpowering odds. Three Wolves had taken on Quincy and his army of hired guns and reduced them to ruin.

"It's all true, ain't it? Everything anybody ever said about Three Wolves is true. I wouldn't have believed it if I hadn't seen it with my own eyes," came a testimonial from one of the awestruck wranglers.

"We better haul these corpses to town," Sunset insisted as he strode over to grab Frank Irving's feet. "Both of these men are wanted for breaking out of jail and killing a deputy in Abilene. I saw the bench warrants myself. There were three of them. Go check around outside and see if you can locate the other escapee."

When the cowboys filed out, Jawbone lingered beside the broken windows that lined the wall, watching the glowing embers, staring at the Comanche moon. The night had finally taken on a peaceful silence. Jawbone reflected on what he had told Miss Jenny that first day she encountered Three Wolves. He had maintained that the dangerous bounty hunter wasn't her kind of folk, that he was law and order's last resort. Jawbone had claimed that when there was nowhere else to turn, law officials called in the wolves . . .

Tonight, Jawbone had seen the shadowy pack of lobos with his own eyes, witnessed the drastic results. *El Lobo Diablo* was more than an incredible legend, Jawbone realized. He was a phenomenon—a wolf man who commanded the powers of Comanche spirits, a shaman of the highest echelon—or whatever title Indians bestowed on men who controlled the forces of nature.

Jawbone pivoted when he heard Sunset striding back into the room. "Do you think he'll ever come back after what happened tonight?"

"Nope."

"Do you think this is the work of the same man Miss Jenny met and married in Dodge?"

"Nope." Sunset glanced over at his long-time friend. "And just between you and me, I'm thinking it was more than just a man who brought all this down on Quincy and his hired guns. Nobody's ever gonna convince me that there's nothing to those Indian legends about men taking the forms of wild creatures to command extra power. You think that sounds crazy, Jaw?"

"Nope," Jawbone said before he turned and walked away.

"Just a few bruises and a mild concussion?" Agatha snorted at the young physician who had examined Jennifer. "And where, I would bloody well like to know, did you earn your medical degree, young man? How can you stand here and tell me that my granddaughter is going to be perfectly fine when she has not opened her eyes or stopped shivering for more than two hours?''

"Calm down, Your Grace," Simpson coaxed. "I do not think it advisable to badger the only doctor within a hundred miles." He turned to the curly-haired physician and smiled politely. "Her Grace is visibly distraught. I am sure you understand, sir."

The lanky physician nodded good-naturedly. "I'm sure you are upset, Your Grace, but Jennifer is not in danger. She received a hard blow to the skull and one to the cheek. She roused momentarily while I was bandaging her head wound, but I gave her a strong dose of laudanum to make her sleep."

Agatha's shoulders slumped in relief. "Well, thank God!"

"Keep Jennifer in bed for a couple of days," the doctor instructed. "You haven't a thing to worry about, Your Grace. She'll be fine in no time at all."

When the doctor exited, Agatha collapsed into the nearest chair. "That tears it, Simpson, I am taking my grandchildren to England as soon as Jen is back on her feet."

"Begging your pardon, Your Grace, but I recall that you made a vow to Three Wolves that Lady Jennifer would be allowed to make her own decision on the matter."

"Blister it, I—"

"You *did* promise," Simpson reminded her gently. "And forgive me for saying so, but now that the worst is over, I must confess that I rather enjoyed all the excitement these past few weeks. It has been a grand adventure that a scant few of our fellow countrymen have ever experienced, now that I think on it."

Agatha stared unblinkingly at Simpson. "What are you trying to say?"

He smiled sheepishly. "True, civilization has not yet caught up with this outback region in Texas. And too true, this place is a world away from the grand parties of London, but there is something about these wide open spaces that has managed to get to me, if you know what I mean, Your Grace."

Agatha stared out the window at the unhindered view of the stars. "I do know what you mean," she murmured pensively

"And is it any wonder that Master Christopher and Lady Jennifer feel compelled to carve their own niches in this place where life has not become regimented by Old World tradition?"

"No, I suppose not," she concurred. "One seems to be able to do whatever one pleases, rather than what one is expected to do."

"Socio-economic lines are not as clearly defined here," Simpson pointed out. "Individuals seek their own destinies. Indeed, they are making history, not following preordained rituals and customs. You may cringe to hear me say it, but I do not feel quite so inhibited in Texas."

Agatha whirled around to gape at Simpson. "Have I contributed to your feelings of inhibition? I never meant to—"

Simpson waved his hand for silence as he sank down on the sofa. He patted the empty space beside him, silently requesting that Agatha take a seat. "Here, you and I have become kindred spirits, battling adversity to save your beloved grandchildren. And I must say, I was impressed to see the whole lot of these cow servants thundering off to save the day. We have had one grand adventure after another."

"Yes, we have."

Agatha smiled, remembering how she had raced to town to rouse Phinneus Albright so he could draw up another contract. Then she had taken the reins to the buggy, determined to do her part in rescuing Jen and Christopher.

Of course, she hadn't realized how effective that half-breed heathen would be when she sicced him on Quincy Ward. She was sure Three Wolves had sent that murdering blackguard straight to hell where he belonged. Three Wolves was a most amazing man, just as Jennifer had insisted he was.

"Far be it from me to tell you what to do, Your Grace," Simpson continued. "But I daresay a woman like you, with your impressive contacts and position in society, could show these Westerners how it ought to be done. You could be the one who guides and directs West Texas into becoming a respectable social and cultural center—''

''Duchess?''

A dusty cowboy, with three days' growth of beard, stood in the doorway of the parlor, toying with his stained hat. ''I just returned from Mobeetie, and Jawbone said I ought to report to you.''

''Report what?'' Agatha questioned the crusty ranch hand.

''We hauled all the hired guns to jail. And don't ask me how it happened, but Quincy Ward was sitting in a cell, curled up in a tight ball, cackling like a hen on boiled eggs.''

Agatha blinked in astonishment. ''What? How did he get there?''

The cowboy shrugged. ''Nobody seems to know, but Quincy was confessing to all his crimes, over and over again. It was like nothing you've ever seen or heard. He admitted to rustling Templeton cattle, robbery, and the murder of Ramsey Templeton. Don't think he'll be right in the head ever again. He's got a strange, vacant look in his eyes and he just sits there and shivers while he's cackling. Tonight must've sent him into the deep end. He keeps yammering about devil wolves sucking the life outta him and stealing his soul.''

Agatha grimaced, remembering that she had almost sold the ranch to the very man who had killed Jen and Christopher's father. Her meddling had nearly been disastrous. How she regretted her foolishness!

Regret . . . Agatha could not recall the last time she had felt so ashamed of herself. She had been too busy living up to her title and rank. Bloody hell, she had become an iron-bound old witch, blinded by her own decrees. It was a marvel that Simpson had remained loyal and steadfast all these years when she had made such a nuisance of herself to him and those around her.

''One more thing, Duchess,'' the cowboy added as he stretched out his hand. ''This was at the marshal's office, attached to a note that indicated it was to be delivered to you.''

Agatha surged from the sofa to accept the gold band she remembered seeing Three Wolves wearing when they first met.

When the cowboy moseyed away, Agatha turned back to Simpson who smiled at her ruefully.

"I do believe Lady Jennifer did love that man dearly," he murmured, his gaze fixed on the ring resting in Agatha's palm. "More's the pity that he does not appear to have intentions of returning to the ranch. Lady Jennifer will miss him, I suspect."

"He was never right for her. We both know that," Agatha said, staring ponderously at the gold band.

"I am not sure it is anybody's place to say who is right or wrong for whom," Simpson put in. "Feelings are the bloody devil to deal with when they come from the heart, are they not, Your Grace? Sometimes, one simply cannot help what one feels. The affection exists and never goes away."

Simpson rose from the sofa and strode over to press a kiss to Agatha's wrist. "Good night, Your Grace. I shall have a cup of tea waiting in your room, as usual."

Somewhere in the distance a lone wolf howled. Agatha gazed out the window, seeing the full moon beam down at her. She wondered if her interference in her grandchildren's lives was more of a curse than a blessing, wondered if she had been too busy commandeering life to actually take time to enjoy and appreciate it.

Fortunately, she had Simpson around to remind her of the things she overlooked. Bless the man. She cannot imagine what it would have been like if she had not had him with her all these years.

Jennifer stirred in laudanum-induced sleep, vaguely aware of the sheltering warmth that replaced the chilling darkness that had engulfed her. She could see the flames burning—fire without heat. She could hear that empty, lifeless voice, smell the suffocating smoke.

Ever so slowly, Jennifer began to distinguish the different aspects of her dreamlike trance. She inched away from the cold, drawing closer to the comforting heat, and inhaled a familiar scent. She knew instinctively that she was protected,

that she would always be safe in the sheltering arms that held
her.

Visions came and went like shifting sands. Memories converged, then scattered. Jennifer could see herself making her
desperate escape attempt from the cellar, see the skipping shadows that lurked around the office. It all came back to her in a
rush.

Jennifer cried out in her sleep, shrinking away from the hazy
shadows so foreign and yet familiar. The eerie image flitted
off into the darkness and the lonesome howl of the wolf echoed
in her mind as one distorted dream gave way to another, then
left her in impenetrable silence.

Trey squeezed his eyes shut when Jennifer trembled uncontrollably, then sagged in his arms. He held her, protected her
from the icy abyss that he himself had thrust her into on a night
that had been thick with the scent of violence and destruction.
Trey needed this last private moment with Jennifer before he
left her in her world and returned to his. He needed to return
from those black depths that entrapped him. Jennifer purified
him, made him feel whole and alive again. She represented all
the good and decent things that he had never been able to find
beyond the cold darkness.

Trey had been desperate to assure himself that all was well
with Jennifer before he went away. He simply could not leave
without seeing her this one last time, without knowing if what
she had witnessed had terrified her so greatly that the thought
of him repulsed her.

Tonight, Jennifer had seen him at his very worst—at the
very deepest level to which he descended to battle the evils
that sought to destroy Jennifer. In the past, Trey had only
allowed her brief glimpses of what he became. But that was
nothing compared to staring at him—staring through him—
tonight. Jennifer had shivered and pulled away when he put
his chilled hands on her shoulders. She had heard the hollow
echo in his voice, seen him deal with Quincy and his hired
guns. Trey had noted the flicker of terror in those expressive

violet eyes, and he had died a little inside when she shrank away from him, as if she couldn't bear his touch.

She had viewed the darkest, most dangerous depths of control—a dimension the Comanche termed the deep sense of knowing and commanding, that place where all thoughts and powers turn inward to summon omnipotent power . . .

When Jennifer stirred, mumbling unintelligible phrases, Trey held her tightly. He knew he had finally shattered her romantic notions of dashing white knights and damsels who wanted to believe in love at first sight and everlasting devotion. He had destroyed the love she thought she felt for him when he allowed her to see him calling in the wolves.

Trey deeply regretted that her last memory of him would be associated with avenging shadows, silver flames for eyes, and a voice as hollow as a chasm. He would have wanted her to remember those magical nights when he made love to her, when she elicited unbelievable gentleness from him, when she surrendered so generously, so sweetly, to him. He longed for her to remember the way he smiled down at her with the inner warmth that she had ignited in his soul.

Yet, now that she knew all of what he was, what he could become when danger demanded it, there was no going back. Jennifer had seen him in the smoke and flame, rising like a hellish phantom, surrounded by the guardian Comanche spirits that took animal form to battle difficult odds. She had been in that deepest, darkest pit with him. She had seen—touched— *El Lobo Diablo,* and she would never forget her terror, never be able to separate him from the frightening memories. He had saved her so he could lose her forever.

And when dawn came, Trey would rise from Jennifer's bed and walk out of her life, because he couldn't bear for her to look at him and know that he wasn't truly the good and decent man she believed him to be. He had made too many trips to hell, had clashed too often with devils who stole a man's heart and soul, until there was nothing left. His own dreams of happiness had been destroyed when Jennifer withdrew from his touch. He had driven her away, tainted her memories of him.

Trey pressed a light kiss to Jennifer's lips, savoring the forbidden taste of her, the fragrant scent of lilacs. He glided his hand over her supple curves, memorizing the feel of her satiny flesh beneath his caress, remembering those times when she smiled up at him, eyes twinkling, and professed to love him.

She was the sun and he would always be the dark side of the Comanche moon. He and Jennifer were as different as day and night, as different as heaven and hell . . .

"Jennifer . . ." Her name tripped from his lips in an agonized whisper as he bent to savor her lips for the very last time. "I'll never forget you, English."

As the first rays of sunlight spilled over the horizon, Trey eased from the bed. Smiling ruefully, he trailed his finger over her creamy cheek. He and this enchanting English beauty had shared so much. Her memory had attached itself to his every thought and would remain with him for years to come. Trey would look back and reflect on those brief, glorious moments when he had basked in sunshine rather than wallowing in darkness. He had discovered pleasure because of Jennifer, but there was no going back now. He had burned all bridges behind him when he allowed Jennifer to see him calling in the wolves.

Trey left Jennifer sleeping peacefully, taking with him the smoky fragrance, the frightening visions, and the feel of flames burning in ice that had left Jennifer disoriented and shivering. He had given her back the warmth that Quincy Ward would never feel again, had given her back the life she fought so hard to preserve for her family and her neighbors in West Texas.

"Have a good life, English," Trey whispered before he melted into the empty shadows.

Jennifer sighed softly as she rolled onto her side, inching toward the warmth that cloaked her like a cozy quilt.

Eighteen

Jennifer groaned groggily and stirred beneath the blanket. She pried open heavily-lidded eyes to see sunlight splashing across her bedroom. Lord, she'd had the strangest dreams . . .

When she realized there was someone ensconced in the corner of her room, she recoiled beneath the quilt and squinted at the fuzzy image.

"Jennifer? It's me. Jonas Rafferty."

She rubbed her eyes, then stared at the man who was sporting a sling on his left arm. "What are you doing here?"

"Keeping vigil," he said with a smile. "I also want to apologize."

"For what?"

"For making life difficult for you." Jonas dropped his head and massaged his aching arm. "I really meant you no harm. I only wanted to protect my property, and—" He glanced at her awkwardly. "Despite what you probably think, my intentions toward you were serious. I admit I did try to discourage your other suitors a few times, but I didn't rough any of them up. That was Quincy's doing."

"I appreciate your honesty, Jonas, but—"

"I want to set things right between us, once and for all," Jonas cut in as he rose to his feet. He ambled over to smile down at Jennifer. "I'm glad you're safe and sound. The duchess is also greatly relieved. She has been popping whips over everybody's head to ensure that—and I quote—'every thing is up to snuff' while you're recuperating."

Jennifer groaned inwardly. Knowing Gram, she would be barking so many orders that the cowboys and household staff would quit their jobs.

"A real character, your grandmother," Jonas said with a chuckle.

"She is definitely that," Jennifer agreed, then gestured toward Jonas's sling. "What happened to your arm?"

"I ended up at the wrong place at the wrong time," was all he had to say on the subject. "I just wanted to see you before I returned to my farm. If ever you need my help, just send for me. I owe you a great debt."

"Owe me?" Jennifer repeated, befuddled.

Jonas leaned down to press a kiss to her furrowed brow and smiled enigmatically. "Your good deed turned another good deed which saved my life."

"What the blazes are you babbling about, Jonas?"

"I'll fetch the duchess," he volunteered without answering the question. "Her Grace insisted that I notify her the instant you roused."

"But what about this 'good deed' business?"

When Jonas tried to make a hasty exit, Jennifer propped up on her elbow. "Jonas Rafferty, do not even *think* of leaving this room until you have told me what the bloody hell has been going on that I do not know about." When Jonas wheeled at the sound of her authoritative voice, Jennifer gestured for him to scoot the chair up beside her bed and park himself in it. "Sit," she commanded.

Reluctantly, Jonas sat.

"Now then, who did you this good deed?"

"Three Wolves did. He saved my life when I swore he came to Texas to relieve me of it."

Jennifer frowned curiously. "Precisely what are you referring to?"

"When my cousin realized I was in the area, I expected him
to—"

"Your cousin?" Jennifer chirped. Blast it, Trey had never
indicated that he recognized Jonas's name when she mentioned
him in Dodge. "Why didn't Trey tell me he knew you?"

Jonas squirmed uneasily. "Well, we weren't exactly on the
best of terms. I tried to kill him after he escaped from the
massacre and came looking for refuge with his white relatives."

Jennifer wilted back to her pillow, gaping wide-eyed at Jonas.
"Whyever would you want to take your own cousin's life?
Drat it, Jonas, no wonder Trey has so little faith in mankind!"

"Well, it wasn't exactly my fault," Jonas said uncomfortably. "It all goes back to the day the Comanche raiding party
attacked the MacTavish homestead. My mother and father
returned to the farm to find my grandparents dead and Glenna
MacTavish abducted. My mother lost her family in the course
of one afternoon and she never forgave, never forgot what
happened. She hated every Indian after that."

Jennifer grimaced. The prospect of walking in on that gruesome scene *would* leave a lasting impression, she imagined.

"Rachael had nightmares about the incident for years. Even
when I was a child I remember hearing her waking up, screaming and crying until my father soothed her back to sleep. When
we traveled to Fort Griffin for supplies, the mere sight of Indians
milling around the army garrison caused Rachael to lapse into
hysterics."

Jonas smiled sadly as he stared across the room, as if gazing
through the window to the past. "After my father was killed
in a farming accident, my mother lost her grasp on reality."

"And then Trey came looking for asylum," Jennifer presumed.

Jonas nodded somberly. "When Three Wolves approached
Rachael, claiming to be Glenna's son, asking after his white
grandparents, Rachael went wild. She tried to stab him with
a butcher knife, but Three Wolves kicked it from her grasp.

I . . .'' Jonas hesitated, composed himself, then continued, ''my mother screamed for me to kill the Comanche who slaughtered her family. I lunged at Three Wolves with the knife.''

''That's what caused the long scar on his rib cage,'' Jennifer whispered. ''Dear God . . .''

''I was just a kid myself,'' Jonas tried to explain. ''Only a couple of years older than Three Wolves, in fact. I was scared half to death, egged on by my mother, who was raving like a lunatic. Although I wounded my cousin, he stumbled away, and Mother demanded that I ride to the fort to summon soldiers to capture the Comanche renegade.

''Not long after that, Three Wolves was hauled off to the reservation. My mother never recovered from the incident. She lapsed into silence and just withered away. She no longer recognized me, wouldn't speak, just lay there staring up at the ceiling. When she died, I joined the Army to get away from the bad memories and I never went back.''

Tears clouded Jennifer's eyes. She realized Trey had lived a life far different from hers, but until now, she was unaware of the full extent of his suffering and isolation. His faith had been tested so many times that it was a wonder he believed in much of anything.

''And then, Three Wolves showed up to save my life last night,'' Jonas murmured as he rose from his chair. ''After what I did to him, after my mother condemned and betrayed him, he still came to my rescue. Three Wolves is one helluva man, Jenny. No matter what anybody says about him, I'm damn proud to call him family.''

When Jonas exited from the room, Jennifer dabbed her eyes and muffled a sniff. Condemnation and betrayal were so much a part of Trey's life that her heart went out to him. And she had behaved no better in that crucial moment of reckoning . . .

Jennifer's tormented thoughts trailed off when she heard approaching footsteps. It was Gram. Jennifer could tell by that clipped, marching gait.

''Well, it is about bloody time, Jen. I was beginning to think that incompetent physician from the fort had mixed a potion to put you to sleep for the next hundred years. Good gad, can you fathom waking up in the twentieth century? There is no telling what the decaying social order of this world will be like then!''

Agatha tramped over to fluff Jennifer's pillow and tuck the quilt under her chin. ''Now, do not fret about a thing, Jen. I am here and everything is under control. Your only obligation is to recuperate. That scoundrel Quincy is in jail where he belongs—a regular basket case, as I have heard it told. Went out of his bloody mind. Conscience must have gotten to the blackguard. I had my solicitor dissolve the guardianship,'' she added offhandedly.

''Thank you, Gram.''

''It was payment owed for a good deed,'' Agatha muttered evasively.

Jennifer frowned at the comment, wondering if this ''good deed'' had anything to do with the one Jonas mentioned.

''Well, I do not have time to fuss over Quincy Ward's ranch indefinitely, now do I?'' Agatha yammered, confusing Jennifer further. ''I have my own endeavors to oversee. Of course, I do not mind filling in for you until you are back on your feet. By the by, I am teaching Christopher to commandeer.''

Jennifer was curious to see how her brother was reacting to learning to boss everybody around with Gram's authority. She hoped her brother didn't take such a highhanded approach.

''Simpson!'' Agatha bugled abruptly.

The devoted butler strode into the room. ''Yes, Your Grace?''

''Have the cook prepare Jennifer's lunch tray. She needs her nourishment if she is to recover her strength. Oh, and did you check on that little matter we discussed this morning?''

''Yes, Your Grace.''

''Everything is in order then?''

''Perfect order, according to your every specification.'' With a polite nod to Jennifer, Simpson performed a precise about-face and took himself off.

Jennifer felt as if she were riding a runaway carousel. Her life was spinning out of control. Gram was ruling the roost, and worse, Jennifer had lost her cheerful enthusiasm. She felt like a sun-baked slug, sprawled in bed.

Although she suspected the sleeping potion was partially responsible for her listlessness, she knew it was far more than that. She felt like a lost soul. A vital part of her was missing . . .

"Jawbone tells me that your shipment of wire and posts has arrived from Dodge City," Agatha went on. "Of course, I don't know what fences are to be stretched where. I put Jawbone—gad, the poor man has been plagued with such a ridiculous nickname! Anyway, I placed him in charge of the project. And you should see Christopher's black eye and puffy lips! The poor boy looks like he went ten rounds with a world champion and lost every bloody round."

"Gram—"

"I have been told that some of your cattle were found in Quincy's herds, so I sent some of your cow servants over there to separate them."

"Gram—"

"Cannot have your stock grazing in the wrong pasture, now can I—?"

"Gram, I get the feeling you are trying to avoid the subject you know I am concerned about. Where is Trey?"

Agatha scowled. "Well, how do I know where he is? I hired him to do a job and he did it. That is all I know."

"You hired him?" Jennifer repeated curiously.

"Of course I did. I wanted you and that hot-tempered brother of yours back, didn't I? And I bloody well paid the price he demanded, do not think I didn't! The rascal! He is the reason the guardianship has been dissolved. Made me swear to let you decide whether to leave or stay in Texas. I could have shot him for that."

"What are you talking about? What bargain did you make with Trey?"

"Ah, Simpson has arrived with your lunch," Agatha announced enthusiastically.

Simpson marched into the room, sporting a beaming smile.

"Lunch is served, Lady Jennifer. I will bring up your tea this afternoon as well. Her Grace has called a halt to activities on the ranch. Everyone will be taking tea at promptly four o'clock."

Jennifer stared, astounded. Since when did Gram cater to those whom she previously considered beneath her socially? "Tea for the ranch hands and household servants?"

"Of course," Agatha harumphed. "Organization is the key to proper management. One works and then one breaks. If civilized society does it, why not employ the policy with the peasants—er . . . whatever. At any rate, the chaps are eager to take a spot of tea and crumpets—or as near as your cook can come to crumpets," she amended.

Good Lord, Gram was turning the ranch into an English estate. Yet, she was mingling with the help in a way that she never would have if she were in England. What had gotten into Agatha? Two weeks ago she would not have given the servants a second thought. Now she was making all sorts of concessions to them. Who would have thought it possible?

"If you are up to seeing more visitors, there is a waiting list of well-wishers who want to pay their respects," Agatha reported. "I will summon your brother first . . . if that meets with your approval."

Her approval? Gram wanted her approval? Amazing.

Jennifer nodded mutely. She barely recognized her grandmother these days. Agatha was behaving as if she were *human*.

Jennifer winced at the thought. Memories came flooding back, along with a deep sense of regret and a consuming sense of loss. Last night Jennifer had retreated from Trey while he confronted Quincy and his henchmen. She knew he had sensed her rejection and alarm. He must have felt her recoil from his icy touch, must have seen the uncertainty in her eyes when she peered up at the smoking image within the shadow.

She, who had sworn unfaltering love . . . had faltered.

Jennifer squeezed her eyes shut and swore under her breath. She had driven Trey away. He was left to believe that she disapproved of what she saw, and felt, when that foreboding shadow swept into Quincy's office. Blast it, she owed Trey her life. In that moment of reckoning, when Trey had done whatever was necessary to save her, she had failed him. No matter how dark or sinister he had appeared, she'd had no right to judge. Trey had done what he had done for her, to ensure her safety, to ensure her property wasn't stolen.

And she had failed him . . .

Tears misted Jennifer's eyes as she munched on her meal. All she could taste was remorse and loneliness. She missed the warmth and security that had encompassed her during the night . . .

Jennifer frowned pensively. Trey must have come to her, she realized suddenly. He was that comforting warmth that replaced the chill that had claimed her since the moment he had touched her in Quincy's office. Trey had come to restore her soul before he went away . . .

Jennifer sat straight up in bed, marshaling her strength and determination. This thing between them was not over! She would refuse to let Trey leave Texas. She would retract that Comanche promise she had forced him to make. Somehow, she would convince him that they belonged together, and then she would beg his forgiveness.

On that positive thought, Jennifer gobbled the rest of her meal and greeted the troop of visitors who filed in and out of her bedroom.

Tomorrow, Jennifer decided, she would have her strength back and her head on straight. Tomorrow she would begin her crusade to assure Trey that *nothing* could change the way she felt about him.

Agatha glanced up when her grandson ambled through the foyer. "And how did you find your sister, Christopher?"

"In amazingly good spirits," he replied.

"That is good to hear. When I was in her room at lunch, she seemed a trifle sluggish. The sedative must be wearing off." Agatha stared steadily at her grandson. "Did she ask you about . . . *him?*"

Christopher shook his head. He wished Jennifer had brought up the subject of Trey. He would have liked to compare experiences, but Christopher hadn't dared, for fear of causing a setback in Jen's recovery.

"I daresay we are making some progress in that department." Agatha snatched up her parasol and pivoted toward the door. "Simpson is bringing the carriage around front. I will be in town overnight. Unavoidable business," she explained hurriedly. "You are in charge, Christopher. Since Jen is back in good spirits, I can leave without fretting about her. Do be a good boy and trot upstairs to tell her I will return tomorrow afternoon."

"Yes, Gram."

"And do not slouch. The man of the house should not slouch. He should be the example and symbol of authority, you understand. Bloody well have to *command* authority if one expects to get it, you know."

With that, Agatha marched off. Christopher reversed direction to convey the message. There was something in Gram's tone that bordered on affection rather than criticism these days. He decided his grandmother wasn't quite the witch he had made her out to be. Her sojourn in Texas had mellowed her.

Bloody good thing, too. Christopher would hate to have to punch out Simpson to keep from pounding Gram flat—which was what he had done the last time he had been angry enough to retaliate.

The thought reminded him that he had yet to apologize to Simpson for knocking the man flat on his back. Spinning around, Christopher rushed outside to apologize before Gram and Simpson drove off to town.

Jennifer pitched camp on the highest plateau on the ranch— right smack dab in the middle of the pasture where Trey could see her if he was inclined to look.

For three days she had waited—and waited—hoping Trey would appear. Her brother and the ranch hands feared that she, like Quincy Ward, had been mentally disturbed by the strange ordeal that had taken place a week earlier, but Jennifer assured one and all that she knew exactly what she was doing.

Although Agatha Reynolds and the ever-faithful Simpson rode out to demand that Jennifer gather her belongings and return to the house, she refused to budge. No matter how long it took, she was not leaving until she spoke to Trey.

When Jawbone, Christopher, and Sunset arrived the evening of the fifth day, Jennifer faced them down with unswerving determination. Jawbone took her aside to explain what he obviously thought she did not understand.

"Now, Miss Jenny," he patronized, "I don't wanna see you living on false hope, and I'm afraid that's exactly what yer doing. After what happened at Ward Ranch, there just ain't no going back. Surely you can understand that."

Jennifer gave her head a firm shake. "Trey will come back, eventually," she maintained.

"No, I don't think he will, not after what happened. He called in the wolves. We all saw them, and you must have seen the changes that overcame him, too. Don't know how you could have helped but notice."

Jawbone led Jennifer through the willows and locust trees that lined Sweetwater Creek. After urging her to sit down on a fallen log, he paced back and forth in front of her.

"I told you in the very beginning that there was something different about Three Wolves that separated him from the rest of us." He pivoted to stare her squarely in the eye. "You know what that something is now, don't you, Miss Jenny?"

"Better than you do," she confirmed.

Jawbone shifted uncomfortably from one foot to the other and stared downstream. "Yeah, I 'spect you do, since you were right in there among them."

Jennifer smiled to herself, knowing what Jawbone was trying to say. "Right in among the devil wolves, you mean? Hell's hounds? Yes, I was definitely among them, not that it has anything to do with—''

''Confound it, Miss Jenny!'' Jawbone erupted, exasperated. ''This has everything to do with that. Do you know which criminals refer to Three Wolves as *El Lobo Diablo?* Well, I'll tell you. It's the ones who barely make it out alive to swing from a noose after they've gone a little crazy. They've had the bejesus scared out of them, just like Quincy Ward has. And I'm thinking you've had a bit of it scared outta you, too.''

''You think I am touched in the head after the incident,'' Jennifer paraphrased.

Jawbone let out his breath in a rush. ''All I'm saying is you need time to put things back in perspective. I know yer thinking Three Wolves will come back, but me and Sunset don't think that's gonna happen, not after what we saw and heard that fateful night. Sometimes things happen that are better forgotten. That night at Ward's ranch is one of those things.''

Jennifer peered into Jawbone's leathery face. She appreciated his concern, she really did. But all the sensible lectures in the world would not change how she felt about that bounty hunter. Part of her attraction to him was her admiration of his bravery, his skills. He was a man among men. She respected his abilities, adored his dry sense of humor and his tenderness toward her. It was the sum total of what Three Wolves was that she loved, and she was prepared to take the good with the phenomenal.

The whole point of camping out in the open was to prove that what she felt would never change, even if she had faltered that one night, even if she had succumbed to a moment of doubt and fear. She wanted the chance to tell Trey that she would never waver again, because now she knew what to expect.

''I am not coming home until I speak with him,'' Jennifer said resolutely. ''Trey saved my life, and at the very least, I intend to thank him for it.''

Jawbone flung up his hands in frustration. ''But he isn't even in the area! No one has seen him for days, not since he called in the wolves.''

He squatted down in front of Jennifer, taking her hands in his. "He ain't coming back, Miss Jenny. When a man takes on an army of hired guns, and does the kind of things Three Wolves had to do to get you and Christopher out alive, he knows it's better just to walk away. He knows what kind of memories and rumors he's stirred up here. Three Wolves ain't coming back," he said slowly and distinctly.

Jennifer smiled, undaunted. "Yes, he is. You'll see."

Jawbone strode off, muttering about Jennifer's stubborn streak. When he stalked up the slope Sunset and Christopher glanced at him expectantly.

"Is she ready to come home yet?" Christopher asked.

"Hell, no," Jawbone grunted. "She's got it in her head that Three Wolves will show up. And there's no telling what might happen to your sister while she's sitting out here all alone. Damnation, she could even be attacked by wolves!"

"I don't think so." Christopher stared ponderously into the distance. "Rustlers might happen onto her, but I don't think she will have to worry about wolves."

"How can you be so sure?" Sunset wanted to know.

"I just know, that's all," Christopher mumbled as he ambled off to speak to his sister.

Jawbone shook his head in dismay when Christopher was out of earshot. "If you ask me, the boy is suffering a few symptoms of loco himself."

Sunset nodded grimly. "I don't know what Christopher and Miss Jenny saw, but I swear it has affected them. Hell, I didn't see the worst of it and it damn sure affected me."

Jennifer watched her brother sidestep down the steep incline, and she chuckled in amusement. "Are you the second wave, Christopher? I suppose I will have to confront Sunset next."

"I suppose you will." Christopher dropped down beside her on the log and stared at the rippling stream shaded by the canopy of trees. "You may not want to rehash this, Jen, but I've got to talk about what I saw and felt that night. You're the only one who really understands."

Jennifer nodded somberly. "You felt the chill and heard the

hollow echo that sounded more like your own thoughts than a voice. It unnerved you and you doubted and feared him, too, didn't you?''

"I'm sorry to say I was frightened. I wasn't sure who, or what, grabbed hold of me after I climbed out the cellar window. There was a strong, overwhelming presence lurking behind me. And yet, it didn't quite feel as if someone was actually there, if you know what I mean.''

Jennifer smiled. "I know precisely what you mean.''

"But then he . . . came back . . . from wherever he was, from whatever he was.'' Christopher shook his sandy-blond head and frowned. "It's bloody hard to explain it.''

"I know. And if you do try to explain, everyone will think you are as mad as I am.'' She looped her arm around her brother's shoulders and gave him an affectionate hug. "Don't you see, Christopher? That is why I have to wait as long as it takes for Trey to return. I have to prove to him that what we saw and felt that night doesn't matter, that we still care about him, still accept him and respect him. I cannot bear to have him go through life thinking we disapprove of him after all he has done for us.''

"But what happened that night matters to him,'' Christopher contended. "Don't you understand that, Jen? When Trey crossed over that line to ensure our safety, and we reacted differently, he thinks we lost respect for him. He thinks we're afraid of him. My God, he was fighting evil with evil and—''

"I prefer to say that he fought force with force,'' Jennifer inserted.

"Evil with evil, force with force, or fire with fire. We can call it whatever we wish,'' he muttered. "But that's why Trey left, I know it is. He doesn't expect us to understand or forgive him because he's so unique. We discovered, firsthand, that all those eerie legends are true.''

"And that is why I have to wait forever if that's how long it takes,'' Jennifer told her brother. "Don't you see? How else can I prove to Trey that you and I may not understand how he wields his power, but that we still care for him? How can I show my loyalty and affection if I am not prepared to wait as long as it takes? This is the only method at my disposal.''

"And what if it takes months before he swings by to see if all is going well with us? What if Trey doesn't expect us to forgive and forget? What if he left the state and never intends to come back at all? He could be anywhere by now.''

"No, he is here—somewhere," Jennifer said with firm conviction.

"Jen, I understand the situation better than the others do, and as much as I like Trey, *I*'m not convinced he wants to come back.''

"That is because you don't love him the way I do. That makes all the difference, Christopher. One day when someone special, *really special,* comes along, you will feel it, just as I do. I knew that first day, that first moment, that Three Wolves was the man I had been waiting for all my life. And you will know, too, just as our parents did, when you find the woman who is meant for you.''

"Miss Jenny!" Sunset called from the ledge above the creek.

Jennifer patted her brother's arm and then urged him to his feet. "I presume Sunset is impatient to have his turn at me. Since I am on my own crusade, you will be in charge of the cattle drive to Fort Elliot tomorrow. The commander is expecting delivery of beef. We Templetons are dependable, after all. We cannot disappoint the commander.''

"Gram is going to chew off both my ears when I return to the house without you," Christopher grumbled. "All that has saved you from her daily lectures is whatever mysterious business that keeps Gram buzzing back and forth to Mobeetie. When her business if finally concluded, you can expect her to be out here railing at you until you give in.''

"If Gram camps out here with me, Trey may never show his face again," Jennifer groaned. "You cannot let Gram do that, Christopher!''

He grinned scampishly. "You're giving me permission to hog-tie Gram? I'll be sure to tell her it was your idea when she lambastes me.''

"Sometimes we must do whatever it takes to see the deed done, don't we, Christopher?"

A knowing smile spread across his handsome face. "I suppose we do at that."

When Christopher took his leave, Sunset replaced him. Jennifer flung up her hand before Sunset had the chance to spout off the lecture he had undoubtedly rehearsed for the past twenty minutes.

"Do not waste your breath, Sunset. I am here to stay, come hell or high water," she assured him.

"Funny that you should mention hell—"

"It was only a figure of speech."

"I used to think so, before *that night.*"

Before Sunset could continue, Jennifer changed the subject. "Christopher will need help herding the beef to the fort in the morning. Please see that he has it, will you, Sunset?"

"Of course, but—"

"I would like to cut Jonas Rafferty in on our arrangement with the fort, too. It will promote relations with our nearest neighbor. It seems to me that Jonas is eager to make a new beginning."

"That's because he owes—"

"Now, if you'll excuse me, I have clothes to wash and supper to prepare." Smiling, Jennifer came to her feet. "Thank you for riding out to check on me. I do appreciate it. But as you can see, I am managing superbly."

"Curse it, Miss Jenny," Sunset complained. "This has got to stop! You could be whisked off by outlaws or renegade Indians or God knows what! It ain't safe for a woman to be camped out here alone."

"I am perfectly safe," she insisted as she hiked up the hill toward camp.

"Only because we've posted guards," Sunset called after her.

"Thoughtful of you, but hardly necessary."

He scowled when Jennifer strode away with her customary cheerful confidence. He would give her another week, he decided. If she didn't give up this lost cause by then, every ranch hand would saddle up and bring her back—kicking and screaming, if need be.

The townsfolk were beginning to talk. Everybody knew about the strange incident at Ward Ranch. Some folks were saying that Jennifer was as touched in the head as Crazy Quincy. And everybody believed Three Wolves was as dangerous as the legends claimed.

In fact, things had simmered down considerably in Mobeetie. Farmers and cattlemen were making efforts to resolve their differences—for fear "the wolves" might be called in.

Miss Jenny had inadvertently accomplished her mission to bring peace to the High Plains, even if she had tipped back a wee bit too far in her own rocker.

As Sunset tramped off, he told himself that Miss Jenny couldn't stay out here indefinitely, pining away for a man who was never coming back.

Trey swore foully as he stared across the pasture to see Jennifer's huge bonfire burning against the night. The damned thing was larger than the one Trey had set when he lured in the Yates Gang. Hell, this fire could probably be seen all the way to Dodge City.

After Trey had bid Jennifer a last good-bye, he had ridden down to Abilene to collect the bounty for Yancy Wyatt, Bernie Giles, and Frank Irving. The marshal, who had lost his nephew in the jailbreak, had been relieved to know the three outlaws wouldn't be bringing down any more victims. After collecting the money, Trey had intended to head north to the Comanche reservation in Indian Territory, but he found himself circling back to check on Jennifer—to reassure himself that she had fully recovered. And there she was, camped out on the prairie, as if she was expecting him to return.

For the past few days, Trey had kept surveillance, expecting Jennifer to give up this futile crusade and go home. But that hadn't happened, even when a procession of concerned family and friends showed up to reason with her.

Well, enough was enough, Trey decided. He couldn't hang around here forever, standing watch over his stubborn ex-wife. Furthermore, the wind had picked up. That fool female would set herself on fire if she didn't watch out!

Grumbling, Trey strode toward the clump of junipers to tame the bonfire that was about to get out of hand.

Nineteen

Determined and optimistic though Jennifer tried to be, disappointment and uncertainty were beginning to take their toll. After a week, there was still no sign of Three Wolves. She sensed he was out there somewhere, but she began to think wishful thinking was influencing her intuition.

Dispirited, Jennifer sank down beside her campfire and stared at the dancing flames. A wave of nausea washed over her, as it had so often the past few days. She was feeling lonely and miserable, but she refused to return to the ranch.

Jennifer stared at the stones she had arranged around the fire—in the shape of a frying pan—as Trey had taught her to do. The grate she used for cooking formed the narrow neck where glowing coals could be raked back, while the outer fire blazed high to provide warmth and light. Jennifer sat upwind from the smoke—just as Trey instructed. Her campfire was as large as the one he had used to lure in his enemies near Dodge, and a man would have to be blind not to see the golden flames and billowing smoke on the open prairie.

Blind and stubborn, Jennifer thought glumly. That described Trey and his unwillingness to approach her.

The sound of approaching riders had Jennifer muttering under her breath. Jawbone, Sunset, and Christopher were probably trotting out to deliver another of their lectures. Blast it, Trey would not put in an appearance when there was a crowd around her blazing campfire.

Jennifer frowned warily when the three riders halted just beyond the light of the fire. Strangers had arrived, she realized as she climbed to her feet.

"Well, look what we have here, boys. Sure 'nuff it's that loony lady folks have been gossiping about in Mobeetie."

When the scraggly-looking hombre, who had designated himself spokesman for the group, tipped back a bottle of whiskey and let it dribble down his unshaven jaw, Jennifer's queasiness became a knot of apprehension. Jawbone and Sunset had warned her that she was an easy target for thieves and thugs. Apparently, their prophesy had come true.

The instant the men dismounted, Jennifer headed straight for her mare. One burly brute snagged her arm before she could reach her horse.

"What's the rush, honey?" he slurred out.

"We thought you might like a little company since your wolf man ran off and left you," the second ogre said as he swaggered toward her.

When all three men closed in around her, Jennifer jerked her arm loose and tried to plow through the human barricade. She found herself grabbed from all directions at once. This revived awful memories of her encounter with the Yates Gang, and Jennifer shrieked and bit and kicked in her attempt to escape—to no avail. She was shoved to the ground, her arms jerked above her head, staking her out like a sacrifice for these lusty cretins.

"Back off . . ."

The hollow, ominous voice caused the cluster of men to wheel around and grab for their six-shooters. Jennifer sagged in relief. She knew that voice. Three Wolves had arrived—and not a moment too soon. Gathering her legs beneath her, Jennifer stood up to peer around the bulky man in front of her. Three

Wolves had taken on that smoky image that had the three burly brutes shifting uneasily, afraid to trust their eyes.

"The last men to lay a hand on Jennifer Templeton became wolf bait," Three Wolves said as he gestured toward the two shadowy images of wolves that circled his legs.

"We were just having a little fun," the spokesman insisted.

"I don't find harassing a woman the least bit amusing, especially not this woman."

The three men backed up a pace when that eerie voice rolled toward them, accompanied by the snarls of the glittery-eyed wolves.

Jennifer surged between the men and headed straight for Three Wolves, smiling up into that hazy image within a shadow. It had taken a confrontation with these hooligans to force his hand, but he was here and that was all that mattered to Jennifer.

Spinning about, she shooed the riffraff on their way. One look over Jennifer's shoulder at the smoky image with blazing silver eyes sent the three men dashing madly toward their horses. The newly converted believers didn't waste time leaving. They thundered off into the night without looking back.

"Bloody hell, English. First you try to set yourself ablaze with that blasted bonfire, then you attract troublesome men," Trey muttered. "Sometimes I swear you don't have the sense the Great Spirits gave a mule!"

Jennifer turned around to stare up at the sleek, masculine form garbed in a skimpy loincloth. She smiled in amusement when Trey borrowed one of her favorite expressions again. He may not have realized it yet, but he could no more sever the ties that bound them together than she could. They had shared the best and worst of times. They had learned to read each other's moods. They had become sensitive to each other's needs. They belonged together forever and always. Now, all she had to do was find a way to convince Trey of that.

"It is about bloody time you showed up," she said. "I have certainly waited long enough."

"Somebody had to show up," Trey snapped as he kicked dirt on the blazing fire. "Rule Number One: Never leave a fire the size of this one burning when the wind picks up. You could get yourself cremated. Rule Number Two: Camping out alone on the prairie is an open invitation to renegades. Go home where you belong, English.''

When Trey wheeled around and stormed toward the tree-lined creek, Jennifer stared at him in disbelief. ''Where do you think you're going?''

''Back to Kansas.''

''You cannot, blast it!''

''The hell I can't! I can do whatever I damned well please. That was our original arrangement. Now that Grace dissolved our marriage, I have no obligation to you or anyone else.''

Jennifer stamped after him. ''Blister it, Trey, you come back here right now! You love me and I will hear you say it at least once before you go!''

Trey halted in his tracks and lurched around. His gaze feasted on the curvaceous silhouette that hovered in front of the banked fire and rolling smoke. Jennifer's chin was tilted to that determined angle he'd come to recognize. Her hands were balled on her hips, and a tangle of blond hair tumbled over her shoulders like a golden cape. Damn, she was stunning. And damn, he had spent more than a week wanting her, refusing to let himself go to her. If not for those three drunken goons, he might have managed to keep his distance until she gave up and went home.

''And what brought you to the conclusion that I love you, English?'' he snapped at her.

She paused in front of him and looked him squarely in the eye. ''You love me, Trey MacTavish. Now say it,'' she demanded.

''Where in the hell did you English people acquire such incredible arrogance?''

''The same place you Comanches acquired it,'' she fired back. ''Now say it.''

Trey gritted his teeth and willed his arms to remain at his sides when they reflexively moved to hold her. He would not—could not—touch her. He had spent the last few days practicing self-denial, repeating all the platitudes. This wasn't the time to crumble. He knew what was best for both of them. He had to get out of Jennifer's life—and stay out.

"Go home, English. You have the peace you wanted. You have your ranch. I have things to do and places to go. We both know our marriage is over. We both know it should never even have taken place. We never were right for each other."

"I know nothing of the kind, so kindly stop telling me what you think I know."

"Why should I?" he countered sarcastically. "You don't hesitate to tell me what you think I *feel.*"

"Come sit down and share a spot of tea with me," Jennifer requested.

"I don't like tea."

Jennifer told herself to be patient. Taming wild creatures took time and effort. "Then at least sit down and join me while I have a cup. I have been short on companionship of late."

"I don't feel like sitting. I feel like leaving."

Jennifer lost her temper. "Hell and damnation, now you listen to me, Trey MacTavish! We are going to talk this out, here and now. I am sorry I reacted the way I did that night, but it does not change how I feel about you."

Trey tensed. The look he had seen in Jennifer's violet eyes had tormented him for days on end. He didn't like to think about it, much less discuss it. She was making a noble effort to reassure him, because she thought it was the proper thing to do. But he had seen and felt her withdraw from him, as if he were a monster. But knowing Jennifer, and he had come to know her exceptionally well, he knew she wouldn't leave the incident alone until they had talked it out.

Trey gnashed his teeth and forced himself to discuss what happened the night he had called in the wolves. "You saw, *distinctly,* what I can become, what life has made of me," he said uncomfortably. "I terrified you and Christopher. I saw your reaction for myself, English. I shattered your illusions."

"No, you only made me realize how much I love you," Jennifer countered. "And if you did not love me, you would have simply let Gram sell the ranch to get my brother and me back. You would not have taken such drastic measures to ensure that I not only survived but was allowed to keep this property. When a man does whatever is necessary, regardless of the risks to himself, then he *does* care. He *does* love. Now say it!''

"No."

Jennifer bowed her neck and came closer so they stood toe to toe. "That Comanche pride of yours is becoming a nuisance. You do not see me balking, just because everybody in the county thinks I have taken leave of my senses, do you? I camped out here to prove to you that I love you and will go on loving you, even if you did frighten me just that once. And honestly, I do not know why you are making a big to-do about my being frightened when you are the biggest coward ever to draw breath."

"Coward?" Trey scoffed into her upturned face. "I've been called many things, English, but *coward* has never been one of them."

"Be that as it may, you are still a coward," she repeated. "You are afraid that admitting you love me will weaken your defenses. But you are sorely mistaken. I can be your greatest strength."

"More English pluck?" he mocked dryly.

"No, English logic."

"I was afraid you were going to say something like that."

Jennifer swatted him on the shoulder. "Oh rot, leave it to a man to make something infinitely simple impossibly difficult!"

"And leave it to you to be unreasonably optimistic."

Jennifer made a quick decision while she stood there staring up into those unyielding features. She had become entirely too predictable, she realized. She had always maintained that she loved Trey, and she made no secret of it, because she believed if she said it often enough *he* would start believing it. He had come to expect to hear that from her, even if the buffalo-headed fool tried to convince himself she had lost her respect for him and that she was only carrying on this latest crusade of outwaiting him to gloss over the incident at Ward Ranch.

It was time to convince Trey—in reverse—she decided. She would lambaste him, ruffle his Comanche feathers, and then she would leave him standing here, contemplating what his life would be like without her in it. Hopefully, the prospect would be distasteful to him as it was to her.

"Fine, have it your way." Jennifer wheeled around and marched toward her horse. "You want it to be over between us, then it will be over." She slung the saddle blanket over the mare's back and fought back another wave of nausea caused by the abrupt movement. "I will return to England and marry whoever Gram selects for me."

She scooped up the saddle and set it on her horse without glancing in Trey's direction. "Maybe love isn't all I hoped it would be. Maybe it is a foolish illusion, just as you claim, just as Gram maintained when my parents married. And maybe I should marry a title, because marrying for love certainly does not appear to be the answer for me."

Jennifer fastened the girth strap and plucked up the bridle. "On my wedding night, I will simply refuse to let myself make comparisons of how it felt to be truly in love with the man in my bed. I will not let myself remember what it was like with you, how gloriously wonderful I felt when you touched me and I touched you in return."

"English—"

"I will continue to be cheerfully optimistic and try to make the best of whatever situation I encounter in England, though I'd prefer to be loved by you rather than tolerating the touch of some foppish, titled duke who bears Gram's seal of approval and has all the right social connections."

"Jen—"

"And when *your* child is born, my new husband will have to become the father, because my *ex*-husband does not want either of us."

"My child?" Trey chirped, staggering to keep his feet after her unexpected comment.

"I will strive to be the best mother and wife I can possibly be. After all, title and social prominence are tantamount in life and love is a fool's illusion—according to you, at least According to Gram, titles are everything and Gram always did think she knew best.''

Jennifer mounted the mare and stared directly at Trey. ''Good-bye, Trey MacTavish. I hope you will be satisfied now that I am riding out of your life. Watching you besiege Ward Ranch did not disillusion me half as much as having you come back as a coward. You want me out of your life forever?'' she asked with a lift of her elegantly-shaped brows. ''Then consider me gone, and consider how much you like knowing that I will be gone forever, gone from the continent!''

Trey stood there like a stone fence post as Jennifer rode off into the night with her full skirts billowing in the wind, her golden hair streaming out behind her like a banner. It took a minute to digest everything she had to say to him in rapid staccato—English style.

Jennifer was removing herself from his life? Just as he had ordered her to do? She had abandoned her absurd fantasies about love at first sight?

Well, it was for the best, Trey tried to assure himself.

So why did he feel as if someone had blasted a hole the size of Texas right through his heart and soul?

Trey stared in the direction Jennifer had taken. Damn it, that woman was making him crazy! He had clung to noble conviction—and hated himself for it. Jennifer had generously offered her love—and now she was taking it back. It was officially over between them. He should be relieved—Grace obviously would be. Instead, Trey felt his insides twisting into aching knots.

Jennifer's words came back to him as he stood there staring off into the darkness. His child. She was carrying his child. He wouldn't be there to comfort her, to care for her. He wasn't going to be around to hold the innocent new life that he had *created* after *destroying* so much evil in this world . . .

Trey frowned suspiciously when a thought suddenly struck him. Was Jennifer truly carrying his child? Or had she said

hat to rattle him? Had she resorted to a devious ploy to break
his firm resolve? Would she stoop to that kind of deception?

Trey scowled as he turned those questions over in his mind.
Jennifer had always been honest with him. It was one of her
most endearing qualities. She *was* carrying his child, he realized.

Good gad! The kid would be a quarter Scottish, a quarter
Comanche and half overly-confident English! With a combina-
tion like that, it would take a strong, persistent hand to breed
the English out of the child. An impossible feat, with Agatha
Reynolds, Duchess of Calverdon, ruling the royal roost and
seeing to the child's upraising.

The thought turned Trey's stomach.

Jennifer smiled wryly as she rode home. She predicted that
Trey was asking himself if she had lied about his child, lied
about tramping back to England to marry whoever Gram
decreed to be Jennifer's social equal.

Sooner or later, Trey would come to the conclusion that she
had never lied to him about her feelings or her intentions. She
had always been honest and straightforward, and had never
deviated from that.

Jennifer slowed the mare to a walk when she reached the
section of the pasture that was plagued with prairie dog holes.
In her condition, she didn't dare risk a fall. She was already
suffering bouts of morning sickness that came and went all
day.

What if Trey never came to his senses? she asked herself
uneasily. If she had to marry another man in England, it would
be difficult to make the best of the situation. She would leave
Christopher in control of Templeton Ranch so she could bring
her child back to Texas whenever she pleased. There was that
escape route, she consoled herself. She could live for her
sojourns to Texas.

A smile replaced Jennifer's worried frown when she speculated on how Trey would feel about having his child raised

under Agatha's holier-than-thou influence. If nothing else, tha'
might be the one thing that sent him charging after her.

"Bloody, blooming hell," Trey muttered as he stamped
toward Diablo. He had a thing—or three—to say to Jennifer
Reynolds Templeton, the ex-Mrs. MacTavish! His child was
not going to be raised by some strutting English dandy, and
Agatha was not getting her hands on *his* baby.

Driven by that thought, Trey bounded into the saddle and
made a beeline toward the ranch house. Jennifer threatened to
take his child to England? No way in hell!

Trey skidded the stallion to a halt in front of Jawbone and
Sunset, who stood on the front lawn, staring at him in amazement.

"I thought you were gone for good," Jawbone said.

"Me, too," Sunset seconded.

"Well, as you can plainly see, I'm not." Trey thrust the
reins at Sunset. "Where is English?"

Jawbone stepped in front of Trey. "I'm sorry, but Miss Jenny
gave us orders not to let anyone near her. She rode back and
said she didn't want any visitors while she was refreshing
herself."

"Don't tangle with me right now, friend," Trey growled
into Jawbone's wrinkled face. "I am not in the best of moods."

"I can see that. But besides Miss Jenny requesting time
alone, there is a highfalutin party going on in the house. The
duchess invited a slew of English ranchers from the area to
join her for dinner. There's also a couple of English investors
that Her Grace met while she was in Mobeetie." He indicated
the line of buggies parked by the barn. "I doubt the duchess
will be pleased if you go stamping in there wearing nothing
but that loincloth."

"I don't give a damn if the king himself is dining with
Grace. I intend to see English . . . now," Trey insisted as he
shouldered his way past Jawbone and Sunset.

Trey tramped down the foyer, then came to a halt when he

saw Christopher dressed in the fashionable trappings of English gentry. When Trey tried to brush past the boy, Christopher flung up his hand and glowered at him. For some reason, Trey's protégé appeared none too happy with him.

"Stay where you are." Christopher stood there with feet apart, arms folded over his chest, imitating the stance Trey had perfected into an art. "My sister said that you wanted nothing to do with her, even after she sat out there on the prairie for a week, waiting for you to come back."

Trey took a menacing step forward but Christopher didn't back off. "Get out of my way, kid. This matter is between me and English."

"English and me," Christopher corrected, lifting his chin in a manner that would have done his grandmother proud. "And I am not a boy. I'm a man. And if you were everything I thought you were, you wouldn't have broken my sister's heart. She loves you, and she is proud enough of the fact to say so. I may not know much about women yet, but I bloody well know you shouldn't trample all over a lady's feelings. If somebody loved me the way Jen loves you I wouldn't tell her to go away and never come back!"

"Is that the version of the story your sister gave you?" Trey questioned.

"No, I'm reading between the lines. Jen didn't say a word to me, but she wouldn't have returned home alone if things were straightened out between you."

"I daresay, Three Wolves, we cannot have those creatures in the house. Her Grace is entertaining distinguished British guests this evening."

Trey glanced over his shoulder to see Simpson trying to shoo the wolves out the front door. The wolves refused to budge.

"Furthermore, if you cannot come dressed appropriately, you will have to leave. A breechclout and breastplate are not proper attire for Her Grace's formal social gatherings."

"Look, Butler," Trey growled, "I don't give a flying fig about what Grace has going. I came here to see English, and I'm not leaving until I do!"

Trey's booming voice brought Agatha to the dining room door. "Good gad, not you again. Blast it, don't you ever wear decent clothes?"

"Not if I can help it, Grace."

"For the umpteenth time, her name is *not* Grace," Simpson corrected.

Agatha waved Simpson off, then gestured for Trey to follow her into the parlor. "Sit down, Hiawatha."

Trey ignored her brisk command. His silver-eyed gaze glittered dangerously when Agatha tried to glare him into submission.

"You are becoming a nuisance," Agatha muttered.

"You ought to know, being an authority on it yourself," Trey said nastily.

Agatha bared her teeth. "I tried to call a truce with you, for all the good it did. I even submitted to your demand to let Jen make her own decisions about this ranch. Now she tells me she is prepared to return to England, because you don't want her. You have offended my family for the last bloody time!"

Agatha stalked up to wag her finger in Trey's scowling face. "I am prepared to make a settlement to get you out of our lives, once and for all. How much will it cost me to see the last of you, and do not neglect to add the cost of a decent set of clothes to your price."

"Grace, there isn't enough money in your damned duchy to buy me off," Trey muttered. "You aren't getting your hands on my child, no matter what!"

"Your child?" Agatha gasped and clutched her palpitating bosom. "Bloody hell! The poor thing will probably be running around in a loincloth if you raise him. He will be communicating in smoke signals!"

"Better than turning him into an English snob," Trey retaliated. "If the baby inherits your charm he'll be doomed for life."

Agatha recoiled as if she had been slapped. "I daresay you do not have enough charm to fill a peephole yourself!"

Trey could stand here all night exchanging insults with Grace, but it would accomplish nothing. The duchess didn't like him. But he had to arrange some sort of working truce, distasteful as the idea was.

"Look, Grace, the fact is that I intend to raise my own child. I am the father, whether you like it or not—"

"Which I don't," Agatha cut in.

"I'm not real fond of my grandmother-in-law, either," Trey flung back, "but folks get stuck with their relatives, for better or worse. Now, you can give me permission to see English or you can deny me, but I'm still going to see her. If you persist, I can sic my wolves on you and your uppity guests. The wolves haven't been fed yet."

Agatha's eyes narrowed as she glanced from the wolves to Trey. "You wouldn't dare."

"Don't challenge me, Grace," he said in his most threatening voice. When Agatha blinked, Trey pressed on. "I am not leaving here until I see Jennifer."

"Your Grace? Your guests are asking what is keeping you," Simpson prompted as he hovered in the doorway.

"Oh, the devil take it," Agatha grumbled. "You have my permission to see Jen, but for God's sake, find some respectable clothes before you venture back downstairs. I will not have my female guests fainting all over the bloody floor when they get an eyeful of you."

"I'll fetch his saddlebag," Christopher volunteered.

Trey regarded the duchess for a long, pensive moment, and then asked himself if he might have become a bit condescending each time he crossed paths with the duchess. He had gone out of his way to aggravate her, usually for the sport and spite of it. Maybe it was time to show the old girl a little respect.

Grasping Agatha's hand, Trey bowed elegantly before her. "Thank you for your permission, Your Grace. And rest assured that I won't embarrass you in front of your guests. Now, if you will excuse me, I would like to have that chat with Jennifer."

Agatha blinked in astonishment when Trey spoke and behaved with the kind of cultured refinement she hadn't thought him capable of. Jen's impeccable manners had obviously rubbed off on him. Why, the man could be utterly polite and charming when he felt like it!

Even Simpson was stunned by Trey's behavior. He stepped aside to let Trey pass and smiled approvingly. "I say, Your Grace. The man does seem to have a few sophisticated qualities after all."

"Life is full of surprises," Agatha murmured as she strode off to entertain her guests. "And I'm going to be appalled if I actually end up liking that renegade."

"It would simplify matters if you did. It looks as if you are going to be stuck with the man permanently, Your Grace."

"You are quite right, as usual," Agatha replied.

He touched her arm in a gesture of reserved affection. "You are going to have to tell Master Christopher and Lady Jennifer about the arrangements you have made. You cannot keep the news under wraps much longer. It would be dishonest and inconsiderate for a woman of your prestige to purposely withhold information that affects your grandchildren."

"I know, Simpson," Agatha whispered as she halted at the dining room door. "I am having trouble working up the nerve to admit that I have been a bloody hypocrite and a snob most of my life."

"Untrue," Simpson begged to differ. "I have always admired you, no matter what the situation."

Agatha suppressed a smile as she drew herself up and walked in to rejoin her guests.

Twenty

Jennifer smiled in satisfaction when she heard three brisk raps on her bedroom door. Trey had made his way through the obstacles downstairs while Jennifer was soaking in her bath. She had also had time to turn down the bed in invitation.

"Come in," she said when Trey hammered impatiently on the door a second time.

Trey burst inside the elegantly-furnished room, but Jennifer was nowhere to be seen. "English?"

"Yes?"

"Where the hell are you? I want to talk to you—"

The evening breeze caused the drapes beside the terrace door to flutter. Trey half turned, and caught his breath when a dark silhouette appeared against the backdrop of a silvery moon and twinkling stars. He stood immobilized, drinking in the alluring sight of the woman who all but floated toward him.

If the seductive black negligee Jennifer was wearing was any indication of English fashion, Trey was quickly developing an appreciation for it. The clinging garment accentuated every luscious curve. If it was her intention to assault his senses and thoroughly distract him, she had succeeded. Trey had never seen anyone so exquisite, so desirable, so spellbinding.

Jennifer smiled to herself. She had gotten Trey's undivided attention. Good. She had taken meticulous care in dressing for his anticipated arrival. She wanted to keep his thoughts centered around her, to make sure his customary cynicism did not cause him to break and run.

"You look lovely, English," he said huskily.

"Thank you. I hope my future husband will find the garment as appealing as you do."

"There isn't going to be a future husband," he declared.

She arched a brow. "No?"

"No. That's what I came here to discuss." Trey closed the door, leaving the wolves as sentinels in the hall. "Come sit down, English."

"I don't feel like sitting."

Trey gnashed his teeth. She was being as contrary as he had been earlier in the evening. "Are you planning to be difficult?"

"No more than usual."

She had always been difficult—to resist, to reason with, Trey reminded himself. And absolutely impossible to forget. Her beauty and charm had forced him to re-cross the one bridge he had never been able to burn behind him. This lively, spirited English aristocrat was the one obstacle he had never been able to overcome. The fact that he had returned to the ranch, and battled his way past a host of family and friends who stood between him and Jennifer, lent testimony to that. When he stared at Jennifer he was staring defeat in the face—always had, probably always would.

Trey glanced around the room. He hadn't realized—until the moment he walked into the house—how much he had missed by not having a place to call home, a purpose other than his dangerous profession. There was something unique about being here—with Jennifer—that brought a deep sense of inner peace and belonging. He hadn't understood what it was like to be loved until he had been loved by Jennifer, either.

She had taught him the meaning of the word, put him back in touch with emotions he had buried two decades earlier.

Love . . . Trey thought as his gaze fastened on Jennifer. He had scoffed at her, denied her feelings for him. Yet, despite the vast differences in their background, she freely admitted she cared for him. And while he taught her the mysteries of passion, she taught him to be gentle and tender. She had believed in him when no one else was willing to see anything in him except a dangerous gunslinger without a heart, soul, or conscience.

How could he let her go when she had become such a necessary part of his existence? How could he live without her now that she had come to mean everything to him?

Trey felt the emotional walls come tumbling down. Jennifer was, he realized with a start, the other half of his lonely soul. She gave him life and made him breathe—not to mention what that sexy negligee did to his pulse rate and his male anatomy. But he didn't just desire her physically. He needed her. She made him weak with wanting.

Bloody, blistering hell! How did he ever think he could walk away from Jennifer and find a reason to go on living? Hadn't he been in limbo the past few days, knowing he should leave—but couldn't?

Jennifer studied Trey closely, watching his expression, watching him watch her. She knew him well enough to know that he had reached a decision. She sensed it in his stance, saw it in the smile that gathered on those full, sensuous lips, felt it in the vibrations that rippled across the room.

"You have finally accepted the truth, haven't you?" she murmured. "Now say it, Trey."

"You are nothing if not persistent, aren't you, English?"

"So I have been told on numerous occasions by my ex-husband."

"You also know you're hell on a man. Of all the battles I've fought in life, you have always been the one I've lost—repeatedly."

"Am I being complimented or insulted?" she asked with a teasing grin.

A slow smile pursed his lips. "I think I've been had."

"Not yet, you haven't," she said saucily. "I am planning on getting to that as soon as you say it."

When Trey sauntered across the room to scoop Jennifer into his arms, she linked her hands behind his neck and pressed a kiss to his lips. "Are you going to say it or not?"

"Damn, woman, you do believe in unconditional surrender, don't you?"

"Yes, and I've had an excellent instructor. Now say it."

Trey treated himself to a taste of her honeyed lips and inhaled the scent of lilacs. Then he silently practiced saying the words he had never spoken to another living soul. "I love you, English. I really do love you," he said softly, sincerely.

Jennifer beamed. "Now, would you like to know when you finally arrived at what I have known since the very first time I saw you?"

Trey chuckled in amusement as he lay Jennifer on the bed and stretched out beside her. "Of course, English," he said, mimicking her endearing accent. "Since you've been determined to get me to say what you know I feel, I suppose it naturally follows that you should tell me when I was sure what I felt for you."

"It was approximately forty minutes ago," she replied as she traced the rugged features of his face. "And I daresay it took you bloody long enough to figure it out. For awhile there, I feared I was truly going to have to marry some English dandy and spend the rest of my life cheerfully assuring myself I was not as miserable as I truly was."

Trey reached out to smooth the silver-gold tresses across the pillow, marveling at the silky texture of her hair, the heady fragrance that filled his senses, the sparkle in those amethyst eyes that bespoke of such depth of character and spirit.

"I couldn't bear to think of another man touching you, loving you," he whispered. "Even though I was certain I had destroyed your respect and affection for me when I called in the wolves—''

Her index finger skimmed his lips, shushing him. Smiling eyes shone up at him. ''None of that matters, Trey. You are the only man I will ever love,'' she assured him. ''You cannot begin to know how it hurt to realize that I had pulled away from you that night. Never again, Trey, I swear it. I just did not realize how incredibly amazing you were until that night. It did not make me love you less. It made me love you more.''

''You did?'' He studied her intently. ''It really doesn't bother you to know that . . . I change drastically when the situation demands it?''

Jennifer shook her head. ''How could I not be flattered that you were willing to do whatever needed to be done in order to rescue me? You didn't fail me, or dim my high opinion of you. I was the one who failed you, and I shall never forgive myself for that.''

Trey peered down into her bewitching face, realizing that she would forgive him anything, except refusing to admit how much he loved her. That was all she had ever asked of him, he realized. It was so simple, really, because loving her had become as reflexive and necessary as breathing. And knowing Jennifer loved him had become his greatest strength . . .

Suddenly he recalled that she had said that very thing to him, and he had called her a foolish romantic. But she fully understood what he was just beginning to discover for himself. The certainty of loving, and being loved, provided an indefinable sense of security and satisfaction that ran soul-deep.

The restlessness that once motivated him seemed a lifetime away. He knew he could be content wherever Jennifer was, because she was his very heart and soul. She was delicate and refined, and yet she was steadfast, devoted, and loyal. She was strong-willed, yet tender and generous. She was also more woman than a man like him deserved. She was everything he needed—and could ever want.

Jennifer reached up to smooth his disheveled hair into place and smiled adoringly at him. ''Love at first sight,'' she said with absolute conviction. "How could I have possibly looked at you that first time and expected to find another man to compare to you? Why, I could not even take my eyes off you when I saw you, could not even find my voice because of the profound effect you had on me. You scoffed at what I knew in my heart to be true, but I felt it, sensed it. All I want is to know that you love me, too."

Not for the world would Trey have tried to convince Jennifer that there was no such thing as love at first sight. How could he? She made him believe in destiny, in that sense of what was right.

Looking back, Trey realized he had been too much the cynic to attach a name to the unfamiliar sensations and emotions Jennifer inspired in him. She had embraced those feelings with a pure heart and deep faith. Jennifer had allowed love to grow while he fought it every step of the way. But no more holding back, Trey decided. He couldn't bear to be without Jennifer's love. It had become too vital to him.

Trey yearned to communicate the maelstrom of feelings bottled up inside him. He brushed his hand over the curve of her breast, feeling the rosy peak beneath the seductive black lace. His lips drifted over her mouth in the tenderest kiss. He inched closer, molding his contours to her soft, luscious body.

"English, I ache to show you just how much I love you, how much I will always love—"

There was a rap on the bedroom door at this most inopportune moment. Trey could have cheerfully shot whoever was standing in the hall. And he seriously considered doing just that when Agatha's brusque voice filled the room. Damn, the Duchess of Calverdon was worse than a curse.

"Hiawatha, I know you're in there. I wish to speak to you and Jennifer—now."

Trey scowled as he pushed upright on the bed. "Why? Are you leaving for England tonight? It's been nice knowing you, Grace."

"No, I am not leaving. I have an important matter to discuss.

As Simpson pointed out to me, I cannot delay the announcement any longer.''

Disappointment clouded Jennifer's features as she rolled off the bed. If Gram was plotting to rout Trey because she didn't approve of him, family fur was going to fly!

"Jen? Meet me downstairs in ten minutes," Agatha ordered—as only Agatha could.

There was a noticeable pause, and voices whispering on the other side of the door.

"And bring Hiawatha with you, of course. Christopher left the saddlebags in the hall. See that the man puts on decent clothes before he comes downstairs.''

Receding footsteps indicated that Agatha and her faithful shadow had traipsed off.

"I hope to hell Grace is leaving on the first stage," Trey grumbled as he stalked off to retrieve his saddlebag. "Texas may not be big enough for the both of us.''

Jennifer rolled her eyes as she scurried off to fetch proper attire. "Please be tolerant. She is my grandmother, after all.''

"You have my condolences, English. I may have been raised as a so-called heathen, but that duchess makes my relatives look like tooth fairies.''

"Gram is not that bad," Jennifer insisted, grinning.

"She certainly has me fooled." Trey thrust a bare leg into his breeches and muttered at Agatha's untimely interruption that prevented him from doing what he wanted to do most— make love to Jennifer until he didn't have the strength left to do it again.

"Gram is fiercely protective of her family and entrenched in Old World tradition. Calling family members together for a conference is standard English protocol. I am sure she has something important to say, or she would not have interrupted.''

Trey cast Jennifer a doubtful glance. He wouldn't put anything past Agatha.

"The last time Grace made an announcement, she dissolved our marriage and wrote up a bill of sale to Quincy Ward," Trey reminded her sourly.

Jennifer grimaced as she wriggled into her gown. "Yes, well, hopefully Gram learned her lesson after that fiasco."

Despite Trey's annoyance, he accompanied Jennifer downstairs. Christopher was seated on the sofa in the parlor, and Agatha was poised in front of the fireplace. Simpson stood directly beside her—as always.

"Good to see that you actually do own proper clothes," Agatha noted as she gestured for Trey to park himself beside Christopher.

When Jennifer was seated, Agatha drew herself up to her full stature and inhaled an enormous breath. "I have spent the past week making arrangements to purchase Ward Ranch."

That got everybody's attention!

"To Simpson's and my surprise, we have discovered that we have found a certain . . . er . . . adventurous appeal about Texas. Granted, civilization has not caught up with the place, but the possibility of molding this backward outpost into a respectable cultural center presents an intriguing challenge."

Trey groaned inwardly. The old girl was here to stay? Damn, and just when he had visions of settling down with a wife to raise his family.

"Simpson and I will be moving into ranch headquarters to oversee the refurbishing of the house." She stared pointedly at Trey. "And of course, there is a new barn to raise, thanks to the destructive fire—not to mention broken glass all over the office."

"I'm sure you and Simpson will be supremely happy in your new home," Trey said, rising from the couch.

Obviously Agatha wasn't finished yet. She glared at him for attempting to take his leave without her permission.

"Sit down. I have another announcement to make."

Reluctantly, Trey plunked down beside Christopher.

"I made other arrangements this week as . . . um . . . well."

When Agatha hesitated, Simpson folded his hand around hers, giving it an encouraging squeeze. Trey frowned dubiously at the affectionate gesture, then glanced at Jennifer, who was smiling for reasons nothing in the conversation could account for. It was as if she knew something that he and Christopher didn't.

Agatha shifted from one foot to the other, then cleared her throat. ''Tonight's dinner party was actually a personal celebration. It is our . . . er . . . first week anniversary.''

Christopher stared blankly at his grandmother. Trey frowned, bemused. But Jennifer's smile broadened and her eyes twinkled with delight.

At Simpson's cue, Agatha blurted out, ''Simpson and I were married precisely one week ago today.''

''Well, I'll be damned,'' Trey wheezed, eyes popping.

My, wasn't Simpson turning out to be an exceptionally good sport. But then, Trey had heard it said that beauty was in the eye of the beholder. If the way Simpson was staring at Agatha was any indication, that gray-haired Englishman saw something very special in the duchess. Who would have thought the hidebound duchess had a spot in her heart soft enough to make her overlook title and position to marry her butler! And to think how she had fussed at Trey for marrying Jennifer. Her tacky remarks had come back to haunt her.

Christopher's mouth opened and shut, but no words passed his lips.

''Congratulations, Gram, Simpson,'' Jennifer said enthusiastically. ''I am happy for both of you.''

Trey wanted to extend sympathy to Simpson, but he kept his trap shut.

''I realize this comes as a surprise.'' Agatha floundered, composed herself, then continued as she clung tightly to Simpson's hand. ''But as dear Simpson has reminded me, there have been many cases of dukes taking brides who do not hold their own inherited titles. And Jennifer's marriage to Hiawatha proved that crossing social lines is accepted in the States. In Texas, it seems, anything goes. Besides, by wedding me, Simpson will become a duke and that makes everything dandy fine.

''Of course,'' she went on, regaining confidence when her family voiced no objections, ''we will have to return to England on occasion to oversee the duchies.''

Trey would be counting the days.

"But we have hired a rather nice chap to manage our ranch, whether we are here or not."

"And who is this *nice chap?*" Trey questioned curiously.

"Well, it is your cousin Jonas, of course," Agatha informed him, as if he ought to have known. "We have to keep this cattle operation in the family, don't we? We bloody well cannot bring in some fob to run the business. We discussed the details over lunch with Jonas today. We agreed to let him run his stock in our pastures, so he would not have to neglect his own herd."

Jennifer was delighted to learn that Gram had included Trey's cousin. Furthermore, she was thrilled to see that Gram had made great strides in broadening her perspectives. Not only had Agatha accepted the fact that she cared for Simpson—and had for years on end—but Gram had dined with a man she would not even have allowed to share her table a month earlier. After all these years, Agatha had finally discovered that titles and pedigrees did not necessarily make the man, that character and integrity mattered most.

"Bloody hell," Christopher erupted when he finally recovered his speech. His blue-eyed gaze swung to Trey. "Do you mean the two of them have been making—ooofff . . ."

Trey gouged Christopher in the ribs before his loosened tongue ran away with itself. "Later, kid."

"But at their age?" he whispered, aghast.

Luckily, Agatha and Simpson didn't hear the exchange. They were staring intently at each other. When Agatha inclined her head, Simpson drew himself up and peered directly at Trey.

"Her Grace and I want to apologize for our regrettable condescension these past weeks. We have behaved rather badly toward you, considering all you have done in our behalf. Lady Jennifer has constantly claimed that you are a good and decent man, capable of impressive deeds. Since we will be neighbors as well as family, we wish to make peace."

Trey was stunned to the soles of his boots. The la-di-da duchess and her bridegroom were accepting him as their equal? Wonders never ceased!

Trey's astounded gaze swung to Jennifer, who was smiling at him with pride and affection. For the first time in years, Trey had a home and a family to call his own. It felt . . . good. It felt damned good.

Even the wolves appeared to be adjusting to their new environment, Trey noted. They were sprawled on either side of the door, their gray heads resting on their oversize paws. They peered at him with eyes of contentment.

Home, Trey thought with a newfound sense of gratification. He would make a place for himself here. He would invest his hard-earned savings in this ranch. With Jennifer at his side, young Christopher to enjoy, and a child on the way, Trey and his wolves could be in heaven!

Of course, there was still the temperamental duchess to contend with occasionally. But if Agatha—under Jennifer's influence—had mellowed this much in a month, the old girl might actually become tolerable in a year—or ten.

"And now if you will excuse us, Simpson and I would like to retire for the night," Agatha declared as she surged across the parlor.

The wolves lifted their shaggy heads when the duchess approached. She paused to glance back at Simpson, who smiled and nodded in answer to her silent question. The duchess shifted her gaze to Trey.

There was a wealth of meaning in the glance Trey and Agatha exchanged. She was silently offering respect and acceptance. He smiled faintly, determined to make peace—for Jennifer's sake.

To everyone's amazement, Agatha bent down to pat both wolves simultaneously, and murmured, "Nice puppies," before she strode through the hall. Simpson did likewise before he followed after his new bride.

Trey nearly fell off the sofa. While he recovered from watching the uppity duchess make one startling concession after another, Jennifer bounded to her feet and rushed off to extend further congratulations to the bride and groom. Trey simply sat there pinching himself, wondering if he dared believe what he'd seen and heard. This was definitely a night of astonishing revelations!''

"I daresay I am glad that is over with." Agatha sighed audibly when Simpson closed the bedroom door behind him. "I have felt like a criminal, sneaking around behind everyone's back since our wedding. My family took the news exceptionally well, didn't they, Simpson?"

He smiled. "Very well indeed. But I knew they would. You have a fine family, after all."

"I do, don't I? Even that pesky half-breed has turned out to be quite remarkable."

"And he seems immensely fond of Lady Jennifer," Simpson pointed out as he peeled off his cravat and jacket. "He proved his devotion the night he rescued your grandchildren. And I say, I *was* impressed when he took all of us on earlier this evening when he came here to speak with Lady Jennifer. We didn't make it easy for him."

"Well, of course we didn't," Agatha replied. "How could I have possibly known for certain that he was seriously devoted to Jen if I didn't badger him until he considered leaving? The man was prepared to take us all on in order to see Jen. That says a lot for his feelings toward her."

"You are extremely shrewd, Your Grace," Simpson complimented. "Testing that rascal again, were you? I must admit, I rather like having him on our side now. These Texans have come to respect his abilities, if the gossip in Mobeetie is anything to go by. Why, the man's name has become a household word after the Ward Ranch affair."

Agatha had come to respect Three Wolves, though she refused to give the rapscallion the satisfaction of hearing her say so. Indeed, she rather enjoyed the verbal sparring matches that kept her wits sharpened . . .

Her thoughts trailed off when Simpson stepped behind her

to unfasten the tedious buttons on the back of her gown. "You and I have wasted too many years, Simpson," she whispered.

"Indeed we have, but I intend to be as devoted to you as always. The only difference is that now I can let you know how I feel about you."

"Oh, Simpson!" Agatha whispered as she turned in his arms to accept his tender kiss.

Christopher stared up the empty stairway, then shook his head in disbelief. "Do you think Gram and Simpson actually sleep together?" he questioned Trey. "At their age?"

The kid had an amazing ability to make Trey blush. He wondered if he had been this inquisitive at Christopher's age. He supposed he had. "I don't think it's any of our business."

As for Trey, he intended to express his affection for his ex-wife, whom he intended to remarry the first chance he got. He couldn't imagine that his feelings for Jennifer would change in the next hundred years, unless they deepened and intensified. But honestly, he couldn't see how it was possible to love her more than he did now. She had become his everything. Time wasn't going to change the way he felt.

"But this is my grandmother we're talking about! Who would have thought—"

"Go to bed, Christopher," Trey broke in.

Christopher grumbled under his breath as he started up the steps. "Everybody around here is doing things I'm still considered too young to experience. Seems to me I'm the only one in this house who isn't getting any satisfaction."

Trey bit back a grin as he watched the kid hike up the steps. "In due time, kid. When the right woman comes along, you'll have all the satisfaction you'll need. I found mine in English, and you'll find yours somewhere along the way."

"Promise?" Christopher asked, staring intently at Trey.

A wry smile quirked Trey's lips as he turned on his heel and strode out the front door. "Comanche promise."

* * *

Jennifer, dressed in her provocative black negligee, paced the bedroom floor, pausing at irregular intervals to stare expectantly at the door. Blister it, where was Trey? She had left him and Christopher downstairs thirty minutes earlier. Surely Gram had not forbidden Trey from returning to her room because of a ridiculous technicality.

True, Jennifer and Trey were no longer legally married, but they had been married. And she fully intended to marry him again. So where the blazes was he?

The cool night breeze whispered through the terrace door leading to the balcony. Jennifer spun around, feeling a presence enter the room. Her heart stalled in her chest when the magnificent form of a man, dressed only in a loincloth and wearing the symbolic feather in the braid on the left side of his head, appeared from the shadows. The wolves were beside him, as always, like an extension of his strength and power.

Here was Jennifer's dashing knight, her warrior, her champion. Trey was everything she had ever wanted, needed, and desired in a man. Trey MacTavish was her fantasy come true. Just peering up at him sent her pulse leapfrogging around her chest. Jennifer longed to spend a lifetime proving to Trey that they were the perfect match—the same perfect match her parents had been.

For all the hell Trey had endured this past decade, Jennifer yearned to give him heaven. There was happiness to be had here, if Trey would let her shower him with inexhaustible love.

Trey felt his knees wobble when violet eyes twinkled up at him. Jennifer's welcoming smile beat anything he had ever seen. He had never felt so wanted, so needed, so loved. She took his breath away when she stared at him like that.

"I love you, English." The words that had once been difficult to speak came tumbling from his lips on a husky whisper.

"Do you, now?" Her lips quirked in an elfin smile. "I daresay I was beginning to wonder if you were going to come back to prove it."

Trey tread silently across the room to sweep her up in his arms. "I had preparations to make first."

Jennifer offered no objection when Trey reversed direction and carried her out the terrace door. After all, the man did his best work in the shadows of the night—so who was Jennifer to question him? She simply snuggled on his lap when he swung onto Diablo's back and reined away from the house.

Minutes later, Jennifer found herself placed gently on a padded pallet beneath a canopy of stars. Seconds later, she felt moist kisses and caresses—administered with the utmost tenderness—whispering over her skin, igniting fires that burned hot against the night.

The feel of Trey's hands and lips moving over her flesh sent waves of heat rippling through her body. Fire sizzled each place he touched, compelling her to return the love he gently offered.

Trey marveled at the pleasure he received from touching Jennifer. When he flicked his tongue against the velvety peak of her breast, he felt her luscious body rise up to greet him. The ache inside him became more pronounced when she responded so sweetly. Trey closed his mind to everything except the overwhelming need to pleasure her, to love her thoroughly and completely.

He came to her, like a shadow consuming the night, and Jennifer clung to him desperately. She was life itself—the air he breathed, the essence of his heart and soul. When he was with Jennifer he knew he had everything a man could possibly want.

When passion flung him into mindless ecstasy, Trey surrendered wholeheartedly. He could feel himself tumbling through time and space, feel that cold, dark core consumed by inexpressible pleasure and warmth. He couldn't imagine how he could ever feel anything but cheerful optimism for eternities to come. Because of her, he doubted he had a cynical bone left in his shuddering body.

"Trey?"

Jennifer's whisper seeped into his thoughts and he smiled languidly. "Mmm . . . ?"

"Do you have any idea how very much I love you?"

Trey shifted, bringing Jennifer down beside him. He cradled her head on his arm and studied the sparkle in her amethyst eyes. "Indeed I do, ma'am," he replied, playfully mimicking her British accent. "And I daresay loving you is right up my street."

Jennifer smiled at his roguish grin, enjoying his teasing mood. "Are you sure you do not have a tad of English blue blood flowing through your veins?"

Trey smoothed his hand over the hilly terrain of her hip, marveling at the silky texture of her skin—more interested in touching her than in idle conversation. "I'll have to consult Jonas Rafferty about that."

Jennifer propped up on an elbow, sending a waterfall of silver-gold hair tumbling over his chest. "And that reminds me, why didn't you tell me that Jonas was your cousin?"

"You didn't ask." Trey didn't want to rehash the unpleasant memories of his youth. The bad times were behind him—and that was exactly where they would stay.

"Is Jonas one of the reasons you wanted to come to Texas? To settle the old grudge with your cousin?"

He flashed her a cryptic smile. "Yes, but fortunately the family reunion turned out much better than anticipated."

Jennifer frowned curiously. "And what about that inadvertent favor Jonas claimed you did for him, because of me? What was that all about?"

"I have more interesting things to do than discuss my long-lost cousin. As far as I'm concerned, my past and future begin and end with you, English."

When Trey's lips moved toward hers, Jennifer dodged the oncoming kiss. "What was the bloody favor?"

Trey sighed in defeat. He may as well answer her, because she wouldn't let up until he told her exactly what she wanted to know.

"Bob Yates followed us to Texas to have his revenge, but Jonas found himself at a bad place at the wrong time. I managed to save my cousin's life before I sent the last survivor of the

Yates Gang to a place where hotter climates prevail. Jonas was exceptionally appreciative."

"Bob Yates?" Jennifer reflexively recoiled when his image flashed before her eyes. "Was he the one who shot Jonas? Why didn't you tell me earlier?"

"Because, at the time, you had hightailed it over to Ward Ranch to rescue your brother," Trey replied. "Now, if you don't mind, could we get back to what we were doing?"

When Jennifer dodged his kiss again, Trey grumbled in frustration. "Now what, English?"

Jennifer's hand swept along the sleek expanse of Trey's chest in an enticing caress. She peered up at him from beneath a fan of long, curly lashes. "Perhaps this isn't the time to ask, but I was wondering if you might have a little chat with Christopher sometime soon. Man-to-almost-man, if you know what I mean. He has become exceedingly inquisitive about certain topics and . . . well, you seem the most likely candidate to enlighten him."

"I've had several chats with him already."

Jennifer blinked. "You have? When was that?"

"While he visited me at my camp on the north range of the ranch."

Jennifer stared at him accusingly. "Then you are admitting that you broke your promise to me."

"No. I left as I promised," Trey clarified. "We simply didn't stipulate how far away I had to go, and whether or not I could come back."

"You are splitting hairs," she pointed out, though her tone was anything but critical.

He tilted her face to his, refusing to let her escape this kiss. "I went only as far as the strings to my heart would stretch, English. Some things, I've discovered, are impossibilities. Leaving you is one of them. You've come to matter too much to me. Although you are entirely too good for me, you are exceptionally good for me. I couldn't let you go, couldn't bear the thought of what my life would be like without you in it."

"Oh, Trey . . ." Jennifer whispered, a noticeable catch in her voice.

"Take back that Comanche promise," he murmured as his hands glided over her supple flesh. "I don't ever want to leave you again. Wherever you are is where I belong, where I want to be. I want to watch our children grow up and discover the same everlasting love I feel for you. I love you more than life itself, Jennifer."

A smile blossomed on her lips and spread across every enchanting feature of her face. "Comanche promise?" she murmured as she moved toward him, giving herself to him— body, heart, and soul.

"Comanche promise," he assured her. "For always and forever . . ."

And in the deepest, darkest hour of the night, a sliver of moon hung against a backdrop of glittering silver stars. The howl of the wolf rose up in a swirl of smoke, condensing and then drifting away in the wind.

Love's promise, tried and true, spread across the West Texas horizon, rising again and again, just as surely as the morning sun burned away the shadows of the night.

A Comanche promise of love everlasting was never broken— not once in all the blissful years to come . . .